Treache

Treacherous Waters

TERESA CRANE

CANELO

First published in Great Britain in 2002 by Little, Brown

This edition published in the United Kingdom in 2019 by

Canelo Digital Publishing Limited
57 Shepherds Lane
Beaconsfield, Bucks HP9 2DU
United Kingdom

A CIP catalogue record for this book is available from the British Library.

Print ISBN 978 1 78863 465 6
Ebook ISBN 978 1 78863 353 6

Extract from *A Passage to India* by E. M. Forster reproduced by kind permission of the Provost and Scholars of King's College, Cambridge and the Society of Authors.

Look for more great books at www.canelo.co

Printed and bound in Great Britain by Clays Ltd, Elcograf S.p.A.

Part One

Spring 1925

Chapter One

'A growing boy needs a father, Annie.' Jane Renault's quiet words broke a long and thoughtful silence and were all but drowned in the restless sound of the sea and the excited barking of the little dog that danced and dashed along the water's edge, snapping frenetically at the waves. The tall young woman strolling beside her nibbled her lip and shoved her hands deeper into the pockets of her baggy jacket, her eyes upon the child who ran with the dog, long bare legs flashing, fair hair flying in the wind. Jane glanced up at her daughter. 'As you just said yourself – he's a good man. And a kind one, I think—?'

Annie nodded, her eyes still on the boy. 'Yes.'

'It's not as if you're rushing into anything. It's more than eighteen months since Charles died.'

'Yes,' her daughter said, again, and then lifted her voice above the sound of sea and wind. 'Not too close to the edge, Davie. Don't get your sandals wet.'

The boy waved to her and swooped off after the yelping dog again. The long wail of a ship's horn sounded across the water. In the near distance the small, picturesque seaside town of Southwold, its skyline dominated by its white lighthouse, perched upon a rise of land unusual on this flat Suffolk coastline. The lad's grandmother watched the running child, smiling. 'He's ten years old, darling,' she said. And then added, gently, 'As I said, a growing boy needs a father.' She eyed her daughter sympathetically. 'Wasn't that why you decided to marry Charles in the first place? That was no grand passion, was it? And it worked out well, didn't it?'

Annie let out an explosive breath. 'I think that's the very point I'm trying to make. And anyway, Charles was eight years ago. Davie's older now. We do very well together.' The words were defensive.

Her mother said nothing.

Annie sighed. 'Oh, I suppose you're right,' she said at last, reluctantly. 'And Fergus is very good to Davie. And to me. I'm very fond of him—'

'Well, then—'

'—as I was "very fond" of Charles.' Annie laid heavy emphasis on the words. She hunched her shoulders a little, scuffed at a stone with her foot. 'And – like Charles – he's a widower and old enough to be my father. Oh, I know, I know' – she held up a hand as her mother opened her mouth to answer – 'the war, the lost generation—' She shook her head. 'Mother, who knows more about that than I do? I was a widow for the first time at the ripe old age of eighteen, remember? And I know a lot of women haven't had the chance to marry once, let alone twice, since the war. I suppose I'm lucky that yet another decent, kindly man wants me to be his wife and is more than willing to treat Davie like a son. It's just… well, I know it must sound ridiculously childish, but it's hardly the stuff of romance, is it? Sometimes – just sometimes – shouldn't there be more to life than… than safety and good sense?' She stopped walking and turned to look out across the restless sea, watching the boat that steamed across the bay.

'The steamer's coming! The steamer's coming!' Davie raced up to them. 'Oh, Mother, I do wish you'd let us go back to London on the steamer. We'd be *perfectly* safe – wouldn't we, Nan? I know you don't like it, Mother – but *please*?'

Annie smiled, but shook her head. 'We've got tickets for the train, you know we have. I thought you liked our special little train?'

'I do. But we *always* come by train. It would be really wizard to come on the boat sometimes—'

Glancing at her daughter, his grandmother ruffled Davie's thick hair. 'You're right, young man. As a matter of fact I've often thought myself that it would be fun to go on the boat. I'll tell you what: if your mother agrees, when next you come to see me, you and I can take the boat together to London and your mother can meet us there. How would that be?'

'Oh, yes, please, Nan!'

Annie opened her mouth to protest, then shut it again. Davie shot off once more. 'Brandy! Here, boy!' The little dog scampered to him.

Jane, watching her daughter's face, shook her head firmly, though there was no lack of understanding in her eyes. 'Don't think about it. And don't worry. I'll look after him, I promise. It'll be an adventure for us both. Darling, you can't wrap him in cotton wool for the rest of his life, you know—'

'I don't,' Annie said, too quickly.

'It's always a danger with an only child.'

Annie cast a sharp, sideways glance at her mother. 'You know as well as I, there's nothing I can do about that. Not that I would if I could, to be honest. Fergus knows that. I wouldn't want any more children, even if I could have them. He understands. For goodness' sake, he's in his fifties, and he's got his own grown-up family.

4

It's hardly likely we'd want a nursery full of babies!' She turned abruptly and began once more to walk towards the little town. The boat had steamed to the end of the pier and several people had disembarked.

'So – is it safety and good sense or not? What will you do?' Jane asked after a pause.

Annie walked on in silence for a moment. 'I really don't know,' she said at last. 'As you know, Charles left the business in trust for us and we have the house in Kew, so we're relatively independent. There's enough to live on more than comfortably, enough to pay for Davie's education, and sufficient over to give him the start in life he will need. On the other hand, as you say, Davie will probably need more help and guidance as he grows up than I can give him alone—'

'Safety and sense do have their attractions.' There was a smile in the words.

'Yes. Charles proved that. Oh, I know it must seem that I'm just being awkward. Most women would jump at the chance Fergus is offering.'

'It's not an easy world for a woman alone,' Jane said softly.

Annie reached for her mother's hand and squeezed it. 'I know.' She pushed the heavy dark hair that was blowing about her face back behind her ears, and looked at her mother with curiosity in her eyes. 'Were you never tempted to marry again?'

Jane shook her head firmly. 'No.'

'Why not?' Annie studied her mother for a moment, smiling. 'Don't tell me you were never asked?' In her late forties, small and dark and with a swift and vivid smile, Jane Renault was still a very attractive woman.

'Indeed I was. Twice as a matter of fact.' Jane spoke calmly. 'But I refused.'

'Why?' The question was mischievous and they both knew it.

'You know why, I think.'

'Because you loved Papa.'

'Yes.' The word was soft.

Annie, as Jane had surely known she would be, was quick to pounce on that. 'Then surely you can see why I'm hesitating? I don't love Fergus. I didn't love Charles. And as for Philippe... we were together for such a little time – just a few weeks – and under such circumstances...' Her eyes, dark as her mother's, went once more to where her son was throwing a stick for the dog, and the words trailed off. The boat shrieked steam once more and pulled away from the pier, riding the rough water. Wind-whipped smoke streamed from its stack as it headed up the coast towards Great Yarmouth. 'I know it would be sensible to marry. I'm fond of Fergus and I know he cares for me.'

'But he isn't Rudolph Valentino,' her mother put in dryly.

Annie threw back her head and let out a sudden, genuinely amused shout of laughter. 'Hardly! But I don't think there's much point in waiting for *him* to knock on my door, do you?' She laughed again. 'And what sort of influence would *he* have on Davie?'

'He could always teach him to dance,' her mother replied, sober-faced.

They had reached the first of the neat rows of beach huts that fringed the wide, sandy beach. The path ran behind them and began to climb a little, up towards Gun Hill. The wind brought the distinctive smell of the famous brewery that was the town's lifeblood to their nostrils. Davie ran up, Brandy at his heels, and slipped a hand into his mother's. His small, handsome face with its eager dark eyes was flushed with the sun and the wind and his bright hair was darkened by the damp salt air. He put his free hand in his pocket. 'Look what I've found!' He held out a narrow, long-fingered hand. On the flattened, sandy palm lay a large and pretty spiral shell. 'I'm going to draw it for you in my book when we get back. Can we buy some cakes on the way through town, please? I'm starving.'

His mother laughed. 'You're always starving. I reckon you must have worms.'

'Ugh! Wriggly, squiggly worms!' Davie crowed with relish, swinging on his mother's hand. '*Disgusting!*'

–

The wind blew night-long, as it often did on this wild, flat coast, dragging ragged tails of streaming black clouds across the face of the moon, cracking and singing through the rigging of the beached fishing boats, driving the white horses of the cold North Sea onto the sand. Annie slept restlessly, the sound of wave and wind in her ears. The moon gleamed fitfully through the open curtains, a pale-lit path from the window to the bed.

Silver pale. Death pale.

The colourless, milky-eyed faces of mother and child, tangled hair streaming and swaying like weed in the strong-flowing water—

No! She struggled against the familiar, terrible image.

The two entwined in death as they must so often have been in life. The bloated flesh sucked and nibbled, the child's mouth, blue-lipped, open as if to cry out—

The wind crashed against the window, rattling the pane. A part of her heard it. A part of her knew she had to get away from this nightmare, from the drowned, dreadful faces, the silent scream of the child; from the paralysing horror that rooted her to the spot.

Water lapped at the bodies, trapping them against the bank, branches entangling them. The woman's head turned, long hair drifting; pale, albescent eyes looked into Annie's. A hand rose, dripping, from the water—

'No!' Choking and shaking, she wrenched herself upright. For a moment the blaze of the moon silvered the room, then the wind-driven clouds covered it and in the darkness she could still see those eyes, the lifted hand—

Annie covered her face with her hands, head bowed, the heavy bobbed hair falling forward over her cheeks. She was trembling violently, sweat slicked her body, the muscles of her throat ached with the memory of her own terrified screams.

Would she never be free of it?

After a moment she reached for the switch of the bedside light. The warm glow was comforting. And at least this time she had not walked in her sleep as she so often did, had not woken panic-stricken at her sleeping son's bedside. Above all she must not frighten Davie; she hated the thought. She swung her feet onto the cold floor and went to the window. The wind whistled, the great moon sailed through the clouded sky, the sea crashed, restless and relentless, on the strand. She leaned her hot forehead on the cold glass. Small, chill draughts whispered around the window. Gradually she was calming, although she knew from long experience that she'd get little more sleep tonight.

8

She stood so for a long time. Then she turned and went to the door. Stopped with her hand upon the knob; shook her head fiercely, closing her eyes for a moment. The child was safe. Of course he was.

Tiredly she picked up the book that lay on the floor beside the bed and slipped back between the sheets.

–

'You'll let me know what you decide?'

'Of course I will.' They were standing beside the little train that ran on its narrow-gauge tracks from Southwold to Halesworth and the main line to London. Boxes of fish were stacked waiting to be loaded; there was a buzz of conversation around them as people climbed aboard.

Jane's dark eyes were quick and bright as a bird's as she looked at her daughter. 'Send me a telegram. Letters are so very slow.' She grinned her quick, almost elfin grin. 'They take a full day sometimes.'

Annie laughed, and bent to kiss her mother's cheek. 'Honestly – you're more of a child than Davie is! And far more impatient.'

The little steam engine wheezed and belched, then shrilled a warning of departure; its idiosyncratic line of maroon carriages settled behind it, ready to go.

'We'd better get on. There seems to be quite a crowd, and Davie insists on travelling third class.' Annie spread her hands. 'He talks to *everyone*.'

'Bully for him. So do I. Both, that is. That's what makes our little railway so special. A pity there aren't more like it. The main-line trains pale in comparison. All those noses stuck in the air; all those whispers behind newspapers and gloved hands.' Jane reached for Annie's own gloved hand, her face suddenly serious, the lightness gone from her voice. 'Think long and hard, Annie. It's your life as well as Davie's.'

Annie eyed her, a little repressively. A cart full of luggage had rolled into the open area that did service as a platform, followed by a pony and trap occupied by a well-dressed couple who were looking distractedly around for someone to assist them. 'Are you suggesting I should wait for Mr Valentino after all?' Annie suggested, a little tartly. 'You seem to have changed your tune?'

'Every woman's prerogative,' Jane said collectedly and bent to hug Davie – though, tall as he was, in truth he was barely a couple of inches shorter than her.

He flung his arms about her, disarranging the old-fashioned bun that coiled at the base of her neck, and all but strangling her in the process. 'Thanks, Nan. I really enjoyed myself.'

She laid a hand against his smooth cheek. 'Come again soon.'

'Oh, yes. We will. And you and I will go back to London by boat. You promised, remember?'

Jane and Annie exchanged a glance. Annie shrugged, her eyes tired. 'Come on, my lad. Or we won't get a seat.'

'Wait.' Jane opened her handbag, brought out a paper bag of sweets, winked at Davie. 'For the journey,' she said.

Mother and son clambered aboard the train, and squeezed onto one of the benches that ran lengthways on either side of the carriage. Davie sat with his legs swinging, his grey socks crumpled about his ankles. 'I met a boy on the beach the other day,' he said after a little while, eyeing their fellow passengers interestedly. 'He goes to *school* on this train. Lucky blighter!'

Annie lifted her eyebrows. Davie pretended not to notice, his bright, dark eyes innocent as a babe's.

The whistle shrieked again; the train, snorting, started to move. Both turned to wave through the window to Jane. Annie glanced at her son. 'Would you like that? To live here, and to go to school on this train?'

He thought about it, face concentrated. Beyond the windows the heathland and marshes of Suffolk chugged by at quiet, comfortable speed. Then, 'No,' he said, and lifted his smiling face to her. 'I like Southwold. It's a lovely place to come and visit, especially with Nan here. But we couldn't leave Kew, could we?' The words were full of absolute confidence. 'Kew's home. And it has the Gardens, and the Gallery.' He wriggled back on the seat and opened the paper bag his grandmother had given him. 'Cor! Gobstoppers.' He popped one into his mouth, rolled it noisily around his teeth. The train was rolling across the bridge that spanned the River Blythe. Davie turned again to look out of the window, his fair, heavy hair flopping across his forehead. The tide was high and the river swirled deep. The sun shone on the lovely coastal flatlands with their creeks and marshes, their lonely heathlands, their long, wild beaches. 'I do like it here,' he repeated, his sun-brightened face serious, 'but really, I always feel a little bit sorry for anyone who doesn't live in Kew.'

Annie laughed. 'It does rather look as if Kew's stuck with us, then, doesn't it?'

Chapter Two

'She really was the most *remarkable* person—' The woman who spoke was the possessor of a booming voice, a large bosom and a bright red cloche hat that clashed garishly with the orange-flowered pattern on her dress. Davie, tongue tucked between his teeth, a frown of concentration creasing his brow, bent over his drawing as the voice went on: '—travelled *all* over the world, you know. A woman alone, and in the nineteenth century. Imagine it, my dear. Africa. America. Australia. Russia. All over Europe – are you listening, Tilda?'

'Yes, Molly.' The large woman's smaller companion bobbed her head obediently. She stood for a moment looking around at the hundreds of pictures that adorned the gallery walls. 'They really are quite extraordinary. So detailed. And so many of them—' She moved closer to a picture, peering at it short-sightedly.

'As I said. A rare and talented woman. What are you *doing*, Tilda?'

Tilda jumped back guiltily. 'Just looking at the picture, Molly. Look, it has a monkey in it – isn't he sweet?'

The loud-voiced one tutted impatiently. 'Oh, do come along. We've no time for that. We haven't been to the Palm House yet. Come along,' she repeated, sweeping to the door. Tilda scurried after her, throwing a mildly apologetic look in the direction of the gallery's only other two occupants. As the door closed behind them, the man who was sitting further along the bench from Davie caught the boy's eye, raised his own eyebrows humorously and grinned. Even beyond the closed door they could still hear the stentorian voice bellowing orders and instructions to the unfortunate Tilda.

The man whistled softly, laughing. 'What a battleaxe!'

Davie grinned back. 'She didn't even know what she was talking about. Marianne North didn't go to Russia. Not so far as I know, anyway. And she didn't do many of her drawings in Europe, either.'

The man glanced around. 'She certainly produced an amazing body of work. And, as poor downtrodden Tilda pointed out, all so beautifully detailed—'

'There are more than eight hundred.' Davie leaned back on the bench, chewing on his pencil. 'I think they're smashing. I like the Indian ones best. Or at least, I think I do. The South African ones are super as well. It's really hard to choose, and sometimes I change my mind. Mother prefers the Australian ones.'

The man glanced interestedly at the sketch pad on the boy's knees, then back up at the earnest face. 'You obviously know a lot about them.'

Self-composedly the child lifted a shoulder. 'I'm going to be a botanist when I grow up. I shall travel all over the world and draw things, like Marianne North did. I hope I'll discover a plant no one's ever seen before, and have it named after me.' The tone was assured. 'And perhaps I'll have one named after Mother as well,' he added.

'Your mother doesn't have a problem with your plans?' his companion asked, in entertained curiosity. 'It seems a slightly unusual ambition?'

'Oh, no. Mother doesn't mind at all. In fact she thinks it a very good idea.'

The man smiled again. Davie, a perceptive child of immediate likes and dislikes, had already decided that he had an extremely nice smile; it crinkled his narrow, brightly hazel eyes in a very infectious way. 'So how are you going to put this grand plan into action?' He sounded genuinely interested.

'I haven't exactly worked it out yet.' Davie was earnest. 'I shall go to university, of course. Mother says I don't have to decide which one yet, and I expect she's right. I read a lot already. And I draw a lot, too.' The boy looked down at his sketch, putting his head on one side as he studied it, frowning a little.

'Would you mind if I had a look?' the stranger asked quietly. 'I know a little about art. I came to Kew specifically to see the North pictures.'

Davie hesitated for a moment.

'It doesn't matter if you'd rather not.' The words, and the smile that accompanied them, were quick.

'Oh, no. Go ahead. Here—' Davie handed him the sketchbook, then watched him with wary, suddenly watchful eyes.

There was a moment of silence; then the man lifted his head, still smiling. 'You have a great deal of talent, young man.' He handed the pad back. 'You get the botany bit right and I don't think you'll have any problems with the pictures!'

'Thank you, Mr—?' Davie, reaching out to take the pad, looked at his new friend expectantly.

'Ross. Richard Ross.' The man extended a large-boned hand.

Davie took it, his own long, narrow hand all but disappearing. 'I'm David. David Sancerre. Everyone calls me Davie.'

Dark brows lifted. 'That's an unusual name. It sounds French?'

'Yes. My father – my real father – was French. I never knew him. He died before I was born. In the war, you know.' Obviously from the matter-of-fact way the child spoke it was a fairly oft-repeated explanation. 'I was born in Paris.'

Richard Ross raised suddenly startled eyebrows. 'Paris? Well, I'll be blowed! My business has a branch in Paris! I have an apartment there. In the rue Jacob. Do you know it?'

Davie shook his head. 'Actually I don't know Paris at all. I've never been there. Not that I remember, if you see what I mean,' he added, with a meticulous accuracy that brought another quick smile.

'Oh?'

Davie turned a page, rummaged in his pocket for a pencil sharpener. 'It's Mother. She won't go there. She's – well, she just won't. She says it's best that I wait till I'm grown up.' He glanced at his watch. 'I can't think where she's got to, actually. She should have been here ages ago. There must have been a queue at the post office. She stopped off to send a telegram to my Nan.'

'So – your mother won't go to Paris? What a pity. It's such a lovely city.'

'It isn't just Paris. She doesn't like boats. But even if she did, I suppose it would make her sad. Paris, I mean. With my father dying and everything.'

'Perhaps. Yes, I can see that.' Richard Ross crossed long legs and leaned forward, his elbow upon his knees. 'So –

tell me about some of the pictures here. Do you have a favourite?'

'Oh yes,' Davie said immediately, pointing. 'It's been my favourite ever since I was a little boy. *And* it's down at the bottom where I can see it properly. It's over there, number forty-two: *Fror Imperiale, Coral Snake and Spider, Brazil.* She painted it in 1873, I think.'

Richard Ross laughed. 'Snakes and spiders. That sounds about right to attract a lad.' He leaned back, stretched his arms along the back of the bench, brown head thrown back as he surveyed the charmingly idiosyncratic exhibition in its equally charming and idiosyncratic setting. The pictures ranged about them, set so close together that the walls between could barely be seen. The artist herself had arranged them so more than forty years before, as she had designed and painted the frieze which ran beneath the splendid clerestory windows that lit the paintings from above, and the intricate decorations that surrounded the doors.

'So what about the paintings right at the top?' Richard Ross asked amusedly. 'Are you saving them for when you grow up, too? Or do you have a ladder?'

Davie laughed. 'Mother used to lift me up, but I'm too big now. I sometimes stand on the benches if there's no one around,' he added with artless honesty, then turned his head and jumped to his feet as the door opened again. 'Mother! There you are! Wherever have you been?'

Annie hesitated a little, smiled. 'There were a lot of people in the post office. I had to wait.'

Richard Ross had risen courteously at her entrance. Annie looked from one to the other, faintly enquiring.

The man held out his hand. 'Richard Ross,' he said quickly. 'Young Davie here has been telling me about the pictures.' His voice was light and pleasant, his bright, flecked eyes suddenly sharp and lit with interest.

Annie, responding to the engaging smile, took his proffered hand. 'Annette Hill,' she said. His hand was warm, the clasp firm. 'How do you do? I do hope he hasn't been bothering you?'

'Mother!'

Richard Ross shook his head. 'Not at all. We've had a very enlightening conversation.' He was, she guessed, in his early thirties, tall, rangily built, dressed in Oxford bags and a sports jacket that were both fashionable and expensive-looking.

'He knows all about art and he likes my picture. Don't you, Mr Ross? Look, Mother – I've been copying the Australian flowers that you like. I'll have to come back, though; they're nowhere near finished. I'll paint them for you if you want. For your birthday.' David held out his sketchbook.

Annie, very aware of the open and undisguised interest in Richard Ross's narrow eyes, withdrew her hand from his. 'Davie – I'm sorry, but I really think we ought to go.'

'What? But you said—'

'We can come back tomorrow.'

'I'm at school tomorrow.'

'After school.' Firmly polite, she nodded to Richard Ross and, turning, held out her hand to her son. 'Goodbye, Mr Ross. It was pleasant meeting you.'

'Goodbye, Mrs Hill. Goodbye, Davie.'

'Bye.' Frowning, Davie turned to his mother. 'Mother, it's not fair – you did say—'

'Home, Davie. Uncle Fergus is coming to tea. He has something to ask you.'

Richard Ross moved to open the door and held it for them, watching as they walked the verdant path away from the gallery, the pleated skirt of Annie's printed chiffon dress swishing about legs that he had already noticed and appreciated. Davie turned to wave. Smiling, he waved back. Annie, tall, graceful, reserved, her dark bob swinging as she walked, did not look round.

–

'Well, young man. What do you say?' Fergus Cameron's deep voice was gentle.

Davie sucked his lip for a moment, and turned his wide eyes upon his mother. The three of them were sitting at the tea table, the remains of the meal still laid upon it.

Annie said nothing, but her own eyes were watchful.

'It will be very nice, I expect,' the boy said carefully, then looked sharply up at the man. 'But we will still live here, won't we? We'll stay in Kew?'

'Certainly. Your mother has already made the point. Your school is here, your friends are here.' Fergus smiled reassuringly. 'The idea is to make you happier, Davie, not to make you miserable—'

'I am happy.' The words were just a little too quick.

Annie opened her mouth, but Fergus spoke first. 'Of course you are. But, surely – there's always room for a little extra happiness in anyone's life, isn't there?'

Davie's face was strained. He had not smiled. 'I suppose so.' The words did not carry conviction.

'Don't you like the idea of having a father again?'

The child nodded.

'Then may I ask you formally for your mother's hand in marriage?' Fergus's eyes were twinkling now. Davie had always thought that, with his white moustache and hair and his rotund figure, Uncle Fergus sometimes looked like Father Christmas dressed up in a business suit. His mother could have done worse, he supposed. She might have ended up marrying someone like Peter Saunders' dreadful father, who never did anything but shout, and who bullied everyone fearfully.

'All right,' he said. 'I don't mind.'

Annie reached out an arm to him. He slipped from the chair and moved to her, putting an arm about her shoulders and leaning against her. 'It'll be fine, darling,' she said softly. 'You'll see.'

He stood for a moment, rubbing a strand of her straight, shining dark hair between finger and thumb in a faintly babyish way that wrung her heart. 'May I go and play in the garden, please?'

'Of course. Off you go.'

He closed the door very quietly behind him, upon silence. Fergus was watching Annie steadily. She fiddled with a teaspoon in her saucer. 'Would you like a fresh cup of tea?'

'No. Thank you.'

'I don't mind making a pot.'

He shook his head.

She got up and went to the long French windows that looked onto the garden. Davie was sitting on his makeshift swing that hung from the branch of an old apple tree, twisting it round and round, then taking his feet from the ground and letting it spin back. As she watched, it stopped, rocked back and forth for a moment, then settled to stillness. Davie sat, arms linked about the ropes, head down, his bare legs swinging.

'He'll get used to the idea.' Fergus had come up behind her.

Will he? Will I? 'Yes,' she said. 'Of course he will.'

There was a small silence; then she felt his hand on her shoulder. 'You've made me a very happy man, my dear. Thank you.'

In the garden Davie, very slowly, was twisting the ropes of the swing again, leaning back, his eyes closed.

–

The spring night was warm, the house very quiet. Annie, propped comfortably upon her pillows, struggled to concentrate on her book. She had read the last sentence at least three times, and had made no sense of it at all. Sighing, she laid the book open and face-down beside her and leaned her head against the pillow, eyes distant.

Fergus was a dear, dependable man. He cared for her and he cared for Davie. He would make a good husband. What was it she had said to her mother on the beach at Southwold? Safety and good sense…

She reached to turn the light off, slipped out of bed and walked to the window, drawing open the curtains. The lino was cool on her bare feet. The garden below was flooded with silver moonlight, the sharp-edged shadows black as ink. Annie leaned her elbows on the windowsill and her chin on her cupped hands. The smell of blossom drifted in through the window, a bird twittered sleepily, and in one of the other gardens a girl laughed softly. On the nearby river a tug hooted. The dazzling lantern of the moon hung motionless in the sky. It was a night to share, a night for lovers.

Davie had been conceived on a night not unlike this, and in a garden.

She shivered a little and closed her eyes for a moment, a taste on her tongue, a haunting shadow in her mind.

Safety and good sense. There was undoubtedly a lot to be said for both...

She remained at the window for a long time before finally straightening, stretching tiredly and turning back to her bed. As she did so she stepped into a beam of moonlight and caught sight of herself in the long mirror on the door of the wardrobe: a tall figure, white-shouldered, full-breasted, the pale satin of her nightdress clinging sensuously to the curve of her neat waist and hips.

The dark eyes that looked back at her were pensive and held, as she supposed they always did, a shadow of remembered pain.

Chapter Three

'—*they said in their hundred voices,* '*No, not yet,*' *and the sky said,* '*No, not there.*'

Annie snapped shut the book and tilted her head back, resting it against the tree under which she was sitting, gazing into the middle distance through half-closed eyes – her attention for once not immediately caught and held by the great glass structure that was Kew's magnificent Temperate House on the far side of this part of the gardens. She had read *A Passage to India* twice in as many weeks; the book fascinated and yet at the same time somehow repelled her. It was – she searched for the word – it seemed a shame to call such a book 'dispiriting', but this was the word that came repeatedly to mind.

Her thoughts distracted, she did not at first see Davie coming out of the Marianne North Gallery accompanied by the tall figure of Richard Ross. They were almost upon her before she noticed them.

She jumped to her feet, brushing her skirt. 'Mr Ross. Good afternoon.'

He smiled his quick, cheery smile. 'Good afternoon. I do hope you don't mind… I came across this young man in the Gallery – I left my fountain pen there yesterday after I had taken some notes and had to return to retrieve it – and we had the mutual thought that a glass of lemonade might be of benefit. What do you think?'

'And a bun.' Davie grinned up at him. 'You did mention a bun—'

'Indeed I did.' Richard Ross looked back at Annie.

Annie hesitated, uncertain. 'I'm not sure that—'

Davie's face dropped. 'But we often go and have a lemonade. Why can't we today?'

Richard Ross's bright, narrow eyes were steady and smiling on hers. He cocked a questioning eyebrow; almost, she might have thought, a challenging one.

'Please?' Her graceless son beamed at her, all confidence that he would get his own way.

She shrugged and gave in. 'All right. Why not? It is very warm.' She tucked the book under her arm, took the folder that Davie held out to her, and turned to stroll beside Richard Ross towards the Refreshment Pavilion, while Davie streaked away across the grass making engine noises. 'In case you're wondering,' Annie said dryly, 'he's a motor car. His one dream in life – apart from being a botanist – is to own a motor car. Until he's old enough he has to put up with pretending he is one.'

The man beside her laughed. 'He told me. In the Gallery. We had quite a chat.' His laugh, like his smile, was quick, warm and infectious.

She smiled up at him. 'Do you have children, Mr Ross?'

He shook his head. 'No.' He hesitated a moment, then added, 'I'm not married. Not...' he hesitated. 'Not any more, that is.'

He spoke with a perfectly easy straightforwardness, yet somehow the confidence disconcerted her, made her feel as if her words had been unmannerly. Annie felt a faint uncomfortable colour rising in her face. She ducked her head to hide it and the book she was carrying slipped from her hand.

He bent swiftly to retrieve it for her. '*A Passage to India.*' He handed it to her. 'I read that last year, when it first came out. What do you think of it? Are you enjoying it?'

Annie, the complexities of the thing still in her mind, thought seriously for a moment. 'Is "enjoy" quite the right word for a book like that? I'm not certain it is. I've read it twice, and no, I'm not sure that I do actually like it. It's marvellously written, but it isn't exactly the most cheerful of works, is it?'

Still smiling, he shook his head. 'Some of the best books aren't. But I do know what you mean.'

'It's…' She hesitated. 'It's a very thought-provoking book.' Suddenly, as she sensed he had wanted, she was at ease again, and laughing. 'I'm just not altogether sure I can organise the thoughts it provokes. Some of the – I suppose you'd call them philosophical – bits stump me entirely. I've read and reread Godbole's piece about good and evil and although I think I can see some underlying sense of what he's saying, I can't really grasp it—'

'Aren't you just proving one of the points the book is trying to make?' he asked. 'East is East and West is West…' He let the words trail off.

'And women are women and men are men, and never the twain shall understand each other,' she supplied wryly. 'Yes. I suppose I am.' They turned and started to stroll towards the Refreshment Pavilion again. 'But – surely – we don't really live like that, do we? No one seems to mean what they say. No one seems to understand their own or anyone else's motives or ideas. Worse, they don't even appear to try. Forster writes as if life is just one big muddle. A misunderstanding. Or worse, a deceit.

People say one thing and mean another. Or say one thing and *do* another, which is horrible. Most of their actions seem predicated on snobbery, ignorance, prejudice or self-interest—'

'Well, I suppose it sounds cynical, but wouldn't you agree that, on the whole, that's often true?' He was watching her interestedly.

She thought for a moment. 'I do hope not,' she said honestly after a moment. They walked a few slow steps in silence. Then, 'Even the relationship that you think is going to survive – the friendship between Fielding and Aziz – doesn't. And again it's wrecked by misunderstanding.' She tilted her head to glance up at him. 'I suppose it's just that the relationships seem all wrong somehow. The whole thing's so perverse and – well, depressing, I suppose. No one seems to *care*.'

'Aren't you really saying that the book is almost too true to real life? People live like that. People are like that. Life *is* messy and contradictory and perverse. There *are* no easy answers, no neat and satisfactory endings. Life on the whole is a muddle. You can never know what another person is thinking, never truly see behind the words he or she speaks. It's the human condition. We tend to expect our books to be different: to offer nice clear beginnings and tidy, explanatory endings.' He grinned quickly, mocking his own sudden seriousness. 'And if possible a well-organised middle. *Passage* doesn't offer that. It offers questions rather than answers.'

They strolled in silence for a moment. The late spring sunshine filtered through the bright-leafed branches above them and touched the freshly cut grass with gold. Davie revved up his motor-car sounds and flew past them, grinning and tooting.

'I suppose you're right,' Annie conceded at last. 'And pessimistic questions at that. Find me one sentence in the entire book that says anything good about marriage, for instance. Wait…' She stopped, flicking through the pages. 'Ah – here – Fielding talking to Adela about marriage. I've read it a dozen times. *It begins and continues for such very slight reasons. The social business props it up on one side and the theological business on the other, but neither of them are marriage, are they? I've friends who can't remember why they married, no more can their wives. I suspect that it mostly happens haphazard, though afterwards various noble reasons are invented. About marriage I am cynical.*'

As she read her words had become slower, her voice quieter. She stood for a moment, staring down at the page.

He waited, watching her, interest in his eyes.

She stood still, head bowed, looking down at the book. 'What is it that Adela asks herself before she goes into the caves?' she asked very quietly, speaking almost as if to herself. *What about love?* What about love,' she repeated, even more quietly, and with a completely different inflection. 'There's a question!' And was herself surprised at the faint but unmistakeably discernible bleakness in the words.

He said nothing.

Annie flushed again, aware that perhaps she had given away more than she would have cared to, and to a stranger.

Suddenly and briskly she snapped the book shut and looked up. 'And then silly Fielding goes and gets married himself! To someone, or so it seems, that he doesn't understand and can't talk to.' She lifted her voice a little. 'Davie – *do* stop tearing around so! You'll wear yourself out in this heat!'

They strolled on. Her companion was obviously enjoying the discussion. '*What about love?*' he repeated. 'A question we could probably discuss for a thousand years and not come up with an answer. But you take my point? In my opinion the whole book is a question. Why do people behave as they do? Why don't we ever learn from our mistakes? Why should one people despise another simply because of their race? Simply because they don't understand them?'

'Will anybody ever understand anybody?' Annie's words were deliberately dry.

'I'm with Forster, I'm afraid. I very much doubt it,' he said, and then laughed aloud. 'Enough, enough! It's too warm for philosophising. Here's the Pavilion. Lemonade and buns, that's the ticket.'

All at once unaccountably light-hearted, Annie flicked a smile at him. 'I don't think even the disillusioned Mr Forster could disapprove of lemonade and buns, surely?'

–

'So – do I understand that you're an artist, Mr Ross?' Annie asked politely a short time later, settled at a table in the Pavilion, pouring tea.

'No,' said Davie cheerfully, around a mouthful of sticky bun. 'He's a solicitor. He works in London mostly, but also in Paris. Don't you, Mr Ross?'

'That's right.' Richard Ross addressed his answer to Annie. 'The law is my living. Art is my passion.'

'A passion I expect you find easy to indulge in Paris?'

'Quite so. My grandfather established the family firm in London some fifty years ago. My father expanded to Paris just after the war.' He accepted the cup of tea she offered. 'Thank you.' He sat in sunshine; as he looked at her, the light gilded his long lashes and glinted green and gold in his eyes. 'Davie tells me that his father was French?' There was a gently questioning inflection in the words.

Annie flicked a slightly repressive look at her son. What other personal details had he divulged to this undoubtedly attractive but somehow increasingly unnerving stranger? 'Yes. He was killed in the first weeks of the war, before Davie was born.'

'A tragedy.' His voice was soft.

'One of many. Like so many other young people, the war wrecked our lives before they had fairly begun. We were far from being the only ones.' She shrugged a little, stirred her tea, eyes downcast, her face pensive.

'You lived in Paris?'

His question reclaimed her attention. 'Yes. Actually, my own father was French. I was born in Paris. My mother is English. Father died just before the war, and after Davie was born Mother and I came to England.'

'Davie tells me you haven't been back to Paris since?'

'No.' The word was short. Davie munched happily on his bun, apparently oblivious to the rather more searching glance his mother had sent his way this time. 'I have no desire to go. There are too many memories. My life – our life – is here.'

'I can understand that.'

'Anyway, I told you – Mother doesn't like ships,' Davie offered innocently.

'Davie, I'm sure Mr Ross doesn't want to be bored by my personal foibles,' his mother said sharply.

Davie finished his bun, licked his fingers, eyed the one that Annie was toying with. 'Are you going to eat all of your bun?' He grinned at Richard Ross. 'Mother thinks I've got worms.'

'You're a growing lad, that's all. Here, have mine.'

'Wow, thanks!'

'Where do you live in Paris, Mr Ross?' Annie asked, trying to bring some order back into the conversation.

'Rue Jacob. On the Left Bank.'

'I know it. We had an apartment on boulevard St Germain. Philippe was at the medical school.'

Richard Ross had leaned his chin on his hand and was watching her with sympathetic interest. 'You must have been very young?'

She shrugged. 'Yes. I suppose we were. We were in Paris. There was talk of war. It was all very... intense. Very chaotic.'

'And very romantic,' he said, unexpectedly.

She looked at him. 'Yes,' she said quietly. 'And very romantic. Almost irresistibly so.'

'I've got a picture of my father,' Davie said. 'He looked just like me.'

'He was a Parisian?'

For a moment Annie found herself wondering how on earth this man was managing – in the most engaging of ways – to extract so much information in so short a time; information that she rarely shared with anyone? 'Yes,' she said, a little abruptly. 'He lived with his father in a house in Billancourt.' A house with an unusually beautiful garden... 'Come along, Davie.' She was suddenly brisk. 'Finish your bun. We're meeting Uncle Fergus at six, remember?' She turned to look directly at Richard Ross. Why she felt compelled to say it she was not sure, but say it she did: 'Fergus is my fiancé.'

He nodded, lips twitching. 'I know. Davie told me.'

This time she was startled into sudden, exasperated laughter. '*Davie!* Honestly!'

'Well, it isn't a secret, is it?' her son asked in a faintly injured tone.

'Of course not, but—' Annie shook her head and gave up. 'Thank you for the tea, Mr Ross. We really must go…' She stood up, reached a hand for Davie's. 'Say goodbye to Mr Ross, Davie.'

Richard Ross too came politely to his feet, opening his mouth to speak, but Davie forestalled him. 'Goodbye, Mr Ross. I'll see you on Thursday,' he said.

Annie looked from one to the other.

'I'm sorry,' the man said quickly, 'I was going to mention it. I should have said something earlier—'

'I'm going to lend him my book about Marianne North. The one you got me for Christmas.' Davie frowned a little uncertainly. 'It is all right, isn't it? He did say he'd look after it.'

'I—yes, of course it's all right.' For a reason she could not, or perhaps did not want to explain, Annie had an obscure feeling that it wasn't all right at all, but she could not bring herself to be so churlish as to say so. She was brisk. 'We'll meet you in the Gallery, then, Mr Ross. About five?'

He hesitated.

'I said he could come and pick it up,' said Davie.

Dark eyes and hazel held each other steadily for a moment. 'I hope you don't mind?' the man asked gently.

'Of course not. Why should I?' She smiled, very brightly. 'Don't tell me – I expect you know where we live?'

He nodded gravely, his eyes laughing. 'Davie told me,' he said.

–

'Is something wrong?' Fergus asked. They were sitting at the open French doors of her sitting room watching Davie play on the swing. 'You're very quiet.'

Annie shook her head quickly. 'No. Nothing. I'm just a little tired, that's all. The warm weather, I suppose.'

He leaned forward and took her hand. 'We have plans to make. Have you chosen a date?'

She shook her head. 'No, I'm sorry, I haven't.'

'It should be in the summer, I think. June? July, perhaps? And the honeymoon? Where would you like to go?'

'I—hadn't thought—'

'I need to know the date, my dear. I have to book time away from the office.'

'Yes, I realise that. I'm sorry. I'll get myself organised in the next few days, I promise.'

'It can only be a week, I'm afraid. I can't trust Smithers to run things for longer than that. He's reliable enough, but lacks initiative—'

'That's all right. A week will be lovely.' Annie put a hand to her head.

'You'll make the arrangements with your mother to take care of Davie?'

'Yes, Fergus. Of course I will.' Her voice had sharpened. 'As soon as we set the date. She'll come to the wedding and she'll stay until we come back.' She rubbed at her head again. In the garden Davie was swinging high, his feet grazing the leaves of the tree. 'Fergus, I'm sorry, you're right. I'm not quite myself tonight. I have a headache coming on. Would you mind very much…?' She let the words trail to silence.

'Of course not, my dear. Would you like me to get you something? A cup of tea? An aspirin?'

'No, no.' She was suddenly desperate for him to go. 'As I said – it's just the heat. I'll get an early night. I'll be quite all right.'

Fergus stood, bent to kiss her cheek. 'Don't get up. I'll say goodbye to Davie and let myself out. I'll pop in on Thursday.'

'No. Not Thursday. We… won't be here. I'm taking Davie to see an old friend in Richmond.'

'Very well. Until the weekend, then.'

'Yes. We'll meet you at Liverpool Street. I thought we'd catch the five o'clock train if that's all right?'

'Of course. I'm looking forward to it.' He kissed her again and went into the garden.

Annie watched as he walked over to the swing. Davie scraped to a halt. Fergus ruffled his hair and said something; Davie smiled half-heartedly. Fergus gave him a push, setting the swing in motion again, turned and lifted a hand to Annie. She waved back, watched him to the garden gate. Why had she lied? Why had she felt that if Fergus had said another word she would have screamed at him?

'A boy needs a father,' her mother had said, and 'he's a good man'.

Yes.

What about love?

'Davie,' she called. 'Come along in. Time for bed.'

Chapter Four

Annie pushed open the dining-room door. '…the wheels are in that box, I think,' Davie was saying. 'D'you mind finding them? I don't want to let go of this until I get the screw in properly—'

'Right you are.' Richard Ross, down on the floor with the boy and apparently equally engrossed in what they were doing, pulled the wooden box towards him and rummaged in it. Neither had noticed Annie standing at the door. The carpet was strewn with pieces of Meccano. The model seaplane that Davie had been painstakingly constructing for weeks had, his mother noticed, become something almost recognisable as an aeroplane in the two hours since he had invited their visitor to 'come and look' at it. She leaned against the door jamb, watching them.

Davie was sprawled on his stomach, fair hair falling across his forehead, tongue caught between his teeth in concentration as he fiddled with the tiny screw. His companion had tired of rooting around in the box and upended it, spilling its contents onto the floor, thus adding to the disorder around them. He had taken off his jacket and tie and thrown them across a chair, turned back the cuffs of his shirt to reveal broad, powerful-looking wrists. Now he raked amongst the bits and pieces with a long, sun-browned finger. 'Ah. Here we are. Which size?'

'That one.' In glancing up, Davie caught sight of his mother. 'Oh, hello, Mother. Look at this – isn't it smashing?'

'It's certainly come on since I last saw it. But then, since it sounds as if you've been using our guest as a dogsbody for the past two hours or so, that isn't too surprising, is it?' She smiled as she said it – and came to an uncharacteristically impulsive decision.

'Mr Ross – may I offer you a drink in exchange for your hard labour?' She glanced out of the window, to where long shadows had crept across the garden. 'Davie's kept you here so long I'd say the sun is well over the yardarm, wouldn't you?'

Richard Ross sat back easily, smiling, his long legs crossed in front of him. 'As a matter of fact, I'd love one. But please – it's a little difficult to be formal sprawled on the floor being out-engineered by a bright lad of ten. Won't you call me Richard?'

'I—' She hesitated, taken by surprise.

Davie's head came up. 'I've already said I will,' he said encouragingly. 'And of course you must call Mother Annie,' he added to Richard. Then, the situation sorted out to his satisfaction, he rested his elbows on the carpet and put his chin in his hands, frowning. 'Could you pass me the screwdriver, please, Richard? And the longest strip you can find—?'

The man threw an amused glance at Annie, smothering a grin.

'What can I get you, Mr—Richard?' Annie corrected herself.

'Would you have whisky?'

Annie hadn't. But Fergus had. 'Yes. Of course.' She laughed a little. 'Will you have it on the floor, or would you rather catch the last of the sunshine in the garden?'

'But Mother, we're—'

She held up a warning finger. 'You, young man, can have another half an hour and then it's bed. You've school in the morning. Milk or lemonade?'

Davie scowled rebelliously for a moment; but even he knew the meaning of that particular tone of voice. 'Lemonade, please,' he said, and then, hopefully, 'and some biscuits.'

'Two biscuits,' Annie said firmly. 'And you can do a bit of tidying up first,' she added for good measure. 'I don't quite see my dining room as a Meccano factory.'

'I'll help,' Richard said quickly. 'I've made quite as much mess as Davie has, after all. Probably more.' Again that open and attractive smile that was so hard not to return.

Davie beamed beatifically, his good temper quite restored.

In the sitting room, ignoring rather than wholly suppressing slight qualms of guilt, Annie opened Fergus's whisky, poured a generous glass and went into the kitchen for Davie's lemonade and biscuits. She could hear them talking and laughing in the dining room. She carried the tray back into the sitting room, put the glass of whisky on it and stood for a moment, undecided. Then, with a quick movement that had a touch of defiance about it, she reached for another glass and poured a small whisky for herself.

Out in the garden the shadows were lengthening across the lawn and the birds were singing. The scent of new-mown grass was on the air. In the far corner a glowing carpet of bluebells caught the last of the sunshine.

An old wooden garden table and chairs were set beneath a gnarled apple tree. It was an evening almost as much of summer as of spring, while the unseasonably warm weather continued. As Annie settled herself into a chair, a nest of baby birds in the branches above her head chirped hungrily and an anxious mother eyed her beadily, head cocked, from a nearby bush.

Richard and Davie came from the house, deep in conversation. Annie sipped her drink, watching them with intent and thoughtful eyes. The whisky burned and spread in her veins, sweet and peaty on the tongue. They stopped for a moment beside the little pond, Davie down on his knees beside it, pointing, Richard leaning forward with hands on knees, peering into the murky water.

Annie, unnoticed, studied him. Tall and lean, long of arm and leg, face narrow and handsomely boned. Not married. What was it he had said? 'Not any more.' A story there, then. She was not the naive innocent she once had been; she recognised too well the signs and signals of danger, of – perhaps – entrapment; certainly of pursuit. Perhaps indeed she was too sensitive to them? Perhaps it was she who was the cynic, rather than the attractive Mr Ross? Or maybe it was just that she knew better than to get carried away by charismatic strangers. Didn't she?

Why had she lied to Fergus about this evening? He could just as well have been here when Richard came to pick up the book. Why had she dressed with such care, changing her frock three times before she was satisfied? How was it that, try as she might to deny it, in their few meetings she had felt a sense of recognition, almost of intimacy with a man she did not know? He had asked her to call him Richard; in honesty she had to admit – to herself if not to him – that in the past couple of days that was already how she had come to think of him.

And she *had* thought of him. She could not deny that, either.

She sipped her drink again.

Richard straightened. Davie jumped to his feet and scampered to her. 'The tadpoles are getting really froggy!' he said excitedly. 'There are *trillions* of them! They're going to be hopping all over the garden soon,' he added with relish, and reached for his lemonade.

'Did you know that some people call them Polliwogs?' Richard asked, murmuring smiling thanks as Annie indicated a chair and handed him his glass.

'*Polliwogs?* What a keen word. We've got a pond full of *Polliwogs!*' Davie rocked with laughter and crammed a biscuit into his mouth.

Annie closed pained eyes for a second. 'Davie, did you leave your manners in the pond with the Polliwogs? Sit down, calm down and eat your biscuits properly. And don't do that,' she added in the same motherly breath.

Davie had been cheerfully gurgling his lemonade through his front teeth. Entirely undaunted he grinned from one to the other. 'It makes it go all fizzy in your mouth.'

As usual Annie could not resist laughter. 'It's already fizzy. You'll give yourself hiccups. Finish your drink and you can play on your swing for a while if you like.'

The child swung his legs. 'In a minute. I'd like to eat my biscuit first.' He caught his mother's repressive expression from the corner of his eye, and 'please,' he added.

Richard sipped his drink, savoured it, lifted the glass to the light that turned the amber liquid to gold. 'Your Fergus is a Scot?'

'Yes.'

He sipped again. 'Single malt, I'd guess—'

'Talisker. It comes from Skye, I believe.' Annie played with her own glass. 'It's Fergus's favourite.'

'Ah.' He smiled slowly. 'A man of good taste, obviously.'

She held his eyes, refusing to play the game. 'Yes,' she said crisply. 'He is.'

'Can I have another biscuit, please?' Davie had finished his lemonade in a long and noisy gulp.

'May I,' his mother corrected automatically. 'Yes, all right. They're in the kitchen.'

The boy slid from the chair and ran back to the house.

'He's a fine lad,' Richard said, watching him go.

'Thank you.' Annie sipped her whisky. 'I do sometimes wonder if I spoil him.'

Richard shook his head, smiling.

The sun had slipped behind the bulk of the house and they were sitting in warm shadow. Dusk gathered beneath the trees. Davie sauntered back out of the kitchen door nibbling on a biscuit, stopped at the pond and hunkered down again, watching the tadpoles.

'When do you marry?' Richard asked quietly.

She found herself avoiding his eyes, studying her glass. 'I don't know. We haven't decided yet.'

He said nothing.

She glanced back up at him, emboldened by whisky and by the sudden intimacy of the fading light. 'And you?'

He cocked his head, widening his eyes and lifting his eyebrows in question.

'You said you weren't married. Not any more?' True curiosity impelled the words.

It was his turn to study the glass he held. For long moments he said nothing, then he shrugged a little, lifted his eyes to meet hers. 'I must admit that I misled you just a little,' he said, 'since I've never actually been married. Not in the conventional sense, that is. Though I have to admit that I had always regarded our union as a permanent one, and tended sometimes even to forget that it actually wasn't.' His tone, whilst perfectly even, had taken on an edge, precariously sharp; close, even, to bitterness. 'Ours was supposed to have been a union that was above such bourgeois, man-made rules and conventions. Pieces of paper and wedding rings were irrelevant, or so my love believed. She would rather live forever free and as a lover than become a mere wife. Respectability did not appeal.' He was quiet for a moment.

'What happened?'

His smile was small and self-mocking. 'What do you think? She left me, of course.'

Annie sipped her drink, watching him.

'She's an artist. A good one. Her name is Isobella. We lived together in Paris. She's' – he hesitated, shrugged – 'wild. Wanton. And, of course – totally enchanting.' His voice was still quiet, and held now an oddly detached note, as if he were speaking of a stranger's life. 'A Bohemian in heart and in soul. She can't bear to be bored; she carries excitement with her like a burning torch. Oh, everyone told me – and I should have known – that I'd never be able to keep her. Never be able to tie her down. No one could. But in the way of such things I had to find out the hard way...' He shook his head a little, lifted the glass to his lips.

'How long were you together?'

'Nearly five years.'

'She's beautiful?'

'Yes. Beautiful. Talented.' He drank again. 'Capricious. Mendacious. And promiscuous. Promiscuity is her second nature. I later discovered that she'd had several affairs while we were together. At least' – he shrugged – 'I told myself that I didn't know until later.'

'That's awful.'

'That's Isobella. She can't help herself.'

'I don't know why,' Annie said lightly, 'but I'm afraid I always find that as excuses go that one has a particularly unconvincing ring to it.' She was aware how close to rudeness that could be thought, but she did not care. The exchange had disturbed her strangely; she wished she had not started it. The contrast between the life that Richard spoke of so easily and her own staid, respectable existence lay like a chasm between them.

Davie had wandered over to the swing and was drifting lazily back and forth, leaning back at arms' length, looking up at the darkening sky. A bird twittered sleepily.

Do you still love her? She nearly asked it. Then, a little alarmingly, she realised that she did not want to know the answer. The silence lengthened. Richard tossed back the last of his drink. 'I ought to go.' He made no move.

'Would you like another drink?'

He held her eyes, unsmiling. 'Very much,' he said.

As she walked to the house she could feel his eyes upon her like a physical touch. 'Five minutes, Davie,' she called as she passed him.

'O-oh—'

'Five minutes,' she reiterated firmly.

When she came back into the garden with the drinks Davie was at the table with Richard.

'…I'm interested in most schools,' Richard was saying, 'but if I had to choose, then I think it would be the Impressionists. They're such an exciting bunch. They took the art world by the throat and gave it a thorough shaking.'

'I'll bet the art world loved that.' Annie set his drink in front of him and sat down.

'Isobella's father was actually a part of it. He knew quite a few of them, was a fair painter himself.'

'That's obviously where she got her… unconventional ideas?' Annie suggested.

'Who's Isobella?' Davie asked, frowning.

Annie opened her mouth, but Richard forestalled her. 'A friend,' he said quickly. 'An old friend.'

Predictably Davie sat stubbornly with them until Richard had finished his drink and taken his leave. Whilst Davie got ready for bed, Annie sat on in the darkening garden, her elbows on the table, her chin in her hands. Around her the sleepy evening noises murmured into the shadows. The air was still warm. In the distance a wireless played tinnily: a Strauss waltz, lilting and familiar.

Annie had never been one to fool herself; she had little patience with self-deception in others and none at all in herself. Richard Ross was attracted to her. She knew it as certainly as if he had put it into words. And she was attracted to him. Very attracted to him.

The waters were getting deeper.

Even in the warmth she shivered a little; where on earth had that particular thought come from?

Fergus. She was to marry Fergus. It was the sensible – the safe – thing to do. She did not know Richard Ross from Adam himself; neither did he know her. A passing attraction could hardly be set against the years of Fergus's friendship.

What about love?

What about it? What was it? Would she recognise it if it walked into the garden and bit her?

She took a deep, sighing breath. The spring night air was fragrant with the scent of flowers.

Davie's bedroom light was on. Time to tuck him in. She got up and walked to the house, going in through the sitting-room windows. Halfway across the room she stopped. A book lay on the sofa table – Davie's Marianne North book. The book that Richard had come to borrow...

She stood looking at it for several long moments.

'Mo-ther!'

'I'm coming.' The words were absent.

'Can I have a drink?'

'I'll bring one.' She applied herself briskly to the tasks in hand. Ten minutes or so later, with a sleepy Davie tucked in and comfortable, she came back downstairs, picked up the book, the whisky bottle and two glasses, went into the garden, sat down at the table and, pensively and precariously balanced between the hope that he would come and the hope that he would not, waited.

–

He came. Half an hour later she heard the latch click on the garden gate. She had left the lights on in the sitting room and the French doors open. Sitting in the shadow of the apple tree she saw his tall figure walk into the patch of light that fell across the lawn. He stood for a moment, a little hesitant, at the open windows.

'I'm here,' she said quietly.

He turned, peering narrow-eyed into the shadows. Seeing her, he came to the table. 'I'm sorry,' he said, his voice nicely rueful, 'I forgot the book.'

Annie had almost finished her glass of whisky. 'No,' she said collectedly, 'you didn't.'

There was a long moment of silence. She saw the glimmer of his teeth in the darkness. 'No,' he agreed. 'You're right. I didn't.'

'It's here,' she said, touching the book.

He did not reach for it but stood looking down at her, his face in shadow.

'Won't you sit down?' She sounded, she realised, quite absurdly like a polite hostess at a tedious tea party.

He sat down, his eyes still on her face, his well-shaped head darkly silhouetted against the spread of light from the windows. In silence she poured him a drink. In silence he accepted it.

'I wanted to ask—' he began.

She waited.

'—if you'd come to dinner with me?' The glimmer of another smile. 'Davie didn't exactly give me a chance.'

There was a long, quiet moment. Annie played with her glass. 'I don't think I should.'

'I didn't ask if you *should*. I asked if you *would*.'

'I don't know. I'm sorry,' she added quickly, 'I'm not being difficult. I mean it: I don't know.'

'Would you think about it?'

'Yes.'

He leaned forward, elbows on the table, looking at her intently. 'May I ask you a personal question?'

She shrugged.

'Do you love Fergus?'

Annie had had far more to drink than was her custom. She turned her head away, looking into the darkness. 'I don't know that either,' she said simply. Then, 'I'm very...' she hesitated '...fond of him.'

'And you're going to marry him?'

'Yes. I am.' Her voice was less certain than the words.

He sipped his drink, watching her. 'Tell me about Davie's father.'

She was silent for a moment. 'There's little to know beyond what I've already told you. I was eighteen, he a year or so older. Summer in Paris. War was coming. In some ways it was... unreal. Feverish. Terrifying and yet... exciting. It was as if the danger-sharpened life, coloured it. As did so many other young people, we rushed into marriage before the war could separate us. We married in August, just before war broke out. He was killed on the Marne in early September; he didn't even know I was pregnant when he died. At the time I wanted to die too. But I didn't.' She turned her head to look at him in the darkness. 'You don't, do you? Mother had contacts at the British Embassy. After Davie was born they helped us get out of Paris and we came to England.' She was silent for a moment, remembering the absolute nightmare of that journey. 'It was a ghastly trip,' she added.

'And you've never been back since?'

She shook her head.

'Paris,' he said, and his voice was soft. 'You know what I love best about Paris?'

'What?'

'The river. The Seine must be the loveliest river in the world.'

Annie said nothing, absent-mindedly rubbed at her bare arms with the palms of her hands. Shivered a little, her skin in goosebumps.

'Those wonderful bridges. The tree-lined walks. Do you remember the chestnut trees?'

'Oh, yes. I remember the chestnut trees.'

'How can you bear never to have gone back?'

'Let's just say that all the memories were not necessarily good ones.'

'No. I can see that.' He had turned a little away from her, his profile silhouetted sharply against the spread of light from the windows. 'But what of the family? Philippe's family?'

'There was only his father... we never did get along very well. We lost touch – the war, the confusion—'

'And you never tried to find him?'

She shook her head. 'By the time the war ended I had remarried. Charles was a widower. Quite a bit older than me, but kind. Very kind. He treated Davie as his own; we were a family. The past was past. And as I said, there was bad feeling...' Shrugging, she let the words trail off, then cocked her head a little, watching him. 'Now, it's your turn.'

'My turn?'

She looked up at him. 'Your war? What was it like?'

He shrugged. 'Unpleasant. Wasn't everybody's?'

'Were you in the trenches?'

He sipped his drink. 'Yes. Ypres. Then the Somme.'

'Were you wounded?'

There was a touch of impatience in his shrug. 'A couple of times. As a matter of fact I was in hospital when the war ended. It was almost six months before I got myself patched up, demobbed and went to join my father in Paris.'

Annie had come across this reluctance to talk of war experience too often to attempt to push him any further. She changed tack. 'Where you met your Isobella,' she said lightly.

'Ah, "my" Isobella.' He put a dry emphasis on the adjective, then fell silent for a moment. 'There isn't a lot more to tell about that than I already have. As I said, she's a lovely, volatile and unconventional woman who tends to make up her own rules as she goes along. And even then she doesn't stick to them. As far as Isobella is concerned, rules – even her own – are made to be broken. I should have realised then – I certainly realise now – that no one will ever succeed in changing her.'

'Did you love her very much?'

'Yes. I did. But when I discovered that I couldn't trust her—' He fell silent for a moment. 'It was almost a relief when she finally left,' he said at last. 'We were living a life based on cheating and lies. It was bound to end as it did.'

The air was becoming cool. Richard tossed back his drink and stood up. 'I'm keeping you out. You're getting cold. You'll think about what I asked?'

'Yes.'

He picked up the book. 'May I bring this back next week? Say, a week today?'

'Yes.' Annie stood up, tilting her head to look up at him, the light falling on her face. For a moment she was certain he was going to kiss her. Then he lifted a hand in quick farewell and stepped back, turning swiftly and walking away to the gate in the darkness. She heard it click shut behind him.

She stood listening as his clipping footsteps echoed away along the pavement before, very slowly, she sank back down onto the chair, put an elbow on the table and leaned her chin on her hand, staring thoughtfully into the shadows of the night-time garden.

She sat there, quite still, for a long time.

Chapter Five

'You are *sure* you won't change your mind about letting me go on the boat with Nan, aren't you?'

'Davie, for heaven's sake! That must be the dozenth time you've asked me that!' his mother said, sleepily. 'No, I promise I won't change my mind, and yes, you may go home on the boat with Nan. Though I can't deny I'll be happy to see you back on terra firma, as you well know.'

'Mother doesn't like water,' Davie confided to Fergus. 'She saw some drowned people once and it frightened her.'

Fergus had heard the story – or as much of it as Annie had cared to tell him. 'Yes. I know.' He looked across at Annie. She had turned her head to look out of the carriage window; the evening sun burnished her dark hair almost to copper and glinted in the sweep of her lashes. Fergus Cameron was no romantic; quite the contrary, he had always positively prided himself upon being a restrained and temperate man. But studying the smooth, pale, intelligent face with its wide cheekbones and soft dark eyes, watching the pulse that beat at the base of her throat, the droop of her eyelids as the drowsy warmth and movement of the train lulled her, he felt – not for the first time – an uncharacteristic surge of excitement. Of real desire. His first marriage had been long, worthy and dull. It had produced two equally worthy and dull children. He had worked hard all of his life, been moderately successful and always irreproachably respectable. Yet in these past months he had discovered that for all the sober, avuncular image he showed to the world he was as capable of love – and of lust – as any other man. The discovery was as exciting as it was unexpected.

Annie sighed, stretched a little. Her full, soft breasts lifted against the bright silk of her dress. She opened her eyes, glanced out of the window, blinked herself awake. 'We're nearly there. Halesworth is the next stop.' She stood up and reached up to the luggage rack for her hat and jacket.

'Let me.' Fergus scrambled to his feet. Smiling, she turned to let him slip her jacket onto her shoulders. As she bent her head to button it her heavy hair fell away and he saw the white skin of the back of her neck, smooth and soft and vulnerable. More than anything he had ever wanted in his entire life, he wanted now to put his arms around her. To kiss her. He cleared his throat and reached for Davie's jacket and cap. 'Here you are, young man.'

It being Friday evening, the little train to Southwold was packed. Davie, inevitably, got into conversation with the woman sitting next to him. By the time they reached their destination, Annie noted with wry amusement that the woman knew who Davie was, where he lived, where he was going and that his Nan's dog was called Brandy, but 'I don't know what sort he is.' He was still talking as they got off the train. 'Nan calls him a Heinz Variety dog—'

'Come on, Davie.' Smiling apologetically at the woman, Annie took her son's hand. 'There is Brandy, look. He's brought Nan to the station to meet us—'

–

'So – have you named the happy day?' Jane Renault looked at her daughter across the kitchen table. They were buttering bread and making sandwiches for supper. Davie and Fergus were in the little front parlour playing ludo. Beyond the window the sun had disappeared behind building clouds; the sound of the distant sea washed through the open door.

Annie sliced cucumber with stoic precision. She did not look at her mother. 'No. We haven't decided yet.'

Something in her tone made Jane cock her head a little as she looked at her. 'So – I don't have to rush out and buy a big hat just yet?'

Annie smiled faintly. 'No. Don't worry. We'll give you plenty of notice.'

There was a small silence. Jane cut the sandwich she had made into neat triangles and arranged them on the plate with the others. 'He's a nice man,' she said softly, her eyes still on her daughter's face. 'I like him.'

'Yes. So do I.'

'He obviously gets on well with Davie—'

'Yes. At least—'

'At least – what?'

'I'm not sure that Davie's really keen on the idea of our marrying.' Annie reached for a slice of bread. She still did not raise her eyes to her mother's.

'Has he said so?'

'Not in so many words, no.'

'Then what makes you think so?'

'Just – I know Davie. I just sense that he isn't happy about it.'

'And is that why you haven't set a date?' Her mother's voice was gentle.

'No. No, of course not. We've been busy, that's all.' The words did not ring true even in her own ears. She buttered the bread ferociously. Brandy, sitting at her feet, cocked his head interestedly and looked hopeful.

'Darling – there isn't anything wrong, is there?'

'No, of course not.'

'Call me an interfering old bat if you like, but you can't let a ten-year-old run your life, you know, even if he is your son. Davie's bound to have some reservations. Children don't like change, and they don't like the prospect of change. The sooner you do it, the sooner he'll come to terms with it—'

Annie lifted her head at last and treated her mother to a swift, rueful grin. 'You're an interfering old bat,' she said mildly.

Unruffled, Jane laughed and reached for the plate. 'Fair enough.' She lifted her voice as she carried the plate to the door. 'Davie? Fergus? Supper's on the table.'

–

When Annie woke the next morning it was raining, a fine, drenching mist of rain that drifted in from the sea like heavy fog. She pulled on a skirt and jumper and went down to the kitchen. Brandy greeted her with a yelp and danced around her ecstatically like a circus dog on his hind legs.

'Ssh! You'll wake everyone up! Wait a minute; let me get my jacket on.' She pushed her arms into the old waterproof jacket she kept by the back door, tied a scarf over her head, slipped her feet into wellington boots and opened the door. With the little mongrel bounding dementedly around her feet, she set off towards the beach.

From a window under the eaves her mother's thoughtful eyes watched her go.

It was very early. The beach was deserted. Annie crunched along the shingle, hands in pockets, collar turned up against the chill air and the melancholy drift of the rain, face preoccupied. As was his habit, Brandy chased the waves, snapping and barking joyously.

As she walked, and as she had been doing almost constantly since Thursday evening, she tried to assemble her thoughts into some kind of rational order.

Richard had simply asked her out to dinner. That was all.

She wasn't married to Fergus. Not yet. She could go to dinner with anyone she pleased.

So – did she want to go to dinner with a virtual stranger?

Yes. She did.

And here, as many times before, in honesty she had to ask herself: what did that say about her relationship with Fergus?

She bent to pick up a handful of stones and stood for a moment absently tossing them into the sea one by one. Brandy came to sit by her side, watching her expectantly. She stooped to fondle the dog's wet ears. 'What do you think?' she asked him. 'Would it hurt? Just once? Something just a little exciting, a little romantic? Where's the harm?' She straightened, pulled a face. 'You know full well where the harm might be, my girl,' she told herself aloud. 'The altogether different question is, do you care?'

Boots scrunching on the shingle, she walked on.

–

As the day went on the weather improved, so after lunch at the Swan Hotel they escorted Fergus on an exploration of the little town, and especially of the lovely old church of St Edmund. Jane, who truly loved the place she had chosen for her home, kept up an informative running commentary, aided and abetted by Davie, who knew almost as much about the place as she did. After the church they strolled towards the sea, and stood looking out across Sole Bay from the low cliffs of Gun Hill, trying to imagine the day in 1672 when a great and bloody sea battle had raged, fought between squadrons of the English and Dutch navies. 'The Duke of York made them break down the bridge across Buss Creek, so the people couldn't run away if the Dutch landed,' Davie said. 'It must have been pretty scary standing here watching, knowing that, don't you think?'

'It certainly must,' Fergus agreed. He was watching Annie, who was looking out to sea with a faraway expression on her face. 'Who won?' he asked.

Annie did not even notice the question.

'Mother.' Davie tugged at her hand. 'Uncle Fergus is talking to you.'

'What? Oh, sorry – I was miles away...'

'I asked who won. The battle?'

Annie looked vague for a moment, then shrugged. 'I don't think anyone did, though both sides claimed they had, of course. By all accounts it was a very fierce affair.'

'There were *tons* of wounded,' said Davie. 'And ever so many died. Where are we going to have tea?'

That evening, at Jane's suggestion, Annie and Fergus went for a stroll on their own. 'Don't hurry,' she said, ignoring Annie's half-hearted protests. 'Davie and I will be all right on our own. Pop into the Crown for a drink—'

It was the last thing that Annie wanted and she was sure her mother knew it. That Fergus knew it too became clear almost as soon as they left the house.

'Annie – what's wrong?'

'Nothing. Nothing's wrong. Why do you ask?'

'You've barely said a word all day.'

'That isn't a crime, is it?' She knew how hurtfully snappish that was. 'I'm sorry,' she added quickly. 'I'm just a bit out of sorts, that's all.'

'Something to do with me?' he asked quietly. 'With us?'

'No. Nothing to do with anyone.' She shook her head irritably. 'It doesn't have to be anything to do with someone, does it? I just got out of the wrong side of the bed this morning, I suppose. That's all.'

They were walking through a small square, its neat garden deserted in the quiet evening light. Fergus stopped and turned to face her, holding her lightly by the shoulders. He studied her face for a long moment. 'Annie – please? Let's settle down, name the day and make the arrangements? I can't tell you how much I want us to be married. Wait…' His hands tightened as she opened her mouth to speak. 'I know I'm not very good at these things, but I want to tell you something. I love you. I hadn't realised how much I loved you. You made me so very happy when you said you'd marry me. Please, Annie, don't have second thoughts. Not now. It would' – he cleared his throat, uncomfortable with the emotive words, but determined to speak them nevertheless – 'it would break my heart, I think.'

Annie was staring at him, astonished – not to say appalled – and completely at a loss for words.

'You aren't going to change your mind, are you?' he asked, unable to keep the anxiety from his voice.

And, 'No. Of course not,' she found herself saying.

'And you will set a date? Soon?'

'Yes.'

He beamed. Drew her towards him. Kissed her, very gently.

Annie closed her eyes and tried, entirely unsuccessfully, to fight off the sense of helpless dismay that was threatening to envelop her.

–

The next day Davie was almost beside himself with excitement at the thought of going back to London by boat. Annie, fiercely anxious and, what was more, faced with the thought of the train journey alone with Fergus and his unexpected – and unwelcome – new eager attentiveness, did her best not to fuss or snap, but it was not easy. Her mother watched her with shrewd sympathy. 'You're sure you won't come with us?' she asked.

They were walking down to the pier, Davie dancing ahead of them. Annie shook her head. 'Mother, I can't. You know I can't. I know it's stupid. But just the thought of the water...' The words tailed off. 'I can't even think about it without getting panicked,' she confessed after a moment. 'I always thought I might grow out of it but,' she shrugged, 'if anything it's worse. I'll never forget the trip across from France. You must remember? I thought I was going to die of fright. It makes me feel ill just to think about it. No, you two go ahead, and enjoy the trip. You've got the key to the house? Just in case we get held up?'

'It's coming! It's coming!' Davie pointed.

'I've got it.' Jane patted her handbag and took Davie's hand. 'We'll see you later. Oh, by the way,' she paused for a moment, 'I forgot to mention that when I took Brandy over to Mrs Ludley she said the parish meeting has been postponed until next week, so I can stay an extra few days if that's all right with you. I thought I might do a bit of shopping in town. Wait a minute, Davie, there's ages yet—'

'We mustn't miss it!'

'We won't. I thought perhaps till next weekend. Is that all right?'

'Yes. Of course it is,' Annie said faintly.

'Bye, Mother. See you later.' Davie flung his arms about her neck. 'And don't worry. We'll be quite safe.'

She squeezed him, dropped a kiss on the top of his fair head. 'Of course you will. I'm just being silly, I know that. Look after Nan for me, won't you?'

Davie beamed. 'Come on, Nan. You will wave to us, Mother, won't you? Like a proper ship?'

'Yes. I'll wave.'

'We can pretend we're leaving Portsmouth or somewhere, to go to America, can't we?' Still chattering excitedly, Davie dragged his grandmother at an unseemly pace towards the landing stage.

Annie, bracing herself to watch them sail away, tried very hard not to think about the unexpected and disconcerting fact that her astute and sharp-eyed mother would not, as she had expected, be discreetly tucked away in Southwold when Richard came for his answer on Thursday evening.

That night, despite having a tired and happy Davie home after his adventure and snuggled safely in his bed, Annie dreamed about the drowned mother and child again. But this time the nightmare went further, as it sometimes did. This time, to the horror of the wan, water-bleached faces was added a haunting and terrible sense of evil, of fear and bitter shame. And this time, when she did wake up, she awoke standing beside Davie's bed, weeping silently.

–

'Richard's coming tomorrow,' said Davie.

His grandmother, standing at the sink scraping potatoes, looked up. 'Richard? Who's Richard?'

Davie was sitting at the kitchen table, his hand in the biscuit barrel. 'A friend. We met him at the Gardens. He's nice; you'll like him.'

Jane flashed him a mildly caustic smile. 'Is that an order?'

He laughed, sorting through the biscuits. 'Yes. Who's eaten all the chocolate biscuits?'

'You have. So, is this Richard the same age as you?'

Davie pulled out a custard cream, and surveyed it critically before biting into it. 'Oh, no. He's a grown-up. I lent him a book. He's coming to bring it back.'

'I see. You'd better make that the last one, now. You'll spoil your dinner.'

'Richard lives in Paris some of the time. In the rue' – Davie hesitated, brow wrinkled – 'oh, I can't remember. The rue something-or-other. You'll enjoy talking to him about that, won't you?'

'Indeed I will. Now come on, rascal, help me lay the table.'

Davie jumped from the stool. 'All right. What have we got for afters?'

Richard, when he came, arrived not just with the returned book but with flowers: not a large and showy bouquet but a pretty nosegay of early sweet peas. Rather more flustered than the small gesture warranted, Annie ducked her head to smell them. 'You're very kind. Thank you. They're my favourite flowers.' She stepped back from the door. 'Do please come in. My mother's here.' Her eyes flickered to his face and away. 'She's very much looking forward to meeting you.' Annie could not suppress a smile. 'Davie's told her all about you, of course!'

She led the way into the sitting room and made the introductions. Annie saw the slight widening of her mother's eyes as she took in the easy charm and rangy good looks of Davie's new 'friend'. She left them exchanging pleasantries while she went to call Davie in from the garden. By the time she came back they were already chatting like old friends.

'—I know it well. Annie's father and I lived just around the corner when we were first married—'

'Richard!' Davie bounded across the room to stand in front of him. 'Come and see my seaplane. I finished it yesterday.'

'In a minute, Davie.' Annie sent Richard an apologetic smile. 'I can't think what happened in this house to the notion that children should be seen and not heard.'

He stayed for barely an hour, most of which he spent chatting easily to Jane or talking to Davie. Annie poured drinks and sat quietly and apparently composedly beside her mother on the sofa, hiding the confusion of her feelings. She had reasoned it out; she had been sensible. Right up to the point when Richard walked through the door she had fully intended to tell him she would not meet him for dinner. The instant she saw him she had changed her mind. Now, perversely, she was afraid that he might have changed his.

She need not have worried. As she saw him to the door he bent his head close to her ear. 'You'll come?' It was only barely a question.

'Yes.'

'When?'

'Tomorrow,' she said collectedly. 'Where?'

'I'll meet you at Waterloo Station. Eight o'clock.' He grinned like a mischievous schoolboy. 'Under the clock.' Before she could move he had bent swiftly, brushed his lips against her cheek, and then was gone.

'What a charming man,' Jane said from the open doorway behind her.

Annie jumped. 'Yes. Isn't he?'

'Charming. Handsome. And the reason you don't want to marry Fergus?' The words were light, the gleam in her mother's eye sharp.

Her daughter turned. She should, she supposed, have known better than to try to hide anything from this shrewd and too observant mother of hers. 'I don't know,' she said. 'But if you don't mind looking after Davie for me tomorrow evening, I'll do the best I can to find out.'

'As long as you let me know,' Jane said, unabashed. 'I do like to know what's going on.'

Annie put an arm about her shoulders. 'You don't say?' she asked in entirely spurious amazement.

Chapter Six

'It was stupid enough to say I'd go,' Annie said, scowling at the clothes-strewn bed, 'but even worse not to have asked where the hell we're going. What on earth am I supposed to wear?'

'I like the green,' her mother said, crisply helpful. 'The neckline suits you. And it has the little black cape. Cape on and it's not too dressy, cape off and it is. It'll take you anywhere.'

'D'you think so? What about a hat?'

'The black velvet, to match the cape. And the black patent shoes. Very fashionable. And the black lace gloves, of course. There! That's that settled.'

'I'm not at all sure that I'm going.'

'Of course you're going, you know you are. Don't be silly.' Jane calmly picked up a dress and put it back on its hanger.

'It's not exactly fair on Fergus, is it?'

Her mother's eyebrows climbed, but she said nothing.

'I hardly know the man.'

'Do you want to know him?'

Annie walked to the window and stood looking down into the garden. 'I…' she hesitated, then, 'yes, I suppose I do.'

'Well, then—' Her mother opened the wardrobe door, hung up the dress and went back to the bed.

'It isn't that simple, is it? I've promised I'll marry Fergus. If he should find out—oh, damn it, *why* did I say I'd go? I didn't *mean* to!'

Her mother put down the jacket she was folding and crossed the room to her. 'You said you'd go because you want to go. It's not a crime. There's nothing to be afraid of—'

Annie swung round. 'There is! Of course there is! That's the whole point! What if I'm making a complete fool of myself? What does he want? I don't know the man! How do I know if I can trust him? I must be mad—'

'Annie, Annie! You're going to dinner with him, not running away to Gretna Green! For goodness' sake! Go and have your bath. And stop worrying.' Her mother smiled suddenly and patted her arm. 'Just make sure you've got enough money tucked in your bag to pay your taxi fare home if needs be. Under these circumstances I always think that's the best friend a girl can have.'

-

If her nerves had not exactly calmed by the time she reached Waterloo Station, at least Annie was fairly confident that they did not show too obviously. She was late enough to ensure that Richard got there first – though not enough for bad manners – and was careful not to hurry as she made her way through the crowd across the elegant new concourse to where his tall figure waited, watching her with a smile. He was in evening dress, which suited him well. It was not lost upon Annie that others thought so too: the interest in the eyes of a smartly dressed young woman who waited a little way away from him – presumably for her own dinner companion – was quite undisguised. As was the pleasure on his face when she joined him. 'Annie. You look wonderful!'

'Thank you,' she said serenely. And, suddenly, she felt wonderful. Wonderful and confident and very, very happy that she had come. She would not spoil this one evening with doubts; she would face the inevitable nagging guilt concerning Fergus tomorrow. She accepted his proffered arm and they strolled out into the busy street.

'Tell me,' he said, smiling down at her, 'do you like to dance?'

Annie laughed. 'It's years since I danced. I used to love it.'

'Good. So do I. And it just so happens that I've booked a table at the Savoy. Have you heard the Orpheans?'

She shook her head.

He grinned like a boy. 'Well, you will tonight. And you'll love 'em!' He lifted a hand. 'Taxi!'

–

He was – as she had guessed he would be – the most charming and attentive of companions. They ate lobster and asparagus, they drank Champagne and they danced. Chandeliers glittered, silver gleamed and candles glinted in crystal. It was, she found herself thinking more than once, a very far cry indeed from her usual prim Friday evening settled quietly by the fire or in her bed with a book. Spinning around the dance floor at dizzying speed, the whole thing seemed suddenly so unreal that she wondered if she might not wake up and find it all some kind of wild hallucination. She leaned back, laughing up into Richard's face. 'I don't think I'd be at all surprised if I turned into a pumpkin or something at midnight.'

He held her tighter, steering her deftly into another turn. 'I hope not. The dancing goes on until two—'

And all the time they talked, easily, animatedly and with laughter, as if they had known each other all their lives.

Annie had never been more sorry to have an evening come to an end.

He took her to her door in a taxi. 'May I get in touch when I come back from Paris?'

'Yes,' she said, with possibly Champagne-induced promptness. The interior of the car was dark; she could not see the expression on his shadowed face. 'Thank you for a lovely evening.'

She sensed his smile. Felt him move a little towards her. She held her breath. He reached for her hand, turned it palm upwards and undid the tiny press-studs that fitted the long lace glove to the wrist. Then, very gently, he kissed the skin he had exposed. 'Good night, Annie. Sleep tight.'

–

As, shoes in hand and head spinning a little, Annie climbed the stairs she noticed the bright strip of light beneath the door of her mother's room. She stopped, her heart sinking. Was something wrong? Had anything happened to Davie? Had retribution struck so soon?

She tiptoed to the door, pushed it open a crack. Jane lifted her head, smiling, laid down the book she had been reading, folded her hands upon it and surveyed her daughter's bright eyes and flushed cheeks. 'No need to ask if you enjoyed yourself, I think?'

Annie crossed the room to sit on the bed. Stuck out her stockinged feet and wriggled them, giggling a little. 'My feet are killing me. Has everything been all right?'

'Everything has been just fine. Davie thrashed me at ludo, and I thrashed him at Beat Your Neighbours Out Of Doors, so honours were even. Where did you go?'

'You'll never guess – the Savoy! We danced *all* night! We ate lobster, and we drank Champagne' – she put a hand to her forehead and rubbed at it a little ruefully – 'a bit too much, I suspect. We talked and we talked—'

Her mother smiled affectionately. 'So you're glad you went after all?'

'Yes. Oh, yes!'

'And what did you discover in all this talking?'

Annie leaned back on her hands, letting her head drop back, heavy hair swinging, addressing her words to the ceiling. 'He lives somewhere in Hampstead. He loves Gershwin and dance music. He's got a motor car, and one of those new-fangled gramophones that don't need a horn. He says it's absolutely marvellous.' She paused for a moment, thinking. 'His father is retired and lives in the south of France. He has a sister in South Africa, married to a farmer; she has two children of whom he is very fond. His favourite food is asparagus. His favourite artist is Toulouse-Lautrec – not the posters and things but the horse pictures—'

'I didn't know Toulouse-Lautrec painted horse pictures?'

'No. Neither did I, but apparently he did. Anyway – where was I? He reads a lot, his favourite writer is Trollope, especially the Barchester novels. He doesn't like the theatre. He smokes the occasional cigarette. He hates Brussels sprouts and rice pudding—'

'Together? So would I.'

Annie laughed. 'Together or separately. He used to play rugby but gave up after he dislocated his neck—'

'A man of sense.'

'He doesn't like shopping and he doesn't like cats, but he's rather fond of dogs and horses.' She wrinkled up her nose. 'I think that's about all I can remember for now. Golly, we certainly did drink a lot of Champagne – my head's spinning like a top! Oh – and he loves opera but doesn't much like ballet, and his birthday is in January. There! I think that really is all.'

'And did he find out as much about you as you did about him?' Jane was amused.

Annie glanced at her, just faintly alarmed. 'Well, yes. I suppose he must have.' She frowned thoughtfully. 'I can't really remember, to be honest.'

Her mother leaned forward and patted her hand. 'I'm glad you had such a good time. Off you go now. You can tell me more in the morning.'

Annie jumped up, kissed her and danced to the door, humming, the pale green lace of her skirt swirling around her ankles. 'Night,' she said from the door.

'Good night, dear. Sleep well.'

Annie laughed. 'I will. I'm sure I will.'

But she did not. Tired as she was, sleep would not come. Her feet ached. And once she lay down, her head ached more. The kaleidoscope of the evening glittered in her mind, restless patterns of light and colour. The same snatch of song rang distractingly in her ears, over and over. She tossed onto her back, lay for a moment staring into the slightly dizzying darkness. Then she raised her arm, turned it a little so that the gleam of the pale flesh caught and reflected the faint light of the moon.

Very slowly she reached her other hand to her inner wrist, touching it gently with her fingertips, shivering a little as she remembered that last moment in the taxi; and, gently, she laid her lips where his had been.

Then with a sudden, violent movement she turned over again, burying her head in the pillow. 'Oh, God!' she said aloud, her voice muffled. 'What the *hell* am I going to do about Fergus now?'

–

The flowers came the next morning, just as Jane was leaving for the station: six white roses, long-stemmed and lovely, wrapped in cellophane and bound together with silken scarlet ribbon. Rosy-cheeked beneath the inquisitive eyes of her mother and her son, Annie took the card from its small envelope, read it and – even rosier-cheeked – tucked it quickly back.

'Richard?' her mother asked.

'Yes.'

'What does the card say?' Davie asked, cheerfully and filially nosy.

Annie shrugged. 'Just "Thank you",' she lied. 'Just "Thank you for a nice evening", that's all.'

'They're beautiful,' Jane said.

'Yes. They are.'

A car horn tooted in the road outside. Jane kissed her daughter's warm cheek. 'I have to go. The taxi's here. I'll drop you a line later in the week and we can finalise the arrangements for Davie to come to stay. 'Bye, darling.' She kissed Davie. 'Be good.'

They stood at the door to wave her off, Annie still holding the flowers. As the taxi turned the corner Davie glanced at his mother and laughed.

'What's the matter?'

'Here comes the bride, here comes the bride...' he sang in a high falsetto.

With her free hand she pretended to cuff him round the ear. 'I'd better put these in water.'

-

The second bouquet of flowers came in the afternoon; identical to the first, six perfect white blooms decked in cellophane and red ribbon.

'Wow!' said Davie thoughtfully. 'You two *did* have a good time, didn't you?'

Annie opened the envelope. Davie watched her curiously as she read the card and slipped it back. When he opened his mouth, Annie lifted a quick, repressive finger. 'It's none of your business,' she said.

Later, with the inquisitive Davie safe in his bed she walked into the cool garden, sat down under the apple tree, took the two cards from her pocket and laid them neatly upon the table in front of her.

'Lovely, lovely evening. Long and thoughtful night. I think that I, at least, may have found the answer to Adela's question...' said the first.

The second was much shorter and to the point: a single sentence which ended with the tiniest of kisses: '*How about you?*'

-

It was all happening much too fast. Annie knew it, yet could do nothing to stop it. All at once she found she was thinking about Richard every waking moment: Richard laughing, Richard talking, Richard watching her with those bright, narrow eyes.

Had he really meant what he'd said on the cards? Was it possible he was thinking of her, as she was of him? Surely not? How could she ever attract such a man?

And what of Fergus?

Restless and uncertain, totally unable to concentrate, she went to a meeting of the Red Cross committee of which she was usually an enthusiastic member and came away unable to remember a thing that had been discussed. She sat down to write a letter to a friend and found herself staring into space with not a word written. She could settle to nothing. Her usual temperate nature deserted her: she swung from happiness and certainty to misery and distrust in seconds whenever she tried to analyse what was going on, which was often. The situation was, of course, made worse by the fact that Richard was in Paris and incommunicado. She would not see him again for a week. Over and over she planned the meeting: what she would say to him, what he would say to her – then what? What did he want? He had not even kissed her. Not properly, anyway. And so it went on – the age-old mixture of happiness and utter misery that the first infatuation of a love affair always brings. And always… there was Fergus…

Who turned up at the house one evening unannounced and unexpected.

'Uncle Fergus is here,' Davie said, from the window seat where he was curled up reading a book. 'He's coming up the path.'

Annie froze. She had been fiddling with the wireless, trying to find some dance music. 'Fergus?' she repeated stupidly, her heart suddenly hammering in something that could only be described as panic. 'Here?'

The doorbell rang. 'Here,' Davie said laconically, and went back to his book. It had been a source of amazement to Annie that over the past few days Davie had apparently sensed nothing of her turmoil. The natural self-centredness of childhood, she supposed, rarely looked beyond its own concerns unless forced to.

The vase containing Richard's roses was standing on the little table in the middle of the room. In a real panic now, she ran over, snatched it up and then stood completely frozen, not knowing what to do with it.

The doorbell rang again.

'Shall I let him in?' Davie asked, shutting his book.

'Yes... No... Wait a minute. I'm—I'm just going to put these out in the kitchen for a moment. I think they need fresh water. I'll answer the door.'

She flew into the kitchen, put the flowers on the table, smoothed her skirt with the palms of her hands, tidied her hair and went into the hall, closing the kitchen door behind her.

It had been pouring with rain all afternoon; Fergus stood patiently on the front doorstep under a large black umbrella. He was wearing a Homburg hat that did not suit him and was carrying a parcel. 'Fergus!' Annie said nervously. 'What are you doing here? Come in. Come in...'

Fergus stepped into the hall, closed and shook the umbrella, put it meticulously into the umbrella stand by the door. When he turned his face was puzzled and a little hurt. 'What am I doing here?' he half-laughed, ruefully. 'I think perhaps I should ask you that.'

'What on earth do you mean?' Annie stopped, both hands going to her mouth. 'Oh, Fergus! How *awful* of me! I forgot! Oh, Fergus, I'm truly sorry – I can't think how it can have slipped my mind—'

'What's the matter?' Davie asked from the sitting-room doorway. 'Hello, Uncle Fergus,' he added politely.

'Hello, Davie. What's the matter is that your flibberti-gibbet of a mother was supposed to be meeting me this evening. We were supposed to be going to the cinema.' He turned a mildly exasperated eye upon Annie.

'I'm sorry,' she said again. 'I completely forgot. Oh, dear,' she added faintly.

Fergus was taking off his coat and hat, hanging them over the newel post at the foot of the stairs. 'Never mind.' He smiled. 'I've had a better idea, anyway.' He turned back to Davie. 'I've got a little something for you, young man.' He handed him the parcel.

'Cor, thanks. What is it?'

'Open it and see.'

Mortified, Annie watched as the boy tore at the brown paper. How *could* she have forgotten? It was unforgivable of her. She was amazed that Fergus wasn't furious with her.

'More Meccano! Look, Mother—' Davie waved the box at her. 'A crane! Gosh, thanks, Uncle Fergus!'

Fergus smiled. 'Why not go and unpack it? I'd like a quiet word with your mother.'

'All right.' Davie ran into the dining room, already trying to open the box as he went.

Annie eyed Fergus with some misgiving.

He smiled. 'Don't look so worried. It's just that I have a little something for you too. First – a drink. I'll get some glasses.' He moved towards the kitchen door.

'No!' Annie slid forward and blocked his way. 'No, no. I'll get them. You go on into the sitting room.' She pushed open the door; once in the kitchen she leaned against the closed door for a moment, trying to compose herself. Richard's roses gleamed almost silver in the dull, rainwashed light. She shut her eyes for a second, breathing deeply, then found two glasses and went back to the sitting room.

Fergus was standing at the window, looking out into the rain. He turned, smiling when she came into the room. As she splashed whisky into the two glasses she was alarmed to see that her hands were shaking. 'There.' She pushed the glass across the surface of the sideboard to him, frightened to pick it up.

He downed it at a swallow and she stared at him, surprised. He grinned. 'Dutch courage,' he said.

She stood quite still, watching him. 'Why would you need Dutch courage?' she asked carefully.

He put his hand in his pocket, pulled out a small square box, snapped it open. There was a long silence.

Annie put her hands to her suddenly burning cheeks and shook her head miserably. 'Oh, no,' she said, very quietly. 'Oh, Fergus, no.'

Chapter Seven

The ring glittered against black velvet: sapphires and diamonds set in gold. An engagement ring. A ring of final commitment. Annie stared at it, unable to look Fergus in the eye.

There was a long moment of silence before he asked, very quietly, 'What do you mean, "No"?'

Her eyes flickered to his face and away. She ducked her head, her hair falling across her face. 'I… I just—' She spread her hands helplessly in front of her, let them fall to her sides.

'Annie? Tell me. What's wrong?'

Still she said nothing. Through its ungainly, rearing horn the wireless hissed and crackled. Glad to have something to do, Annie crossed the room and turned it off. The ensuing silence was absolute.

'Annie!' There was a trace of sharp impatience in Fergus's voice now. 'Will you answer me?' He still held the open box towards her; the ring, catching the light as his hand moved, sparkled with a blue and crystal fire.

With a quick, nervy movement she fairly snatched the box from him, snapped the lid shut with a sharp click and all but dropped it on the table, as if it burned her fingers. Then she lifted her chin to look at him, hands clasped in front of her. 'Fergus—I can't marry you,' she said, her voice unsteady. 'I'm sorry, but I can't. It—wouldn't be right.'

It took a moment or so to sink in. Then, 'What the hell do you mean?' She had never heard him speak so harshly. His usually pleasant face was thunderous. 'What the *hell* do you mean?' he repeated. 'What – wouldn't be right – about it?' He emphasised the words with sudden suspicion.

'I...' Miserably she turned away from him to stare out into the rain. 'I just can't, Fergus. I can't marry you.'

'*Why not?*'

Annie spun on him. 'Because I don't love you! That's why not. I am extremely fond of you. Truly I am. But I don't *love* you. I'm sorry. I've tried. Really I have—'

To her surprise and alarm he stepped to her and caught her wrist bruisingly hard, pulling her towards him, forcing her to look at him. 'There's something more to this,' he said, suddenly quiet.

She shook her head stubbornly. 'There's nothing. I just know I can't – shouldn't – marry you.'

He was watching her steadily. 'Davie?' he asked. 'Is it Davie?'

She wrenched her wrist from his grasp, precariously close to tears. '*No!* It isn't Davie! It's me! I'm sorry! – I'm sorry, I'm sorry, I'm sorry! – I should never have agreed to it in the first place—'

'But you did,' he said grimly.

'Yes. I did.' All at once she felt her own temper rising. 'How many times do I have to apologise? I made a mistake. And I've hurt you. For that I truly am sorry. But I can't compound the mistake and the hurt by going ahead. It won't work, Fergus. Believe me!' Her voice had risen and was shaking. She took a deep, fierce breath, knowing with certainty that Fergus would misinterpret any sign of tears as weakness. 'You can't make me marry you,' she said. 'Under the circumstances you'd be stupid to try.'

He was watching her narrowly. 'I still don't believe I know the circumstances,' he said slowly.

She made a sharp, impatient movement with her hand. 'You do! I've told you—'

He shook his head. 'I don't believe you.'

'Believe me or not, I don't care. Please, Fergus!'

'Mother? What's wrong?' Davie had appeared in the doorway, was looking from one to the other in bewilderment.

Annie swallowed, steadied her voice. 'Nothing, darling. It's all right.' She held out an arm, and her son came to her side. 'Uncle Fergus and I are having' – she glanced at Fergus and away – 'a discussion.'

'It sounds more like a quarrel,' the boy said doubtfully. In Davie's world grown-ups didn't quarrel. He found it distinctly unsettling.

'Yes, Davie.' Fergus picked up the ring box and slipped it in his pocket; he stalked into the hall, face thunderous, to retrieve his raincoat and the unbecoming hat. 'That's how it sounds to me too.' Clumsily he struggled into the wet coat, shrugged it onto his shoulders. His face was black with confusion and fury. He came back to the sitting-room door, glaring in understandable but somehow self-righteous anger at Annie. 'When you come to your senses,' he said stiffly, 'you know where I am.' He turned with no further word. The slamming of the front door behind him shook the house.

'What was the quarrel about?' Davie asked hesitantly, after a moment.

'It was about getting married.' Annie drew a deep breath, half-smiled, shaking her head ruefully. 'Or rather, about not getting married,' she corrected herself. She turned him fully to look at her, studied his small, solemn face. 'Davie – would you mind if I didn't marry Uncle Fergus?'

He stared at her. 'Mind? Of course I wouldn't mind. I'd rather you didn't. I thought you knew that? I mean,' he added hastily, 'he's very nice, and I like him quite a lot, but…' He let the words trail off.

Annie pulled him towards her and hugged him tightly. 'That's exactly how I feel,' she said into his thick, smooth hair. And then, 'Poor Fergus,' she added. And truly meant it. But could not deny in her heart of hearts that her predominant feeling was one of profound and growing relief.

She wrote to Fergus that night, apologising yet again, telling him how much she had always valued their friendship, pointing out as gently as she could that friendship alone was not sufficient basis for a marriage.

She did not mention Richard.

Perhaps understandably, she received no reply from Fergus.

–

Richard Ross opened the door of the quiet, shadowed room and, with his hand still on the knob, turned to look back towards the bed. 'I'll be back as soon as I can,' he said softly.

The reclining figure that he addressed regarded him with serene dark eyes, smiled faintly, but said nothing.

Richard pulled the door shut behind him, and a moment later was stepping from the cool, sweet-smelling darkness of the silent house into the sunshine of the flower-filled, fountained courtyard. As he let himself out through the little gate into the narrow street, the smell of fresh coffee came to him from the small pavement cafe on the corner. In the distance, between the buildings, the River Seine glittered, a serene and lovely silver ribbon of light that reflected, shimmering, the graceful bridges and elegant buildings that lined it. Hands in pockets, Richard strolled towards it, his face very thoughtful. A street market in a side street was a kaleidoscope of colour; the smell of newly baked bread was mouth-watering. A small donkey cart rolled and rattled up behind him and he stepped out of its way, acknowledging the dour greeting of the driver. Drifts of pink petals from the blossoms of the chestnut trees that lined the river's banks blew in the faintest of breezes. Paris was at her best. Richard walked halfway across the Pont des Arts and stood leaning, elbows on the parapet, looking downriver towards the verdant Île de la Cité and the twin towers of Notre Dame. It was his favourite view in his favourite city, but for once it failed to enchant. He drew a silver cigarette case from his pocket, extracted a cigarette, lit it, blew smoke pensively into the bright air.

He had been kicking his heels in Paris for nearly a week. Long enough? It should have been, he reckoned. It would have to be. Time was running out. He could wait no longer.

With a suddenly decisive movement he dropped the cigarette and ground it out with his heel.

It was time to get back to London. And to Annie.

–

'Mother! Richard's here—' Excitedly Davie raced into the garden. 'He's outside. He's come in his motor car!'

It was the first Saturday in May; the afternoon sun was high and bright. Annie, who had been on her knees weeding a flower bed, sat back on her heels, pushing her hair from her eyes. 'Richard? Are you sure?'

'Of *course* I'm sure. I'll go and let him in—' He shot off again without waiting for her to reply.

Annie dropped her trowel and scrambled to her feet, frantically brushing at her shabby gardening skirt with a dirty hand. 'Damn it!' she said aloud. 'Of all the times!' She heard the sound of laughter coming from the house. Then Davie danced out through the French windows beside the tall figure of Richard Ross and her heart turned over.

She had lectured herself sternly in the days since she had broken with Fergus. She had warned herself time and again not to jump from the frying pan into the fire, not to read too much into a single, pleasantly flirtatious evening, not to make a fool of herself. All to no avail. As he came towards her, smiling, she found herself blushing furiously and as tongue-tied as any schoolgirl with a crush.

'Hello,' he said. He was immaculate in flannels and a blazer; his skin had darkened a little in the Paris sunshine.

'Hello. You're back then?' Her colour deepened. Sparkling repartee, this.

'Yes. Arrived back yesterday.'

'Did you have a successful trip?'

'Yes, indeed.' Richard was carrying a brown paper carrier bag that Davie was eyeing with interest. 'I bought you both a little something. I hope you don't mind?'

'What is it?' asked Davie, straight to the point as usual.

'Take a look.' Richard reached into the bag and pulled out a brown paper-wrapped parcel that was quite obviously a large book. He laughed. 'No prizes for guessing what it is, but open it up – I think you might like it—'

As Davie ripped enthusiastically at the paper Richard turned to Annie and handed her a small, exquisitely wrapped package. 'For you,' he said.

She took it, held it for a moment, touching the ribbons and tiny paper flowers that adorned it. 'I haven't had a chance to thank you for the flowers yet,' she said softly.

'Did you like them?'

She looked up quickly. 'Oh, yes! They were lovely. Thank you.'

'Golly, look at this!' Davie had discarded the wrapping on the grass and dropped to his knees, laying the book in front of him, leafing through the heavy pages with their tissue dividers with – for him – great care.

'Richard! You really shouldn't!' Annie peered over her son's shoulder. 'What perfectly lovely illustrations!'

'I found it in a second-hand bookshop. Couldn't resist it. Apparently the artist travelled all over Africa, cataloguing and drawing the flora and fauna for the French Botanical Society. Splendid, isn't it?'

'It's *wizard*!' Davie said.

Annie smiled at Richard. 'And they don't come any better than that, I can tell you. Davie – what do you say to Richard?'

'I was going to.' Davie was injured. 'You haven't given me the chance. Thank you, Richard.' He dropped his head to the book again, instantly absorbed.

Richard smiled his acceptance of the thanks as Annie tousled her son's hair. 'Sorry. Who'd have a mother, eh?' She straightened, pushing back her hair.

'Aren't you going to open yours?'

She laughed a little. 'It's too pretty to open.'

'I cheated,' he admitted cheerfully. 'The shop girl wrapped it for me.'

Very carefully she unwrapped the little present. Her eyes widened. 'Chanel Number Five!' She was utterly delighted. 'Richard! How extravagant! How very kind! Thank you.'

'It's a pleasure.' He was looking at her quizzically, as if waiting for something.

She unstoppered the small, stylish bottle and breathed in the perfume. 'It's *lovely*!'

He put his head on one side, his eyes holding hers. With a quick movement she stepped to him, put her hands on his shoulders and kissed him on the cheek, swiftly and lightly. His skin was taut and warm beneath her lips. 'Thank you again.'

'Thank *you*.' The emphasis was different, and dry.

Davie looked up suddenly. 'Can I have a look at your motor car? It's a Wolseley, isn't it?'

'Yes, it is. The new thirty-five-horsepower saloon.'

'They're smashing cars, aren't they? My friend Robert's father's got one. Can I have a look?'

'You can have a ride if you'd like.' Richard laughed at the delight that lit the boy's face. He looked at his watch. 'Tell you what – get your glad rags on, the pair of you, and we'll take a spin in the country. Who knows – we might even find someone who'll oblige us with a cream tea! Would you like that?'

Davie needed no more persuading than that. He jumped to his feet and gathered up his book, cradling it like a baby in his arms. 'I can wash and change in less than five minutes,' he said.

Annie laughed. 'Well, I can't! So you're just going to have to wait for me, aren't you?'

'For as long as you like,' Richard said. And if the words were innocent enough, Annie saw with suddenly quickened breath that the look in his narrow eyes was not.

–

'This is really very kind of you,' Annie said, stirring her tea. 'I haven't seen Davie so excited in a very long time.'

'Show me a boy who doesn't get excited about motor cars.' Richard looked out into the pretty garden of the tea room where Davie, unable as usual to sit still for long, was leaning over the railings of a little wooden bridge, watching the goings on in the stream below. 'When they grow up his generation will probably know more about the internal combustion engine than we do about how a steam engine runs.'

She glanced up at him, smiling. 'That wouldn't take much in my case. I haven't the foggiest notion how either works.' Her eyes followed his: Davie had crouched down and stuck his head through the rails, peering intently down into the water.

Annie frowned suddenly, nibbling her lip.

Richard, seeing her expression, touched her hand lightly. 'Don't worry. He's all right. He can't fall.'

'No.' She did not take her eyes from her son.

'And if he did he probably wouldn't hurt himself. It's only a couple of feet and the stream's very shallow—'

'You can drown in two inches of water,' she said quickly.

He put his head on one side, watching her, curiosity in his eyes, but said nothing. After a moment, sensing his gaze, she looked back at him. Her whole body had tensed. 'I'm sorry,' she said. 'Water frightens me. That's all. I…' She took a breath. 'I found a drowned woman and child once. In the Seine. It was the most dreadful thing you can imagine. It haunts me still. I dream of it sometimes – usually when something reminds me, or if I'm upset or unhappy—' She stopped, looked down sightless into her teacup. *Drifting hair. A child's bloated hand. Fish, darting and nibbling*— She shuddered, suddenly chill.

Again he touched her hand, and this time held it lightly. 'I see. That does explain it. How old were you?'

She looked up again, her face very pale. She shook her head. 'Do you mind if we don't talk about it? I only mentioned it to explain…' She glanced out of the window again. Davie had left the bridge and had found a wooden swing. Annie relaxed. 'It's stupid, I know,' she said, quietly. 'I just hate water.'

'Understandable under the circumstances.' Richard's hand still lay upon hers. Beyond the garden the rolling Surrey countryside lay tranquil beneath an evening sky that was beginning very faintly to show the rosy glow of sunset in the west. Richard's hand tightened slightly for a moment, then he let hers go.

She smiled, faintly apologetic.

'Are you in any great hurry to get home?' Richard asked after a moment. 'We could explore a little further if you'd like? Does it matter if our young man there is a little late in bed tonight?'

She shook her head. 'No. As a matter of fact he's on holiday. It's Founder's Week – they always have a few days off. I'm taking him up to Southwold on Tuesday, to stay with his Nan until the weekend.' She laughed a little, fondly. 'And since, as you can probably guess, Mother isn't exactly a martinet when it comes to bedtime, he might as well start now. He'll be thrilled. He'd probably stay up all night if it meant driving around in your car.' Davie had slowed down the swing and was looking in their direction. When Annie waved and beckoned to him, he slipped from the swing and ran to the window. 'Richard wants to know if you'd rather go home to bed, or drive around the countryside for a little while longer,' his mother said, straight-faced.

Davie laughed.

Richard reached for the road map that was folded up on the table. 'Let's see where we'd like to go.'

They cruised around the country lanes for an hour or so, with the energetic Davie bouncing on the back seat and conducting an excited running commentary for them that brought to their attention everything from sheep, cows and horses to duck ponds and thatched cottages. Finally they rolled to a stop just below the crest of a hill. The sky was ablaze as the sun touched the horizon and began to slip beneath it. 'Fancy stretching your legs for a minute or two?' Richard asked.

Davie put his head over the back of the seat. 'Can I sit in the driver's seat?'

'As long as you don't touch the brake.'

'I won't. I promise.' He scrambled from the car and climbed into the seat Richard had vacated. Annie walked around the car to stand by Richard, smiling as her son pretended to steer the car, making loud engine noises as he did so. 'Looks as if Wolseleys have trounced all rivals in the motor-car popularity stakes.' She turned to look at the sunset. 'What a wonderful view! England is so very lovely at this time of the year, isn't it?'

'Yes,' Richard said, 'it is.'

Without looking at him, she was acutely aware that he was looking not at the view but at her.

Together they strolled the little way to the hill's crest, stood looking out over the rolling fields and woods that were bathed in the glow of the sunset. Behind them Davie's engine noises were getting ever more enthusiastic. 'It occurred to me—' Richard began, and then stopped.

'Yes?'

'You said Davie was on holiday – that you were taking him down to Southwold on Tuesday?'

'Yes. He always goes to stay with my mother for a few days when he's on holiday. They enjoy being together. And I feel it's good for him to be in someone else's company rather than mine all the time.'

'It's just… well, it so happens that I could be free on Tuesday. I wondered – would you like me to drive you there? Davie seems rather taken with the car.'

They both turned to look back at the big green and black car and its small occupant. 'Oh – we really couldn't impose on you…' Annie began, doubtfully.

'It isn't an imposition.' His voice was quiet. 'It's an offer. But I quite understand if it makes things difficult for you—'

'Difficult?' Genuinely puzzled, she turned to look at him.

'Your Fergus. I expect you think he would object?'

There was a very long moment of silence. Annie cleared her throat. 'I… don't have a Fergus any more,' she said, turning back once more to watch the glowing palette of the evening sky that now was darkening by the moment.

'I beg your pardon?'

'Fergus. We aren't getting married.'

83

'I'm sorry.'

'There's no need. It was my decision.'

'I see.'

As she started to walk back to the car, he fell into thoughtful step beside her. 'It wouldn't have worked,' she said, and flashed him a glimmer of a smile. 'I blame Mr Forster,' she added, 'and his cynicism. He made me think.'

'And your conclusion?' They had reached the car. Richard held the door open for her.

She stood for a moment. '*It begins and continues for such very slight reasons*,' she quoted. 'Remember?'

'Indeed I do. What's the other bit?' He frowned, pondering. 'About his friends and their wives?'

'*I've friends who can't remember why they got married, no more can their wives*,' she quoted promptly.

'My.' The word was soft. 'You have taken it to heart, haven't you?'

She shrugged. 'I just realised that if I had married Fergus, good and kind man though he might have been, there would come a time when I would feel exactly like Forster says. I don't want that.'

'What do you want?'

She looked him straight in the eye. 'I don't know.'

'Fair enough.' He handed her into the car, stood looking down at her, smiling. 'At least that's no bad place to start.'

–

They arrived back in Kew long after dark, Davie sleeping soundly curled up on the back seat. As the car purred to a halt outside the house Annie turned to Richard. 'Thank you. It's been a lovely afternoon. And all the better for being unexpected.'

84

'I'm glad you enjoyed it,' he said. 'And you'll let me take you to Southwold on Tuesday?'

She laughed a little. 'You saw Davie's reaction when you suggested it to him. I think he'd run away from home if we disappointed him now!'

He grinned. Davie stirred a little.

'I'd better get him in to bed,' Annie said, but did not move.

'Yes.' He was watching her steadily. In the darkness, very slowly, she lifted her loosely curled hand, brushed his cheekbone with the backs of her fingers. 'Thank you again.'

For a moment he did not move. Then he leaned towards her and very gently brushed her lips with his. She closed her eyes briefly, every sense concentrated on the exquisite pleasure of the touch. After a long moment he sat back. Neither of them spoke, nor did they touch each other again. 'I'd better wake Davie,' she said at last. 'Will you come in for a drink?'

He hesitated. Then, 'No,' he said. 'Not tonight, I think. You need to get young Davie to bed.'

She was taken aback – and more than a little disturbed – by the sharpness of her disappointment; and just as unprepared for the lift of her heart, the faint prickle of excitement when he suggested, softly, 'Perhaps on Tuesday?'

Annie smiled. 'Tuesday,' she agreed.

Chapter Eight

A little disappointingly, if not exactly unexpectedly, the British weather lived up to its deserved reputation for unreliability and they set off for Southwold the following Tuesday beneath lowering grey skies that would have done as much credit to November as to May.

'You are sure you don't mind?' Annie asked, for the half-dozenth time, as Richard stashed Davie's small suitcase on the back seat of the car.

Davie, fidgeting impatiently, threw his mother a look of pure disgust. If you *keep* asking that, it said as clearly as words, then he'll say 'Yes' and that will be that!

Richard shook his head. 'I'm looking forward to it. It's years since I've been to Suffolk, and this young lady' – he patted the car – 'likes nothing so much as a good long run.'

'It's really very kind of you.'

'I do think she's a real cracker.' Davie was running a finger along the long, gleaming green bonnet.

Richard smiled.

'Have you had her very long?'

'A few months. I must say I think she's the best I've had.'

'She's absolutely wizard,' Davie said, ignoring his mother's expressively rolled eyes. 'Can I sit in the front?'

Richard glanced at Annie, eyebrows raised in question. She shrugged, smiling. 'If you don't mind, why not? I'll be in the front all the way back, after all. Mind you – I don't talk the hind leg off a donkey the way Davie does. Well, I don't!' she added, mildly injured at the laughter that had brought.

The big Wolseley purred slowly through the congested streets of London, through the trams and the buses, the plodding horse-drawn vehicles and the shiny modern motor cars. The pavements bustled with pedestrians, and bicycles wove their precarious way through the traffic. Davie was ecstatic.

'That's a Morris Oxford, isn't it? It isn't as nice as your car, is it? How fast will she go, Richard? Have you ever driven her really fast? Oh, I know you're only supposed to go at twenty miles an hour, but that's silly, isn't it? No one bothers about it, do they? Hey – look at that motorbike! What a smasher! Look, Mother – d'you see?'

Annie, settled comfortably on the luxuriously soft leather of the back seat, propped her elbow on the armrest, leaned her chin on her hand and watched the busy, crowded streets through half-closed eyes.

'That's a Ford. My friend Tommy's father's got a Ford. But, d'you know what? He only takes it out on Sundays.' Davie crowed with laughter. 'That's *really* silly, isn't it? What's the point of having a car if you're only going to use it on a Sunday? D'you know, they go by bus on the other days of the week, just like anybody else!'

Annie smiled a little at her son's excited chatter, turned her head to look at Richard. His thick, neatly cut reddish-brown hair grew to a point at the nape of his neck. His hands were big and relaxed on the steering wheel. He turned his head a little, half laughing, to answer Davie, and the light caught the line of his jaw, the lean planes and angles of his face, the narrowing of his eyes and the flicker of his long lashes as he smiled.

'We're going on the Lowestoft road, aren't we? Mother and I looked it up on a map. It's more than a hundred miles from London to Southwold. How long will it take, do you think? How much petrol will we use? We go past Chelmsford, and Colchester – the Romans were at Colchester, did you know? – and Woodbridge, and—' He hesitated, frowning. 'Somewhere else that starts with W. I can't remember – where else, Mother? Mother? What was the other place in Suffolk that starts with a W?'

Annie was still looking at Richard. It came to her suddenly that there was something absurdly, and perhaps dangerously, intimate in being able to study him so closely and unobserved. 'Sorry, darling?'

'The place we go through that begins with a W. In Suffolk. It's got two words.' Her impatient son bounced in his seat. 'What's it called?'

'Oh – something Market. Wickham Market,' she said absently.

'That's it. I say – look at that! A Rolls-Royce. With a *chauffeur*,' he accented the word exaggeratedly, pushing his small nose in the air with his finger. 'Pooh, pooh, pooh!'

That was too much. Annie straightened in her seat. 'Behave yourself, Davie.'

Davie, surprised if the truth be told that he had got away with as much as he had, subsided, for the moment at least.

Annie put her chin on her fist and looked out of the window again, very thoughtfully.

The crowded working-class areas of the east of London were made no more picturesque by the grey dullness of the weather. No Rolls-Royces with chauffeurs here. Even Davie found little to exclaim about, apart from the looming bulk of the Tower of London – which prompted a few interesting asides about executions and torture – and the towering cranes of the docks, which Richard admitted exerted a romantic lure for him far beyond the harsh reality of the gruelling everyday realities of life at sea, or in the docks themselves. 'Silks and spices from the East, Davie,' he said. 'Cotton from America. Tea from Ceylon. Sugar from the West Indies. This is where they all come to. The greatest docks in the world.'

'Together with the greatest exploitation in the country,' Annie said tartly, but so quietly that she did not expect him to hear her.

But his hearing was sharp. He glanced at Davie, then across his shoulder, amused and enquiring. 'You're a Labour supporter? You surprise me.' His glance was quizzical.

'I'm a labour supporter – small "L". I'm not actually political at all. But I read the papers. I talk to people. I make up my own mind. And – yes – I do think it's wrong that decent men and women should be exploited so that the likes of you and me can live – relatively at least – the life of Riley. I didn't know anything about the casual labour system until I read about it last year during the dock strike. Whatever your politics, you can't approve of a system that treats men no better than work animals, that pauperises families and prevents them from caring properly for their children. Not just in the docks. In the mines; on the railways. No wonder they strike. I don't blame them. Yet all the government can do is order out the army to shoot them. Very constructive, that.'

He laughed a little. 'Well, well – sounds as if we've a real little revolutionary in the back there, Davie. We'll be in for it when she can vote.'

'Well, while we're on the subject, there's another thing,' she replied with mild asperity. 'Why can't I? What makes the great and the good believe that a man of twenty-one can use a vote sensibly while a woman must wait until she's thirty? It's patently ridiculous.'

Richard swung the big car out onto a main road, edged his way into the traffic. He was grinning broadly. 'Looks as if we're going to have an interesting journey,' he said.

As at last they drove out into the flat, green Essex countryside the traffic eased, and the road cleared. The car was warm, the ride smooth and comfortable. Half listening to Davie and Richard as they talked, Annie found herself dozing.

She woke up some time later, stretching and yawning. The sky had cleared a little and the sun gleamed fitfully between clouds. 'Where are we?'

'We've just gone through Ipswich.' Davie had a map spread on his lap. 'I'm the navigator,' he added. 'Richard says I'm very good at it.'

Not for the first time, it occurred to Annie that for a man who had no children of his own Richard appeared to have an almost uncanny knack of knowing exactly how to keep Davie happy and interested; a knack that Fergus, for all his efforts, and despite being a father, had never managed to acquire. 'How much longer, do you think?'

Richard flicked a glance at her through the rear-view mirror. 'An hour or so, I should think. Are you comfortable? Do you want to stop?'

'No, no. I'm quite happy.' She yawned again, sleepily.

Richard laughed, and the undisguised affection in the sound warmed her heart. 'Go back to sleep. Davie's doing an excellent job. We'll wake you when we get there.'

They drove into Southwold at about half past midday. The weather now had cleared completely: the sun shone and a cool breeze blew from the sea. Jane was waiting for them, a simple lunch on the table. 'I thought you might like a stroll along the beach before you go back?' she suggested. 'It seems a shame to come all this way and not to stretch your legs.'

Annie glanced at Richard. 'Would you like that?'

'Very much.'

'I'll come,' Davie said, around a mouthful.

'I rather thought, Davie,' his grandmother suggested, 'that you and I might do some shopping. At Mr Goffin's. Essential supplies for a grandson's visit, so to speak.' She grinned like a child herself. Mr Goffin it was who ran the sweet shop that was famous county-wide for its gobstoppers.

'Oh. Yes, please.' Davie looked at his mother. 'You don't mind, do you?'

Annie shook her head solemnly. 'No, no. You go ahead. We'll be quite all right.'

–

'I really like your mother,' Richard said later as they strolled along the water's edge, feet scrunching on the shingle.

Annie glanced up at him, smiling. 'I'm fairly fond of her myself.' They had left behind the huts and the fishing boats of the longshoremen, together with the bathing machines and the picnicking, sandcastle-building families on the town's popular beach, and were strolling north along the wide, empty stretches of the deserted coastline, the waters of Sole Bay glittering restlessly to their right. Brandy, having raced around like a mad thing for the first half-hour, now trotted docilely at Annie's heels. Shrimp boats bobbed, far out on the water.

Richard tilted back his head and took a deep breath of the cool, fresh air; then suddenly he stopped walking and turned to Annie, both his hands outstretched.

With no hesitation she took them. It was as if she had been waiting for the gesture.

'Thank you,' he said.

She laughed, startled. 'For what?'

'For letting me bring you here,' he said lightly. 'For walking with me. For sleeping in the back of my car.' He glanced down, and all at once the laughter was gone. 'For taking my hands,' he said quietly. 'For being Annie.'

In the silence the sea washed almost to their feet, then rippled away again, restlessly tumbling the shingle as it went. Annie said nothing.

Still holding her hands he drew her close to him, bent his head, kissed her very gently. Annie stood quite still, his lips on hers. She tasted salt. The breeze ruffled their hair, the sea rushed and murmured, above them a seabird wheeled and called, mournful and haunting; and still, gentle and undemanding in the cool air, he kissed her. After a moment he released her hands to lift his own and cup her face. She closed her eyes; in that moment it was as if every sense she possessed was more vivid, more acutely tuned than she had ever known before. It was as if the world had stopped. The sound of the sea and of the bird call, the brush of the sea breeze on her skin, the touch of the man's salty lips on hers: the moment was perfect.

Too perfect. Painfully perfect. When finally he lifted his head she leaned to him and he wrapped his arms about her, holding her to him, looking over her head to the shimmering distances of the sunlit sea. She rested her head against his shoulder, the rough, sea–damp tweed of his jacket scratching her cheek.

Neither spoke for a long time.

'I'm sorry,' he said at last. 'I really shouldn't have done that.'

She stirred, opened her eyes, lifted her head to look at him. 'Why not?'

He looked down at her. 'I wouldn't want you to think—' He stopped.

'At the moment,' she said softly, touching his lips with her finger, her words almost lost in the sound of wind and sea, 'I'm actually not thinking at all.'

His arms tightened around her; he laid his cheek against her hair. And Brandy, bored, suddenly shot yapping along the beach to chase off a huge seagull that had had the temerity to land at the water's edge nearby. The spell was broken. Laughing they stepped apart, hands still linked, turned to stroll back towards the town with the dog trotting proudly beside them. Neither broke the silence that had fallen between them; but when they arrived back at Jane's cottage they were still holding hands.

–

'I got your letter,' Jane said quietly, a little later. She was standing at the kitchen window, cup and saucer in hand, watching Davie and Richard in the garden playing an arcane and apparently rule-less game involving sand buckets, spades and tennis balls.

93

Annie looked up. 'And?' she asked quietly.

Her mother shrugged, glanced a smile across her shoulder. 'I can't say I was actually surprised.'

'Do you think I did the right thing?'

'Would it matter if I didn't?' Jane was genuinely amused.

Annie shook her head and stirred her tea. 'No.'

'That's what I thought.' Her mother joined her, sat down across the table from her. 'But for what it's worth – yes, under the circumstances, I think you did.'

'Circumstances?' Annie made only a half-hearted effort at innocence. She knew her mother too well.

Jane did not even dignify that with an answer; she simply raised wry brows and smiled.

Annie tinkered with her spoon in her saucer. Her mother watched her in patient silence. Annie raised her eyes, opened her mouth to speak, shut it again.

'What?' Jane asked.

Annie shrugged. 'I don't know. It's just… things seem to be happening rather quickly.' She lowered her eyes again, blushing a little. 'Richard just kissed me. On the beach.'

'I rather thought he had.'

'I don't understand.' Her daughter spoke in a rush. 'I don't know what he sees in me. Oh, I don't mean' – she stopped, shook her head – 'I don't think I know what I *do* mean.'

Jane laughed softly. 'That,' she said, 'sounds very much like the onset of love. Or, of course,' she added, 'of infatuation?'

'Exactly.' Annie was quick to pick that up; it was the thought in the forefront of her own mind. 'How do you tell the difference?'

'An age-old question, that, and not an easy one to answer.' Jane got up, took her cup and saucer to the sink and ran it under the tap. Then she turned, leaning on the sink with arms folded, surveying her daughter. 'Annie, darling, you're a grown-up woman. Just a few weeks ago you were bemoaning the lack of romance in your life—'

'I know. That's the trouble, can't you see? How do I know that—'

'You can't *know* anything,' her mother interrupted gently.

In the garden outside Davie was laughing so hard he could hardly speak. 'Oh, come on, Richard – *nobody* can be as cack-handed as that—'

'Oh, no? Try me – why do you think I'm a solicitor and not a brain surgeon? – blast it, missed again!'

'What are you afraid of?' Jane asked softly. 'Why shouldn't he be attracted to you? What else could he possibly want? He's obviously not short of money, so it can't be that. He's a very attractive man…'

'The most attractive I've ever met.' Annie's eyes went to the window; there were more shouts of laughter from the garden.

'He gets on well with Davie and Davie with him.'

'Yes.'

Jane came to her, rested a hand on her shoulder. 'Then just enjoy yourself. And give it time. You don't have to rush into anything. I suppose that's the answer to your question; if you're falling in love, time will tell. Infatuation doesn't last. You like him very much, don't you?'

Annie lifted her head and her face broke into a dazzling smile. 'Yes. I do.'

Her mother dropped a quick kiss on the top of her dark head. 'And so do I, if that helps at all.' She grinned impishly. 'I could quite fancy him myself, as a matter of fact.'

'Mother!' They were still laughing at that when Richard and Davie appeared in the doorway. The man's arm was resting across the boy's shoulders in an easily companionable way, and they were both smiling; Richard's eyes were warm on Annie's. 'Time to go,' he said.

'I'll get my things.'

A few minutes later Jane and Davie stood at the door waving as the big green and black car pulled away. Annie's shining bob blew in the wind as she leaned from the window to wave back. 'I expect Richard will look after Mother while I'm away,' Davie said.

Jane looked down at him affectionately. 'Oh, I'm sure of it,' she said, smiling. 'Now – what do you say to toasted buns for tea?'

–

The big Wolseley purred along the quiet country lanes towards the main London road. For a long time neither Richard nor Annie spoke. She sat with head averted, watching the passing countryside, apparently absorbed but actually taking little in. She could feel – physically feel – the man's presence beside her. Without the protection of Davie's relentless and distracting chatter she was suddenly stricken by an odd and confusing combination of excitement, apprehension and an almost paralysing self-consciousness. She could think of absolutely nothing to say.

Richard sat easily, hands relaxed on the wheel, humming quietly to himself as he drove. They turned a corner, came up behind an ambling horse and cart. Richard slowed the car to a patient crawl, glanced at her with a smile. 'Penny for them?'

At that moment she had been wondering if he would stay for the evening. If he would kiss her again. Her cheeks warm, she shook her head quickly. 'They aren't worth it.'

The lane widened. Richard swung the car carefully out to overtake, lifting an acknowledging hand to the cart driver, who nodded, unsmiling, lifting his ancient whip. The car surged forward again, Richard settled back in his seat. 'May I ask you something?' he said, after a moment.

She looked at him enquiringly.

'Will you truly never go back to Paris?'

The question took her entirely by surprise. She thought about it for a moment, then gave a small shrug. 'No, I shouldn't think so. There's no real reason why I should.'

'It seems such a pity. I know she holds unhappy memories for you, but I truly believe she is the loveliest and most romantic city in the world. Hasn't enough time passed for you to forgive her?'

Annie said nothing, but gave the tiniest, stubborn shake of her head.

Richard glanced at her again. 'Davie was born there. Won't you take him back to see his birthplace?'

'We've already discussed that,' she said evenly. 'Davie understands. He knows how I feel about the city and he knows how I feel about crossing deep water. He'll go eventually, when he's grown up. It doesn't seem to bother him at the moment.'

'Paris in June,' he said musingly. 'Coffee and croissants at a pavement cafe. Shuttered windows on a hot afternoon. The sun shining on the river. Sacré Coeur gleaming on top of her hill…' He shook his head as he pulled out onto the main road and headed south. 'I don't see how you can resist going back, I really don't.'

Annie's fingers were clasped in her lap and she had dropped her head a little, her eyes fixed upon them. Her mouth, suddenly, was set in an obstinate and unhappy line.

Richard did not appear to notice her silence. 'Think of Paris at night.' He smiled suddenly. 'Was there ever such a combination of fairytale and madhouse? Grand opera. Grand passion. Pretty girls in feathers and spangled tights. The Champs Élysées glittering like a string of diamonds. Bars packed with destitute artists and writers wrecking themselves with cheap absinthe, falling in love, falling out of love, putting the world to rights. The rich and the fashionable promenading on the boulevards, the down-and-outs clutching their bottles and bedding down under the bridges…' He stopped speaking for a moment as he negotiated a tight corner. Annie turned her head to stare again sightlessly out of the window. 'You knew Paris before the war,' he said quietly. 'You grew up there. You were young – beautiful—'

She turned, startled, to look at him, but his face, like his words, was matter-of-fact. His eyes were on the road, his voice was quiet. 'I know it ended in tragedy. As it did for so many. But you must, surely, remember the good times? The beauty, the life, the love? It was ten years ago, Annie. A war, and a lifetime, away. Wouldn't you think of coming back to Paris? With me?'

'I…' For a fraction of a second she hesitated. Then, 'No,' she said, shaking her head, her heavy hair swinging about her face. 'I'm sorry.'

'So am I.'

She struggled for a moment. 'You'll never understand,' she said at last, flatly. 'In fact I don't even want you to try.'

There was a small silence. Then, 'Fair enough,' he said lightly.

They motored on. The sun, moving westward, lit the underside of suddenly gathering clouds to a picturesquely lurid glow in the wide East Anglian sky.

'Tell me something?' Richard asked.

She turned her head.

He smiled, not looking at her. 'Am I invited to supper?'

Her heart lurched. 'Yes. If you'd like.'

He glanced at his watch, then at her, eyes glinting. 'Then when we get to town, best I find a sensible off-licence, wouldn't you say?'

'Sensible?'

He grinned. 'One of the kind that sells Champagne,' he said.

–

'That was splendid. Thank you.' Richard laid his knife and fork on his plate and pushed it a little away from him.

Annie shook her head. 'It wasn't exactly the Savoy.' Richard leaned back in his chair and lifted his glass. 'Who needs it? Suffolk ham, new-laid eggs and Champagne. A feast, no less!'

She smiled. 'The Champagne certainly adds a certain something, doesn't it? I seem to have run right out of lobster and asparagus. Perhaps next time?' Despite her barely acknowledged apprehensions, the evening had been a delightful one. Richard had been an easy, entertaining and attentive companion. She felt light-hearted and not a little light-headed; they were already on their second bottle of Champagne. It was, she reflected wryly, becoming something of a habit.

Richard grinned. 'Perhaps.'

The candles on the table flickered a little. In the darkness beyond the dining-room window rain had begun to fall, steadily and heavily.

Annie started to collect the plates. 'There's fruit if you'd like some?'

He shook his head, still smiling. As she reached for his plate he caught her wrist lightly. 'Leave it,' he said, 'for now. We'll do it later.'

There was a small, somehow slightly precarious silence. In the dancing light of the candles Richard's eyes were very steady on hers. Her skin tingled beneath his light touch; she nibbled her lip. He smiled, a sudden flash of mischief in his face. 'Anyway,' he said, letting go of her wrist, 'you can't use the sink yet. There's another bottle of Champagne in it. It wouldn't do to waste that, would it?'

Annie sat down again, leaned her elbows on the table and her chin on her cupped hands, watching him, eyebrows raised a little. 'Are you trying to get me tiddly?' she asked.

He laughed, shook his head. 'That's the last thing I'm trying to do.'

She surveyed him for a long moment, then reached for her glass and held it up to the candlelight, studying the glittering effect with apparently absorbed interest. Then her eyes flickered back to his. 'Oh?' she asked innocently. And with a daring touch of no doubt Champagne-induced impudence, 'So, what's the first thing?'

His eyes gleamed appreciatively. 'Right now?'

'Right now.'

He reached across the table for her hand again. 'First this,' he said, turning her hand and kissing the palm gently. 'Next – with your permission – a cigarette and a drop of your excellent whisky. Then I should like to turn on the wireless and dance with you.' He stood up. 'You bring the Champagne,' he said, 'I'll bring the candles.'

She had lit the fire in the sitting room earlier, against the chill of the damp evening. Whilst Richard set the candles on the little table and went to fiddle with the radio, Annie poked the embers into life and tossed on a small log. Flames leapt and flickered. She straightened to find that he had come up quietly behind her. Before she could move he had slipped his arms about her, drawing her towards him, burying his face in her neck. She tipped her head back onto his shoulder and closed her eyes. They stood for a moment, swaying to the quiet sound of the music that did not drown out the thunder of the rain. Then, perfectly naturally and entirely without thought, she turned around in his arms and put her own arms about his neck.

Later she thought that, whatever had gone before, that kiss was her undoing. Perhaps she had willed it to be so. Perhaps after the years of sober responsibility, straitlaced respectability and stubborn self-denial, it was inevitable that the genie, once released from the bottle, could not be reconfined. They did not dance. They made love, on the floor in front of the fire, a thing she had never done in her life before.

'What do you mean?' he asked, smiling down at her when she told him so. He had sat up, propped his back against an armchair, a cigarette in one hand and the other stroking her hair in a shining fan across his thigh. She was lying naked upon her back, arms outstretched, her head in his lap, watching him. The firelight flickered upon her skin. It was still raining.

'I've never made love on the floor before.' She lifted a hand, ran a finger down the sharp-angled curve of his cheek. 'Only ever in bed.'

He drew once more on his cigarette, tossed it in the fire. Smiled down at her. 'You like making love in bed?' he asked softly, tugging at her hair a little. 'Come on, then. Let's go to bed.'

This time, at his gentle insistence, their lovemaking was more leisurely. 'Wait, my darling,' he whispered, tongue and fingers rousing and teasing. 'We have... all... the time... in the world—' He had turned on the bedside lamp. Helpless, she watched the play of light on his face and could have wept in the wonder of what she saw there. Indeed, in the end, weep she did. He leaned above her, resting on an elbow, bent to kiss her wet cheek. 'I'm sorry. Did I hurt you?'

Smiling, she shook her head, tears still welling. 'No. Far from it.'

He watched her carefully for a moment longer, then he too smiled. 'Time for that other bottle of Champagne, I think?'

—

Beyond the drawn curtains of the window the rain still fell in sheets. The room, lit by its single lamp, was an intimate cocoon enclosing them. Annie put her tall glass on the bedside table, threw her head forward so that her heavy hair covered her face, and teased at it with her fingers. 'I must look an absolute *mess!*'

He shook his head, smiling, but said nothing. The smoke from his cigarette coiled in the air. He sipped his whisky.

Annie threw back the sheet, reached for the silk robe that was draped on the chair next to the bed.

'Please,' he said, 'don't do that.'

'What?'

'Cover yourself. Hide from me. You don't need to. You're beautiful.'

A fiery colour rose in her cheeks. She hesitated.

'Please?'

She nibbled her lip; then slipped from the bed and walked, naked, to the dressing table, perched on the stool and reached for a hairbrush.

Outside, a wind was lifting. The rain was being driven in gusts against the window.

He watched her. 'Annie?' he said quietly.

The slow, lazy brush strokes ceased; she turned her head a little, her face bright, to look at him in the mirror. 'Yes?'

'Will you marry me?'

Shock froze her. She looked at him in complete incomprehension. 'What?'

'I said – will you marry me?' His voice was gentle. 'I would have thought it a simple – and time-honoured – question?'

'Marry you?' she repeated blankly.

'I do believe that's what I said.' His voice was patient.

'But – Richard – I… we can't! Not just like that! We hardly know each other!'

He lifted his eyebrows, glanced around the disordered room.

She flushed, swung the stool round to face him, looked at him for a long time, her arms suddenly and defensively crossed over her bare breasts. 'Don't you think this is just a little... premature?' she asked uncertainly. 'We've only met half a dozen times. Oh – I know—' She shook her head sharply at his significantly lifted brows. 'I know we've made love. And it was wonderful. But – marriage?' Suddenly she was fighting something very close to panic. She walked to the bed and, forcing herself not to fumble, slipped on her silk dressing robe and belted it firmly before turning to face him.

Richard was watching her calmly. 'I could have asked you the very first day I met you,' he said, with tranquil certainty. 'That, I agree, would certainly have been "a little premature".' He smiled. 'If you ask me, I think I've been very forbearing.' He stubbed out his cigarette, leaned forward and held out both hands to her, his smile disarming. 'I love you,' he said simply.

She shook her head again in confusion, desperately – and belatedly – wishing that she had not drunk so much Champagne. Of all the things she had hoped for – expected, even – this was the very last. 'I—'

'Yes?'

'Richard, it isn't that easy! You must know that. We can't simply get married! Not just like that! It isn't reasonable. It—wouldn't be right!' She was all too aware of the sudden narrowing of his eyes, the tightening of his long mouth, but stumbled on stubbornly, the words tumbling over each other. 'We need time to get to *know* each other. There are... things that you don't know about me. Things that I don't know about you. We can't just ignore that.'

'Why not?' The words were cool and quiet. Then, 'Don't you trust me?' he asked, in the same tone.

'It isn't that!' she said quickly.

'Then what is it?' He was implacable.

She stared at him helplessly.

'I've told you. I love you. I want you to marry me. That's simple enough, isn't it?'

'*Simple!*' Faintly hysterical laughter rose; she fought it down. 'Look, Richard, I'm flattered and—and delighted that you feel…' she trailed off.

'I don't want you to feel flattered and delighted,' he said flatly. 'I want you to say "Yes". You may not have thought about this, but I have. I don't want us snatching time together like this when Davie's away—'

'Davie,' she said, snatching gratefully at that straw. 'We do have to think of Davie. We can't just—'

'I've thought of Davie. He won't mind. You know it.' The quiet words were all but lost in a sudden squally blast of rain and wind against the window.

She said nothing for a moment.

'Annie?' he asked.

She stood up, walked over to the window and drew back the curtains a little, looking sightlessly out into the drenched night.

'One of the things you don't know,' she said, almost steadily, 'is that I… can't have any more children.'

'I don't want children,' he said, immediately and with no pause for thought. 'I want you. And Davie.'

She swung round, hands outstretched. 'Richard, please! Don't be so unreasonable! At least give me time – time to think, time to—'

'Time to find excuses?' he interrupted. He stood up, reached for his shirt. 'I'm sorry to have upset you. I'm sorry to have… embarrassed you so. I should have known. You've made your opinion of marriage quite clear—'

His movements as he dressed were sharp and fierce. 'I'm sorry if you find this' – he made a curt gesture at the tumbled bed – 'so much more romantic, more desirable.' He hesitated. When he spoke again his voice was stiff and held the faintest edge of bitterness. 'I've made a fool of myself. Again. I should have recognised the likeness—' He stopped abruptly.

She swung to face him. 'What do you mean?' she asked fiercely. 'Likeness? To whom?'

'Never mind.' He picked up his tie, cracked it like a whip to smooth the creases, stalked to the mirror.

'I do mind. Likeness to whom?' Her own temper was beginning to slip.

'I said never mind.' Stone-faced, he fixed and straightened his tie, then reached for his jacket. He stood looking at her for a long moment. 'The fact is, as I said, you don't trust me. You want me. But you don't trust me.'

'That isn't fair! It isn't so!'

'Isn't it?' He took one long step towards her, caught her shoulders in his hands and jerked her roughly to him. 'Think about it,' he said, and kissed her, hard, and with not the faintest trace of tenderness, before striding to the door. There he paused. 'Think about it!' he said again, and was gone, running fleetly down the stairs, his very footsteps sounding angry.

'*Richard!*'

The front door crashed closed.

Annie turned back to the window, watched bemusedly as the tall, obviously furious figure wrenched open the door of the car and flung himself inside, slamming the door behind him. She could not understand – could not believe – the abrupt and bizarre turn the evening had taken. What in God's name had happened? And how – *how?* – had it happened so suddenly?

She watched in miserable disbelief as the big car slid, gleaming, from beneath the lamplight and into the sodden darkness; then she turned, looked around the room. The smell of his cigarette still hung in the air. His empty glass stood on one of the bedside tables. As she moved she caught a gleam of gold from the floor beside the bed. Moving slowly and tiredly, she bent to retrieve a small, heavy cufflink with an ornately etched 'R' upon it. She laid it carefully upon the dressing table. Her mind was all but blank with misery; she hadn't, she discovered, even the energy to cry.

A half-empty bottle of Champagne stood on the other bedside cabinet.

She picked it up, carried it into the bathroom and, upending it over the basin, bleakly watched the frothy sparkle of it as it ran down the plughole.

Part Two

Summer 1925

Chapter Nine

For most of what was left of the night Annie tossed and turned unhappily in the darkness, listening to the rain that drove in torrents against the window. Tired tears came and went; a sodden and dreary dawn light was seeping into the sky before, at last, she slept.

She awoke with a vilely queasy stomach and a brutal headache. Groaning, she curled up and buried her hot face in the pillow. It took a moment or so before she fully remembered the events of the night before; when memory did return she sat up, altogether too suddenly. The room tilted and spun, her stomach roiled again. With extravagant care she swung her feet to the floor and lowered her face into her spread hands. She felt sick enough to die. What fool, she wondered numbly, had put about the rumour that Champagne did not induce a hangover?

It was a long time before she lifted her head and squinted groggily through a curtain of hair at the bedside clock. 'Good God!' she mumbled. 'It can't be.'

The rain had stopped, the wind dropped. With enormous care she stood up and, fingertips pressed to her burning eyes and thumping forehead, moved slowly to the window and drew back the curtains. There was the faintest suggestion of brightness in the heavy sky. She flinched from it, screwing up her eyes, and turned back to survey the room. Her clothes were still dumped untidily on the chair; the bed looked as if a bomb had hit it. The single gold cufflink lay upon the dressing table. Still moving very cautiously, and wincing at almost every step, she went to the dressing table, lowered herself gingerly onto the stool and picked up the gleaming thing. Last night she had watched Richard's long fingers as, deftly practised, he had slipped it from his cuff. Last night those same fingers had touched her, stroked her, coaxed her to abandon. Last night…

She lifted her head to survey her own all but colourless face in the mirror. Unsurprisingly she looked ghastly. Even more unsurprisingly, she felt worse. She ran distracted fingers through her unkempt hair. Her eyes were reddened, her mouth felt like a desert.

Last night Richard had left her in anger. In anger and in hurt. What was it he had said? *'I've made a fool of myself. Again. I should have recognised the likeness…'* She had hated that. Likeness to whom? The fickle Isobella, who had so obviously betrayed and wounded him? That wasn't fair. It wasn't! *'You don't trust me,'* he had said. *'You want me. But you don't trust me.'* Was that true? Hollow-eyed, she stared dejectedly at her reflection. In all honesty she didn't know. In all probability she would now not have a chance to find out. Richard did not strike her as a man who would stand still to be slapped twice.

But – marriage? What in the world had possessed him to spring such a suggestion upon her so precipitately? And to take so badly what she perceived to be her very natural inclination to caution? Had he truly expected her to give no thought, no deep consideration to his proposal? Had he planned to ask her? Or had it been some kind of Champagne-induced impulse? The more she thought about it the more confused she became; and, yes, the more miserably and self-defensively indignant – an indignation, however, that was at the moment powerfully diluted by her fragile physical state. She desperately needed a cup – a pot, perhaps two – of tea and an aspirin. She almost as desperately needed to go back to bed – if possible, she thought with a touch of bleak humour, to die.

Sighing, she hauled herself to her feet, reached for her dressing gown and went down to the kitchen.

–

The hangover lifted at least a little; the gloom did not. She trailed dejectedly around the house for the rest of the day, crushingly tired, unable to concentrate on anything, missing Davie.

Davie. How was she going to tell Davie that she and Richard had quarrelled?

Every time the thought occurred she quashed it firmly. She could not bear to think about it. Her first instinct – once at least the physical effects of the Champagne and the emotional upheaval of the night before had eased – had been to take a taxi to Liverpool Street and the first and fastest train east, to the calm, comfort and reassuring good sense she knew would be waiting for her. But to do that meant breaking the news of the quarrel to Davie – since he would certainly demand to know what she was doing there – and she wasn't up to that. Not yet. And anyway, deep in her heart she could not quite kill a tenuous, almost unacknowledged, hope.

There might in the end be no *need* to tell him?

In her imagination she visualised it a million times: a car pulling up outside, quick footsteps on the path, the door flung open – *'Darling, I'm sorry… I'm so sorry—'* Or more white roses, perhaps? Another tender, clever message? A telegram, even? Abject apologies – an invitation to dinner maybe? A smart lad, pencil in hand: *'Will there be a reply, Madam?'*

No such thing happened, of course. The day dragged on. It put her at a huge disadvantage that she did not even know where Richard was, let alone what he might be doing. She had never been to his apartment, nor to his office; indeed, had only the vaguest idea of where either was situated. He on the other hand knew exactly where she was and, she suspected, probably had a fair idea of the way she was feeling. Rebelling at that thought, halfway through the afternoon she flung on her coat and went for a walk in the Gardens, dawdling along the still-wet paths, noting with an unwontedly indifferent eye that the colours of early summer were beginning to splash in the beds and that the trees were in bright and vigorous leaf. The damp air blew at least some of the cobwebs away. She stopped for a pot of tea, avoiding almost without thought the table at which she had sat with Richard and Davie. She played a superstitious game with herself: the longer she stayed out, the more likely that there would be a message when she returned…

There wasn't. It was nearly six o'clock by the time she got back to the house; a house that seemed echoingly empty as she shut the front door and stood in the hallway taking off her coat and hat. She slung them across the banisters and wandered into the kitchen, opening and shutting cupboard doors. She felt half-heartedly hungry, but could not be bothered to cook anything. In the end she settled for toasted cheese, which she ate in the sitting room, listening to the wireless. Two hours later she was in bed; and a half-hour after that she was sound asleep.

–

At least Annie felt physically better the next morning, the direst effects of the hangover having worn off. She sat at the kitchen table, toying with a piece of cold toast and seriously considering taking flight to Southwold. Then she remembered: it was Thursday. The day of the Red Cross Bazaar at the Town Hall. She had promised to help with the refreshments for the morning.

She closed her eyes. 'Blast it!' she said aloud. '*Blast it!*'

In the event, however, the bazaar turned out to be just the tonic she needed. It was difficult to mope in the friendly, if wearing, atmosphere amidst steaming urns of tea, freshly made sandwiches – which seemed to disappear just as fast as she could make them – and home-made cakes. She did not get back to the house until mid-afternoon. There was no message, no sign that Richard might have called. Annie shrugged; her hope that he might have done had been a half-hearted one at best. She went into the kitchen, stood at the back door, pondering. It was too late to try to get up to Southwold today; she'd go tomorrow. Meanwhile, her gardener's eye was already noting the damage the wind had done to the garden, the way that rain and sun had caused a surge of growth, especially, as so often seemed the way, among the weeds. John, the man who helped her in the garden once a week, would be coming tomorrow, but there was nothing to stop her making a start today...

She was engaged in ruthless attack against the stinging nettles that were doing their best to invade the large border that ran alongside the fence when, through the open back door, she thought she heard the doorbell. She sat back on her heels, cocking her head, listening. She had changed into an old skirt and jumper, donned socks and wellingtons and an old pair of leather gloves.

The bell rang again.

Richard...

'Oh, Lord, just *look* at me!' But her heart was beating like a drum. She scrambled to her feet, pulling off the gloves, brushing the dirt and moisture from the sleeves of her jumper. 'I'm coming,' she called. She ran to the back door, kicked off her boots, grinned at the sight of the heavy brown socks – one of which had a hole in the toe – and ran through the house to the front door.

The man on the front doorstep looked a little startled at her tousled appearance, but he was nowhere near as taken aback as Annie was.

'Fergus,' she said, blankly. 'Hello.' The disappointment that was welling inside her was all but unbearable. It couldn't be Fergus, it couldn't be.

Fergus doffed his hat. 'Hello, Annie.' The words were absurdly awkward. She had forgotten how plump he was, how thin his hair.

There was an embarrassing moment of silence. 'I... was passing,' he said. 'I thought... I'd pop in and see—' he cleared his throat 'how you were—'

She stepped back, holding the door open. 'Come in,' she said. 'Do come in.' The words, like her smile, were over-bright. She could have wept. She wanted to scream. 'Tea?' she asked.

The hour that followed was an excruciating one. Annie did her best, but the cold stone of disappointment that seemed to have settled in her stomach did not make for sparkling conversation. She wanted Fergus to go, to leave her alone to nurse it. She had tried; she had almost succeeded. But it was impossible to deny that fierce surge of happiness which had so betrayed her, and had made the dashing of her suddenly raised hopes so hard to endure.

Fergus perched uncomfortably on the edge of the sofa, his cup and saucer balanced on his knee. 'You look a little pale,' he said.

'I've had a couple of late nights,' she said absently, stirring her tea, and completely missing the sudden sharpness of his glance at her. 'And I spent this morning serving tea and cakes to what felt like half of Kew and all of Richmond, so I've been on my feet all day. I'm a bit tired, that's all.'

He glanced around. 'Where's Davie?'

'At Southwold with Mother. It's half-term. You know they like to have a few days together.'

He nodded. 'It must be... lonely for you without him?' he suggested tentatively.

Annie shrugged. 'Would you like another cup of tea?'

'Yes, please.'

She stood, took his cup and saucer and walked to the table. 'How are things at the office?' she had begun politely, when there came the clatter of the letterbox.

Her heart lurched.

Fergus leaned to look out of the window. 'Postman,' he said. 'I'll go.' Annie was astonished at the quick stir of resentment brought by this assumption of a familiarity that in her mind no longer existed. But she bit her tongue and said nothing.

He left the room, returned carrying a letter: a plain, heavy cream envelope addressed in a neat and regular hand that Annie recognised immediately. She had last seen it on the flyleaf of the book Richard had bought for Davie in Paris. Fergus held it out to her. She took it and, with a composure that she herself could scarcely believe, glanced at it and then tucked it behind the clock on the mantelpiece. 'It's nothing important. I'll look at it later. I was saying, how's business going?'

Poor Fergus had known from the moment she opened the door that the impulse which had brought him here had not been a sound one. He struggled on for a while longer before ostentatiously glancing at his pocket watch. 'Well – I mustn't keep you any longer.' He stood up. 'It's been nice to see you.' The words were wistful.

On impulse she kissed his cheek lightly. 'And you.'

'But...' he hesitated, 'but you haven't changed your mind?'

She shook her head gravely, suddenly torn with sympathy for him. 'No, Fergus. I haven't.'

He nodded, smiled a small rueful smile, reached for his hat. Annie followed him out into the hall. 'Do call again,' she found herself saying, 'if you're passing. We shouldn't lose touch.'

Fergus fingered his hat brim, watching her for a moment, then he settled it on his head and smiled brightly. 'No, of course not. Goodbye.'

'Goodbye, Fergus.' Annie watched the stout figure down the path, then closed the door and leaned against it for a moment. Through the open door of the sitting room she could see the mantelpiece, the clock, the envelope tucked behind it. From the moment she had seen it she had been all too aware that there could be no foregone assumptions about its contents. An apology? A goodbye? More bitter recriminations and hateful comparisons? She clasped her hands behind her back and walked to the mantelpiece, stood looking at the envelope. At last, carefully, she reached for it. Even then she did not immediately open it. Almost superstitiously she fingered it for a moment; while unopened, it held threat and promise in about equal shares. Once opened, there would be no going back.

The letter was short and to the point. It was not effusive, and contained only the mildest hint of an apology, though the tone was pleasant enough and the touch was light…

> Dear Annie,
>
> I neglected to ask, before my somewhat precipitous exit the other evening, if you might find it interesting to visit the new 'Modern Foreign' exhibition at the Tate? I've visited it once – it's quite wonderful, much too much to take in all at once. Cézanne, Degas, Manet, Van Gogh, Matisse, Renoir, Lautrec – they're all there. What do you think? I would, of course, be the last one to blame you should you have discovered over the past couple of days that your enthusiasm for the Impressionists and all their works had waned a little. Or even a great deal. That would be a pity. In the hope that it has not, I'll wait at the entrance tomorrow (Friday) afternoon at three.
>
> Love,
> Richard.

Annie re-read the letter, then lifted her head to regard herself in the mirror that hung above the mantelpiece.

'*Love, Richard,*' she said, indignantly. 'He's got a bloody cheek! If he thinks I'm going to his beastly bloody exhibition with him at the drop of a hat—' She stopped, laughing aloud at herself.

Perhaps, after all, she would give a little more serious consideration to her decision to go to Southwold tomorrow...?

Humming, and still in her stockinged feet, she went into the kitchen to prepare herself some supper. Suddenly, and unexpectedly, she found that she was famished.

–

It was a cool, sunny afternoon, with a slightly chill breeze blowing from the river. Annie, determined not to be early, sauntered along the Victoria Embankment, pausing every now and again to lean against the parapet and watch the bustling activity on the Thames. She was wearing green and cream, a pretty, short-skirted dress that she knew showed off her legs to good advantage, and a hip-length matching jacket. As a gust of wind blew again from the water she lifted a gloved hand to her narrow-brimmed hat, entirely unaware of the appraising glances of a group of young men sitting on one of the elaborate cast-iron benches that were set at intervals beneath the trees lining the wide pavement. A pleasure boat crowded with sightseers chugged by. She watched it for a moment before turning to continue to stroll towards Westminster and the Houses of Parliament. She glanced at her watch. Five to three. Despite herself, faint anxiety lifted. Perhaps she shouldn't be too late? She quickened her pace.

Richard saw her coming before she saw him. One of the first things he had noticed about her was the way she walked: straight-backed, long-legged and graceful. Her heavy, straight hair blew a little in the breeze, and her cheeks were bright with colour in the wind. He smiled. The cream and green outfit, with its carefully matched accessories, was very becoming, very fashionable. But, no matter how she tried, Annie's special charm did not fit the conventions of the day. She was too tall for fashion, and too shapely. Her face was too open, her smile too quick; she was no sophisticate, nor ever could be. Yet that unconsciously graceful walk was almost provocative. His blood stirred.

She caught sight of him, smiled a little awkwardly as she joined him.

He had anticipated that. He kissed her lightly on the lips. 'An apology,' he said, before she could speak, 'then the exhibition. Then we'll talk. How does that sound?'

She watched him steadily for a moment, then nodded. 'Right. The apology first. I'm sorry I hurt you the other night. I didn't intend to, I promise. I got... carried away. A little too much Champagne, perhaps—'

Ruefully she put a hand to her forehead. 'You can say that again.'

'I had no right to lose my temper with you. I had no right to say some of the things I said. Can we start again?'

She did not have it in her to prevaricate. 'Yes.'

He smiled, held out his hand. 'Good. Let's go and look at the pictures.'

–

'I'm not sure about Van Gogh.' Annie shook her head thoughtfully. 'He's too...' she hesitated, 'violent. He must have been a very strange man.' They were strolling by the river now, outside the Gallery. The sun was dipping and the breeze had died a little. The city's Friday evening traffic was building up.

Richard smiled wryly. 'Cutting off your own ear and then going mad and shooting yourself couldn't exactly be considered normal, I suppose,' he conceded. 'Even for a foreigner,' he added with a small grin. 'But I must say I find his paintings fascinating. Who did you like best?'

'Degas,' she said promptly. 'And Renoir. I didn't like the Gauguin much. You?'

'If I had to choose, then it would be Lautrec. It always would be – I've told you before, he's my favourite painter. No one comes near him for me. But Monet runs him a close second.' He looked at his wristwatch. 'It's early for dinner. How do you fancy a real old-fashioned cream tea?'

She eyed him, faintly wary. 'Is this the talking bit?'

'It is.'

She shrugged. 'All right.'

'I know just the place. And here comes a taxi, right on cue.'

–

The large, panelled room was opulently comfortable: heavy curtains, expensive rugs upon the polished floor, deep cushioned armchairs and big, brass-bound wooden tables. The place was fairly full, the air filled with the chink of cup upon saucer, the murmur of well-bred voices, occasional laughter. Annie looked up with a smile as the black-and-white-uniformed waitress delivered tea, scones, thick yellow cream and jam. 'Thank you.' The girl bobbed a half-curtsey.

Annie arranged the plates, the gleaming knives, the cups and saucers, the scones, cream and jam, very precisely on the table. She did not look at Richard. She pulled the silver tray containing the teapot, milk jug and sugar bowl closer, rearranged them too to her satisfaction.

Richard watched her, a faint, warm gleam of amusement in his eyes.

'Sugar?' she asked politely.

'Yes, please,' he said gravely.

She poured the tea. 'This is a lovely place,' she said. 'The jam looks home-made.'

'It is. The hotel is renowned for it.'

'Oh.' Annie set his teacup in front of him, picked a warm scone from the dish and set it on her plate. The silence was not an easy one.

'Will you start, or shall I?' Richard asked after a moment, gently teasing.

She ducked her head, reached for the dish of cream. 'After you.'

He was quiet for a moment, marshalling his thoughts as best he could. 'I'm not going to apologise for asking you to marry me. I know you think it rash. And despite what I said the other night I do understand why. I took you by surprise, and for that I *do* apologise. To be utterly honest I rather took myself by surprise.' He leaned forward, his face intent. 'But I meant what I said, Annie. I love you. I want you with me. I want to care for you. For you and for Davie. And – given the society in which we live – there's only one satisfactory way to do that.'

Annie was watching him, uncertainty in her face.

'I've never believed in love at first sight,' he said, his voice calm, almost analytical, 'until now. I can't explain it, but it's happened. I'll say it again: I love you. And if I love you it follows that the last thing I want to do is to hurt you. But I *will* hurt you – and possibly hurt Davie more – if we start something… underhand. Can't you see that? Can you imagine the salacious gossip, the outrage if… when… people discover what's going on between us? And they will. Sooner or later they will. You know it.'

She opened her mouth to protest.

He shook his head, held up his hand. 'You're going to say you don't care. You're going to say that we don't have to tie each other down. That we're different—'

She lifted her chin, a touch defiantly. 'I suppose I was going to say something along those lines, yes.'

He leaned forward. 'And Davie?' he asked quietly. 'What of him? What of the first time he hears the gossip? At school perhaps? From one of his friends? Or – worse – from someone who isn't a friend? You know how cruel children can be.'

'But… we'd be careful—'

'No!' His suddenly raised voice attracted attention from a nearby table: a plump woman in tweeds and pearls turned her head, eyebrows raised. Richard took a breath, spoke more quietly. 'No,' he said again. 'Annie, don't be so naive. You *know* that, sooner or later, there'll be talk. Curtains twitching. Knowing looks and raised eyebrows every time my car turns into the street. And I won't – I will *not* – play that kind of hole-in-the-corner game with you. Hotel rooms and weekends in Brighton? No. I can't. You're worth better than that—' Abruptly he stopped, and laughed with infectious amusement. 'Who the hell wrote this script, do you suppose? Aren't these supposed to be your lines, my darling?'

She was watching him uncertainly. 'I… suppose so, yes. But—'

The laughter died. 'But you don't love me?' he asked.

'Yes! I do! At least' – she spread helpless hands – 'I *think* I do…'

'Not good enough,' he said softly. 'Annie, what are you afraid of?'

She laughed, a little shakily. 'Deep water,' she replied.

Richard half-smiled, acknowledging the point. 'And commitment?' he asked.

Annie fiddled with her napkin, not looking at him.

'Annie?'

She shrugged a little but would not answer.

Again he leaned forward, his face intent. 'Annie, listen to me. I love you. I mean it. And the other night was wonderful. But I won't go on like that. If you're frightened to commit yourself to me, then you don't love me. And if you don't love me' – it was his turn to shrug – 'then best we call it a day before one of us gets hurt.'

'No! Richard – please – won't you try to understand—'

'I do understand.' He pushed his cup to one side, reached for her hand. 'Look at me.'

She raised her eyes to his. 'I want there to be no secrets and no lies between us or around us. I want utter trust and utter commitment…'

'Is that all?' Her voice was wry, her face very sober. 'Don't we all have secrets? Don't we all lie sometimes?'

He ignored the words, his hand tightened on hers. 'Utter trust. Utter commitment. From both of us. I will not live a lie. I want you to marry me.'

She was quiet for a moment. 'Tell me something? Honestly?'

He raised enquiring brows.

'Has this' – she paused, searching for words – 'has this got anything – anything at all – to do with Isobella?'

Very subtly his face changed. He studied her for a long moment. Then, 'No,' he said shortly. 'I can see that it might seem so to you, but no, it hasn't.'

'Are you so sure?'

He took a breath, then shook his head. 'All right – no – I suppose I can't swear to that with my hand on my heart. Does it make a difference?'

'I'm… not sure.'

'If you're looking for an excuse, Annie,' he said quietly, 'then surely you can come up with a better one than that?'

She flushed a little.

'Drink your tea,' he said, letting go of her hand and sitting back in his chair. 'It's getting cold.'

They drank their tea in a pensive silence. Annie crumbled a scone and picked at it.

Richard waited, watching her. 'You need time,' he said at last, gently.

She looked at him quickly. 'Yes. Please.'

He shook his head, his straight mouth unsmiling. 'I shouldn't have rushed you the way I have. I'm sorry. It's only that I feel so very strongly – not only about you but about Davie too. I already love him as if he were my own, Annie. To lose you both—' He stopped, sudden undisguised pain in his eyes.

'Richard, please, don't! There's no reason why you should lose either of us—'

'It seems to me that there is.'

Her heart wrenched. At that moment, to make him smile again, to bring back the warmth into his eyes she would have done anything. She opened her mouth.

'I meant what I said.' He spoke before she could. 'Tuesday night was wonderful. If you never give me anything else I thank you for that.'

'Richard—!'

He raised his hand. 'Enough, my darling. You're right. You need time to think. Perhaps to talk to Davie. I'll be as patient as I can. But please – don't take too long. And while you're thinking, think on this. It's so simple, really. I want you to be mine, openly and honestly mine. I want you on my arm, in the sunlight. I want to say, "This is my wife." Is that so bad?'

She shook her head. 'Of course not.'

'We'll leave it at that for now, then, shall we?'

Annie nodded.

'But you haven't forever to think about it. I need an answer.'

'Yes.'

'And now, just to confirm your low opinion of me, I have some bad news, I'm afraid.' His face was rueful.

Annie was startled. 'Oh?'

'I've been called away. To Paris. I have to leave tomorrow.'

'Tomorrow?' she asked blankly. 'Saturday? But—'

'Yes, I know. I was supposed to take you to pick Davie up on Sunday. I really am sorry. But this is business. Lucrative business. A—' he hesitated, '—demanding client.'

'How long will you be gone?'

'Three… four days.'

'Davie will be terribly disappointed.'

'There'll be other trips. Tell him we'll take him to the seaside next weekend; that'll cheer him up.'

Annie set her cup carefully upon its saucer, not looking at him. 'When are you sailing exactly?' When he did not reply she lifted her eyes to his.

He was watching her with quizzically understanding eyes. 'I'm taking the early morning boat train. The ferry sails at about noon, I think. Annie – don't worry—'

'I can't help it.' She shook her head, impatient at herself. 'I know it's irrational. I know it's stupid. But I simply can't help it.'

He leaned forward, took her hand again. 'It is irrational. It isn't stupid. Marry me, Annie; you'll be safe with me, I promise, and between us we'll beat this fear of yours. You and Davie will walk aboard a ferry with me. You'll walk the streets of Paris holding my hand.' He tightened his fingers on hers, then laughed. 'I'm sorry. I've already broken my promise not to push you. You see what you've done to me? Come on, time to go.' He lifted a finger to summon the waitress. 'There's a taxi rank outside the hotel.'

The taxicab wove its way through the busy streets. As it turned onto the bridge to cross the Thames, Richard's warm hand found Annie's and he linked his fingers through hers, his thumb gently and rhythmically stroking her knuckle. The simple gesture almost stopped her heart. She kept her head turned, looking out of the window, apparently watching the busy traffic on the river. Then, sensing that he was looking at her, she glanced at him. His narrow eyes were watching her with an expression of such intensity that she could not look away. The silence between them lengthened; then she cleared her throat. 'You'll… come in for a drink?' she asked, not nearly casually enough.

He did not answer for a moment; then, his eyes still on hers, he shook his head. 'No.'

Her eyes widened, startled and disappointed.

He shook his head again. 'No, Annie,' he repeated gently. 'I've told you, I won't do that. You aren't the only one who needs time to think, you know.' He smiled suddenly, trying to lighten the moment. 'Anyway – I have to be up early in the morning.'

The depth of Annie's disappointment appalled her. 'You wouldn't have to stay,' she found herself saying quickly, almost pleading.

Wordlessly he shook his head yet again. She turned away from him. The busy world beyond the car window was suddenly just a little blurred. Fool! she berated herself, *fool!*

The touch of his hand was like fire on hers.

She would not ask again.

The rest of the journey continued in silence. As they drew up outside the house Richard pulled her to him and kissed her. 'Don't sulk, darling. It doesn't suit you.'

'I'm not sulking.' The words were stiff.

'Then kiss me properly.'

She did.

He smiled. So did she. 'That's better. Look – I'll be in touch just as soon as I'm back. Oh, and...' He drew out his wallet, extracted a couple of cards. 'I do think it's time you could get in touch with me if you needed to, don't you?' He handed them to her. 'My address and telephone number, both at home and at the office. If I'm not around Miss Brownel will take a message.'

'Who's Miss Brownel?'

'My secretary. She's an absolute tyrant,' he said cheerfully. 'She frightens the life out of me sometimes, but she's *very* efficient.'

'She sounds terrifying.' Annie was making conversation, she knew, and did not care. Anything to prevent his leaving.

'She is.'

'Richard?'

'Yes?' He was still holding her hand.

'You will be careful, won't you?'

Impulsively he pulled her to him and kissed her again. 'Annie, Annie, don't worry so! I've been to Paris a thousand times! What makes you think that the boat's going to sink this time? Annie?' His voice was suddenly full of concern. Her face had drained of colour; she had snatched her hand from his. 'Annie... I'm sorry—' He was full of contrition. 'It was only a joke. A joke in very poor taste.' He put his arm about her shoulders and drew her to him. 'Come on, now. I'll be back next Tuesday or Wednesday. I'll see you then.'

She lay against him for a moment, then drew away. 'Fine,' she said, brightly. 'Oh – it's all right...' Richard had reached for the door handle. 'I'm a grown woman, you know. I'm perfectly capable of seeing myself to my own door.' She dropped a light kiss on his cheek and got out of the car. 'Bye.'

She stood on the pavement and watched as the cab drew away and turned the corner. Then she walked up the path and fitted the door key into the lock.

The house was very quiet; it had never felt so empty. She sighed, restlessly dispirited. For almost the first time in her entire life the thought of her own company did not appeal. The evening – and the night – stretched ahead endlessly.

There was, of course, now nothing to prevent her from going to Southwold tomorrow, a day early. Her mother would welcome her, there was nothing more certain than that.

The problem was that honesty demanded she acknowledge the fact that, suddenly, the company she truly craved was not in Southwold.

Chapter Ten

'So – you see the problem?' Annie set down her glass of lemonade on a small, somewhat rickety table and leaned back in the deckchair, closing her eyes. 'He says he loves me. I think I believe him. And I'm crazy about him, I can't deny it. But we've only known each other for a few weeks, and for some reason he's absolutely insisting that we get married. Now. Right now. Which seems an incredibly big step to take so soon, don't you think? Why rush things so? How do we know what we feel isn't infatuation? It would be so awful to make a mistake. I really, really don't know what to do. What do you make of it?' She and her mother were sitting in fresh, clear sunshine in the cottage garden.

Jane, who was knitting, laid her work on her lap and was silent for a moment. 'I grant you it does seem a little strange for him to be so insistent,' she said at last, thought-fully, looking at her daughter over the top of her glasses. 'I don't know him well, of course, but Richard didn't strike me as being – well – that impulsive a person. On the other hand—' She laughed a little. Annie opened her eyes to look at her enquiringly. 'Well,' Jane said, delicately, 'whilst I suspect that most men wouldn't be pressing so soon to marry you, they might well be pressing for… some other arrangement, shall we say?'

Annie's face was already sun-reddened; she could only hope that her mother could not see how it now burned.

She could tell Jane a lot of things, but she had not been able to bring herself to say that she and Richard had already made love. That this, indeed, was the greatest of her problems: it was as if their lovemaking had opened a door within her, a door through which light, laughter and breathtaking excitement streamed, a door of promise that she could not bear to close again. But if she refused to marry him, Richard was ready to close that door, of that she was certain. She shifted in the deckchair, straightening her back and leaning forward, her elbows on her knees. Above them a gull wheeled and called; the gentle sound of sea and shingle was soothing. 'He lived with someone in Paris,' Annie said quietly, after a moment. 'An artist – a girl called Isobella.'

Jane cocked her head. 'That's relevant?'

'I think it might be, yes. She wouldn't marry him, you see. Wouldn't commit herself. I gather she didn't believe in marriage. Thought it bourgeois. Unnecessary. She hurt him badly, I think. To be truthful she sounds to me like a thoroughly nasty piece of work. She had affairs. And she was a liar. Richard can't bear deception—'

'Can any of us?' Jane's voice was quiet.

Annie did not for the moment reply. Then, without looking at her mother, she asked, suddenly sombre, 'Don't we all lie, or deceive, sometimes? Can any one of us truly say we don't? Aren't there times when it's better to deceive than to tell the truth? What if the truth is unbearable? What if the truth can only cause hurt? Aren't there times when deception is the kindest thing?'

Jane was watching her, brow faintly furrowed. Annie did not look at her. 'Annie?' her mother said at last, half-smiling, mildly questioning. 'You make it sound as if you're harbouring some dark and guilty secret yourself?'

The words were light, but her eyes were bright and searching on her daughter's face.

Annie paused before replying. She was sucking her lip, her expression distant and preoccupied.

'Annie?'

She jumped from her reverie. 'I'm sorry?'

'I said – you make it sound as if you're harbouring some dark secret—?'

Annie shook her head sharply. 'No, of course not. How could I be?' She gave a small, caustic laugh. 'In order to have dark secrets I imagine you have to have lived a rather more interesting life than I have.'

'I suppose so.' Jane did not sound entirely convinced, and she was still watching her daughter with thoughtful eyes.

'Oh, don't be silly, Mother. Now look – in a nutshell, this is it. Richard wants me to marry him. If I'm absolutely honest with myself, I want to marry Richard—'

'Put like that,' her mother smiled composedly, 'there's a fairly simple answer there somewhere. And perhaps I'd better go out and buy that big hat after all.'

Annie grinned suddenly. 'Do behave! And listen. It just seems such a big step to take so soon. Yet, the way Richard spoke yesterday, nothing else will do, and I think there's a very real danger that I'll lose him if I don't agree.'

'He's that set?'

'Yes.'

'Difficult.'

'Yes.'

Jane cocked her head. 'This Isobella you mentioned? Am I wrong, or do you think that she's somehow involved in all this? Is it she who's worrying you? You think Richard is… well, on the rebound, so to speak? Or something worse than that?'

Annie pulled a small face and sighed. 'I don't know, I really don't. But yes, both thoughts have obviously occurred to me. It's quite clear that the way she treated him has influenced the way he feels about us – about me – and no, I suppose whatever's behind it I don't like that very much.'

'Well, my dear.' Jane wrapped her knitting around the needles and stuffed it into the bag that hung behind her on the chair. 'I don't see that there's much to be done about that. You must make up your own mind, trust him to have done the same, and decide from there what you want to do.'

Annie looked at her with mock indignation. 'A fat lot of good it's done me coming to *you* for advice! I could have worked that out myself!'

Her mother smiled and shook her head slightly. 'You know very well there's nothing else I can say. By all means talk, if it helps sort things out in your head, but in the end no one can make the decision but you.' She stood up. 'I made a Madeira cake yesterday. Fancy a slice?'

'Yes, please.' Annie hauled herself out of the deckchair and followed her mother into the sunny kitchen. 'Who are these people Davie's gone to the beach with?' she asked.

'The Millers. Lovely family.' Jane spoke over her shoulder. 'They're from Reading, I believe. They've two boys and a little girl. We met them a couple of days ago – they're here for the week and they've got a beach hut. Davie and the boys got on like a house on fire the moment they met, so they invited him down for the day today. He'll be back after tea.' She glanced at the clock, then a little mischievously back at Annie. 'Which gives us,' she said with an amiable smile, 'just about time to have a nice big glass of sherry with our cake. I do so enjoy a sherry with Madeira cake.'

—

'I'm back, Nan!' Davie flew through the kitchen door in a clatter of buckets and spades and a shower of sand. 'The Millers said they couldn't come in because—' He stopped. 'Mother! What are you doing here? You aren't due until tomorrow—' He ran to her, flung his arms about her and kissed her. Then as he stepped back and glanced around, the implication of her presence here alone hit him and his face dropped. 'Where's Richard? Is he coming in the car tomorrow?'

Annie shook her head. 'I'm sorry, Davie, no, he isn't. He sends tons and tons of apologies, but he got called away on business. To Paris.'

Davie could not hide his disappointment. '*Business?*' he said disgustedly. 'At the weekend?'

Annie laughed. 'He's got a living to earn, Davie. Anyway, he said I was to tell you that he promises to take us both to the seaside next weekend.'

Davie's face brightened, and his eyes fell upon the cake. 'That'd be wizard,' he said. 'Can I have a piece of cake, please, Nan?'

Jane picked up the knife. 'Of course. How big?'

Davie eyed the wedge of cake judiciously. 'About half that, I reckon,' he said. 'With some jam, please.'

'*Davie!*' his mother exclaimed.

He smiled at her disarmingly, his dark eyes shining in a nut-brown, handsome face. 'I'm ever so hungry,' he said. 'The Millers are very nice, and John and Luke are smashing, but their picnics aren't like yours. They only had paste sandwiches and biscuits. And not many of them, either. I'm starving.'

'I somehow doubt *that*,' his grandmother said crisply. 'But you are a growing boy, so here, tuck into that and then you'd better go and have a bath – you're shedding half of Southwold beach onto my nice clean floor!'

–

The train slowed, huffing steam, and pulled into the station with a screech of brakes. The elderly gentleman who had shared their carriage from Halesworth put his hand through the open window to turn the door handle, then doffed his hat courteously to Annie before stepping onto the platform and slamming the door shut behind him. The distinctive, acrid smell of steam and coal fumes wafted into the carriage. There was a bustle of activity on the platform and then the shriek of a whistle. The huge engine hauled itself forward, belching smoke and steam like some great mythical monster, and they were off again, running smooth and fast through the green countryside. Annie stood up to slide the window shut, fastened the leather strap, then sat down and studied her son, who was sitting in the window seat opposite her, absorbedly reading a comic.

His week on the beach had bleached his thick hair and eyelashes almost to silver, his skin was smooth and brown. Sensing her eyes on him he glanced up and smiled, then dug in his blazer pocket for a crumpled paper bag. 'Would you like a humbug?' he asked, proffering the bag. 'They're spiffing. Ever so strong.'

She shook her head. 'No, thank you.'

He extricated one of the sticky things and popped it into his mouth, licking his fingers. Then he looked out of the window. 'Where are we?'

'Just south of Colchester. Not long now.' She hesitated. 'Davie?'

'Hm?' His nose was back in his comic.

'You… like Richard, don't you? Very much?'

'He's smashing. So's his car.' The answer was distracted. The boy giggled at something in the comic and rolled his humbug noisily around his mouth.

Annie tried again. 'Do you like him enough to… well, that is, do you think you would mind if—' She stopped.

She had his whole attention now. His wide, lustrous eyes fixed suddenly on her face, and he stopped chewing.

Annie fidgeted a little; took a breath. 'Look – Davie – I know you weren't too keen on my marrying Fergus. Could I ask you something?'

The boy nodded, a little warily.

'Was that because of Fergus, or because you didn't want me to get married again?'

Davie looked a little uncomfortable. 'It wasn't that I didn't *like* Uncle Fergus exactly,' he said carefully, after a moment. 'I just – didn't like him *enough*.'

His mother nodded. 'I can see that.' She took a deep breath. 'And… Richard?' she asked tentatively. 'How much do you like him?'

Davie stared at her for a moment. '*Richard?*' he asked, his eyes suddenly, sharply, alight. 'You mean you're going to marry *Richard?*'

'I didn't say that,' she said hastily. 'But – well – there is some suggestion that—'

'But that's *wizard!*' Davie exclaimed. 'Will he come to live in Kew? Will he bring the car?'

'Davie!' Annie laughed exasperatedly. 'I've just said – I haven't made up my mind. I just wanted to know how you'd feel about it if I did, that's all. But for goodness' sake, child, if I do get married it will be to Richard, not his wretched car!'

Davie grinned blithely. 'I know *that*. But it would be fun, wouldn't it? James Barton would be *green* with envy!'

Annie gave up. 'So – you wouldn't mind?'

He looked at her in genuine surprise. 'Mind? It'd be smashing!'

'It's just… well… it all seems to be happening rather fast—'

Her sometimes too-astute son's grin widened. 'Lots of things happen fast, Mother,' he reassured her. 'Look how fast I broke my arm when I fell off my bike!'

Annie laughed, then sobered. 'It took a lot longer to mend,' she said quietly. 'Remember?'

'Of course, but…' Davie lifted his left hand and flexed it encouragingly, 'it's as good as new now.'

Annie could not resist a smile. 'I'm not sure Richard would be too flattered to hear you comparing my marrying him with falling off a bicycle!'

Davie was silent for a moment, his face pensive. Then, out of the blue, 'Mother – was my real father anything like Richard?' he asked.

Annie stilled, and for a moment did not answer the unexpected question. When she spoke it was slowly and with a certain care. 'I… no, not really, not as I remember him. He was… much younger of course.' The words sounded stiff and awkward, almost wary, in her own ears, but Davie did not seem to notice.

'Yes, I s'pose he was.' Davie brightened a little. 'P'raps he *would* have been like Richard if he'd managed to get a bit older? Anyway – don't worry – I think Richard would make a topping father,' he added with beguiling directness, and, apparently unconcerned, went back to his comic.

Annie leaned back in her seat and turned her head to watch the flying countryside with suddenly shadowed eyes.

–

Richard sipped his coffee. The sun was warm, the wide, tree-lined pavement busy; a young couple wandered past hand in hand, utterly absorbed in each other. He watched them for a moment. The girl had hair as dark as Annie's, and as she tilted her head to smile bewitchingly up at her companion, it moved, silkily heavy, as Annie's did. He set the small cup back in its saucer, reached in his pocket for his cigarette case. The girl swung away from her young man, laughing, their hands still linked. They were the very picture of carefree love and laughter.

What was he doing?

His face expressionless, Richard bent his head to light his cigarette, the lighter flame cupped in the palm of his hand. For the dozenth time, in his head he heard the distinctive, quietly husky voice, almost a whisper: 'After all, Richard, in the end isn't it only love that counts? Not money. Not possessions, but love?' Richard had shaken his head. 'How can you of all people say that? Love is transient,' he had said, glancing around the lovely, shadowed room. 'Love fails. Art endures.' He could see the faint smile. 'No.' The answer was very soft. 'Love is all. Even, perhaps, the transient kind. What does your Shakespeare say? *Better to have loved and lost…*? Experience' – again that faint, almost mischievous smile – 'experience tells me that is true. You'll come to know it in time. Believe me.'

Richard narrowed his eyes against the drift of cigarette smoke. Why the philosophy? he asked himself for the umpteenth time. Was there a touch of suspicion there?

The lovers had stopped beneath the canopy of a huge chestnut tree. The girl's arms were lightly about the young man's neck, their bodies very close. She tilted her head to look into her sweetheart's face and, with unaffected tenderness, he kissed her smiling lips.

Richard averted his eyes, looking down at the hand that held the cigarette. It trembled very slightly. 'Shit,' he muttered under his breath, shaking his head. 'Oh, *shit*!'

–

'When's Richard coming home?' Davie asked. He was sitting at the kitchen table, drawing. He looked up to watch Annie, chewing on the end of his pencil.

'Don't do that, darling,' Annie said automatically, as she slid the cake she had just mixed into the oven. 'You know it isn't good for you. Tomorrow, I think. Or perhaps the next day. I'm not sure.'

He cocked his head, eyes bright. 'Have you decided?'

'Decided?'

He shook his head impatiently at her assumed innocence. 'You know! Whether you're going to marry him or not.'

Annie smiled a little wryly. Put like that, it sounded so very simple. As indeed it had seemed in the middle of the night as she had lain, sleepless and alone, aching for the touch of Richard's hand, the sound of his voice, the smooth length of his body beside hers. For what seemed like the dozenth time then, she had taken a firm decision: she could not – would not – risk losing him. He had turned her humdrum life upside down, had shown her a world of warmth and excitement; what possible risk could there be in agreeing to marry him? Why had she even hesitated? Yet, once again, here in the cool light of day the doubts were nagging...

Davie sighed and rested his cheek on one hand, watching her. 'Honestly, Mother,' he said with frank exasperation, 'don't you think you should make up your mind before he comes back?' His brow furrowed, a little worried. 'He might go and find someone else.'

Annie had to laugh at that. 'There is always that possibility, I suppose,' she agreed; something else, she had to admit, which had occurred to her in the middle of the night. She sat down opposite the child, leaning her elbows on the table and her chin on her linked hands. 'You really would like to live with Richard, wouldn't you?' she asked softly.

He nodded vigorously. 'Wouldn't you?'

Her smile was slow and wide. 'Yes. I do believe I would.'

'D'you know what?'

'What?'

'I'd even move if he wanted us to.'

She sat quite still, studying his small, earnest face, then said at last, 'And d'you know what?'

'What?' There was a small glint of excitement in her son's eyes.

'I think I would too.'

They held each other's smiling eyes for a moment. Then, 'Hooray!' Davie shouted. 'We're going to live with Richard!'

'And his motor car,' Annie added, straightfaced.

'Oh, yes, and his motor car. I wonder if he'll run me to school sometimes? James Barton's going to be greener than grass!'

–

Irritatingly but she supposed inevitably, the decision taken, Annie began to worry. Tuesday came, and then Wednesday and there was no news of or from Richard. She wrote to Jane telling her that a big hat might well be in order after all, and received by return of post a prompt and openly delighted reply leavened with a touch of motherly leg-pulling: *'Even as a child you were always a little slow on the uptake, but I have to admit that you usually get there in the end…'* She smiled as she tucked the letter behind the clock on the mantelpiece, and as she did so her eye was caught by the two neatly engraved cards that were already there. She took them out and looked at them thoughtfully. She had no telephone of her own, but she knew the whereabouts of one that she could use. Was Richard home? Annie so wanted to hear his voice… so wanted to tell him… She flicked at the cards with her fingernail for a moment. Looked at her watch. Davie would be home in ten minutes or so. She would leave it until tomorrow. If she had heard nothing by then, she would telephone. At least, surely, his secretary would be able to tell her when he was expected back? Humming light-heartedly, she went to the window to watch for Davie.

–

She waited until the afternoon, still half-hoping that he would arrive on the doorstep, but the day dragged on and nothing happened, so, armed with the cards he had given her, she made her way to the small office around the corner that was run by the Red Cross.

'All right if I use the telephone, Judith?' she asked. 'I won't be long.'

'Of course. Help yourself.' The plump little woman who was sitting at the desk tallying two long rows of figures straightened her back, stretching a little, and put down her pen, waving a hand at the battered black Bakelite sit-up-and-beg telephone on the desk. 'I'll make myself scarce for a bit, if you'd like. I could do with a cup of tea.'

Annie tried the home number first, to no avail. 'There's no reply, Madam,' the bossy-sounding operator informed her, entirely unnecessarily. Annie gave her the office number.

'Mr Ross's office.' The voice was clipped and precise.

'Is Mr Ross there, please?'

'May I ask who is calling?'

'It's Mrs Hill. Annette Hill. I just wondered when Rich—Mr Ross was due back from Paris?'

'He returned two days ago.' The words were crisp and cool. 'Do you wish to make an appointment to see him?'

Annie's heart seemed to have stopped entirely.

'Mrs Hill? Are you there? Do you wish to make an appointment?' There was a touch of impatience now.

'Yes, I'm here. And no, I don't wish to make an appointment. I'd like to speak to Mr Ross, please.'

'That won't be possible, I'm afraid. He isn't in the office.'

'Could you tell me where he is?'

There was a small silence. 'I'm afraid I'm not at liberty to do that, Mrs Hill.' The voice was openly sharp now.

'If you wish to speak to Mr Ross, I'd advise you either to make an appointment or to telephone tomorrow.'

'I—thank you. I'll do that.' Annie, never completely at home using the telephone, seemed to have lost the ability to think clearly. She felt as if she had been reprimanded by a disapproving schoolmistress.

'Very well. Goodbye, Mrs Hill.'

'Please – would you tell him I rang?'

Another small and, Annie felt, faintly hostile silence. 'If you wish,' the other woman said. 'Goodbye, Mrs Hill,' she repeated.

'Goodbye.'

She replaced the receiver very carefully on its hook, stood staring down at it with blank eyes. The disappointment was crushing; and as the implications sank fully into her mind, mortification all but choked her. Two days! He'd been home for two days and had not come near nor by her. Anger struggled with misery. How could he? How *could* he…?

'Everything all right?' Judith had come back into the room, carrying a sheaf of papers and a cup of tea.

Annie smiled, very brightly. 'Yes. Yes, everything's fine.'

'Fancy a cup? There's a pot made.'

'No, thank you.' Desperate to get away, Annie shook her head. 'I've got some errands to take care of before Davie gets home. I'll see you next week.'

'Good.' The other woman gave her a quick, friendly smile and addressed herself to her paperwork.

Annie stepped out into the street. It was crowded and very busy. The noise of the traffic seemed suddenly deafening. She walked quickly; all she wanted was to get home. To be on her own. To think.

Why hadn't he called? Or even dropped a short note to let her know he was back? Why hadn't Miss Whatever-her-name-was recognised her name? Obviously Richard hadn't even mentioned it to her. And yet – he had asked her to marry him. And – chagrin brought warm colour to her cheeks – she had told Davie and her mother...

She hurried up the garden path and let herself into the quiet house, flinging off her coat and hat, kicking off her shoes in a sudden savage spurt of temper. How dare he? How *dare* he make such a fool of her?

She stalked into the sitting room, threw herself into a chair, nibbling at her thumbnail, trying desperately to keep the goad of her anger white-hot. Trying not to feel the awful, physical ache of disappointment. She rubbed at her hot cheeks with the palms of her hands. Why should she care? She hadn't really made up her mind to marry him anyway. Defiantly she lied to herself, fighting off the miserable tears. One thing she was resolved upon: she would not be telephoning his crabby old bat of a secretary again. Not for anything.

Unable to sit still, Annie scrambled from the chair, walked on stockinged feet to the French windows, looked out into the early summer garden. She took a deep, calming breath. She was letting her thoughts run away with her, she knew it. He'd come, of course he would. There must be some explanation, some reason for his silence. She dashed a quick hand across her eyes. There had better be, she told herself a little grimly.

It was two hours later, and she was sitting in the garden trying to read a book when she heard the sound of the front doorbell. Sighing, she laid the book aside and stood up. Davie was forever mislaying his door key. She went through the house to the front door, opened it and blinked.

'I'm sorry, Mrs Hill – these came for you this after-noon, when you were out. The lad asked me to take them in for you – but then I had to go out myself...' The woman who stood there, rather awkwardly clutching a bunch of long-stemmed roses, was small and bird-like, with a twittering voice. Her eyes, behind rimless glasses, were bright with curiosity. She lived in the house across the road. 'I've only just come back, and I said to myself, "I must deliver these straight away" – lovely flowers – I did put them in water...'

Annie's heart had lifted. She reached for the flowers. 'Why, thank you, Mrs Dobson, that was very kind of you.'

Mrs Dobson had her nose buried in the blooms, sniffing noisily. 'Lovely smell, too. Flowers do make such a lovely gift, don't they? Is it your birthday?' Again that bright, curious glance. 'Are congratulations in order?' The words were coy and questioning.

Annie shook her head, trying to contain her impa-tience. 'No. No congratulations, just a present from a friend, I suspect.' Again she reached for the flowers. Reluctantly the woman gave them up.

'Thank you again.' Annie stepped back, began to close the door.

Mrs Dobson leaned forward confidentially. 'Have you heard the news?' she asked.

'News?' Annie's face was blank. There was a small envelope attached to the flowers. She pulled it off, her fingers itching to open it. 'What news?'

'The Pattersons. The whole road's talking about it.'

'Pattersons?'

'You know – at number eight. It seems,' she leaned even closer and her voice dropped, 'it seems she's in the family way. Again.' She nodded her head in an odd and smugly satisfied way.

'Oh.' Annie fingered the envelope distractedly. 'That's nice,' she added, since the other woman was patently expecting some kind of reaction.

Mrs Dobson sniffed. 'Four mouths to feed seems quite enough to me, when you're only a bank clerk,' she said, righteously pious. 'Mr Dobson and I were saying so just the other day.'

Annie's temper was rising. She opened her mouth to speak and then, over the woman's shoulder, caught sight of Davie, satchel swinging, school cap at a rakish angle on the back of his head, socks wrinkled about his ankles, dawdling down the road. 'Here comes Davie,' she said. 'At last! His tea is spoiling. Thank you again for taking in the flowers.' She lifted her voice firmly, and beckoned. 'Davie, do come along. You're late again.'

Davie, lifting his eyebrows in faint but unconcerned surprise, quickened his pace infinitesimally. 'Hello, Mother. Hello, Mrs Dobson.' Then he saw the flowers and his face lit in a wide grin. 'They from Richard? He's back then?'

Mrs Dobson cocked an interested head. She still had not moved from the doorstep. Davie slid round her, dropped his satchel on the hall floor and tossed his cap towards the newel post, missing it by a yard and leaving it where it lay. 'What's for tea?'

Annie smiled sweetly at Mrs Dobson, raised her eyes to heaven. 'Boys!' she said, and shut the door in the inquisitive woman's face.

Davie had perched himself on the stairs, his elbows on his bare knees, watching her. 'Well?' he asked, nodding towards the envelope she still held. 'What does he say?'

She slit open the envelope. 'If it has anything whatsoever to do with you,' she said mildly, 'I'll tell you. Here – hold these for a minute.'

He skidded across the hall floor and took the proffered flowers, stood watching her with expectant eyes.

Annie read the note. Twice. Davie hopped from foot to foot. She lifted her smiling eyes to his. 'The first part is not your concern.'

'What about the second?'

She grinned. 'The second says, "*Pack your bags and your buckets and spades. I'll pick you both up at nine on Saturday morning. P.S. Bring the green thing and the little black hat.*"'

'What's that supposed to mean?'

'It's a joke. About a dress.'

'Oh.' Davie shrugged, dismissing such silliness. Then his face lit up. 'Where are we going, do you think?'

She shook her head. 'I've no idea.'

He dumped the flowers back into her arms and turned to dash into the kitchen. 'I hope it's ever so far away.' His voice came back to her and she heard the pantry door open. 'A really, really long drive. Is Scotland too far, do you think?'

'Just a bit.' Looking back at the note, she smiled, tucked it into her pocket. There came a clattering crash from the kitchen. 'Davie, what *are* you doing?'

'I just dropped the biscuit tin.' His voice was cheerful. 'But it's all right. They're only a bit broken. I can still eat them. I'm famished!'

Chapter Eleven

'I did threaten you with a weekend in Brighton, remember?' Richard said with a mischievous tilt of his brow. 'What do you think – are you up to it?' Grinning, he relieved Annie of the large leather suitcase she had hauled to the front door and strapped it on top of his own on the fold-down luggage carrier at the rear of the car.

'How far's Brighton?' Davie asked. He was swinging energetically on the garden gate, scooting it back and forth with his foot.

'About sixty miles.'

'Can't we go somewhere further away?'

'*Davie!* Behave yourself! Get off that gate and go and fetch your bucket and spade and the other things. And don't forget your paddling sandals,' Annie called after her son as he scurried up the path and through the front door. She shook her head ruefully as she looked after him. 'I do apologise. He's been *so* excited—'

'About going to the seaside?'

'No, don't be daft – about going in the motor car!' Annie laughed. 'He suggested that we might go to Scotland.'

'That could be arranged,' he said quietly.

She turned to look at him. His narrow eyes were steady on her face. The expression in them brought a faint flush of colour to her cheeks. She flashed him a quick smile.

'Did your disapproving Miss Brownel tell you that I rang?' she asked lightly.

He nodded, laughing. 'Oh, yes. The disapproving Miss Brownel tells me everything that goes on in the office. That's what she's there for.'

'She sounded as if she was there to protect you from man-eating female clients.' The words held a faintly caustic edge.

'I think she does feel some responsibility in that department.' Richard nodded gravely. 'She's been with me for a very long time, and before that worked for my father.'

Annie could not contain her curiosity. 'How old is she?'

He considered, his head on one side. 'Oh – about a hundred and eighty, I'd say,' he said, straightfaced. 'But her shorthand is very good.'

Annie giggled a little. 'Don't be silly.'

'Next time you phone she'll know who you are. I explained to her that ours was something rather more than a working relationship.'

'You hadn't already told her?'

He looked at her in surprise. 'No. Why should I? Miss Brownel and I don't have that kind of conversation. Or at least, even if I wanted to, Miss Brownel doesn't. She's run that office for upwards of thirty years, and I know absolutely nothing about her private life. Miss Brownel "keeps herself to herself" as she frequently puts it.'

'Mo-other. Do I have to bring my sun hat?' Davie had appeared at the front door, arms full of buckets, spades and sandals.

'Yes,' his mother said firmly, 'you do.'

'O-oh!'

'Get on with it, Davie,' she said, with crisp patience, 'or we'll leave without you. The hat's on the kitchen table.' She turned. Richard was holding open the car door for her.

She hesitated. He saw it, shook his head, smiling. 'Davie,' he said, 'can take a back seat for a change. I want you beside me.' As she climbed into the car she saw Mrs Dobson's curtains twitch. She ducked her head to hide her smile. Mrs Dobson was undoubtedly adding two and two together and coming to a very satisfactory four. Anyone in the road who was unlucky enough to miss their departure would not, she guessed, be left in such a state of deprivation for long.

'I rang you at home as well,' she said on impulse as he opened the back door and stood waiting for Davie. 'There was no reply.'

'I wasn't there.' The words were easy. Richard's eyes were on the open front door; for a moment she thought he would say no more. Then he glanced at her. 'My sister – the one in South Africa? – is sending her son back here to England to school. She asked me to check out a couple of schools for her.'

As simple as that. Why had she been so silly? So suspicious?

Davie came out of the door, crashing it shut behind him. 'All right, young man. Give me those while you climb aboard.' Richard took the assorted bits and pieces from Davie, helped him into the car and piled his possessions on the seat beside him. The heavy diabolo rolled across the leather seat and thumped on the floor. Richard grinned. 'Have you brought the entire contents of your toy cupboard?'

'More or less.'

'Would you mind locking the door for me?' Annie had taken a key from her handbag. Richard took it, went to the front door and locked it, dropped the key in his own pocket before coming back to the car and swinging with practised ease into the driving seat. Well, Annie thought, as she settled herself comfortably in her own seat, *that* should give the meddlesome Mrs Dobson something to think about. For an amused moment she considered waving as they drove away, but – with enormous self-restraint – resisted the temptation.

As they pulled away from the kerb Richard glanced at her. 'I hope you don't mind, but I've taken the liberty of booking rooms in a small family hotel I know. It's run by a very nice couple – the Suttons – and is near the sea. I've also booked dinner for us tonight at the Grand. I've already checked with Mrs Sutton and she says she'll keep an eye on Davie for us—'

'Can't I come?' asked the sharp-eared Davie from the back seat.

Richard shook his head. 'Today is your treat, tonight is your mother's.'

'Does that mean I can do as I like today?' the lad asked hopefully, glancing at Annie.

'Within reason,' Richard conceded. 'Which way do you want to go? The main roads or the pretty route?'

'Which way will take longest?'

'We'll travel faster on the main roads, despite the speed limit. The pretty route will take longer.'

Davie settled back in his seat. 'Let's go that way then.'

Annie, laughing, glanced over her shoulder at her son. 'Doing what you like,' she said, 'does *not* include driving around in the car all day.'

'I don't want to drive *all* day,' he reassured her. 'Just quite a lot of it.'

Richard manoeuvred out into the main road. 'That reminds me,' he said over his shoulder, 'I've got a book for you in my suitcase. I think you might enjoy it. It's called *By Car to India* and it's a true story written by a Major Forbes-Leith who drove his Wolseley over eight and a half thousand miles, to India—'

'Gosh!' Davie leaned forward eagerly. 'How long did that take him?'

'About five and a half months,' Richard laughed. 'I guess that would be a long enough journey even for you?'

It was a lovely day, warm and sunny with cotton-wool clouds dotting the blue sky. Before long they had left the congested streets of London and the suburbs behind and were driving with the windows open through the rolling wooded countryside, talking, telling jokes, singing songs. They wove their way through the winding, narrow streets of bustling market towns and quiet rural villages, passed cottages and grand houses, streams and pastures, patch-works of hedgerows and neatly tended fields. Richard and Davie kept up an almost unbroken stream of chatter; Annie for the most part was content to listen, and to smile. She had never felt so happy. Acutely aware of the man beside her, catching his eye every now and again as he turned to glance at her or reached briefly to touch her hand, any doubts or fears she might have been harbouring simply and suddenly evaporated. Why had she made it so difficult for herself – and for him? People did meet and fall in love. Of course they did. There was no statutory timescale, no litmus test to prove it one way or another; it happened, and had to be taken on trust.

Davie was singing at the top of his voice. '*One man and his dog, went to mow a meadow—*'

'Penny for them?' Richard asked, raising his voice against the sound of the wind through the open window, his quick, smiling glance warm.

She shook her head. 'I was just thinking what a lovely day it is. I think I'd like it to go on for ever.' Impulsively she laid her hand on his arm. 'Thank you. Thank you so much.'

His smile answered the words.

'You aren't singing!' Davie bellowed without taking breath.

Richard, grinning, obediently joined in. '*Two men, one man and his dog, went to mow a meadow—*'

It was coming up to lunchtime when the great South Downs loomed in the distance. 'What do you want to do?' Richard called against the warm wind that blustered through the open windows. 'We can stop for lunch somewhere or head straight on into Brighton – which do you fancy?'

Annie turned questioningly to her son. Davie bounced on his seat. 'The seaside,' he said immediately, having obviously already given the matter some thought. 'We can have fish and chips. In newspaper.'

Annie rolled her eyes to heaven, Richard laughed and put his foot on the accelerator. 'Very well. Fish and chips it is!'

'In newspaper,' Davie repeated firmly.

'In newspaper.'

–

The day was, without a doubt, one of the most enjoyable Annie had ever spent. Richard entered into the spirit of

Davie's day with an energy and enthusiasm that would have done credit to a child. They ate their fish and chips – in newspaper and well doused in vinegar – sitting on a bench on one of the town's two piers, with the sea sucking and slurping beneath them. Afterwards, shepherded by Davie, they played the penny machines, rode on the fairground rides, bought sugared almonds at a pretty kiosk, and watched a hurdy-gurdy man with a dancing monkey. They hired deckchairs and sat on the beach. Davie rode three times on the donkeys, his sandalled heels drumming against the flanks of the shaggy, docile beasts in a completely futile attempt to make them gallop. They built a huge and intricate sandcastle and paddled in the shallow water, picking up stones and shells for Davie's collection. Davie and Richard had a diabolo competition, which Richard won, while Davie outsmarted both the adults at quoits on the smooth, tide-washed sand. It was a hot and somewhat dishevelled party who gathered their belongings at last and trailed to where the car was parked to dump them untidily on the back seat. The car, having stood in the sun for the best part of four hours, was hot as a cooking stove.

'I'll open a couple of windows,' Richard said, 'and we can round off the afternoon with an ice cream, if you'd like. I told the Suttons we'd be there at about five, so we have time.'

They wandered back towards the pier. 'There's a "Stop-me-and-Buy-One",' said sharp-eyed Davie, pointing.

'Here.' Richard reached into his pocket for a coin. 'Go and get yourself one.'

He looked enquiringly at Annie, who shook her head, smiling. 'I think I'd better save myself for dinner.'

'We've got tea to get through yet,' he grinned. 'Mrs Sutton's cream teas are famous, and I can't see Davie allowing us to miss that!'

She laughed. 'Well, he'll just have to eat mine as well – which he is, as you know, perfectly capable of doing. Oh, look—' She stopped, pointing. 'A fortune teller!'

He looked at her quizzically, eyebrows raised.

She shook her head, laughing again. 'I know it's silly, but I've never been able to resist a fortune teller. When I was a little girl in Paris there was a woman – a clairvoyant – who used to visit our apartment block; a friend of mine lived upstairs and her mother wouldn't move a step without consulting her. My mother thought it was a hoot, of course, as you can imagine. She used to call her the Delphic Oracle. But I was fascinated. Claudette – my friend – believed absolutely every word she said; and honestly, she was very often right. I lost a ring and she told me where to find it. I never did understand how she did that.'

'Didn't that impress your mother?'

Annie laughed. 'Oh, don't be silly! You'd have to do a lot more than *that* to impress Mother.'

'I'd noticed.' He smiled, nodded towards the fortune teller's booth. 'Do you want to have a go?'

Annie hesitated. 'You wouldn't think I was being silly?'

'Of course not. It can't do any harm; it's only a bit of fun.' He dug into his pocket, pulled out a small coin. 'Here. Cross her palm with silver. I'll stay here and wait for Davie.'

She took the coin, tossed it into the air and caught it. 'Why not? I won't be long.'

'Where's Mother?' Davie asked as he joined Richard a few minutes later, cornet in hand. His eyes fell upon the fortune teller's booth. 'Uh–oh, all right, you don't have to tell me.' He licked at the ice cream, neatly and meticulously smoothing it with his tongue. 'She can't walk past a fortune teller's.'

'So she told me.' Richard grinned. 'There are worse vices.'

Davie held out the ice cream. 'Would you like a lick?' he asked in a friendly tone.

'Er, no, thank you. Look, there's a bench over there. Let's sit down while we're waiting.'

A few minutes later Annie emerged, smiling, from the dark little booth. Richard stood up as she joined them. She eyed him speculatively. 'You're tall, all right,' she said contemplatively, 'and you are quite dark. But—?'

Eyes dancing with mischief, she let the rest of the sentence hang in the air.

He laughed and kissed her. 'Perish the thought you should fall for my looks,' he said. 'Where would that leave me in twenty years? Come on, you batty little thing, time to go.'

The hotel was situated on the front at the quieter end of the town. The house itself was charming – built, like so much of Brighton, in the Regency period. Its wooden floors were polished to a glossy sheen, and the tall, elegant windows were draped in velvet; but for all that there was a welcoming air of homely comfort about it. There were flowers everywhere, and in the sitting room the armchairs were large and soft and the shelves were full of books and games.

The couple who ran the hotel were as charming as the establishment, and the smartly dressed maids were efficient and cheerful. 'It's delightful,' Annie said sincerely, over a cup of tea in the elegant dining room. 'I didn't expect anything like this!'

'My room looks over the sea,' said Davie, through a mouthful of cream scone, 'and it's ever so big. Mr Sutton said there's a toy train set in the attic that his son used to play with. He says he'll show it to me tonight, while you two are out.'

'That's kind of him.' Annie nibbled her lip for a moment, casting a small, doubtful glance at Richard from beneath her lashes. 'It must be very... expensive?' she ventured.

Richard shrugged. Smiled. 'Nice things usually are, I find,' he said gently.

'But—'

He shook his head sharply and held up his hand. 'No. No, no, no. This is my treat. All I want you to do is enjoy it. How much it costs is nothing to do with anything.'

'Does that mean I can have another scone?' Davie asked innocently.

–

'Are you having a good time?' Richard's voice was quiet, his mouth very close to Annie's ear.

Annie drew closer to him and shut her eyes for a moment, her head on his shoulder. 'Wonderful.' As they had discovered before, they danced together in perfect, unthinking harmony. The band swung into a foxtrot, and a young man stepped to the front of the stage and began to croon. Annie leaned back in Richard's arms and looked up into his face with a smile. The dance floor was crowded, the Grand Hotel and its glittering clientele were both the very height of stylish elegance. The clatter of cutlery and the hum of conversation and laughter sounded a counterpoint to the syncopated swing of the dance band. Richard's arms tightened about her. 'Come and sit down,' he said. 'There's something I want to ask you.'

She giggled delightedly. They were on their second bottle of Champagne. 'Something you asked me once before?' she asked, her head on one side and grinning like an urchin.

He tried to suppress his laughter. 'Yes.'

'Then that's the answer. Yes. Yes. Yes.' She leaned back, her hair swinging, and let him lead her into a deft and practised spin. 'Yes,' she added again for good measure, as they moved smoothly into the steps of the dance.

He was laughing now. 'You don't know what I'm going to ask you,' he protested.

She put her head on one side again. 'True,' she said, with the solemnity of the very slightly tipsy. 'All right. Let's sit down, so you can do it.' She stopped dancing so suddenly that he almost lost hold of her, and another couple narrowly missed colliding with them. 'Come on.' She took his hand in hers and led him off the dance floor to their table, where she sat down, put her elbows on the table, her chin on her folded hands and looked at him enquiringly. She was wearing the green dress and had flowers in her hair. Her eyes sparkled with happiness, her cheeks glowed with it. Her creamy shoulders were smooth as satin.

Richard sat wordless, an odd, suddenly unfathomable look on his face. 'Is something wrong?' she asked, puzzled.

There was a moment of silence, then, 'You're beautiful,' he said. 'Do you know that?'

She had had enough to drink to have lost all trace of the self-consciousness that so often plagued her. 'Thank you,' she said simply. 'So are you. And yes, please, I would like to marry you.'

He shouted with laughter, took her hand. '*Annie!* I haven't asked you yet!'

'You are going to, though, aren't you?' she asked composedly. She was aware that diners at other tables were watching them, their attention caught, and cared not a jot.

He lifted her hand to his lips, kissed her fingertips. 'Yes, I am.'

She waited. 'Well, go on, then,' she said encouragingly, after a moment.

He was laughing so much he could hardly speak. 'My darling – will you marry me?'

'Yes,' she said.

'When?'

She shrugged. 'Whenever you like.'

'How about the day after tomorrow?'

That – as he had obviously intended – took the wind out of her sails entirely. She stared at him. 'You're not *serious*?'

'Perfectly,' he said calmly. His eyes were steady.

She put her hands to her cheeks. 'But – how? We can't—?'

'Special licence,' he said. 'I enquired.'

She took several deep breaths, watching him. 'I wish I hadn't drunk so much,' she said, plaintive but honest. 'I'm having a little bit of difficulty keeping up with this.'

He laughed, reached for her hands. 'Silly,' he teased, 'I'm joking. Of course I wouldn't rush you into it like that.' He put his head on one side, contemplating her with narrow, amused eyes. 'You can have a week,' he said.

She opened her mouth, shut it again.

Richard reached for the Champagne bottle, leaned across the table and refilled first her glass, then his own. Annie was still staring at him, dumbstruck. He picked up his own glass, nodded smiling towards hers. She picked it up. Richard toasted her: 'To us!'

'To us,' she agreed a little distractedly. Then added inconsequentially, 'Having a special licence doesn't mean you can't wear a big hat, does it? If it does, Mother will kill me.'

–

'All right,' Richard said later, 'a fortnight. That's surely plenty of time? After all, it's not as if we're getting married in Westminster Abbey with a dozen pageboys, is it?' They were walking hand in hand along the dark beach, the sea washing to their feet. Annie's inhibitions, to her own surprise, appeared to have deserted her entirely. She wandered barefoot on cool, sandy feet, her shoes and her stockings tucked into the pockets of Richard's dinner jacket.

'Where will we marry?' she asked curiously.

'The Register Office in Kew, I would imagine.'

She swung round to look at him in the sparkling lights of the promenade. 'And where will we live?'

'We don't have to decide that, do we? We're lucky enough to have a choice. Davie obviously wants to stay at Kew during term time. My place in Hampstead will be handy for town. Why change that?'

'It all seems too good to be true, doesn't it?' Despite herself, her words were just a little anxious.

He stopped walking, turned and drew her into his arms. 'No. It doesn't.' He kissed her, a long, tender kiss that made her suddenly tremble.

When he lifted his head she stayed in the circle of his arms, looking up into his face. 'I don't suppose—' she began, and then stopped, her cheeks warm in the darkness.

'What?'

She shook her head, giggling a little. 'No, we couldn't. It would scandalise that nice Mr and Mrs Sutton.'

Catching her drift he threw back his head and laughed, but then sobered. 'And Davie. Don't forget Davie. Darling – in a couple of weeks we'll be man and wife. Don't let's spoil that.'

She nodded, linked her hand with his again and they walked slowly on. 'Are we going to have a honeymoon?' she asked.

'Well, of course we are.'

'Where?'

'Where would you like?'

She shrugged a little. 'I... don't know. You choose.'

There was a moment's silence. Then, 'I don't suppose,' he asked carefully, 'that you would consider Paris?'

She stiffened. 'No.' She turned her head, not looking at him.

They walked on in a silence that was not as easy as it had been. 'Annie,' Richard said at last, 'isn't it time you tried to do something about this phobia of yours? I spend a lot of time in Paris. Dammit, you're half French, and so is Davie. Is it fair that he's never seen his father's city, the city in which he was conceived and born?'

There was an overly long and rather difficult silence. Then, 'I can't help it,' she said quietly. There was a stubborn note in her voice, an obstinate set to her chin. She turned to look out over the sea. In the far distance a ship was passing, forging through the Channel waters; her decks were lit like a Christmas tree and light streamed from her portholes. 'Don't you think I would if I could?' There was a kind of desperation in the words. 'I've told you, I know it's irrational. But I can't help it. Davie went on a school trip a little while ago, to the Tower of London. They went by river boat. I worried myself sick. I swear I very nearly had a nervous breakdown. I know it's irrational. I hate it. If I could cure it I would. But I can't. Please, Richard, leave it be.'

He put a reassuring arm about her shoulders and bent his head so that his cheek touched her hair. 'All right, all right. I'm sorry. But tell me one thing – if there were a way to cure it, would you try?'

'Of course I would.'

'Well, we'll see.' He paused. 'It's just, well, I've been thinking. I have a friend—' he went on. His eyes were watchful, a little wary. 'A very good friend. A doctor, who specialises in' – he hesitated – 'in this sort of thing.'

Still on the defensive, she picked that up sharply enough. 'What do you mean "this sort of thing"? You make it sound like some kind of aberration!'

He shook his head impatiently. 'Of course I don't mean any such thing. You said you'd be willing to try. I know someone who might be able to help, that's all—'

She sighed. 'I'm sorry. I didn't mean to jump like that. Of course I'd be willing to talk to your friend.'

'Well, we don't have to think about it just yet, do we? I'll have a chat with him, see what he says. For now, the important thing is the honeymoon. North, south, east or west – which would you prefer?'

She was quiet for a little while longer, then shaking off her moment's sombreness she raised her head, smiling again. 'I told you. I really don't mind.'

'A surprise, then?'

She looked up at him in delight. 'What a lovely idea! Yes, please.'

'Right. Well, I suppose we need to be practical. Big wedding? Small? Fancy? Simple? Trillions of guests or none at all? It's entirely up to you. We can pick up a couple of witnesses from the street if you like; it's all just as legal.'

She thought for a moment. 'I'd much prefer it small, and simple. It's going to get terribly complicated if we try to invite everyone, isn't it? And all at such very short notice. Shall I tell you what I'd rather do?'

He waited.

'I'd like a really small wedding – just us, Davie, Mother, someone for you – and then a bit later in the year, after we're settled, we can throw a great big party to introduce our friends to each other. And to us, if you see what I mean. Whatever you say, it has all happened rather fast. There'll be some very surprised people about. We may as well give them the chance to get used to the notion—' She stopped.

'That you're marrying me and not Fergus?' He was gently amused.

'Well – yes – I suppose so.' She cast a sly glance at him. 'Most of my friends thoroughly approved of Fergus,' she said with mock primness.

He grinned. 'And you don't think they'll approve of me?'

She squeezed his arm. 'As Davie would say – they'll be green with envy.'

They had almost reached the hotel. Richard handed Annie her shoes, held her steady, laughing, as she squeezed her damp bare feet into them, and they started up the beach to the roadway. Just before they reached it Annie stopped and turned, surveying the moonlit beach, the silvered, shimmering water, the glittering lights of the piers. 'I'll always remember this moment,' she said, and then was in his arms, fierce and demanding, trembling with need.

Richard it was who, at last, gently but very firmly put her from him, shaking his head a little. 'Time to go in.'

'Must we?'

'Yes.' She sensed rather than saw his sudden grin. 'Don't forget that Davie's room overlooks the beach. It might be just a little embarrassing if he's waiting up for us!'

—

They broke the news to Davie the next day, over an excellent breakfast. While unsurprised he was clearly delighted, beaming at the pair of them in a positively proprietary way. 'Now we can be a proper family,' he announced with satisfaction; and for a short and surprising moment Annie found she was in danger of shedding a tear.

Richard looked at her, faint concern in his eyes. 'You're very quiet this morning? And pale. And you haven't eaten your breakfast. Are you all right? Didn't you sleep well?'

She smiled a little wanly, shaking her head faintly, pushing her plate away. 'Too much Champagne, I expect,' she said, touching her fingertips to her head. 'Again. You really are getting me into bad habits, you know.'

'That was smashing,' Davie announced, taking a crust of bread and cleaning the very last vestiges of a breakfast that would have defeated many a grown man from his plate. 'Can we go down to the beach, please? I'd like to collect some more shells and things.'

'Of course. We don't have to go back to London until this afternoon.' Richard pushed his chair back from the table. 'I'll fetch my camera. I wanted to get some pictures.'

Annie still had her hand to her head. 'Would you mind very much if I didn't? I really didn't have a good night. I think I'd like to lie down for an hour or so.'

Richard peered at her, concerned. 'Are you sure you're not unwell?'

'Oh, no. Of course not.' She forced a smile. 'I told you, I'm tired, that's all. You go ahead. I'll meet you later if you like. How about the Grand at eleven for coffee?'

'That'd be wizard,' Davie said enthusiastically. 'I expect they do great biscuits in a place like that.'

'Come on, monkey.' Richard ruffled his hair affectionately and stood up. 'You are sure you don't mind?' he asked Annie.

'No, no. Off you go. I'll see you at eleven.'

'I'll go and get my bucket and spade.' Davie raced off and then, remembering where he was, slowed to a sedate walk before taking the stairs two at a time and flying along the corridor to his bedroom.

When he got back downstairs his mother had gone and Richard, in blazer and flannels, was waiting for him in the hall. They crossed the road and went down on to the beach, freshly washed by the receding tide. The air was clear and salty and still held traces of an early morning chill. The wet sand and pebbles glistened in the sunshine, and a breeze blew in from the sea. Davie ran to the water's edge and in no time was absorbed in his hunt, eyes intent upon the sands, every now and then hunkering down to examine some find, poking with his long, sun-tanned finger before scooping it up, washing it in the lapping water and dropping it into his brightly coloured tin bucket. Richard watched him with a smile. With his long bare legs and tousled, sun-bleached hair – he had managed to evade his mother's rules on the hated sun hat this morning – he was the very picture of mischievous, innocent boyhood.

His face suddenly sombre, Richard reached into his pocket for his cigarette case.

Later, as they were sorting through the boy's finds, Richard said casually, 'Do you know, I don't know when your birthday is?'

Davie, intent upon a tiny crab that was rather more lively than the pebbles and shells with which it shared the bucket, did not look up. 'It's in March. Do you think Mother would let me take this little crab home? I could keep it in a bowl or something.'

Richard pretended to give the matter some thought. Then, 'No,' he said, 'I'm fairly sure not. And it wouldn't be very fair to the poor little chap, would it?'

'No, I s'pose not.' Reluctantly Davie picked up the fragile thing and set it carefully on the sand.

'How old were you? On your birthday?'

This time the child did look up, with one of those wide, flashing smiles that were so characteristic of him. 'Ten. That's quite big, isn't it? I'll be going to upper school next term.'

'Ten! My, my! That's a pretty important birthday, eh? Starting on your second decade. It's a shame I wasn't around then. I'll tell you what, seeing as how we're family now' – Richard winked at him – 'how about a special treat, a belated birthday present and a big thank you for letting me marry your mother? How does that sound?'

'Can you think of one?' Davie asked eagerly, his attention caught.

'Oh, I'm sure I will. Leave it to me. Though I say it myself, I'm good at surprises.' Richard stood up. 'Hello, there's the Wall's man. Fancy an ice cream?'

'Yes, please. Hey – I read some of that book you lent me before I went to bed last night. It's a corker, isn't it? I couldn't work out – was the car like yours?'

From the window of Davie's room Annie watched as the tall, rangy man and the long-legged boy scrunched up the beach towards the ice-cream man. The sun was very bright; she closed her eyes against it, feeling fragile and out of sorts. She had not expected the dream last night; indeed it had been the last thing she had anticipated. Nor had she expected to find herself jumping awake here in this room, beside the soundly sleeping Davie's bed, disorientated and trembling with fear. It had been such a wonderful evening. She had been so happy. Last night the world had seemed a perfect place. So why the dream? Why the terror? Would she never be free of it?

In the shifting, haunted darkness behind her eyelids two faces swam, a current swirled, and hair drifted like seaweed.

Chapter Twelve

For the whole of the next week it seemed to Annie that her feet barely touched the floor. A telegram to Jane brought her mother up to London by Tuesday, to help with the preparations and, as Jane herself readily and breezily admitted, to go into her interfering old bat routine with regard to what the bride should wear – about which she had some very firm opinions. She also quietly and efficiently took over the running of the household, coped with a Davie who was so excited he could barely keep his fingers out of anything, and remembered things like wedding cakes, cars and flowers. No matter how small the wedding, in Jane's opinion it should be a day to remember, and for the right reasons rather than the wrong ones.

'We must find the outfit as soon as possible,' she announced to Annie over breakfast on the Wednesday morning.

Annie, smiling inwardly at the 'we', to say nothing of the capital letters that she found herself mentally envisaging in that sentence, nodded.

Jane munched toast and marmalade thoughtfully. 'Harrods, do you think?' she asked. 'Or Debenham and Freebody? I did hear that Selfridges is very good this year? But no – Harrods, I think.' The words were firm.

Annie pursed her lips doubtfully. 'Harrods is very expensive,' she ventured.

'Oh, don't be ridiculous, child.' Jane mounted her motherly high horse and dismissed that out of hand. 'Richard will expect you to look your very best.'

'Mother, it's a wedding, not a bathing belle contest,' her daughter objected with mild asperity.

Jane raised a brow.

Annie laughed. 'All right. We'll try Harrods first. But I mean it. I'm not spending a fortune on something I'll probably hardly ever wear again.'

'We'll see,' Jane said smugly.

And a couple of days later, as she had guessed, smug she could afford to be, Annie having fallen head over heels in love with a sumptuous cream- and coffee-coloured silk outfit with a matching hat and a price tag to freeze the blood.

'It looks just wonderful, darling,' Jane beamed. 'It's exactly right.'

Annie surveyed herself in the huge mirror a little worriedly. Her mother was right: the dress might have been made for her, and for the occasion. A wide boat neck with a coffee-coloured collar set off her shoulders perfectly. The slim-fitting sleeves belled slightly at the wrists, the cuffs, too, bound in coffee silk. A wide sash of the same colour settled with artful neatness about her hips, and the fashionable knee-length skirt was as short as decency would allow. The pale coffee hat was wide brimmed and decked with cream silk ribbon and cream roses.

Jane clapped her hands together delightedly. 'Cream roses,' she said firmly. 'Of course. Cream roses to match the hat, with lots of trailing foliage. A perfect summer bouquet.'

'It is awfully expensive,' Annie observed, doubtfully.

The black-clad shop assistant, hands clasped dutifully before her, ignored the last words completely and nodded approvingly. 'If I may say so, the outfit suits Madam very well indeed. Might I suggest that I send for someone from the footwear department to wait upon Madam? It's so very difficult to visualise the whole effect without the right accessories—'

In the end of course she bought not only the dress, hat, shoes, bag and gloves, but pale silken underwear as well. Travelling home in a taxicab full of beautifully and expensively wrapped boxes and parcels, she looked at her mother, half-laughing, half-accusing. 'Fancy letting me do that!' she said, her indignation only partly assumed. 'I thought you were supposed to be the practical one in this family! You just wait. I'm coming with you when you go to buy your hat, and I'm going to make sure you get the most expensive one in the shop!'

Jane leaned forward and touched her hand, smiling. 'The outfit is my wedding present to you, my dear. I didn't say anything before, because I knew you wouldn't spend that kind of money if you thought I was paying. You have your home, you have your pretty things. There's nothing you need—'

'Mother – you can't!'

'Indeed I can.' Jane was collected. 'Now – we have to think about Davie. I was wondering – he is very tall for his age – do you think we might allow him his first long trousers?'

Annie saw little of Richard that first week until the Saturday evening, when, leaving Jane and Davie at home in Kew, he took her out to dinner, to draw breath and to compare notes. They went to a quiet restaurant in Chelsea. 'I've asked Charlie Draper to be my witness. He's a good friend, as is his wife Katrina.' He glanced up at her over the rim of his wine glass. 'He's the doctor I mentioned, do you remember? The one I thought might be able to help you?'

She opened her mouth to speak and he held up his hand, laughing.

'That is *not* why I've asked him! He won't be holding a consultation on the steps of the Register Office, I promise. As I say – he's a very good friend. He's been dying to meet you. They both have.' He grinned again. 'Especially Katrina. Any professional contact will be made through the proper channels later. But only if you want to. I thought it might be best for you to meet socially first. Now – the telephone will be connected whilst we're away—' Annie pulled a small face, and Richard laughed. 'I know you don't like them, but I do need to be in contact with the office and if we're going to be spending a good deal of time at Kew—'

'Yes, I know. There's no need for me to use it if I don't want to, is there?'

'My darling,' he said, amused, 'I give you a month – no, a fortnight – before you're on the thing all day long. The honeymoon is booked, as is lunch at the Savoy for the wedding day, and a room for us for the night. I pick up the special licence on Monday.' He paused, thinking.

'What sort of clothes should I pack?'

He smiled. 'Are you angling?'

'Not at all!' She was indignant. 'I was just wondering.'

He waved an expansive hand. 'Anything you like. If you can't get it in a case, there's the whole of the back seat of the Wolseley free. Now; your turn.'

They returned to the Kew house to find Jane nodding in an armchair, an open book on her lap. 'Richard, my dear.' She came to her feet, stood on tiptoe to kiss his cheek. 'How are you standing up to all of this rush?'

'Very well. Thank you so much for coming to help.'

'Don't be silly. I'm thoroughly enjoying myself. Well' – she stood, as though considering, her head on one side – 'apart from tonight, that is.'

'What?' Annie's eyes were wide with concern. 'Davie? Has he been naughty?'

'No, no. Far from it. He's been reading to me.' She rolled her eyes. 'All evening!'

Richard had begun to laugh. '*By Car to India?*' he suggested.

'Quite.' Jane was tart. 'The sainted and dauntless Major Forbes-Leith and his tedious machine en route through thick, thin and just about everything in between, to the subcontinent.' She pointed a caustic finger. 'I hold you entirely responsible, Richard, and consider that the least you can do is to ensure a constant stream of Champagne at the wedding lunch.'

'Done,' he said, grinning. 'You shall have your very own bottle!'

'There's no need to go to extremes,' she said primly, her eyes gleaming with laughter. 'Did you know that wretched man covered two hundred and forty-nine miles over railway sleepers when he ran out of road?'

'Did you count them, one by one?'

'It feels so. Annie – what about a nightcap? I don't know about Richard, but I could certainly do with one.'

Annie regarded her mother with solemn eyes. 'Ovaltine?' she suggested.

'Whisky for me, thank you.' Jane was unperturbed. 'Though Richard might like the Ovaltine,' she added helpfully.

Later, as they stood at the door, Richard gathered Annie into his arms and kissed her, very gently. 'This time next week,' he spoke quietly into her hair, 'we'll be man and wife. And setting out to live happily ever after.'

She leaned back to look at him. It was a sultry night; the air hung heavily and the sky was dark and starless. 'We really will, won't we? Live happily ever after?'

His arms tightened. 'Yes,' he said simply. Then after a moment he added quietly, 'Annie?'

'Hmm?' She was standing sleepily in the circle of his arms, her head on his chest.

'Will you promise me something?'

She had nodded, smiling, before the sudden intensity in his voice registered. Again she lifted her head to look at him. 'What is it?'

He hesitated. 'Whatever happens. Anything. You will believe that I love you, won't you?'

She shook her head slightly. 'I don't understand. What's going to happen?'

'Nothing. Nothing. I'm not saying—' He stopped, caught her close again. 'I just want you to know that I love you.' The words were very quiet.

She laughed a little. 'Why, of course you do. Why else would you be marrying me? Lord knows I'm not that much of a catch!'

This time the tightening of his arms took her breath away. 'So long as you know.'

'I know.' And even at that moment she was surprised at the certainty of her own feeling. She *did* know. It must be so. Or the world would end.

With a finger under her chin he tilted her head and kissed her lightly on the lips. 'This time next week. A brand-new start. For both of us. Oh – and the honeymoon?'

'Yes?'

The odd tension seemed suddenly to have left him. He grinned that boyish grin, hazel eyes crinkling and glinting gold in the light of the street lamp. 'Bring your paddling sandals. And your sun hat. Oh, and your walking boots – don't forget your walking boots.'

She watched him drive away, stood for a long time leaning against the door jamb, unwilling to close the door against the slightest breath of air that stirred in the night street. Next week. A brand-new start. For both of us.

She had to tell him. The thought came from nowhere and shook her to her soul. Then she lifted her head sharply. She couldn't tell him. There was no need. The secret had been hers for so long...

A brand-new start. For both of us. How did secrets fit into that?

She stood quite still, biting her lip, carefully examining the chasm that was suddenly opening before her.

Then she shook her head and, suddenly tired, closed the door against the sultry night and climbed the stairs to bed.

In the bedroom her wedding outfit was hanging on the wardrobe, the material gleaming softly in the lamplight; it really was quite the most exquisite dress she had ever owned. She put out a hand and touched it gently with her finger. The silk was heavy and smooth, the colour of clotted cream. She drew it to her face, looked in the mirror. Her mother was right, the colour suited her beautifully.

She had worn white when she married Philippe. A hastily acquired dress that had not fitted her well – there had been no time in those last precious, pre-war days to have it altered. Her lace veil, delicate and fragile as a cobweb, had belonged to Philippe's grandmother. Philippe – tall, golden-haired, his face bright with love as she joined him at the altar – had looked, even to her eyes, very young. That had been just ten days before war was declared and the world had descended to horror, brutality and death.

She sometimes thought it had been the worst day of her life.

Thunder rolled distantly.

A new start. Brand new. Clean. Oh yes, that, indeed, was what she needed.

As she slowly undressed and slipped on her satin nightdress, she did not bother to wipe away the tears that all at once were sliding soundlessly down her cheeks.

–

'Something old, something new, something borrowed and something blue. How are we doing on that?' Jane asked next day over the breakfast table. The morning had brought no freshness to the weather: the clouds still hung low, the morning was airless.

'Hadn't thought about it.' Annie was at the sink, filling the kettle. Her voice was distracted, almost irritable. She had not slept well.

'You could borrow my pearls, if you'd like. They suit you well, and would go beautifully with the outfit.'

'Thank you.'

Her mother glanced at her sharply. 'Annie? Is something wrong?'

Annie almost jumped. 'No. No. Of course not. I'm quite all right.' She tried to focus her whole attention on what her mother was saying, but could not. During a sticky, sleepless night her courage had ebbed and flowed as violently as a spring tide. What had seemed right one moment had appeared totally wrong the next. The morning had brought no answers.

'What about something old?'

'I'll wear my sapphire ring. That's old, and it's blue. It'll do for both.' The words were absent.

'Perfect.' Jane's gaze was still on her, sharp and faintly puzzled.

Annie put the kettle on the gas ring and stood watching it with troubled eyes. Beyond the open back door the storm clouds gathered and billowed in the sky.

–

She stood outside the tall, elegant house and looked up uncertainly at the second-floor windows. Perhaps she had got the wrong address? And even if she hadn't, Richard probably wasn't in. If he were not, then the gods would have intervened. It would be a sign. She would go home, and leave it at that. If he were…? She drew a deep breath. The pretty, narrow street with its tall, elegant buildings and heavy-leafed trees was sunk in a warm, Sunday quiet. Thunder rolled over the Heath. The air was very still. A middle-aged woman in a light, flowery dress and fashionable straw hat came out of the door and walked down the steps, a tiny dog, little more than a bundle of silken fluff, tucked under her arm. She looked at Annie with undisguised, even slightly disapproving curiosity. 'Good afternoon.' There was faint enquiry in her voice.

'Good afternoon. Please – could you tell me if Mr Ross lives here? Mr Richard Ross?'

'Indeed he does. His apartment is on the second floor.'

'Thank you.' Annie was finding it strangely difficult to breathe in the oppressive atmosphere. She felt the woman's eyes upon her as she mounted the steps and entered the hallway. It was cool, and gloomy. Polished wood shone and a long mirror glimmered in the shadows. A wide, curved staircase led up to an equally dim-lit landing. Annie took a deep breath and began to climb it.

Richard's door was at the far end of the landing; his name was on the small brass-mounted card beside the knocker.

For one last second she hesitated. And then she knocked.

For a long moment nothing happened. Her heart calmed; he wasn't there. She was about to turn away when the door opened.

'Annie!' His face lit with surprise and pleasure. 'What on earth are you doing here?' And then, in sudden dawning concern, 'Is something wrong?'

'I—' She stopped, her courage failing her at the last moment. 'No. Of course not. Mother's taken Davie out for the afternoon. I… it's silly, but I just wanted to see you. I was' – she hesitated – 'I was lonely.' Her eyes held his. 'I've never been lonely before. Never. See what you've done to me? I always used to enjoy being alone. Now…' She shrugged, did not finish the sentence. 'Anyway,' she added, smiling hesitantly, 'I decided it was time to come and find your lair.'

His own smile was gentle. 'To beard me in my den?'

'Exactly.'

He stepped back, laughing. 'Welcome to Bluebeard's Castle!' He was wearing slacks and an open-necked shirt, the sleeves rolled up in the heat. As always the sight of his smile, the look in his eyes all but stopped her heart. She didn't *have* to tell him. The thought was almost defiant. What had past secrets to do with present happiness?

She followed him into a long, well-proportioned hallway with a polished parquet floor. It was lined with pictures that were lit by bright, modern lighting, and several doors opened out of it.

'This way.' He ushered her to an open door to her right.

She stopped on the threshold, eyes wide. 'Richard! What a delightful room!' The drawing room was very large, very light and positively exuded comfort and simple good taste. At one end was a large open fireplace, its currently empty fire basket hidden by a large screen exquisitely embroidered in modern style. The rugs on the wooden floor and the heavy curtains at the window were also of modern design, as was the furniture. The walls were hung with perhaps a dozen paintings, most of them in Impressionist style. A bowl of roses on a low table in the centre of the room scented the air. 'You like it?' Richard asked.

'I love it.' She went to the window, which looked out over what appeared to be a tiny park, though closer examination revealed that it was actually a large communal garden with lawns and benches, a pond and several huge and ancient trees. She turned back to survey the room. Richard had moved to a cabinet and was standing with a record in his hand. She watched as he slipped it from its cover and put it on. Ragtime filled the air; Richard turned down the volume and lifted his head, smiling.

'I'm glad. I was afraid you might not like the style.'

'I love it,' she repeated. 'It does seem strange, doesn't it? That I haven't been here before?'

'There hasn't been time, that's all. Come.' He took her hand, drew her to him and kissed her lightly. 'I'll show you the rest of the place.'

Every room in the apartment was to scale with the drawing room. The kitchen was vast – rather intimidatingly so, Annie found, though she did not say so – the bathroom luxurious. The main bedroom was panelled in light, beautifully grained maple, and the – again modern and beautifully designed – furniture was fashioned in the same wood: a large wardrobe, a chest of drawers, a tallboy and the biggest bed Annie had ever seen. It was the most masculine of rooms; a fact that she somehow found unexpectedly comforting. No woman had had a hand in this.

As so often happened, Richard seemed to sense her thoughts. 'We can change it,' he said quietly. 'You'll need a dressing table, a wardrobe of course—'

'There's room,' she said absently. 'It isn't important.' Her eyes on the bed, she was suddenly very aware of his closeness. The window was open. Sultry air drifted in, carrying the scents and sounds of the garden. She turned to him.

He was watching her, smiling. She opened her mouth to speak; said nothing. Their eyes locked. He lifted his hand, brushed the back of it very gently upon her cheek. She turned her head a little, laid her lips upon his knuckles. His skin smelled as it always did, a familiar and to her almost intoxicating mix of sharp citrus soap and nicotine.

The moment stretched, seemingly endless. 'I'll show you Davie's room,' he said at last, and cleared his throat.

She did not move.

The music had stopped. The apartment was very quiet.

His hand dropped to her shoulder, then moved to her breast. She took a small, shuddering breath and closed her eyes. 'Annie, I didn't want to do this – I wanted us to wait – that's why I hadn't brought you here before—' His voice was suddenly harsh with strain. She could feel the trembling of his body. She curled her arms about his neck and kissed him.

There was nothing gentle about their lovemaking, nothing of tenderness. It was an alleviation of hunger, an assuaging of thirst – quick, fevered, almost brutal. They lay afterwards for a long time, half-dressed, dishevelled and slick with sweat in the humid air, saying nothing, drained yet oddly unsatisfied. Eventually Richard rolled onto his stomach, burying his face in his arms. 'I'm sorry,' he said, his voice muffled.

Annie came up on one elbow, looking at him, tracing the curve of his back and shoulder with the light touch of her finger. 'Don't be silly. Whatever for?'

'I told you. I didn't mean that to happen. And certainly not like that.'

'I enjoyed it,' she said, simply and candidly.

He lifted his head, rubbed big hands through his already furiously disordered hair. 'So did I! Of course I did. It's just… Annie, I told you – and I mean it – I want us to do things the right way.' He turned his head to glance up at her, the sudden rueful laughter back. 'And grabbing you like a demented adolescent a week before I marry you doesn't really fit that particular bill, now does it?'

She smiled a little, swung her legs to the side of the bed, reached for her clothes. They dressed in silence.

'Drink?' he asked, watching her in the wardrobe mirror as she pulled a comb through her tangled hair.

She smiled faintly at his reflection. 'Yes, please.'

'Martini?'

'Would be perfect.'

As he went out she studiously avoided her own eyes in the mirror. A moment later she heard music coming from the drawing room again, a soft, crooning melody of love and moonlit seduction. She cast a quick glance at the messily rumpled bed. Her smile was wry as she left the room.

Richard had the drinks waiting, the cocktail shaker and the stemmed, frosted glasses sitting on an ornamental black lacquer tray. Annie took hers, thanked him with a smile and went to the open window. In the past half-hour the sky had darkened ominously; there was the unmistakeable feeling of a storm in the air. As she watched she caught the faint, distant flicker of lightning. A woman's voice called sharply; a child's answered and Annie caught a glimpse of a small boy running from under a tree just as the first huge drops of rain splashed through the leaves. 'It's raining,' she said.

'It's been threatening all day.' She heard the clink of glass behind her.

Thunder rolled.

'Annie?' Richard's voice asked from behind her. 'What's really wrong? Why did you really come?' There was a quiet certainty in his voice that defied her to lie.

She did not turn. 'To tell you something,' she heard herself say.

There was a small, wary moment of silence. 'You – haven't changed your mind?' he asked, his voice very even.

'No. No, of course not. How could you think that after...' She let the words trail off, bent her head to look at her glass. Her hands were shaking. She tossed back what was left of her drink, the dry bite of it catching in her throat. 'It was something you said – something you've said more than once – about fresh starts, and honesty and not deceiving each other—'

'Well?' The word was tense.

The last, plaintive notes of the love song died. She took a breath. 'What would you say,' she asked, 'if I told you that Philippe wasn't Davie's father?'

This time the silence was so long, and so fraught, that she turned to face him – and flinched from the expression on his face. He was staring at her; to her astonishment he had actually paled. 'What do you mean?' he asked.

'What I said.' Suddenly she was desperately composed. 'I was pregnant when I married Philippe. He didn't know it; he never found out.'

It was a long, long time before he spoke. She saw the struggle in his eyes, the final understanding. Then, 'How could you?' he asked. 'How could you have married him knowing...?'

She was regretting the impulse already. Too late. 'Oh, for heaven's sake, surely you can *see* how?' She shook her head, closing her eyes for a moment. 'Sorry. I didn't mean to snap. Darling – please – try to understand. I was eighteen years old—'

'You loved him,' he interrupted her. 'You told me that you loved him.' He was watching her intently, his expression suddenly unfathomable.

'l did. At least, insofar as I knew what love was, yes, I did.'

'Then, how—'

She turned from him sharply. 'I can't tell you that. Please try to understand. I just can't.'

'And Davie?' There was a tight edge of something close to anger in his voice. 'Does Davie know?'

'No.'

'Will you tell him?'

The question that had haunted her for more than ten years. She hung on to her self-control by a thread. 'One day, I suppose I'll have to. Richard, please – *please!* – don't make me sorry I told you. Don't let it make any difference to us. I just felt I had to tell you.'

The room had become very dark. Outside the window a sudden intense flash crackled through the clouds and lit the sky. Annie jumped.

Richard reached for the cocktail shaker. 'Another?' he asked. His voice was cool. It was, she thought, as if he spoke to a stranger. She hated the sound of it.

'No. Thank you.'

He poured one for himself. She could not see his face. 'Richard?' she ventured. 'You aren't... angry with me? It was all so long ago – it feels like a different lifetime—'

For a long moment he did not speak, then he turned, and to her relief the unnervingly chill look had gone from his face. 'Of course I'm not angry with you. Why should I be? As you say, it was a long time ago. How could I be angry about something that happened long before we met? You were eighteen – and I'm willing to bet a not very experienced eighteen. I remember Paris in those last months before the war. It wasn't the most calm or chaste of environments, as I recall.' He put down his glass and came to her, putting his arms about her, drawing her to him. Thunder rolled and crashed. 'I'm glad you told me,' he said.

She drew a deep breath. 'So am I.'

'Tell me something – does Jane know?'

Annie shook her head against his chest. 'No. No one does.' She closed her mind to the thought that this might not be entirely true; she had said enough.

'You'll have to tell Davie. One day.'

She bit her lip and said nothing.

'Annie?'

'Not now. Not yet,' she said.

'Of course not.'

She stepped back, looking up at him. The long dark lashes were wet with unshed tears. 'You are sure it hasn't made any difference?'

He had taken a cigarette from his silver case and was tapping it on his thumbnail. 'I'm sure. It… was a shock, that's all. As I said, I'm glad you told me. I don't want us to have secrets. Now – we don't have to speak of it any more. Thank you for telling me. Thank you for being so brave. It couldn't have been easy.'

She smiled a little shakily. 'I think,' she said, 'if you don't mind – I'll have that drink now.'

Outside the heavens had opened; the sound of the rain all but drowned her words. They stood at the window watching the storm. Lightning split the sky, gusts of wind tossed in the treetops, the world was drenched in the ferocious downpour. Darkness shadowed the room around them.

The telephone rang.

Richard cursed mildly, picked it up. 'Hello?'

Annie, sipping her martini and watching the streaming rain, did not see the sudden sharp glance he threw her when he heard the answering voice. He turned his back, spoke quietly. 'It's a bit difficult at the moment' – another bellow of thunder – 'plans have changed… Yes… Look, old man, I'll ring you tomorrow – fill you in. Sure. Talk to you then. Thanks. And you. Bye.'

He hung the receiver back on its hook and rejoined her. 'If there's one problem with the telephone, that's it,' he said easily. 'Some people just never stop working. Now – another small one while we wait for this to clear, then I'll call a taxi for you. Jane will be thinking you've been kidnapped.' He nodded ruefully at the sheets of rain that were blowing against the window. 'Or drowned.' He saw the flicker in her eyes at that and shook his head gently. 'Don't be silly,' he said, 'I'm joking. That's all. We're going to get you over that, aren't we?' He bent to kiss her lightly.

'If you want, I'll try,' she said. And meant it. At that moment she would have done anything in the world he asked.

'Good.' Richard went to the gramophone, picked up a record. 'Ambrose and the Embassy Club.' He smiled across the room at her. 'Fancy a dance?'

An hour later the storm had died, and a taxi had pulled up outside the house. Richard escorted her downstairs and out onto the wet pavement. The storm had cleared the air and the birds were singing. 'We'll need to get together one day this week to make the final arrangements,' he said. 'How about Wednesday?'

'That suits me.'

Richard opened the taxi door for her but, before she could get in, clicked his fingers and turned her to face him. 'I've had an idea.'

She looked at him enquiringly.

'Davie. Do you think he'd like to come and stay with me on Friday night? Some friends are taking me out on Thursday, but I've kept Friday free. I never could see the point of turning up hungover at your own wedding. I'd love to have Davie's company. He could see the apartment, it would get him out of your way, and he could really do his best-man bit – get me to the church on time! What do you think?'

'He'd love it,' Annie said. 'I think, much as he loves us, his women are rather getting on his nerves.' She laughed. 'He can bring that wretched book with him and you can read it together to your hearts' content. What a splendid idea!'

'Good! Tell him I'll pick him up after school. He can bring his glad rags and we'll get ready together.'

'I'll tell him.' She kissed him, got in the cab, waved through the window as it pulled away.

Richard lifted a hand, stood watching as the taxi drove off.

Then, as it turned the corner he reached into his pocket for his cigarette case, and the smile faded from his face to leave it totally expressionless, the eyes cool and very, very thoughtful.

Chapter Thirteen

'I wish *we* could go on an adventure like that, don't you?' Davie closed the book he had been reading and ran a finger over the cover. He was lying on the floor on his stomach, knees bent, sandalled feet waving in the air. He put his chin on his cupped hands and looked up at Richard, who was sitting in an armchair reading *The Times*. Richard folded the newspaper and dropped it to the floor, smiling. 'D'you think we could one day?' the boy persisted. 'When I'm grown-up, perhaps?' He paused, frowning slightly. 'You wouldn't be too old then, would you?' he added, a little doubtfully.

Richard threw back his head and laughed. 'I don't suppose you're ever too old for that kind of adventure.'

'It would be smashing, wouldn't it?' Davie's dark eyes were shining. He squirmed round and sat up, holding an imaginary steering wheel and making engine noises. 'Brrm, brrm – we're in Persia. Look at the desert! Brrm, brrm – we're crossing the Alps – look at the mountains! Brrrm! – now it's Turkey – look at the turkeys!' He curled up with laughter at his own witticism.

'I've got a strong feeling you're going backwards,' Richard observed dryly. 'Best you take a course on map-reading before we leave, I think.'

Davie scrambled to his feet, still gurgling with laughter. 'Oh, we'd be all right. We could just lean out of the window and ask "Which way to India?"' he said breezily.

Richard laughed again. 'I must say I think that might be just a little haphazard,' he said. 'And besides… in my dotage, as I obviously will be, I'm not sure I'd be able to go all the way to India. Eight and a half thousand miles might be a bit much for an old codger. No, I really think that the trip I did last year was exciting enough for me.'

Davie draped himself leggily over the arm of the chair. 'Last year? What did you do last year?'

Richard smiled into the eager face. 'I drove to Paris,' he said.

Davie stared. '*Paris?* You *drove* to *Paris?*'

'Indeed I did. Not in the Wolseley, of course – I didn't have it then. I reckon it would be even more fun in that, don't you?'

'But – how did you get the car across the Channel?'

'They crate it up and put it in the ship's hold.'

Davie blinked. 'Gosh!'

'And then they unload it the other side – and Bob's your uncle, off you go.'

'Just like that?'

'Just like that.'

The boy looked at him, dawning delight in his face. 'Could we do that?' he asked slowly, his huge eyes entranced upon Richard's. 'Could we?' There was an almost breathless pleading in the words.

Richard shrugged. 'One of these days, I expect.'

'When? When could we?'

Richard cocked his head, his face thoughtful. For a moment he did not reply.

'Soon?' the boy prompted excitedly.

'Your mother said that you wanted to go to Scotland – I'd been half planning—' He stopped.

'But Paris would be *much* more exciting!' The meaning of the words suddenly registered and Davie jumped to his feet. 'What had you been planning?'

Richard hesitated. 'Your special treat, remember?' he said. 'I promised you a special treat – to make up for missing your birthday, and as a man-to-man thank you for letting me marry your mother. I was going to suggest that – after the honeymoon, of course – we could take you on a trip. Anywhere you wanted.'

'I want to go to Paris,' the boy said with neither hesitation nor a moment of thought. 'I want to see them put the car on the boat and take it off again—' He stopped abruptly.

Richard eyed his suddenly stricken face sympathetically. 'Exactly,' he said.

'Mother wouldn't come, would she?' Davie ambled over to a chair and threw himself into it. 'And – even if she agreed to let me go with you on my own, she'd worry so... Oh, blast it!' He eyed Richard a little warily.

Richard let the forbidden expletive pass without comment. He was tapping a finger pensively on the arm of the chair. 'There is one possibility,' he began at last, slowly.

Davie cocked his head to look at him.

'Your mother has agreed to talk to a friend of mine about this phobia of hers. He's a doctor – a psychiatrist, actually – and a good one. I've spoken to him about it. He thinks he can do something for her. If he did...'

'We could go,' Davie said excitedly. 'Couldn't we?'

Richard nodded. 'Yes, we could.' He paused, his brow still furrowed in thought. 'There's a problem, though.'

'What?'

'We'd have to go during the summer holidays, of course. And that's only a few weeks away. Unfortunately these things take a bit of arranging. If we could persuade Annie, I'd have to book a place for the car. Fairly soon. There would be all sorts of things to arrange – passports, tickets—'

Davie glanced at him from beneath the long curling fringe of his eyelashes. 'Couldn't you... book it all first and persuade her later?' he ventured hopefully. 'Sort of... as a surprise for her?' The suggestion was shamelessly less than artless and they both knew it.

Richard frowned a little, thoughtfully.

'If she knew it was booked, it might help her to make up her mind?' the lad suggested helpfully.

Still Richard said nothing.

Davie contained himself, and waited.

'Leave it with me,' Richard said, after a long moment. 'But' – he lifted a warning finger – 'don't get your hopes too high. I don't want to disappoint you. It obviously depends on your mother.'

'Shall I ask her?' His voice was eager.

Richard shook his head quickly. 'No. Not right now. She's got quite enough on her mind at the moment. Leave it to me, and to Charlie Draper. He says that an awful lot depends on her co-operation – on whether she really wants to be cured.'

'Oh, I'm sure she does. She's often said so.'

'Well, we'll see. Just don't say anything yet, all right?'

'I promise.' Davie said it in his best grown-up voice, but his eyes gleamed with a very boyish excitement.

Richard stood up, walked over to him, ruffled his hair with a smile. 'That's my man. Now – why don't you thrash me at chess again? Or at least give me a chance to get my own back?'

Davie eyed him a little suspiciously. 'You didn't let me win last time, did you?'

'Of course not. Why would I do that?' Richard pulled him to his feet and put an arm about his shoulders. 'That's hardly the sort of thing a good father would do, is it?' he asked quietly.

'No.' Davie shook his head, his face shining with happiness. 'Not a really good one.'

Richard grinned. 'At least I'm on the right track, then?'

The boy's eyes were suddenly solemn. 'I think you're going to be the best father anyone ever had,' he said stoutly.

Richard caught a sharp breath and drew the boy to him for a moment. But he said nothing.

Even though he was satisfactorily late to bed that night Davie found it hard to sleep, though it was neither the thought of the following day's ceremony nor the until now much-anticipated prospect of grown-up lunch at the Savoy that kept him awake. Despite Richard's cautions the suggestion, however vague, that they might drive to Paris had fired his boyish imagination and roused an excitement that no amount of down-to-earth common sense could quell. It would be an adventure of the finest order. Surely – surely! – his mother would see that? So rarely did she refuse him anything that by the time sleep finally did claim him he had all but convinced himself that the only decision to be taken was when they would go. When Richard came to look in on him before going to bed himself the boy lay with arms outflung, long fair lashes curling against the still-childish smooth roundness of his rosy cheeks, a faint smile curving his mouth.

Richard stood for a long time looking down at the sleeping child before very gently brushing the tousled hair from his forehead and bending to kiss him. Davie stirred, muttered, settled. Richard went to the door, stood for a moment longer watching him before quietly leaving the room.

–

'Do I look all right?' Annie asked nervously for at least the dozenth time.

'Darling, you look gorgeous.'

'What time is it?'

Smiling, Jane glanced at her wristwatch. 'Five minutes later than it was when you last asked.'

'Oh – I'm sorry. I knew I shouldn't have got ready so early.' Annie prowled restlessly about the room, stopped to look in the mirror, made an infinitesimal adjustment to her wide-brimmed hat.

'You can sit down, you know,' her mother pointed out.

'I don't like to. I don't want to arrive all creased.'

'Are you planning to stand up in the car?' Jane asked innocently. She checked her own appearance in the mirror, smoothed the neatly coiled bun of her hair, adjusted the fox fur that was draped around her shoulders.

Annie giggled. 'Don't be silly.' She came up behind her mother and their eyes met in the mirror. 'You look awfully nice,' she said sincerely. 'That colour suits you so well.'

'Thank you, darling.' Jane smoothed the flared skirt of her emerald-green suit, smiled reassuringly at her daughter's reflection. 'Soon be over,' she said.

Annie turned and wandered to the window. 'It's all happened so quickly that it seems rather like a dream,' she said slowly. 'I honestly thought that being swept off your feet only happened to dotty heroines in romantic novels. I do hope—' She stopped abruptly. Behind her she heard the chink of glass and she turned to find her mother holding two glasses. Jane grinned and offered her one. 'Just a splash,' she said. 'Dutch courage. You can always suck a peppermint in the car.'

Annie took the glass, tossed back the contents in one swallow and promptly choked. By the time that emergency had been taken care of, the wedding car had arrived and it was time to go.

-

'Gosh, Mother, don't you look swagger!' Davie's eyes were wide with what Annie thought could only be regarded as unflattering surprise.

'Well, don't sound so astonished,' she said in a mildly injured tone, replying to her son but with her eyes on Richard, handsome as she had ever seen him in morning suit and grey top hat, a cream rose that matched her own bouquet in his buttonhole. The sight of him steadied nerves that had threatened to overwhelm her. She smiled a little shakily, looked at the man who stood by his side.

'Annie, darling, you look wonderful.' Richard doffed his hat, bent a little carefully, dodging her hat brim to kiss her, then straightened and turned. 'I'd like you to meet Joshua Foster. He's a very old friend of mine. An art dealer. He's very kindly agreed to be my witness.'

Annie shook hands with the rather patrician-looking Mr Foster. 'How do you do?' She glanced back at Richard enquiringly. Had he not said that his doctor friend was to be his witness? She was certain that he had.

Richard caught her glance, sent her the shadow of a wink and shook his head very slightly. 'Well,' he said, 'seems we're all present and correct.' He grinned at Annie. 'Shall we go and take the plunge?'

The ceremony was short and simple. So quickly did it seem to go that Annie found herself wondering a little bemusedly how such a momentous change could take place in such a short time. In Paris the ceremony had seemed interminable, and even when she married Charles there had been friends and relatives and church blessings and photographs – what had in fact felt like a whole day of to-ing and fro-ing. Now, in what seemed to be the twinkling of an eye she found herself ensconced comfortably in the back of a taxi, Richard's hand in hers, the bright gold ring gleaming on her finger. 'Are we really married?' she asked in not wholly assumed astonishment.

Smiling, he ducked under her hat again and kissed her. 'Indeed we are, Mrs Ross. Were you nervous?'

'Yes.'

'Are you nervous now?'

'No.'

'Good. I'd hate you not to enjoy your lunch. I have to tell you, by the way, that Davie was planning what he was going to eat over the breakfast table. He intends to make the most of it.'

She laughed, turned her head to look at the following taxi that held their guests. 'That reminds me… didn't you say that your doctor friend – what was his name? – was going to be your witness?'

'Draper. Charlie Draper. Yes, he was, but unfortunately a crisis blew up – he has a very classy practice, his patients are of the kind who think that everyone, even an eminent psychiatrist, should be at their beck and call – so he had to pull out. He sends his abject apologies. Thanks for not mentioning it when I introduced Joshua. I didn't want him to think that he was second choice, that's all.'

She snuggled close to him. 'Do you know what?'

'What?'

'You're a *very* nice man.'

'I do my best,' he said modestly.

–

Joshua Foster, his sober and even somewhat supercilious appearance notwithstanding, turned out to be unexpectedly good company. He quickly discovered Davie's artistic ambitions and charmed the boy with a series of wicked – not to say scurrilous – anecdotes about the foibles and pretensions of some of the artists with whom he dealt. He won Jane's heart entirely by waxing lyrical about her much-loved east coast, which he clearly knew well, and wondered aloud, wittily and often, whatever hidden qualities his friend Richard might possess that he had managed to capture such an enchanting bride. The food was excellent, the Champagne cool, crisp and plentiful, the service attentive. More than once Annie found herself wondering if she had not wandered into an especially luxurious and self-indulgent version of Alice's Wonderland.

Davie it was who brought the celebrations to an end. In the middle of the afternoon, having eaten everything that had been put in front of him and partaken of far too much Champagne, he suddenly lost interest in the proceedings, put his head on the table, closed his eyes and was sound asleep in a moment.

'*Davie!*' Annie was mortified.

Joshua Foster laughed and touched the boy's shoulder gently. 'You'll have to develop a better head than that if you mean to be an artist, young feller-me-lad.'

Davie stirred. Briskly Jane poured a glass of water. 'Come on, Davie. Up you get.'

Davie sat up abruptly. 'What's up?'

His grandmother put the glass of water firmly in front of him. 'Drink that, my dear. All of it.'

A hovering waiter smothered a smile, his eyes sympathetic.

'Time for a bit of air, I think,' Jane said. 'Richard, thank you for a quite superb lunch. We really should go.'

'A stroll along the Embankment, perhaps?' Joshua Foster suggested. 'That'll bring the young man to his senses, I should think. I'd be honoured to accompany you, dear lady.'

'But—' Annie was looking anxiously from one to the other.

Her mother patted her hand. 'Don't worry, darling. He's all right.' She smiled at Joshua Foster. 'And thank you, we'd be delighted with your company.' As she stood up, a positive army of waiters sprang to draw back chairs and assist the party to rise, hurrying off for coats and wraps. Within moments Annie found herself in the large, elegant foyer making her farewells.

Davie, chin firm, flung his arms about her. 'Bye, Mother. Have a lovely time.'

She hugged him tightly to her. 'It will only be for a week or so,' she said very softly, and then coloured as she saw from the small affectionate rise of Richard's eyebrow that he had heard her.

'I'll be all right,' Davie said reassuringly, though there was a suspiciously damp look about his dark eyes. 'Nan and I will have a really good time.'

'That we will.' Jane kissed Annie crisply, turned to plant a kiss on Richard's cheek. 'You two have the most lovely honeymoon.' She took Davie's hand. 'Air,' she said firmly.

Joshua Foster bowed over Annie's hand, shook Richard's firmly. 'What an extraordinary woman,' he said appreciatively, mischievously leaving it to his listeners to decide to which woman he was referring.

'I like him,' Annie said as they watched the others through the huge revolving doors that led out onto the Strand.

Richard turned her to face him. 'And I like you,' he said. 'Now – one more bottle of Champagne here? Or a bath and a rest upstairs?' He smiled. 'There's dining and dancing this evening, remember.'

'Richard! I couldn't possibly eat or drink any more today!'

This time his smile was deliberately and lazily suggestive. 'Sounds as if, like Davie, you need some exercise, Mrs Ross? But not on the Embankment, do you think? I'm sure we can think of something more… imaginative?' He took her hand. 'If we want to look at the river,' he added innocently, 'there's a very good view of it from the window of our room.'

–

'Tired?' Richard asked.

Annie smiled sleepily and yawned again, snuggling into the comfortable leather car seat. 'I am a bit, yes.'

'Not surprising.' Richard slowed the car a little, steering it one-handed as he reached into his pocket for his cigarette case. 'We've been going since six this morning and yesterday was a very busy day.'

Annie smiled at him. 'To say nothing of not getting to bed until two o'clock—'

'—and not getting to sleep until a good deal later.'

Annie blushed a little, turned to look out of the window. The flat road stretched ahead of them, the wide Wiltshire plain reaching from horizon to horizon. 'Am I allowed to know where we're going yet?' she asked after a moment. 'Is it much further?'

He laughed. 'You sound like Davie. Yes, of course I'll tell you. We're going to Cornwall. To a little fishing village called Tregeeth, not far from Helston. It's very quiet and very beautiful. Do you know Cornwall at all?'

She shook her head. 'No. I've never been there, though I've always wanted to.'

'Then you've a treat in store. My sister and I used to go every year with our parents. It's a magical place. Cliffs and coves and tiny sandy beaches…'

'I've seen pictures.' Despite her effort not to, she yawned again.

He lit his cigarette, glanced at her, smiling. 'Why don't you try to have a little snooze? We've a long way to go yet.'

–

'There,' Richard said several hours later, rolling the car to a halt on the narrow clifftop road. 'What do you think of it?'

Annie looked down at the tiny harbour beneath them and clapped her hands together in delight. 'Oh, Richard! It's lovely!'

The road dropped steeply away, zigzagging down the cliff to a sheltered little cove in which, along the narrow banks of a tumbling stream, nestled a cluster of white-painted cottages. Several small fishing boats were drawn up on the sandy beach, and nets were spread upon the harbour wall to dry. Through the open car windows Annie could hear the sound of the restless sea as it creamed and curled about the rocks, and surged, foaming, across the flat, golden sand. There was the smell of seaweed in the air. She scrambled out of the car. The soft breeze was warm; the sun, low in the sky behind them, danced on the moving waters. Seabirds wheeled in a sky of cobalt blue. 'It's idyllic,' she said, as Richard climbed a little stiffly from the car to join her. 'Absolutely idyllic. Like a picture postcard.'

Smiling at her enthusiasm, Richard pointed: 'That's where we're going to be staying. See? The long thatched place next to the harbour. It's an inn called the Ship. It isn't the Savoy' – he flashed her a laughing glance – 'but it ought to be fairly comfortable.'

She slid her arm through his. 'I'm sure it's going to be perfectly wonderful,' she said confidently. 'The very place to begin living happily ever after. Wouldn't you say?'

She tilted her head back, shutting her eyes against the glimmer of sun on water.

Her husband kissed her. 'I certainly would,' he agreed.

The landlady of the Ship was a plump, motherly woman called Mary Tregowan, who greeted them as if they were long-lost family. Indeed, since she remembered Richard from his childhood visits, it seemed that they almost qualified as such. 'My father was running the place then,' she informed Annie, in her rich Cornish accent. 'Afore the war it was, of course. And Mr Ross here and his family always used to take Polrun House, up there on the cliffs, for a month in the summer. Isn't that right, Mr Ross?' She puffed her way up the narrow staircase.

'It certainly is. It was the highlight of our lives. My sister Dolly and I used to run completely wild – swimming, fishing, picnicking on the cliffs. For a couple of town children like us, it was absolute bliss.'

'There.' Mrs Tregowan pushed open a door, stood back for them to pass. 'I do hope it'll suit.' She sounded a little anxious. ''Tis all we have that's big enough—'

'It's delightful!' Annie ran to one of the two little dormer windows that peeped out from the thatch. 'Richard – look – what a lovely view! Right across the bay!' She turned and surveyed the room. It was large, clean and very simply furnished; the pillows and bedspread on the huge bed were crisp white cotton, the bunch of bright cabbage roses in a vase on the table matched those that twined across the wallpaper. A large china jug and bowl, also rose-covered, stood upon the washstand.

Mary Tregowan beamed. 'I'll send Tom up with your cases, then, shall I?'

'Yes, please.'

'And I daresay you could do with a jug of warm water, to freshen up with?'

'That would be lovely,' Annie said. 'Thank you.' As the landlady left the room she turned to Richard and threw her arms about him. 'Oh, Richard, this is perfect!'

'You are sure? It isn't too' – he glanced around, grinned a little at the glimpse of a chamber pot under the bed – 'primitive for you?'

'Of course not! I love it.' She took off her hat and tossed it onto the bed. 'Come on, let's get changed and take a walk round the harbour. I want to see everything, absolutely everything.'

–

'Wouldn't Davie just love this?' she asked later as they leaned in the late evening light with their elbows on the harbour wall. A small fishing boat bobbed out on the water, the lights from its lamps dancing on the rippling surface. The waves slapped gently against the wall, and out on the point beyond the harbour the sweeping beam of a lighthouse was beginning to move across the sky. Even though it was not yet fully dark the moon hung in ghostly splendour over the sea.

'We'll bring him,' he said. 'But for now, it's ours. I did so want you to see it.'

She reached out to squeeze his hand.

They had dined simply but well, on fresh-caught fish and home-grown vegetables washed down with cider. The contrast with their meal the evening before had only increased Annie's delight. They pushed themselves away from the wall and, hand in hand, strolled on to the end of the harbour and stood for a moment in silence, breathing in the salt air and watching the bobbing fishing boat.

'We'll walk along the coast tomorrow,' Richard said. 'There's another village just round the point there. And inland there's a famous ring of standing stones above a village called Mallagan. My father used to hire a pony and trap and take us there. Dolly and I would play for hours up there. They always used to have a summer fair – about this time of the year, I suppose it must have been. I'll ask Mrs Tregowan. Now – who's ready for bed?'

She sighed happily, closed her eyes and laid her head on his shoulder. 'I thought you'd never ask,' she said.

'Does the summer fair still visit Mallagan, Mrs Tregowan?' Richard asked the next day as he tucked into the biggest breakfast Annie had ever seen in her life.

Mrs Tregowan placed another heaped plate of toast on the table. 'It surely does. 'Tis on now, as a matter of fact. It'll be up there till at least the end of the month.'

'We'll go later on in the week, if you'd like?' Richard looked at Annie. 'It isn't just a fair – it's a market, too. You'll enjoy it, I think.'

Mrs Tregowan was hovering, eyeing the boiled eggs and toast that Annie had asked for with something close to disapproval. 'Are you certain that's all you want, Mrs Ross?' she asked.

Annie laughed. 'Yes, thank you.' She shook her head a little, glanced again at Richard's plate that was piled so high with ham, eggs, sausages and bacon that it just might, she thought, have defeated even Davie. 'Quite certain.'

'I'll get in a couple of nice crabs for supper if you'd like?'

'That would be lovely.'

Annie was enchanted by the picturesque Cornish coastline with its towering cliffs, its coves and inlets, and small, white-painted cottages. That morning they rambled along the cliffs and around the point, passing the lighthouse, to yet another village further down the coast, where they stopped at the pub for a leisurely lunch of bread and cheese and a pint of beer for Richard before setting off back to Tregeeth. This more or less set the pattern for their days. Mostly they walked, sometimes drove further afield; often they sat on the beach reading, talking, or simply watching the sea and the activity around the tiny harbour. The packed lunches that Mary Tregowan provided would, as Annie pointed out, easily have fed four. 'She thinks you don't eat enough,' Richard teased.

'If we stay much longer I'll finish up as fat as butter!' Annie nibbled on a hard-boiled egg. They were sitting on a rug spread on the sand, their backs against a rock. The sun was high and very hot. Richard, in his shirtsleeves and a casually tilted straw panama, was tucking into a huge Cornish pasty with considerable gusto. Annie, dressed in a pretty, short-skirted sundress and a wide-brimmed straw hat, smiled at him affectionately, shaking her head a little. 'I just don't know where you put it.'

'Hollow legs.' Richard finished the pasty, brushed the crumbs from his fingers and shirt, reached for his cigarette case. 'Oh, damn it!' he said mildly.

'What's the matter?'

He was looking at the open case. 'I'm nearly out of fags. I'd forgotten that. I'll have to drive into Helston. What a drag!'

Annie began to gather up the picnic. 'Don't they sell cigarettes in the local shop?' she asked, surprised.

'They certainly do. Woodbines, Woodbines, Woodbines or Woodbines. Not quite up my street.'

She laughed. 'I'll come with you.'

He shook his head. 'There's really no need. You'd have to pack everything up, change – no, it isn't worth it. We've only got another couple of days, and we're going to Mallagan tomorrow. You don't want to waste time in the car today just because I've got a memory like a sieve.' He stretched his long legs. 'Besides, you're enjoying your book.' He grinned. 'Again,' he added. 'I'm surprised it isn't falling to pieces.'

Annie glanced to where the much-thumbed book lay. 'I've told you before – I'm not sure "enjoy" is quite the word to use about *Passage*, but at least I think I'm beginning to get to grips with it.'

He leaned forward, kissed her slightly sunburned nose. 'And his views on marriage?' he asked lightly.

'Are interesting,' she said primly.

He scrambled to his feet, picked up his jacket, swung it across one shoulder. 'I won't be long.'

She watched his tall figure striding across the sand towards the harbour road. When he reached it he turned and waved. She lifted a hand. Once he had gone she picked up her book. 'Interesting, but wrong, Mr Forster,' she said aloud, very firmly.

–

'Do me a favour?' Richard asked the following morning, watching her from the bed as she stood at the washstand.

Annie turned, towel in hand. 'Mm?'

'Wear your red dress today? It suits you so well.' He smiled. 'Your skin has gone the colour of honey.'

She laughed. 'I was going to wear the blue—'

'I prefer the red.'

'Very well.' She crossed to the wardrobe, dropping a kiss on the top of his head on the way. 'The red it must be, I suppose. Tell me – are you ever going to get up? Or are you planning to spend the day in bed?' It was another in a string of lovely mornings, the air was fresh and saltily tangy, the sun streamed through the window, the seabirds cried above the sound of the waves.

Richard leapt, naked, from the bed and caught her about the waist, sweeping her into a spinning waltz. She could feel the warmth of his hands through the silk of her dressing gown. She squealed with laughter. 'Richard! Put me down.'

'No,' he said, 'not until you've given me a kiss. Two.'

They were late for breakfast.

'Goin' to the fair, then?' Mrs Tregowan asked, eyes twinkling as she observed the faint, becoming flush of colour in Annie's cheeks. 'Saturday's a good day. There'll be plenty goin' on.'

'Yes, we are. And then we thought we might go on up to the north coast.'

'Aye. It's quite nice up there, so they say.' Mary Tregowan's tone was disinterested to the point of dismissiveness. 'Though I wouldn't bother myself.'

'Do you honestly think that she's never been to the north side of the county?' Annie asked later as they drove away.

Richard grinned. 'She's probably never been any further than Helston,' he said.

They arrived at Mallagan late in the morning, when the market was in full swing. They strolled along the rows of stalls selling everything from bolts of cloth and kitchenware to vegetables and fresh-caught fish, to where the animals were penned: calves and piglets and lean moorland sheep. The fairground beyond was only just stirring, though a few children and young people were riding the horses on a giant roundabout whose cheerful barrel-organ music boomed above the chatter of the hawkers and their customers. Gaily coloured swing-boats, worked by tasselled ropes, stood in a row. 'Take the little lady for a ride, sir?' The man wore a flat cap and a bright bandanna; his smile was wide and very white. 'Only a penny a go.'

'Fancy it?' Richard asked.

'Why not?'

They scrambled up the steps and settled themselves in the gondola seats. The man set them off with a push, Richard hauled on the rope and the swing-boat went higher and higher, above the heads of the crowds. 'If Davie could see us now!' Annie called, laughing, holding onto her hat.

Richard grinned. 'Why should children have all the fun?'

They wandered the fairground hand in hand. Richard tried his skill at the coconut shy with no luck at all; Annie kissed him and told him she didn't like coconuts anyway. They rode the bounding horses of the brightly painted roundabout, Annie seated decorously side-saddle; they rolled ha'pennies and won a celluloid doll in a stiff net skirt – which Richard presented to a wide-eyed little girl whose face lit up as if Christmas had come; they ate sticky, too-sweet candyfloss and had to lick their fingers clean like a couple of children.

'Uh-oh,' Richard said, pointing. 'Look what I spy!'

Annie turned. Laughed. 'A fortune teller!' she said. 'Gypsy Valentino, no less!'

'Want to visit him?' Richard asked.

'Of course! Coming?'

He shook his head. 'I can't keep a straight face. I put the bad ones off and if I ever come across a real one he'll probably put a hex on me. You go ahead. I'll see you over there by the rifle range. I'll bet you didn't know I had secret yearnings to be the next Buffalo Bill, did you?'

He watched her as she slipped into the darkness of the gypsy's booth, her red dress bright in the shadows, then strolled over to the rifle range.

Ten minutes later, a small felt doll attached to a safety pin in his hand, he turned to find her standing silent beside him. 'Hello, I didn't hear you arrive. Look what I've won for you—' He stopped. 'Annie? Is something wrong?'

'No,' she said quickly. 'No, of course not.' She took the little brooch, bent her head to pin it to her dress.

He took it back, frowning, fastened it for her. 'You're shaking,' he said.

'It was chilly in the tent. I'm quite all right. Please don't fuss.'

He eyed her but said nothing. She turned away. 'I'd like to walk up to the standing stones, please,' she said.

The stones stood on a rocky outcrop above the village. They climbed the steep and narrow path in silence, the sounds of the funfair dying behind them. Annie leaned against one of the ancient dolmen, her eyes on the distant sparkle of the sea.

'Annie, what's wrong?' Richard asked quietly.

She shook her head. 'Nothing, honestly. I think I may have had a bit too much sun, that's all. I have quite a bad headache.'

He put a concerned arm about her shoulders and drew her to him. 'Do you want to go on to the north coast? Or would you rather go back?'

She lifted her head; her eyes were shadowed. 'Could we? Go back, I mean? Would you mind?'

'Of course not. We'll go back to the Ship – I'll get some aspirin in the shop – and you can have a quiet lie-down. How does that sound?'

She smiled wanly. 'If you really don't mind—?'

He took her hand. 'I really don't mind,' he said gently. 'Come on, we can be there in an hour and you'll be right as rain in no time.'

She hardly spoke during the ride to Tregeeth, but lay with her head thrown back on the seat, her eyes closed. Back at the inn, she took the aspirin that Richard had bought and allowed him to lead her up the stairs to the bedroom, where he drew the curtains. The room was cool and shady. She kicked off her shoes and lay down on the bed, one arm thrown up to shield her eyes.

'Do you want to get into bed?' Richard asked.

She shook her head, smiling a little. 'No, I'm quite happy like this. Once the tablet works and the headache goes I'll be much better. Why don't you go for a walk? There's no need for you to sit around with me.'

'You're sure?'

'Of course.'

'Perhaps I'll take a stroll around the harbour then.' He stopped at the door. 'I'll see you later,' he said, a little uncertainly.

She did not open her eyes. 'Yes.'

Annie heard the door close behind him, and his light, receding footsteps. The nagging headache that she did indeed have was fading a little. For a long time she lay very still in the warm, sea-washed quiet, eyelids drooping. The curtains moved in the gentle breeze from the water, that also stirred her hair against her cheek…

Milky eyes and nibbled flesh. Gaping mouths and thin, decaying fingers, reaching – reaching…

Davie? Davie, where are you?

The cold and pitiless water, lapping and shifting; filling lungs and ears and eyes; deep, deep water, endless, bottomless, no light, no warmth, no hand or toehold – clutch at your loved one – you cannot save him – you cannot save yourself—

Davie!

'Annie – for Christ's sake! What the *hell* are you doing?'

208

She jumped awake, found she was standing at the top of the narrow stairs, Richard's horrified face on a level with her own. He stood a step or so below her, holding her arms in a painful grip. Confused, she swayed, and his hands tightened further.

'Christ Almighty – if I hadn't come back—' He stopped, his mouth tight.

Annie pulled away from him, turned and walked back into the bedroom, sat on the bed and dropped her face into her hands, sobbing. She could still see those faces, there behind her eyelids, still feel – physically feel – the chill, dead weight of the water, the sucking and the cold suffocation…

'Annie!' Richard was speaking urgently. He took her wrists in his hands and, none too gently, forcibly pulled her hands from her face. '*Will* you tell me what the hell's going on?'

She sat for a moment, fighting for control. 'I'm sorry,' she whispered at last.

'What happened? What's the matter? Annie, you were right at the top of the stairs – you could have fallen… You could have—' He stopped.

'I'm sorry,' she repeated. 'It was the dream. The drowning dream. I had to find Davie—' The tears came again and she bowed her head.

He sat beside her on the bed, drew her head onto his shoulder, his movements gentle now. 'But, darling, why? Why should the dream come back now? You're not unhappy, are you?'

She did not speak for a moment, then, 'It was the gypsy,' she said, her voice muffled.

'*What?*'

'The gypsy,' she repeated, pulling a little away from him and sniffing. 'He said—' She could not go on.

Richard took both her hands in his. 'Darling, look at me,' he said. 'You aren't telling me that you really believe in that nonsense, are you? God Almighty, if I'd thought that I'd never have let you—'

She was shaking her head. 'You weren't there,' she told him.

'So tell me. What was it he said?'

Annie drew a deep breath. 'At first it was just the usual stuff. He had a crystal ball that sparkled and lit like a rainbow when he touched it. He said I had recently found happiness—'

'He saw your bright new wedding ring, no doubt,' Richard interrupted dryly.

Annie shrugged. 'Perhaps. He said I had an… an aura of gentleness—'

'Well, of course you have. It doesn't take a bloody charlatan fortune teller to see that.'

'Richard – please—'

He shook his head. 'Sorry. Go on.'

'Then suddenly the globe went… milky. Dark.' She shivered. 'He looked at it for what seemed ages without speaking. Then he lifted his head and looked at me. He didn't smile, as he had before; his eyes seemed to go right through me. When he spoke, his voice had changed, too—'

'Changed?'

'It was deeper. Sort of… echoing.' She stopped, swallowed.

'What did he say?'

'He said, "You do well to fear the treacherous waters. Not for others, but for yourself."' Her voice shook as she spoke. 'Then he said something about the happiness and the gentleness being treasures, treasures to be preserved, or looked after' – she made a rapid gesture with her hand – 'something like that. He said they were not to be squandered amongst the damned souls of the drowned.' Her voice had fallen to a whisper. 'Richard – how did he know?' she asked.

'Oh, this is bloody ridiculous,' Richard snapped. 'I'll break the bastard's bloody neck. How *dare* he turn a party trick into such dangerous drivel?'

'But – *how did he know?*'

'He *didn't*, you silly thing. He guessed. It was a coincidence. Oh, for God's sake – do you think you're the only one who's afraid of drowning? It's not hard to play on it, is it? He could just as easily have picked on fire, or illness. We all have our ogres. We all have our fears.' He drew her close to him again. 'I'm sorry. I don't mean to shout. I honestly didn't realise just how deep this thing went. No more fortune tellers. And I think we'd better forget Charlie Draper as well. Lord only knows what could happen if he stirs things up, as he's bound to do. Sleepwalking is dangerous. You could have broken your neck. What on earth does it matter if you hate boats? It isn't the end of the world, after all—'

'No,' she said firmly, straightening her back.

He looked at her questioningly.

She lifted her chin. 'You're right. This is absurd. And it's gone on for too long. I'm a grown woman, not a silly frightened child. I will go and see your Mr Draper. I want to, I want him to help me. I won't let this ridiculous thing dominate me—'

'But—'

'Please, Richard. I've made up my mind. As I say, I'm not a child. And if he can help me, at least I want him to try.'

He looked at her for a very long moment, then sighed. 'If that's what you want then I can't stop you, of course. But I must say I've changed my mind. I don't think it will help, and it might do a great deal of harm. I wish I'd never bloody suggested it!'

'I don't care,' she said, and her voice was stubborn. 'You can surely see – I've got to try.'

He gathered her to him. 'If you say so, my darling,' he said softly. 'If you say so.'

Chapter Fourteen

'Mother!' Davie threw open the door of the car and flung his arms about his mother as she stepped onto the pavement. 'I was watching for you. Have you had a lovely time? We have. We've been on the river, and had tea at the Ritz, and we went to the zoo—' He caught her hand, danced ahead of her up the path to the open front door. 'Hello, Richard!' He waved back to the smiling Richard who had climbed a little stiffly from the driving seat and was unstrapping the luggage from the carrier on the back of the car. 'We went to the museum and saw the mummies – *gruesome!* – and I rowed Nan on the Serpentine—' He stopped just short of the door, still holding her hand, and the tumble of words quieted. 'Now you're to close your eyes,' he announced, his eyes bright with expectation.

Annie looked at him, startled and more than a little suspicious. 'What? Why?'

He almost jumped in impatience. 'You'll see. In a minute. Just close your eyes. That's right. Now, mind the step – no peeping – Nan!' He raised his voice. 'They're here!'

Annie allowed herself to be led into the hall. Somewhere close by she heard her mother's laughter.

'There,' Davie said. 'You can open them now.'

Annie opened her eyes and looked around a little warily. Nothing, so far as she could tell, had changed.

'What—?' she began, then stopped as her mother stepped into the hall from the sitting room. She stared. 'Mother!'

Davie giggled delightedly. 'Doesn't she look just swagger?'

Jane cocked her head a little and the short, fashionably cut bob of her hair swung about her face. 'Do you like it?'

'It's lovely! Absolutely lovely! It makes you look ten years younger!'

'That's what Uncle Joshua said,' Davie put in.

'Uncle Joshua?' Annie's eyes went from one to the other.

'You know, Richard's friend. The one who was at the wedding. He came to the museum with us. And took us to tea at the Ritz. That was when he suggested that Nan should have her hair cut.'

'He did not!' Jane said, mildly acerbic.

'Well, sort of, anyway.' Davie was unapologetic.

Annie raised amused and mildly questioning brows and looked back at her mother. A very faint colour had risen in Jane's cheeks.

'He came on the Serpentine with us, too. He said I was a *very* good rower. Didn't he, Nan? Up for a Blue, he said.'

'Indeed he did.' Jane's voice was just a little too composed. Her daughter's smile widened delightedly. 'Would you like a cup of tea?'

'Well, I'll be…' Richard had come into the hall, carrying the cases. His eyes on Jane, he put them down and straightened. 'Jane! What have you done to yourself?'

'I hardly did it myself, Richard. In fact I paid quite a handsome sum to have someone else do it. Don't you like it?'

'It's fantastic. It makes you look—'

'—ten years younger,' Jane finished for him, a little tartly. 'So everyone says. No one, however, has mentioned how old they thought I looked before.'

'Apparently it was Joshua's idea,' Annie said, straight-faced, her eyes dancing as she glanced at her husband.

'Joshua's—?' Richard stopped and his grin suddenly matched hers.

'I don't quite see what you both think is so funny?' Jane enquired repressively, her small chin lifting.

Annie took off her hat, flung her arms about her mother and kissed her soundly.

'We had a telephone call,' Davie said proudly. 'Nan answered it.'

'Gosh. That was even braver than having your hair cut.' Annie had forgotten about the new telephone. 'Where is it?'

'In the sitting room. On the sofa table. You can't miss it. It stands out like a sore thumb. A gentleman called Charles Draper rang—'

Richard, who had been about to haul the big leather case up the stairs, stopped and turned. 'Charlie? What did he want?'

'He said he had the tickets that he'd spoken to you about. He said he'd ring back in a day or so.'

'Thanks.' He bent back to the suitcase.

Annie shook her head. 'Leave that for a minute, darling. Come and have a cup of tea. You've been driving for hours.'

'Lucky things,' said Davie.

They sat around the kitchen table exchanging news. Glancing surreptitiously at Richard, Annie was sure that she was not the only one to note how many times Joshua Foster's name came into the conversation.

'It doesn't sound as if you've missed us at all,' she smiled at last, putting down her teacup.

'Don't be silly.' Jane reached for it, filled it again. 'Another, Richard?'

'Please.'

Jane poured the tea, handed it across the table to him. 'I gather the tickets your friend rang about are for Covent Garden?'

Richard, who had for the moment been lost in thought, nodded a little absently. '*Bohème*, I believe.'

'How lovely. It's one of your favourites, isn't it, dear?' Jane asked her daughter, laughing a little. 'The first time I took her to see it, as I remember, she cried almost all the way through it,' she confided to Richard. 'I must say your friend sounded very nice.'

'He was the one who was supposed to come to the wedding,' Annie said, stirring her tea. 'The psychiatrist.' She smiled mischievously. 'I must say that it sounds to me as if you might think it a stroke of luck that he couldn't get there.'

Once again a faint, unusual but unmistakeable blush of colour tinged Jane's cheeks.

Davie was dipping his ginger nut into his tea. Sidetracked, he glanced up at Richard. 'Is he the one who's going to cure Mother so that we can go to—?' he asked unthinkingly, then stopped suddenly, biting his lip. The sodden ginger nut broke and dropped into the cup; he ducked his head and began fishing for it with his teaspoon.

'Oh, for goodness' sake, child! Here – give it to me – I'll pour you a fresh one.' Jane reached for his cup.

'So that we can go to where?' Annie asked quietly, her eyes not on Davie but on Richard.

'Nowhere,' Davie said, hastily and obviously untruthfully.

Annie raised her eyebrows and looked from her son to her husband, unspeaking.

'It was just... a conversation that Davie and I had,' Richard said carefully. Davie did not look at him.

'A conversation. About what?' Annie looked at her son. 'Well?'

'About going to Paris,' he mumbled. 'In the car.'

She stared at him. '*Paris?* In the *car*? Don't be silly, Davie. You can't drive to Paris in a car from here.'

The boy's face lit up. 'You can! You *can*! Richard's done it, haven't you, Richard? He told me about it. They put the car in a great big crate and use cranes to stow it in the hold, and then they land it on the other side and' – he tried out a tentative smile on Richard – 'and Bob's your uncle,' he finished. 'Oh, please, Mother. It would be such fun. It would be like Major Forbes-Leith—'

'Oh, heavens, spare me that,' Jane said dryly, putting his fresh cup in front of him.

Annie was looking thoughtfully at Richard, who had the grace to look slightly abashed. 'I'm sorry, darling,' he said. 'I did point out to Davie that your' – he hesitated – 'your problem made it highly unlikely that you'd agree—'

'But you said your friend could make it better,' Davie said stubbornly. The subject now broached, he was not going to give up so easily.

Richard shook his head. 'I said he *might* be able to,' he corrected the child. 'And,' his eyes were serious on Annie's face, 'you know – I'm not sure that I'm not having second thoughts.'

Annie did not speak for a moment but sat stirring her tea, watching the liquid swirl in the rose-patterned cup.

Then she lifted her eyes to Richard's. 'Well, I'm not,' she said firmly. 'What harm can it do? You've said many times that Charles is a popular and respected practitioner. He may be able to help. I'll never know if I don't try.'

Davie was looking from one to the other with bated breath.

'But – after what happened the other day—'

Jane frowned a little, looked at her daughter enquiringly.

Annie flushed and shook her head. 'That was just stupid. I see it now.'

'What happened the other day?' Jane asked.

Annie's colour deepened further. 'I went to a fortune teller,' she admitted sheepishly. 'He... frightened me. That's all.'

Practical Jane's eyebrows almost shot up to her hairline. 'Oh, Annie!' The expressive words were a mixture of exasperation and disbelief.

'I know, I know. That's what I'm saying; the whole thing is absurd. And I'm going to do something about it.' Easy to say, here in the warm, sunlit kitchen, the floor firm beneath her feet... She stood up briskly, carried her cup to the sink.

'So – can we go to Paris?' Davie asked, cautiously but with the ferocious single-mindedness of childhood.

'We'll see.'

'But you see, Richard has to book the passage for the car – and get passports and tickets and things—' Davie jumped as his mother swung round on him with her finger raised in warning.

'Enough,' she said.

Davie subsided. 'Yes, Mother. Sorry,' he said. But his eyes were still brightly eager.

His grandmother stood up. 'Come along, young man. Leave your mother and Richard alone to get unpacked. Some help with the washing-up would be greatly appreciated.'

--

When the telephone that stood like an oddly shaped candlestick on the sofa table in the sitting room rang a couple of days later, Annie was alone in the house. As it happened she was actually sitting on the sofa when it rang; the suddenness of it made her all but jump from her skin.

She stared at the instrument in alarm, much as she might at a snapping dog.

It rang again, imperiously.

At last, very gingerly, she unhooked the receiver, surveyed it for a moment before putting it to her ear. 'Hello?' The word came out as a whisper. She cleared her throat. 'Hello?' she said again, this time much too loudly.

'Mrs Ross? Mrs Richard Ross?' The pleasant voice was deep and rich, almost melodic.

'Yes.'

'Charles Draper here. I'm a friend of your husband's—'

'Oh, yes. He's told me about you. Did you want to speak to him? I'm afraid he isn't here. But you'll probably find him at the office. If you can get past the fearful Miss Brownel, that is.' Ridiculously nervous as she was, she was quite proud of the small joke.

The man laughed. 'No, no. I'm just as happy to speak to you.' His chuckle, like his voice, was infectiously warm and attractive. 'He's spoken to you about the tickets for Covent Garden?'

'Yes. I'm looking forward to it. My mother said they were for *La Bohème*? It happens to be one of my favourites.'

'Good, good. They are for next Thursday. I do hope that's convenient?'

'Yes, I'm sure that will be all right. My mother's staying until the weekend, so we can be free any evening.'

'I thought perhaps dinner after the performance? Shall I arrange it?'

'That would be very nice. Thank you.'

'My wife and I are both very much looking forward to meeting you.'

'And I you.'

It was more than the niceties of good manners. If the owner of the voice was even half as charmingly likeable as he sounded, it should, Annie reflected, be a thoroughly enjoyable and entertaining evening. She clicked the earpiece back into place with a faint feeling of pride at having won her first skirmish with the telephone, and also with a small sigh of contentment. Not for the first time she found herself astounded at the change in her life which had been wrought since her first meeting with Richard. A bare few months ago she had been contemplating with no great enthusiasm the prospect of a dull, respectable existence within an even more dull, respectable marriage. Now she had Richard, charming, unconventional Richard, who loved her, and the future positively glowed with enchantment and promise.

Annie stood, danced a few steps about the sunlit room, humming to herself softly, stopped in front of the mirror above the mantelpiece, smiling at her reflection. As she stood there she remembered those last, nervous moments in this room on the day she had married, and the thought brought her mother to mind. The smile widened. She had the strongest feeling that hers was not the only life which had changed direction after that fateful meeting in the Marianne North Gallery. In the last couple of days the urbane and articulate Joshua Foster had visited the house twice; Jane was at this very moment attending an art auction at Sotheby's with him. 'Purely out of interest,' she had asserted, in answer to her daughter's sly enquiries. 'I've never been to one before. You know my philosophy: try anything once. You'll never know what you like unless you try it.' And that, Annie thought now, explained why Jane had taken the entire morning to get ready and borrowed Annie's prettiest earrings to set off the haircut!

Laughing, she went out to the kitchen to prepare for the return of her hungry – or as he would undoubtedly put it, 'starving' – son from school.

-

'Are you enjoying it, my dear?' Charles Draper handed her a slender glass full of bubbling Champagne and spoke above the babble of voices around them.

'Very much.' Annie laughed a little self-consciously and dabbed at her eye with a gloved finger. 'But I'm afraid you'll have to forgive me: I shall be in floods of tears by the end. I always am. I only have to hear the music on the wireless and it makes me cry.'

Katrina Draper drew on the cigarette she had fitted into a long ebony holder and cocked a thin, supercilious eyebrow. 'Personally I find it all just a little hard to take,' she said. 'Isn't consumption supposed to make you thin? Our little seamstress is a little – shall we say – too substantial for the part, don't you think? And as for all this love-at-first-sight nonsense...' She shrugged and let the sentence trail off.

Disappointingly Annie, who had taken to Charles Draper as immediately as she had thought she might, had just as quickly taken a dislike to his wife. Katrina Draper was tall, fashionably and elegantly slim, undoubtedly beautiful and, Annie thought, infuriatingly patronising.

Charles sent a cool look towards his wife, not the first that Annie had observed. She looked at Katrina curiously. 'Don't you believe in it? Love at first sight, I mean? Or at least something like it?' she asked.

Katrina shrugged slim shoulders and shook her auburn head. 'Of course not.'

Annie smiled at Richard. His eyes gleamed, suddenly bright and warm as he looked at her. 'I do,' she said firmly.

Katrina sighed ostentatiously.

The crowd around them was beginning to thin. Richard glanced at his watch. 'The last act begins in five minutes,' he said. 'Drink up.' He smiled at Annie in mischievous affection, produced from his pocket a large, pristine white handkerchief. 'I think you're very probably going to need this!'

She did. As later they shuffled out onto the pavement with the glittering, chattering crowds, she was still surreptitiously mopping at her eyes. Richard, his arm about her shoulders, laughed and pulled her to him, dropping a quick kiss on her hair. 'Chump,' he said gently. 'You're supposed to enjoy it, you know.'

'I did!' She was indignant. 'I loved it!' And then, sniffing, she joined in his laughter.

He was peering over the heads of the crowd. 'Over there, look! Charlie's managed to bag a cab.'

The restaurant, like the streets around it, was crowded with theatre- and opera-goers in evening dress. Jewels sparkled in the light of the chandeliers, rings glittered on slim, gloved fingers, animated conversation rose and fell around them. Yet despite the noise Annie's head was still ringing with Puccini's glorious music and with the sound of the voices that had so beautifully performed it.

'You're very quiet, my dear?' Charles was smiling at her. He was a square-built, handsome man with dark curling hair and the brightest of blue eyes. There was a calm and benevolent warmth about him that was almost mesmerising.

She shook her head, laughing a little. 'I'm afraid I'm still listening to Rudolfo.'

He put his head on one side, watching her intently. 'You can still hear him?'

She nodded. 'As if he were standing on that stage singing.' She nodded towards the low platform where a small string ensemble was preparing to play.

'That's interesting.'

She cocked her head enquiringly. 'It is?'

He smiled.

'What are you two whispering about?' Katrina asked, her eyes sharp.

'We are discussing sensitivity, my dear,' Charles said dryly. 'Not a subject that I think would greatly interest you.'

'Were we?' Annie asked, surprised.

'Indeed we were.'

Katrina was completely unabashed. 'If it's insensitive to like my stories to bear at least a little resemblance to reality, the characters to look at least a little as if they're starving in a garret or dying of consumption – if that's what they're supposed to be doing – and to find it difficult to believe that the awful Mimi, having trailed around Paris like a pathetic puppy behind a man who's deserted her, can sing her heart out flat on her back on her deathbed, then yes, you're very probably right,' she agreed blandly, fitting a fresh cigarette into the ebony holder.

Despite themselves, that brought them all to laughter. Pleased, Katrina leaned forward, smiling, for Richard to light her cigarette. 'You have to admit that Musetta's the only halfway decent character in the whole thing.' She sat back, gently blew out a stream of smoke. 'At least she knows what she wants and how to get it. You wouldn't find *her* dying of consumption in a Paris attic, I know.'

Charles obviously decided it was time to change the subject. He looked across the table at Richard. 'How *is* Paris?' he asked.

'Still pretty wonderful the last time I saw her.' Richard, who had picked up the menu to study it, glanced up smiling. 'And my own particular garret is' – he gestured with his hand and his wedding ring gleamed – 'marginally more comfortable than the one we just watched poor Mimi die in.'

Katrina leaned forward, her elbow on the table, her delicate chin resting upon curled knuckles. Her long black gloves made the skin of her upper arms and shoulders look almost translucently pale. 'Somehow,' she said thoughtfully, 'I can't see you living in a garret.' The words were soft, the tone suddenly and unmistakeably coquettish.

Her husband sent her a look like daggers. 'He doesn't,' he said shortly. 'As you say, that's hardly Richard's style. Now – shall we order? I do highly recommend the smoked salmon – they have it sent down from Scotland daily, you know. Splendid stuff. Quite the best I've tasted in London.'

–

The taxi eased into the stream of traffic that crawled along the Victoria Embankment; lights gleamed upon the dark waters of the river. Annie, snuggled against Richard, her head on his shoulder, sighed happily. 'Wasn't the opera lovely?'

'It certainly was.'

'The music of *Bohème* always has to stand entirely on its own, doesn't it? I mean – there are no fancy costumes or spectacular backgrounds like most operas have. It may be set in Paris but there isn't much sign of that really, is there?'

He shook his head.

She was quiet for a moment. 'Richard?'

'Hmm?' His hand lifted to her hair, stroking it gently.

'What *is* your Paris apartment like?'

He thought for a moment, then laughed a little. 'Much like the Hampstead one, I suppose.'

'Except it has shutters?' she asked after a moment.

'Yes.'

'Long ones?'

'Yes.'

She turned her head to look up into his face. 'And a balcony?'

She saw him smile in the flickering light. 'Yes. And a balcony.'

'With geraniums?'

'Yes. With geraniums. The only thing Madame Colbert does unstintingly and without complaining is water the geraniums. How did you know?'

'I just guessed.' She snuggled her head back onto his shoulder, closed her eyes. 'And Madame Colbert is your concierge,' she added after a moment. 'Is she as much a dragon as Miss Brownel? They usually are, as I remember.'

He laughed. 'She's worse. As you say, blood kin to Miss Brownel – but twice her age and harbouring three times as much malice. Rumour has it she eats small children for breakfast.'

Eyes still shut, Annie smiled reminiscently. 'Paris concierges!' she murmured. 'We had one just like that.'

His arm tightened around her, and they fell to silence for a moment. It was Richard who broke it. 'What did you think of Charles?' he asked quietly.

She stirred, opened her eyes. 'I liked him,' she said slowly. 'I really did. But—' She stopped.

'Yes, I'm sorry. Katrina is a bit difficult to take, isn't she? I should have warned you.'

Annie yawned. 'I must admit I didn't like her very much,' she said. 'And she did have an awful lot to drink. Does she always flirt like that?'

He laughed a little. 'I wouldn't exactly call it flirting.'

'I would. She couldn't keep her eyes off you.' There was amusement rather than rancour in the words.

He grinned.

'Anyway – I don't have to like her, it's Charles that I'll be seeing.' She shifted her head again to look up at him. 'I got the distinct feeling that he was – well – watching me. Not nastily, but… attentively.'

'You don't miss much, do you? You're right. He was.' Richard hesitated. 'Apparently there are certain types of people who are more likely to benefit from treatment by hypnosis than others. He was explaining it to me. He was very interested to hear that you occasionally sleepwalk. And had guessed that *Bohème* would make you cry.' He fell silent.

'Go on,' she said, interested.

He said nothing for a moment.

'Richard? Go on – what did he think, having met me?'

'He said… we had a word, while you and Katrina were in the powder room. He thinks you're an all but perfect subject. He—he really thinks he can help you. But – Annie – seriously, I'm still not sure—'

'Good!' She interrupted him, snuggled her head onto his shoulder, closing her eyes. 'Good. Maybe we will get to Paris after all.'

Richard turned his head away to look out of the window. He said nothing. His face was sombre in the darkness.

–

'Liverpool Street Station, love?' The taxi driver picked up Jane's case, dropped it, picked it up again.

'Yes, please.' Jane winced and looked after the man's retreating back in some irritation. 'That's bad news.'

'What is?' Annie handed her mother her gloves.

'He called me "love". That probably means he'll want to chat all the way to Liverpool Street. It's a sure sign.' Jane kissed her daughter's cheek warmly. 'Now – you will let me know how it goes, won't you? Tell you what – I'll telephone you. From the pay telephone in the post office. On Tuesday afternoon. You can tell me all about it. I must say this telephone business could turn into quite good fun.'

'You'd better take the Hampstead number too, then. I'm not altogether sure where we'll be.' Annie laughed a little. 'Having two homes is all very well, but it can get a bit confusing. Hold on a minute, I'll get it for you.' She disappeared into the sitting room, came back with a slip of paper. 'There.'

Jane took the paper and tucked it into her handbag. 'Will Richard be going with you?'

Annie shook her head. 'No. Charles wants to see me alone. He says that having someone else there would be distracting.'

Jane hesitated for a moment, a faint crease furrowing her brow. 'Annie, darling… I haven't said this before – but are you absolutely sure about this? You do hear of such charlatans. To be honest I can't deny that I'm… a little uneasy about it.'

'I'm absolutely sure.' The words were firm. 'I've quite made up my mind. You of all people know how much Davie wants to make this wretched trip. He's talked of hardly anything else since he let it slip the other day. And I know it isn't fair for me to hold him back. It's never been fair that I haven't been able to take him back to the city where he was born. Up until now he's been as good as gold about it. But since he's met Richard, and talked about it, things have changed. You mustn't worry, Mother. I'm sure everything will be perfectly all right. Neither Richard nor Charles would do anything that would harm me. I've met Charles; you haven't. I trust him implicitly.'

Jane sighed, put a sympathetic hand on her arm. 'And – if it doesn't work?' she asked. 'From what I gather there's no guarantee that it will. What then? Would you let them go without you?'

Annie hesitated. 'I don't know. I hope it won't come to that. But' – she pulled a small, wry face – 'but yes, I think I would. You know Davie. Once he gets his teeth into something he rarely lets go. And yes, I know, it's I who have spoiled him. I just don't think I'd be able to bring myself to disappoint him so.'

'Jane—' She looked up. Richard was standing above them on the stairs. Smiling, he ran quickly down to her side and hugged her. 'Goodbye. Have a good trip. Come back soon.'

Jane beamed. 'I will.'

'I'll bring them down to see you soon, I promise.' He smiled slyly. 'Perhaps Joshua would care for a spin to the country?'

Jane pulled on her gloves, avoiding their eyes. 'Actually, he's already suggested it.'

Annie kept a straight face. 'You mean that he might like to come with us to see you?' she asked innocently.

Her mother pulled a decidedly impolite and unmotherly face at her. 'You know very well that isn't what I mean,' she said. 'I'm sure he'd be delighted to come with you if you invite him. But he's coming next weekend anyway. He fancies a weekend away from the city.'

Richard laughed delightedly. 'He fancies a weekend with you, you mean, Mother-in-law,' he said.

'Richard, please!' Jane was pained. 'Don't call me that. It smacks of bad music-hall jokes.'

'Anything less like a music-hall joke than you I can't imagine.' Richard kissed her. 'Off you go, the meter's ticking. We'll see you soon.'

They watched her down the path, waved off the taxi, closed the door.

Annie turned to go into the kitchen.

Richard put out a detaining hand. 'And just where do you think you're going, Mrs Ross?'

'I was going to start supper.'

He shook his head. 'Davie isn't due home until four. You've plenty of time to start supper.' Gently he drew her towards the stairs. 'It just so happens that I've got a much more imaginative idea...'

Chapter Fifteen

'I'm sorry to disappoint you, Mother, but I truly can't tell
you anything because I hardly remember a thing about
it. Charles did warn me about that. All I know is that he
seems very pleased with me, that he was rather more than
cautiously optimistic and that I have an appointment to
see him again in three days' time.'

'You don't remember anything at all?' Jane's voice was
surprised. 'Not even, well, what his office looked like, or
anything like that?'

Annie laughed, cradling the receiver in one hand as
she picked up her teacup with the other. 'Well, of course
I can remember what his office looked like, silly! I mean
I don't recall anything that happened during the session.
Charles says I'm an excellent subject – suggestible, I think
he called it – and he's fairly sure he can do the trick in
two or three sessions. You wait – we'll be on that steamer
to come and see you in no time. Won't Davie love that?'

'And you don't feel any after-effects?' Jane asked curiously. 'Not even faintly?'

'Not even faintly. Far from it, I feel perfectly well. I *feel*
as if I'm going to beat it. Charles says that's half the battle.'

'Yes, I suppose so.' Jane still sounded doubtful.

'Don't *worry*, Mother. Charles isn't some kind of witch
doctor, I promise you. Look – sorry – I have to go. Davie's
got a concert at school later this afternoon and if I don't

get there early I'll finish up sitting right at the back and missing his two minutes of glory. I'm seeing Charles again on Friday, in the morning. You can ring again in the afternoon, if you like, but I doubt there'll be anything else to report. Anyway – must go, darling—'

'Give my love to Davie. Tell him to break a leg.'

'I will. Bye.' Annie put the phone down, took the cup into the kitchen and then, humming, went to fetch her coat and hat.

–

'Did you think I was good?' Davie skittered a stone off the pavement and into the gutter with his foot as they walked.

'I thought you were stunning. Don't do that, dear.'

Davie, who had taken aim at another pebble, thought better of it and skipped into step beside her. 'Better than Thompson?'

She smiled down at him. 'Much, much better than Thompson.'

'It's a smashing poem, isn't it?' Davie, his cap set at a rakish angle on the back of his head, swung round a tree, his satchel flying. Still full of the adrenalin of public performance, he struck a declamatory pose. '*If you can keep your head when all about you Are losing theirs and blaming it on you, If you can trust yourself when all men doubt you But make allowance for their doubting too*—'

Annie, who felt as if she had heard the wretched piece at least a thousand times in the past few days, and who could have recited the thing herself standing on her head, winced. 'I don't think we need to hear it again, dear,' she said.

Davie took another turn about the tree, ran to catch up with her. 'It's a shame that Richard couldn't have come.

231

Perhaps I'll recite it for him tonight, when he comes home. It's his sort of poem, isn't it? *If you can meet with Triumph and Disaster, And treat those two impostors just the same—'*

'*Davie!* Do calm down! You were very good. I enjoyed it. But I don't think the whole of Kew wants a free public performance of Rudyard Kipling. Not on a Tuesday afternoon.'

Davie giggled, hitched his satchel higher onto his shoulders. 'I thought Jamie Saunders made a good job of "Wings of a Dove",' he said judiciously, after a moment.

'That's very magnanimous of you,' his mother said dryly. 'And indeed he did.'

'I thought Form Three were the best at—oh, no!' Davie clapped a hand to his mouth. 'Sorry. I forgot.'

'*Now* what are you talking about?'

'Today was your day for Mr Draper, wasn't it?'

She nodded.

'How did you get on?' He was watching her eagerly.

'Very well, it seems. Charles was pleased at any rate.'

'What about you?'

She smiled. 'I don't actually remember much about it. I remember getting there, and I remember having a cup of tea with Charles and then leaving. But the bit in between is a bit of a blank. All I know is that Charles said that he was optimistic, that he thought I was a very good subject and that he was sure he could help me.'

'But – that's *wizard*! That means we can—'

Davie stopped as his mother shook her head sharply. 'Don't go jumping to conclusions yet,' she said. 'I don't want you to be disappointed.'

'But it's better than if he'd said he *couldn't* help you, isn't it?' Davie ventured, ever hopeful.

'Yes,' she conceded, 'it is.'

'When will we know?'

She smiled a little at that 'we'. 'I'm seeing him on Friday morning, and then again early next week. He says we should have a good idea by then if it's worked or not.'

Davie cocked his head on one side. 'How will we know?'

'He's suggested that when he thinks I'm ready we should go for a trip on one of the river boats. That way, I'll know that if I'm frightened I can get off, so it won't worry me so much.'

'So when will that be? Next week?' The eagerness was back. 'It's only just over a week to the summer hols. Richard says he'll have to book — and there are passports and things—'

'*Davie!*' The word was exasperated. 'It's a long way from a trip on the river to the Tower of London and a fully fledged crossing of the Channel! Wait and see!'

Davie subsided, but his mother glanced at the bright, ardent face with a sinking heart, and not for the first time wished that her son were not quite so relentlessly single-minded.

—

The clock in the sitting room struck seven. Annie went to the French windows and called across the garden to where Davie was sailing a tiny paper boat on the little pond. 'Bedtime in half an hour, Davie.'

Without turning his head Davie lifted a hand in acknowledgement, his attention fixed on his small, frail craft. The evening had chilled a little; goosebumps lifted on Annie's arms as a fresh breeze stirred the curtains.

She rubbed at her skin briskly; she had left her cardigan upstairs.

To reach the main bedroom she had to pass Davie's room; the door stood ajar. As she passed she glanced in and was startled to see Richard standing by the bed with his back to her, looking at something he held in his hand. She pushed the door open a little further, took breath to speak; and then, seeing what he held, exhaled it softly and slowly. Quietly she walked into the room, came up behind him. She knew he had heard her, but he did not turn. For the moment, neither spoke.

'May I ask you something?' he said after a moment, still without turning.

She waited in silence.

He looked down at the blurred photograph in its battered silver frame. 'Davie once said that he had a picture of his father and that the picture looked like him. It does. Does that mean that this isn't Philippe?'

'No,' she said, her voice expressionless, 'it is Philippe. The likeness is coincidental. Davie's father was fair, and the boy inherited my dark eyes. That's all. When Davie found that photograph and decided it looked like him I didn't have the heart not to let him keep it. Perhaps I was wrong. I don't know. I can't see that it does any harm, really.'

Richard studied the photograph. A tall, slim young man, thin-faced, with a mop of fair hair and dark eyes, leaning on the parapet of a bridge, laughing into the camera. The image was blurred and faded. 'Annie?' he asked very quietly, very gently, his back still to her. 'What did happen? Who was Davie's father?'

Her mouth tightened stubbornly. 'Richard, it's irrelevant. A world and a lifetime away. I don't want to talk about it. Not now. Not yet. You promised.'

'Yes.' Sighing, he turned, the photograph still in his hand. 'Just one thing. Do you think he's still in Paris?'

She shook her head. 'I doubt it. I imagine he's dead.' Her voice was entirely unemotional. 'There's been a war, remember. A lot of men died.'

'A lot of us didn't,' he said gently. He held her eyes for a long moment, then put the frame in her hands and left the room. At the door he paused and turned. 'I'm sorry, I forgot to tell you – I have to go to Paris for a couple of days early next week. With any luck, once I get back – if Charles is right – we can try that river trip, if you'd like. Oh, and just in case you do decide to try for Paris, I've got someone looking into the passport situation for both of you. Seems better than leaving it to the last minute.'

Annie nodded silently, her eyes still on the photograph.

She heard him run lightly down the stairs, heard Davie's voice lift as he joined him in the garden. She stared down at the picture, closed her eyes for a moment. Then she bent to put the frame down on the bedside cabinet, set it with careful precision at the right angle and left the room, closing the door quietly behind her.

–

The next session with Charles Draper increased Annie's confidence further. That evening she, Richard and Davie went for a walk by the river. Davie watched her with unabashed curiosity. He had lived with his mother's terror of water for so long that it had come to seem a natural part of her. The thought that it might be cured greatly intrigued him. 'Do you feel any different?' he demanded.

They were standing on the towpath, leaning on the wooden railing, looking out across the river. Richard, too, was watching her with interested eyes.

Annie looked down into the water that swirled giddily against the muddy, overgrown bank. The level was high. Grass and weed streamed in the current. She frowned a little. 'Yes,' she said, then added slowly, 'that is – it's really hard to say. I mean, I don't feel anything. And that's unusual in itself. I'm not frightened, certainly. I'm not afraid I'm going to fall. Look…' She lifted her hands from the rail and held them before her, perfectly steadily. 'My heart isn't racing. I can breathe perfectly normally—'

A tugboat churned past them in midstream. Its wake widened in a surge to slap and suck at the bank beneath them. Davie looked at his mother a little anxiously; he knew how she hated that particular movement in water. She smiled at him and he positively glowed with happiness. 'You're *cured*!' he crowed. 'We can go! We can drive the car to Paris!'

'Hey, hold on, young man.' Richard put an affectionate arm about his shoulders. 'Don't let's get too carried away.' He smiled over the boy's head at Annie. 'Wait until next week. One more session with Charles and when I get back, if you feel happy about it, we'll take a trip on one of the steamers. If that works – well, yes, I should think we can safely say that we can start making plans. What do you think?'

She nodded. Looked down into the water again, deliberately trying to conjure those terrifying images that had haunted her for so long. Faintly they came to her, like echoes of a half-forgotten sound. Drifting hair. Pale, translucent skin. She looked up. The green banks of the river were solid, beautiful, comforting. There was nothing in the water, nothing to threaten her. She caught Richard's eye and smiled.

–

Paris was hot, the atmosphere stiflingly close. Richard sat in his shirtsleeves in the all but airless room, his elbows on the desk, studying the document laid out before him. Even with the shutters closed he could sense the sweltering heat of the street outside. It was very quiet. He dropped his face tiredly into his hands for a moment, rubbing his eyes with the flat of his palms, then ran his fingers through his already damply disordered hair. After a moment he lifted his head, turned the page, trying to concentrate, and reached without looking for his cigarette case that lay on the desk beside him. A fly buzzed. The room was very still. He stretched a little in his chair, settled down to work again.

An hour or so later he stubbed out his third cigarette and leaned back, rolling down his sleeves and sighing with relief. He neatly stacked the documents he had been working on, tied them with a narrow ribbon and tucked them into a folder, then looked at his watch. Over three hours until the train left. Richard stood up, straightened his tie and pulled on his jacket, picked up the small case that stood ready packed by the door, tucked the folder under his arm and, with a last look around the quiet apartment, went out onto the dark, stifling landing, locking the door behind him.

The dumpy, black-clad concierge opened her shutter at Richard's tap and looked up at him with flat, unfriendly eyes. Madame Colbert had little time for men, and for good-looking men no time at all. 'Yes?' Her voice was indifferent.

Richard held out the folder. 'Someone from my office will be here in an hour or so to collect this.' His French was perfect and near-accentless. 'Perhaps you'd be kind enough to give it to him? His name is Laroche. Pierre Laroche.'

She grunted, put out a claw-like hand and took it from him. 'Why not? I do everything else. Run errands. Take messages. Feed cats. Call plumbers. Why not be a postbox too?'

'You're very kind.'

She grunted again.

'If there should be any problem – if anyone needs to contact me within the next couple of hours – I'll be at the house on rue Descartes until about two o'clock. You have the telephone number, I think?'

'I have the number.' The small, black eyes gleamed, knowing and cynical. Madame Colbert had her own ideas about why this too-handsome Englishman spent so much time in the rue Descartes. Men were all the same, weren't they? Good for nothing.

With no 'goodbye' she closed the shutter in his face.

Despite himself, Richard grinned. In a city famed for its harridans, this one stood head and shoulders above most of them. A moment later he was in the hot, deserted street striding towards the rue Descartes.

–

A drenching mist of summer rain drifted across the river that moved sluggishly in the dull light. Annie strolled slowly along the muddy towpath, her eyes on the water. That she could even walk, unconcernedly, along the unprotected bank with the path beneath her feet slick and slippery with mud, would have been unthinkable just a few short weeks ago. For all her words of caution to Davie she was certain in her own heart that she was free of her fear at last. There had been no nightmares, no sleepwalking – at first she had suffered a nagging anxiety that Charles's probing of her subconscious might trigger the terrible dreams – and now as, hands in pockets, she turned to look down into the water she felt nothing. On the contrary there was something almost comforting in the steady, melodic running of the river.

The rain drifted softly into her face, settled in a spider's web of tiny gleaming droplets on the shoulders of her jacket. The trailing branches of a nearby willow tree drifted in the current. And though she flinched from the memories that the sight of it brought, she felt no panic, no terror. She took a deep breath. Richard would be home later that night. Home from Paris. The city she had once loved; the city she knew that, if she let herself, she could love again. Over the past weeks and months, fuelled by Richard's gentle promptings and Davie's enthusiasm, she had allowed herself to remember; and had discovered to her own surprise that most of what she remembered was a source of delight and happiness. For too long she had allowed the dark shadows of fear and guilt to obscure the brightness of the sun. She would go to Paris, with Richard and with Davie. They would buy flowers in the Place du Tertre, breakfast on croissants and coffee at a pavement cafe, stroll with the other lovers along the banks of the Seine…

Smiling, her eyes distant, she turned and retraced her steps. Davie would be home soon. Only a day or so and his long summer holiday would start. They would try the river boat first, as Charles had suggested. Then she would take him by steamer to Jane's for a few days. And then – the three of them would go to Paris. Unexpected excitement lifted her, and she quickened her footsteps.

–

'Are you all right?' Richard squeezed Annie's hand reassuringly as the little steamer turned out of the mainstream of the river and chugged towards the landing stage on which they stood. She nodded without speaking. Truth to tell, at that moment she was in a state bordering on blind panic, but she was not about to admit it at this late stage. She glanced at Davie; her son was watching her with such a transparent mixture of concern, pleasure and pride on his face that her heart turned over. 'I'm fine,' she told herself through stiff lips. Her legs were trembling so that she found herself seriously wondering, as the little boat surged towards them, how she would ever summon the courage to step onto the gangplank, let alone board her.

Richard's hand tightened further on her cold one; Annie concentrated on controlling her shaking legs. Water lapped and splashed beneath the jetty where she stood. The handful of people who had been waiting with them shuffled forward. The lad who had sold them their tickets caught a flung rope and hauled on it. Richard smiled encouragingly.

'All right, folks. All aboard the *Skylark*, as me old dad used to say. Tickets, please. Morning, Sir; morning, Madam. Hello, young man – taking Mum and Dad on a trip, are we? Mind 'ow you go there, Sir, we don't like to lose our passengers – not the minute they get on board, any road—'

'Where would you like to go?' Richard asked, his hand firmly on Annie's elbow. 'Inside?'

She shook her head. 'Charles said to stay outside, to stand by the rail as we pull away, and to keep my eyes on the bank. Will you… stay with me, please?'

'Of course I will.' Richard took his place at her side, his arm lightly about her waist. Davie leaned over the rail, watching the churn of the water as the boat began to move. Annie resisted the temptation to reach out and grab him.

The strip of water between the steamer and the jetty widened. Despite the instructions Charles had given her Annie found her eyes being irresistibly drawn to it. For a moment she was transfixed; then, slowly, slowly, she found that her heartbeat was calming. She took a deep breath. Her legs had stopped shaking. The water foamed and streamed around and beneath them. And that was all it was: water. There was no threat. There were no drowned faces, no ghosts. Just the exhilarating feel of the wind in her hair and on her skin, the cool feel of the spray in the air. The little boat swung in a wide arc, weaving through the river traffic, and headed downstream towards the city. Annie relaxed her iron grip on the rail. To her amazement she found herself perfectly at ease, moving almost unthinkingly with the motion of the vessel. She had never seen London from the river before; fascinated, she watched as houses and gardens, factories, wharves and workyards, parks and palaces streamed by. With growing confidence she stepped a little away from Richard and stood, one hand lightly on the rail, watching the panorama of the riverbank unfold. A pair of cyclists on the towpath at Hammersmith waved, and gaily she waved back. To her delight she discovered that not only had she overcome her tyrant fear, she was actually hugely enjoying herself. They chugged under bridge after bridge, pointed out the picturesque names of the riverside wharves – Rose, Crabtree – speculated on the contents of the Harrods repository, waved to the people on the piers waiting for the upstream steamer.

'Look!' Davie was jumping up and down with excitement. 'There's Fulham football ground! We'll be coming up to Putney Bridge in a minute. Oh, Mother, isn't it fun? Aren't you glad you came?'

Annie leaned closer to Richard, glanced up at him, smiling. 'Yes,' she said, 'it is. And yes, I am.'

'No fears? No problems?' he asked softly.

She shook her head. 'None.'

His arm tightened about her. 'Well,' he said, looking past her to Davie's happy face. 'Looks as if I might be able to get cracking and book those tickets, eh?'

Davie clambered up onto the rail, leaned, shouting, into the wind. 'Hooray! We're going to Paris.'

His mother took a firm grasp of a handful of pullover and hauled him back. 'We'll be going nowhere, young man,' she said, 'if you fall overboard and drown.'

And that, she thought with perhaps a faintly perverse pride, isn't something I could have said a few weeks ago...

They disembarked at Charing Cross Pier and went happily off to lunch.

'Game for the trip back?' Richard asked her, over coffee.

'Can't wait,' she said.

Davie looked from one to the other, beaming.

–

'Mr Easton says that when we come back I can tell the class all about driving to Paris next term. Like Jenkins did, when his parents took him to Rome last term. But he only went on the train. Didn't he just think he was swagger, though?' Davie spoke with some satisfaction around a mouthful of fruit cake, licked his sticky fingers.

Annie, who was peeling potatoes at the sink, looked around in surprise. 'But, darling – you're moving on to upper school in September. Oh, for goodness' sake – don't do that! Here, wipe your fingers.' She tossed him a tea cloth.

He caught it deftly. 'Yes, I know. But Mr Easton says he can fix it with the new teacher. He says that travel broadens the mind and helps us to understand other people. He says there wouldn't be anywhere near so many wars if people got to know each other and their countries. Mr Easton was in the last one. He shakes a lot.' The words were matter-of-fact. Davie's was a generation that had grown up with the human consequences of war. 'He had a brilliant idea. He said I should take lots of photographs, and collect maps and postcards and things and make notes, and drawings. Wouldn't that be wizard?'

Annie had turned and was leaning on the sink, knife still in hand. She smiled. 'It certainly would. I'll tell you what, we could make a scrapbook. Two scrapbooks – one of the journey and one of our stay in Paris. You could use them for your school project and then we'll have them as souvenirs for ever.' Suddenly she found her own enthusiasm rising to meet his. 'It would be fun. You can have my old camera if you like.'

'Thanks! And I can do lots and lots of drawings. Jenkins can't draw for toffee.' They beamed at each other. 'I'm really excited,' Davie said. 'I think this is the most exciting thing that's ever happened to me. Can I have another piece of cake, please?'

'I've written to Mother to tell her that we're catching the boat from London Bridge on Saturday.' Annie cleared the dishes from the table and stacked them in the sink.

Richard nodded, his face preoccupied.

'How are the arrangements for the French trip going?' she asked over her shoulder.

He did not reply.

'Richard?'

'I'm sorry?'

'I asked how the arrangements for the trip to Paris are going?' She turned on the tap, ran her fingers under the water.

'Oh, very well. Yes.' He hesitated. 'Annie – leave that for a moment. Come and sit down a minute, would you?'

She raised her eyebrows a little in surprise. 'Why yes, of course.' She dried her hand, came and sat down opposite him with her elbows on the table, her eyes enquiringly on his.

It was a long time before he spoke. When he did he reached out and took her hands in his. 'Annie – I wanted to ask—' He stumbled a little. 'That is... are you absolutely sure about this? Do you think perhaps... you should give it more time?'

Annie was looking at him blankly. 'What do you mean, "more time"? What difference will time make? You're making the arrangements. We've told Davie. We can't possibly let him down now. We can't! He's told everyone at school. His teacher wants him to talk to the class about the trip next term. Richard, for heaven's sake! We can't disappoint him now! He'd never forgive us!'

Richard shook his head. 'I know. I understand that. It's you I'm worried about. Suppose we're jumping the gun here? Shouldn't you perhaps see Charles a couple more times – over a couple of months, perhaps – to make sure—'

She pulled her hands from his and stared at him. 'A couple of months? What good would that do? I've told you – Davie's to do a project for the school. He'll never live it down if he doesn't go after all he's been saying. You *know* how cruel children can be! And it's his first term in the upper—'

He caught her hand again. 'Listen.' His voice was oddly urgent. 'Why don't we go – Davie and me – just for a few days? I could arrange for you to see Charles again – just to be absolutely sure – and then we can all go to Paris for Christmas. Together!'

She stood up, unsmiling, looked down at him. 'We are going together,' she said, 'in a couple of weeks' time. Would you like some apple pie?'

Richard took a long breath, forced a smile. 'Yes, please.' He bowed his head for a moment, pressing his fingers to his eyes.

She hesitated. 'Richard? Are you all right?'

He nodded, lifted his head. 'I've been working hard, that's all. I'm tired. Had a couple of headaches lately.'

She smiled. 'This trip is going to do us all good,' she said, turning away from him to take the pie from the oven.

Richard did not reply.

-

The saloon of the MV *Shamrock* was spacious and comfortable. As the vessel pulled away from the pier at London Bridge just before nine in the morning Davie knelt up in his seat, craning his neck to look out of the window. Annie watched him, smiling. As the only one of the party who had been on the trip before, albeit in the other direction, he had taken on the role of unofficial – and slightly superior – guide.

'Tower of London coming up,' he said, pointing. 'Gosh, I wonder what it was like to be a traitor going there to be executed?'

'A little worrying, I should think,' his mother conceded.

They passed the great water gate, with its intimidating portcullis, which had served for centuries as Traitor's Gate.

'Clang!' Davie said with mordant resonance. 'Off with his head! Swish! Clunk! I say, look' – he had laid his cheek against the window and was looking ahead – 'Tower Bridge is open. There must be a really big boat coming up.' He turned again to the near bank. 'Richard, what are those docks?' He pointed. 'Are they the ones we passed when we were in the car?'

'St Katharine's,' Richard said, a little absently. 'And yes, they are the same ones.'

'What's in those warehouses, do you think?' Davie leaned to the window, cupping his hands above his eyes to keep out the light. The great blackened, yellow-bricked buildings towered above the wharves, making the men and vehicles around them look disproportionately small in contrast.

'Oh – tea, rubber, wool, sugar maybe.' Richard made an obvious effort to rouse himself.

Annie looked at him fondly across the table that separated them. She had woken in the middle of the night to find his lips gentle but insistent on hers, his hand on her breast, his strong, warm body urgent against her. With no words they had made love; long, tender and fierce. She had fallen asleep with his breath in her ear. 'I love you,' he had said softly. 'You'll never know how much I love you.' Sleepily, a little while later she had stirred, reached for him and found him gone. He had been standing by the window, his cigarette glowing in the darkness. 'Richard? Is something wrong?'

He had turned. 'No, no, my darling. Nothing. Go back to sleep.'

Watching him now as he discussed the rights and wrongs of free trade with Davie, she thought he looked tired, a little drawn. He was working too hard. A rest would do him so much good.

The steamer ploughed on downriver, out of the city with its wharves and cranes and warehouses and into the flat estuary countryside. They were scheduled to stop at Gravesend in Kent before they turned north to run up the coast.

'Gravesend!' Davie said, hanging over the side to watch the new passengers climb the gangplank. 'What an absolutely gruesome name! I wonder why it's called that?' He glanced hopefully at Richard.

Richard laughed, shook his head. 'I'm afraid I haven't got the faintest idea.'

'Oh, well.' Davie was philosophical about his usually impeccable source of information being stumped. 'Can I have some ginger beer and cake, please?'

They went below again, into the saloon, as the ship's hooter sounded and she pulled away from the landing stage. It was very warm after the fresh air on deck. Annie leaned her head back on the seat and closed her eyes, lulled by the movement and the monotonous throb of the engines. The sound of voices and laughter around her rose and fell like the sound of the sea. An odd, comforting murmur filled her mind; she felt warm, secure.

She dozed.

When, disorientated, she jumped awake, she had no way of telling how long she had slept. Bemusedly she turned her head to look out of the window, and her heart lurched. The close and comforting banks of the river had gone, their place taken by a flat coastline in the far and misty distance. Between her and the land stretched an infinity of grey, restlessly moving water; the sunlight on the choppy waves glinted and flashed cruelly into her eyes like shards and splinters of glass. She could feel – *feel* through the suddenly painfully tense bones of her feet – the unfathomably dark, icy, pitiless depths beneath her. She began to tremble.

There was a voice in her head. Quiet. Insistent. Real.

Panic rising, she put her hands to her ears. No. *No!*

'Annie? Is something wrong?' Richard had leaned across the table towards her, his face concerned.

The room swam. It was hot and airless; yet the sweat on her skin was icy.

You do well to fear the treacherous waters.

She shook her head desperately, stumbled to her feet.

'Annie!' Richard had hold of her arm.

In blind panic she tried to tear away from him. 'I need some air. I think I'm going to be sick—'

The world tilted dizzily about her.

You do well to fear the treacherous waters.

'Come. I'll help you.'

The chill air struck at her like a whip. She staggered, grabbed hold of the rail. The water – endlessly moving, endlessly sucking, endlessly threatening – the perilous water, that decayed and devoured, in which there was no life, no warmth, no safety, swirled beneath her. And to her horror they were there: the mother and child, in ghastly embrace. Corrupt and livid flesh and milky eyes. The helpless horror of the gaping mouths. The reaching, grasping, fleshless hands.

For a moment it was as if her blood had frozen, her very life left her. She could neither move nor breathe. Then the cold air rushed to fill her lungs and, tears suddenly streaming down her face, she began to scream.

She screamed as she had screamed once before; in mindless shock and terror, the pain of it tearing like knives in her throat.

'Annie! Darling!' Richard's arms were tight about her. His face and voice were distraught. 'Oh, God! *Annie!* Stop it! Please! Darling, what's wrong?'

And still she screamed; long, echoing, desolate screams, as if she would never stop.

Chapter Sixteen

The water wasn't cold, after all. It was still, and it was dark, but it wasn't cold. Annie drifted, weightless, unthinking. Lost. She felt nothing. There was no sound. It was as if time itself was suspended.

And then, at last, there was the faintest opalescent glimmering of light somewhere above her. She took a deep, gasping breath. The darkness shifted, a rosy glow pulsed through her eyelids.

When she opened her eyes, she was lying on a hard, narrow little bed in a white room that smelled of disinfectant and was bright with sunshine. To her right a dark shadow was silhouetted against a blaze of light.

She struggled to sit up. 'Where am I? What happened?'

The figure at the window turned and hurried to her. 'Annie! Annie! Are you all right?' Richard sat on the bed beside her, caught her hand in his.

'I—' She put a hand to her head. 'I... don't know. I have a terrible headache. And my throat feels like fire.'

'I'm not surprised.' His voice was gentle. He looked dreadful, the skin of his face grey, dark rings beneath his eyes.

'Where am I?' she asked again.

'The cottage hospital, at Southwold. The doctor on the *Shamrock* sedated you. There was nothing else he could do. You were absolutely beside yourself; I was terrified you were going to throw yourself overboard. Annie, what in God's name *happened*?'

She shook her head, closed her eyes for a moment. 'I don't know. Truly I don't. I was all right, I was! And then...' She shuddered; the voice echoed again in her head: *You do well to fear the treacherous waters.* 'I saw them,' she said, as calmly as she could manage. 'The drowned mother and child.' She gripped his hand fiercely, willing him to believe her. 'Richard, I *saw* them. It wasn't a dream.'

'There, there,' he said, stroking her hand. 'Darling, your imagination was playing tricks on you. You panicked and you thought you saw—'

'No!' she interrupted him fiercely, '*No!* I tell you I saw them—' She broke off as the door opened and a nurse came into the room: a tall, grey-haired woman, needle-thin and with a mouth like a trap. She moved briskly, her starched uniform rustling.

'So, we're awake, are we? Off the bed, please, sir.' Her voice was sharp. 'Would you wait outside for a moment?' It was a command rather than any kind of question.

Richard opened his mouth, shut it again at her quelling glance and let go of Annie's hand. 'I'll only be outside.'

'In the waiting room if you please.' The words were repressive. The nurse took a thermometer from her pocket, shook it sharply and inserted it under Annie's tongue. Without even glancing at Richard to ensure that he complied with her orders, she took Annie's wrist in her sharp, cold fingers and lifted the watch that was pinned to her breast.

Richard shrugged, sent Annie the smallest of sympathetic smiles, bent to pat her hand. 'Don't worry about Davie. He's with your mother. I'll see you in a minute.'

As the door closed behind him the nurse eyed Annie with open disdain. 'Are you with child?'

Taken aback, Annie, unable to speak around the thermometer, shook her head, flushing.

The woman removed the thermometer and studied it for a moment. 'In my opinion there can occasionally – rarely – be an excuse for hysterical behaviour,' she said, coolly. 'But not often.'

'I was not hysterical.' Annie was suddenly shaking with anger. 'I—' She stopped.

The woman looked at her unhelpfully, brows raised.

Annie's mouth tightened. 'May I leave now, please?'

The woman stood up, checking the thermometer again. 'Well, there certainly doesn't seem to be much wrong with you physically. But you'll have to wait until Doctor can see you, to make sure.'

'Please!' Annie was desperate. 'There's nothing wrong with me. I want to go.'

'You'll go, young woman, when Doctor says you can.' The disapproving trap of a mouth folded firmly.

Fuming, Annie subsided.

The doctor, when he came, was at least initially a little more kindly disposed – until in the course of her story she mentioned Charles Draper and the hypnotherapy. Interrupting her he stood up, his face cold. 'Well, Mrs Ross, if you will meddle with such mumbo jumbo I'm afraid you can't complain at the consequences. I suggest that it might be sensible in the future both to stay away from the sea – which obviously disturbs you – and such... questionable... non-medical practices.'

'May I go, please?' Annie's voice was tight.

'You may. You appear to be in good health, physically at any rate. I would recommend that you rest for a couple of days. I'll give you a prescription for a tonic. It will be at the desk in Reception in five minutes; you may pick it up on the way out. Please be good enough to leave your address. Goodbye, Mrs Ross.' He inclined his head coolly.

'Goodbye, Doctor.' Annie pulled a ferocious face and stuck her tongue out at the door as it closed behind him.

'Good Lord,' said Richard, laughing despite himself as he opened the door in time to catch the furious, childish gesture. 'It looks as if you're feeling better! What did he say?'

'That I was an unstable hysteric who was wasting his valuable time and deserved no better than she got. And could we leave our address at the desk so that he can charge us an outrageous sum for giving me the benefit of that opinion.'

Richard raised his eyebrows.

Annie shrugged. 'Well, that was clearly what he meant anyway. Please, Richard, get me out of here.'

–

'*Mother!*' Davie's small, handsome face was pale, his eyes red-rimmed with crying. He flung himself upon her as she walked through the door. As she caught him in her arms she was alarmed at the way he trembled. 'Mother, you *frightened* me!'

'I'm sorry, darling. I'm sorry.' She hugged him close, laid her cheek on his thick hair. 'It's all right now. See, I'm back. No harm done. It was just a silly panic attack. I'm better now.'

He lifted his head. 'You were supposed to be cured.' His fears calmed by the sight of her, there was now just a trace of almost truculent accusation in the words.

She sighed. 'I did warn you that I might not be.'

'But *why*? You were all right. You weren't frightened or anything! What happened?'

She shook her head. 'I don't know. I really don't know. I went to sleep, I remember that. And then when I woke up—' She stopped. Despite herself, her flesh crawled.

'Sit down, dear.' Jane's voice was crisp. 'I'll make a cup of tea. Davie, fetch the biscuits for me, would you? They're on the sideboard in the parlour.'

Annie dropped into a chair, put her elbow on the table and rubbed her forehead with her fingertips, closing her eyes for a moment. 'You wouldn't have an aspirin, would you?'

Her mother looked at her with sympathetic eyes. 'In the medicine cupboard in the bathroom—'

'I'll get them,' Richard said quickly.

Jane filled the kettle, set it on the gas ring, turned to rest her hands lightly on Annie's shoulders.

'I feel such a fool,' Annie said, after a moment. 'Such a bloody fool!'

'Don't be silly.' Jane began setting out cups and saucers. 'You couldn't possibly have known what was going to happen.' Ruefully she smiled a little. 'I must admit it was a bit of a shock to come to meet the boat and to find you being carted down the gangplank on a stretcher.'

Annie put a hand out to her. 'I'm sorry. Did Davie take it very badly?'

Jane shrugged and avoided her eyes. 'He was… upset, yes. And frightened. From what I can gather you were—' She stopped.

'Totally hysterical. Yes, Richard has told me.' Annie shook her head. 'I just can't make it out.'

Her mother stood for a moment with cup in hand, looking down at her, her dark eyes soft. 'If you'll take my advice you won't try. You've done your best. You've done everything you can to beat this... phobia, or whatever it is. For goodness' sake, it's hardly the end of the world if you can't get on a boat—'

There was a sound by the door. Annie lifted her head. Davie stood there, the brass-banded biscuit barrel in his hands, two large tears rolling down his cheeks. She held out her hands to him. 'Davie – please don't cry. I'm all right, I promise you.'

'Yes,' he said, not looking at her. He put the biscuit barrel on the table.

'Would you like one?' Jane asked gently.

He shook his head.

Annie sighed. 'Davie,' she said quietly, 'I'm sorry. About Paris.'

His head jerked up. The dark eyes gleamed with tears. The combination of shock, relief and disappointment was too much; he lost his temper. 'I don't care! *I don't care!* Who wants to go to smelly old Paris anyway? I don't! I *don't*!' He wrenched away from her reaching hand, ran to the door and flung himself through it, slamming it behind him.

Annie half got to her feet. A firm hand pressed her down again. 'I'll go and talk to him,' Richard said. 'Here. Take a couple of these.' He put the pack of aspirin in front of her. 'I won't be a minute.'

In the garden Davie was sitting on a low wall, sullenly throwing stones at a small flowerpot that Jane had hung upside down on a raspberry cane. Annie watched as Richard came up behind the boy, put an arm about his shoulders. Davie unsuccessfully tried to shrug it off.

Richard said something; the boy shook his head stubbornly, threw another stone. Richard spoke again, at some length. Davie ducked his head and his shoulders shook.

Hot tears came to Annie's own eyes as she watched.

Suddenly Davie dropped the stones he was holding, turned to Richard, flung his arms about his waist and buried his head in his chest, sobbing as if his heart would break.

Jane looked with sympathy at her daughter. 'Perhaps it would be best if you had a lie-down?' she suggested gently. 'I'll bring your tea up to you.'

'Thanks. I think perhaps I will.' Annie made no attempt to wipe away her own tears. Tiredly she stood, kissed her mother's cheek and left the room.

–

The next day she felt better. The events of the day before had taken on the quality of a bad dream, parts of which flickered now and then in her memory like the jerky, grainy, early films she remembered seeing as a child, and parts of which she could not remember at all. Since there was no question of taking the boat back to London, they decided to catch the evening train. After lunch Jane suggested a walk along the beach.

'You don't mind?' She eyed her daughter curiously as they strolled along the water's edge. Ahead of them Richard and Davie were kicking a ball about, a frenetic Brandy chasing around their feet, threatening imminently to trip them up.

'Mind?'

Jane nodded towards the water. 'The sea. You don't mind being near it?'

Annie shook her head. 'No. I can look at it. It's being *on* it that I can't stand. Or rather – having it underneath me, if that makes any sense?'

Jane thought about it for a moment, then nodded slowly. 'Yes. I think I can see that. But – you never used to be like that as a child. We were always going on the Seine, remember? You never showed any signs of fear then.'

'No.' Annie's voice was very quiet. 'It was... after I found—' She stopped.

Fleetingly her mother's hand touched hers. 'I'm sorry. Don't think of it. I shouldn't have said anything.'

'No,' Annie said quickly, 'it's all right. It was just so strange that the dream was involved in what happened yesterday. And the words that I heard in my head – so clear, so real—' She stopped suddenly, frowning.

Her mother looked at her enquiringly. 'What is it?'

Annie shook her head. 'I don't know. I can't put my finger on it. Something... odd.' She shook her head again. 'No, it's no good. It's gone.'

Jane slipped an affectionate arm about her waist. 'Well, good riddance to it, say I. Wherever it's gone, leave it there. Forget about it.' They strolled on in silence for a moment. Ahead of them Richard and Davie were taking it in turns to throw the ball for the indefatigable little dog. Davie had been very quiet since his outburst the day before. When he had come downstairs this morning there had been signs of more tears in his face, despite his obvious best efforts with soap and flannel. Jane watched him now for a moment, thoughtfully, before saying, suddenly and impulsively, 'Annie, don't you think you should—?' She stopped, flicked up an apologetic glance at her daughter. 'Sorry. Interfering old bat time again!'

Annie stopped walking and turned to face the sea, her hands in her pockets, her eyes pensive. 'I know what you were about to say.'

Jane waited.

'You were going to suggest that I ought to let Davie go to Paris with Richard on his own.'

'Yes.'

Annie pulled a wry face, shrugged, turned to start strolling on again, her eyes on the sand. 'I've been thinking about it on and off all night,' she said at last. 'I know you sometimes think I spoil Davie, but even you can see how desperately disappointed he is this time. I really don't think I can stand it. With the school project and everything – it isn't fair of me to prevent him from going just because I can't go, is it? Richard has already offered to take him on his own. I don't really see what else I can do, do you?'

Jane shook her head slowly. 'No. To be absolutely honest, I don't. To have raised his hopes so high…' She let the words trail to silence, then suddenly smiled. 'Look – tell you what – if you'd like, I'll come up to town and spend a few days with you when they're gone. We'll spoil ourselves – breakfast in bed, lunch at Harvey Nichols. A good old weepy film matinee. We could go to the ballet, if you'd like. What do you say?'

Annie smiled very brightly. 'I'd say it was a splendid idea,' she said. Then, determinedly and without giving herself time for further thought, she raised her voice to carry above the sound of the waves. 'Richard? Davie? Have you got a second?'

–

Davie's excitement and happiness at knowing that he was after all to experience what to him seemed like the adventure of a lifetime almost made up for Annie's own disappointment and for the anxiety she resolutely hid. The boy sang around the house, discussed every detail of the trip with her, traced every possible route on maps and atlases, avidly read everything he could lay his hands on about northern France and Paris. He even, to his mother's amused amazement, took an interest in what clothes to pack, quizzing Richard about where they would go and what they would see.

'I've truly never seen him so excited,' Annie told Richard. 'When he saw his name on your passport I thought he was going to burst.'

'You don't mind? That he's on my passport?' Richard eyed her seriously. 'You know it's only a purely legal, technical thing? As his guardian' – he smiled a little wryly – 'as his male guardian... I would have to give permission for him to travel abroad with you even if I had had him put on your passport. It just seemed simpler—'

'I don't mind. Of course I don't.' The words were quick. They were sitting in the garden, nightcaps on the table before them. Summer dusk gathered around them. 'It was very clever of you to get it all fixed up so quickly. Do you know everyone in the entire world?'

He smiled a little, shook his head. 'Only about half!'

'Well, they certainly seem to be the influential half.' She turned her glass in her hand, her eyes reflective. 'It's just such a shame that I won't be using the one you got for me.'

He reached out a hand to touch her arm.

'When will you know when you're going?'

'In a couple of days.' He grinned that engaging grin. 'I've got a friend looking after things for me.'

She laughed softly.

He leaned to kiss her. 'I'll take care of him, my darling. I promise you.'

'Oh, I know that.' The words were quick and obviously sincere. 'It's just – well, he and I have never been so far apart before. Oh, he goes to Mother's, but that's different somehow. I know where he is, what he's doing, who he's with. And you – I hate it when you go away. It seems such a' – she hesitated, searching for words, then laughed again – 'such a waste of time. It's as if… as if there's a hole in my life.' She shrugged, sipped her drink.

There was a moment of silence. Then Richard took her free hand and stood up, gently pulling her with him. 'Bring your drink,' he said softly. 'Let's go to bed.'

–

Two days later, early on the Saturday morning, the telephone call came. Richard took it in the sitting room. 'Bernard, hello,' Annie heard him say. 'Yes. Yes. Splendid! When?' A pause. 'As early as that? Wonderful. You're a grand chap. No, no, that's fine. Yes, all arranged. You'll send the necessary paperwork to the office? Many thanks. We will. Thanks again. Bye.'

Davie, tucking into boiled egg and soldiers, had all but stopped breathing. He sat in a state of suspended animation, the spoon halfway to his mouth. Egg yolk dripped.

'Davie!' Annie said. 'Do watch what you're doing!'

The boy lowered the spoon, his eyes on the door.

Richard appeared in the doorway, smiling. 'Well,' he said and then, teasingly, hesitated.

'What?' Davie's eyes were shining with excitement. '*What?*'

'Wednesday. We leave on Wednesday.'

Davie let out a little wordless screech and dropped his spoon.

'This Wednesday?' Annie asked faintly.

He nodded.

'And when do you come back?'

'Saturday week. So, young man, now we can really start making plans and plotting routes. Best you get packing, eh?'

Annie was suddenly brisk. She reached for the teapot. 'Best you eat your egg first,' she said. 'You won't get boiled egg and soldiers in Paris!'

-

The next few days flew by. It seemed to Annie no time at all before suddenly neatly packed suitcases were being carried downstairs, travel documents checked, last-minute details sorted out. Davie, scrubbed and shiny as a new pin and looking as if he had not slept for twenty-four hours – which his mother knew for a fact he had not – danced on the doorstep with impatience as Richard and Annie said their goodbyes.

Richard held her tight, crushing her to him. 'You're not to worry. If I can I'll telephone you, but you know how difficult it can be. You sometimes have to book a call days in advance. If you don't hear, don't fret.'

'I won't.' She clung to him for an instant, closing her eyes.

'Jane is coming today?'

'Yes. Around lunchtime.'

'Good. Now you two have a really good time, you hear me? Hit the town. Spend some money.'

She lifted her head, gave him a slightly wobbly smile. 'We will.'

'Come on, Richard.' Davie was looking at his wrist-watch. 'It's nearly eight o'clock. You said we had to leave by eight—'

Richard grinned. 'I'm coming.' He kissed Annie fiercely. 'Davie, come and say goodbye to your mother.'

'I've already...' Davie took one look at his mother's face and thought better of that. He ran to her, submitted to yet another kiss, another rearrangement of his hair.

'Now, you be good,' Annie admonished him for at least the dozenth time. 'And be careful. Stay with Richard. Do as he says. Don't talk to strangers. Remember that in France the traffic travels on the wrong side of the road—'

'Oh, Mother!'

'I know. I know.' She dropped a quick kiss on his cheek. 'Just one more thing,' she added.

Davie sighed. 'What is it?'

'Don't get too used to sitting in the front seat of the car. That's mine.' Laughing, she gave him a little push. 'Off you go! Have a good time.'

She stood at the door waving until the car turned the corner; then, sighing a little, she turned back to the quiet and very empty house.

–

Within seconds of arriving Jane was organising their week with military precision. 'I've got tickets for the ballet for Friday night. I ordered them by post the moment I got your letter. It's *Coppelia*. I do love *Coppelia*, don't you? I thought we might go to the cinema this afternoon, and then spend a quiet night in. What do you think? What's on – do you know?'

'Er... something with Charlie Chaplin, I believe—'

'Oh, good. That'll make you laugh. You always liked him, didn't you? Silly little man. And then tomorrow – tomorrow I thought we might go shopping. In the West End.' Jane had removed her hatpin and then her hat. She stood for a moment looking down at them, thoughtfully, before lifting wide and artless eyes to her daughter's face. 'I hope you don't mind,' she said, a touch too composedly, 'but I thought it might be nice to have a visitor for dinner tomorrow night. I thought it might… distract you a little.' She had the grace to colour very faintly at the laughter that lifted in her daughter's face.

'Joshua?' Annie suggested.

'Joshua.'

Annie laughed aloud. 'He'll be more than welcome. As are you. Come in, come in. I've been ordered to indulge myself. And you. So – a small glass of sherry before lunch? In the garden?'

Jane slipped from her light summer coat and hung it on the newel post. What a very splendid idea,' she agreed.

–

To her own surprise Annie did not actually worry about Davie as much as she had expected to; she trusted Richard implicitly, knew the boy could not be in safer or better hands. By the morning following their departure she knew that the boat which had carried them across the Channel had not sunk, for such an event would certainly not be missed by *The Times* – she had to laugh at herself with her mother at that piece of motherly deduction – and she did not suppose that the roads of rural France were any more or less dangerous than those of rural England. The thing that surprised her most, however, was how very much she wished she were with them, and not simply because she missed their company. Over the past few weeks, as she had gradually started to believe that her paralysing phobia had been cured, she had positively come to look forward to revisiting the place where she had spent the many long and happy years of her young life. With Richard beside her, the tragedy and horror that had blighted the end of those years could surely have been put behind her. Through all the precious years of Davie's life she had carried deep down within her a sense of guilt, of worthlessness, a smothering and agonising fear that the conventional, unremarkable but above all safe life she had built for herself – and for him – was a building with foundations in sand. In deception, and worse than deception. But was it really so? Was there no such thing as a fresh start, a clean slate? If Richard had given her anything, apart from his love, it was a sense of proportion. More and more she had come to see Paris as what she really was – not as she, Annie, in her paranoia had perceived Paris to be. A lovely, light-hearted, beguiling city, no more, no less. A place. A beautiful, vivid, heartwarming place – not a devil's den of deceit, iniquity and haunted shadows. She laughed at Charlie Chaplin, enjoyed her mother's company, looked forward to the ballet. But in her heart she longed to be in Paris with the two she loved most in the world.

–

Joshua, leaning back in his chair and placing spoon and fork precisely together upon his empty plate, surveyed Annie with bright, questioning eyes. 'That was truly delicious, my dear. Thank you.' He hesitated for a moment. 'I must admit that I hadn't realised just how badly you wanted to accompany your menfolk on this trip.' He glanced at Jane, his smile mischievous. 'I had simply assumed that you were happy to be rid of them for a while, to enjoy some more amenable and civilised feminine company?'

Annie shook her head. She was well aware that she had drunk too much of the excellent wine that Joshua himself had supplied, and had perhaps spoken with more passion than was usual for her. 'I always love to spend time with Mother.' Her own smile matched his. 'Who wouldn't? But I can't deny it's been a terrible disappointment to me not to be able to go.' She began to collect the dishes. 'Brandy, Joshua?'

'Please. Yes.' He cocked his handsome silver head to one side, watching her. 'I assume,' he said as she stacked the dishes on the sideboard and brought the brandy bottle to the table, 'that the great adventure of the journey which has so caught the imagination of your son is not of any great interest to you?'

She shrugged a little, reaching for glasses. 'Not really.' She laughed a little. 'But unfortunately I don't have a magic wand. Or a fairy godmother. If you want to go somewhere the journey is inescapable, isn't it? And I wouldn't want to disgrace myself again. Not yet, anyway. Brandy, Mother?'

'Yes, please, dear,' Jane said comfortably. She was watching Joshua intently, an interrogatory crease on her brow.

Joshua watched as Annie poured the brandy, lifted his glass, swirling the golden liquid in its bowl. 'Then why don't you join them, my dear young thing?' he asked at last, face and voice faintly perplexed. 'I say, do you mind if I smoke?'

'No, of course not.' Annie was now looking at him with much the same expression as her mother. 'What do you mean?'

'A cigarette, my dear—'

'No, no. I mean – how could I possibly join them?'

He reached in his pocket, brought out a gold cigarette case that gleamed dully in the candlelight. Cigarette unlit between nicotine-stained fingers, he looked from one to another with the faint dawn of amused enjoyment in his eyes. 'Annie – a clever girl like you – you surely know there are always more ways of killing a cat than choking it with butter?' He looked at Jane. 'I'm surprised at you, my dear. I had you down as the resourceful one.'

Jane reached for her glass, shook her head. Her eyes held a mixture of curiosity and laughter.

Joshua lit his cigarette, stood up. 'May I use your telephone, my dear?'

Annie stared at him. 'Why – yes. Of course.'

'You are serious? About going to Paris?'

'Yes,' she said again. 'Very. But I don't see—'

He held up his hand, smiling, and left the room.

Annie and her mother eyed each other.

Joshua's head reappeared around the door. 'You do have a passport?'

'Yes.' Annie had given up. She looked at her mother. Jane shrugged, shook her head.

'And you have your husband's full permission to spend money?'

'Yes.'

'Which is only as it should be,' he said approvingly. 'Just give me a moment.'

'You've got the address?'

Annie nodded nervously.

'Passport?' Her mother was counting on her fingers.

'Yes.'

'Money?'

'Yes.' Annie hefted the heavy winter coat that hung over her arm. 'I must admit I feel a bit silly carting this about on such a lovely afternoon.'

Joshua, who had turned up unexpectedly to see her off, smiled. 'You'll need it, my dear. Believe me.'

Jane opened the front door. 'Ah. Here's the taxi.'

Annie glanced in the mirror, adjusted her hat. 'Do I look all right?'

'You look lovely. Are you nervous?'

'Very.'

Jane laughed. 'I'm sure you'll be all right. I envy you. What an adventure! Give them my love.'

'I will.'

Her mother made a little shooing movement with her hands. 'Well, go on then. Off you go.'

Annie picked up her small case, hesitated for a moment longer. The taxi driver hooted his horn. Impulsively she kissed her mother, and then Joshua. 'Thank you so much for your help. Bye, Mother. See you next week.' She hurried down the path, handed her case to the driver and climbed into the back of the cab.

'Where to, love?'

She took a breath. 'Hounslow Heath, please,' she said. 'The aerodrome.'

As they drove off she turned to look through the rear window at her mother and Joshua. And even nervous as she was, could not resist a smile to see how closely they stood to each other, Joshua's arm lightly about her mother's waist; and how bright was Jane's face as she tilted her head to look at him. No fears at all that she had blighted Jane's few days in London by leaving so precipitately. The ballet tickets would not be wasted.

She settled back in her seat and tried not to think of what she was about to do.

Conclusion

Paris

Chapter Seventeen

The aeroplane was delayed – an event which Annie gathered from her fellow passengers was by no means unusual – and a late dusk was gathering as the taxi finally drove into the centre of a Paris sweltering in the warmth of an August night, and glittering with a spangled mantle of light that rivalled, indeed outdid the brilliantly star-lit sky. Annie, suddenly animated, leaned forward to look out of the window. The flight had been nothing like she had anticipated; nothing, she thought to herself wryly, remotely like the advertisements that graced the pages of the fashionable newspapers and magazines. She had expected to be nervous – if not downright terrified. Despite Joshua's warnings, and the coat he had assured her was absolutely necessary whatever the weather, she had not expected to be quite so cold, quite so uncomfortable nor subjected to so much noise that her ears still ached with it. Yet there had been an unexpected elation, too, a sense of excitement and adventure. She smiled to herself as she anticipated, not for the first time, Davie's astonishment when he saw her, his envy when he discovered how she had managed so to surprise them.

The taxi had slowed to a crawl; the streets and pavements were thronged with people; tables and chairs were set beneath the trees; a babble of talk and laughter came to her through the open window of the cab. Gradually her ears were attuning to the sound of a language that had once come as naturally to her as her English. Looking out over the wide tree-lined boulevards, the pavement cafes, the glittering river with its graceful bridges, she suddenly felt a catch in her throat. This had been the city of her childhood and her youth. She saw herself as a small girl, skipping beside Colette, their maid-of-all-work, in early morning sunshine, going to the *pâtisserie* to buy croissants and *pains au chocolat* for breakfast. All at once, she remembered vividly the demure young woman of the pre-war years, in sprigged muslin, heavy hair swept up beneath her wide-brimmed hat, walking with careful dignity beneath the trees of the Champs-Élysées, well aware of the impression she was making upon the young men who lounged at the pavement tables. She saw too, suddenly and crystal clear, a tall, fair, dark-eyed young man with an enchanting smile and an endearing gentleness about him; remembered the stolen meetings, the touch of his hand beneath a table, the first tremulous kiss on the banks of this very river that sparkled and glittered through the trees and buildings as they approached it.

She blinked and sat back a little, into the shadows.

The Place de la Concorde was crowded, a moving mass of horse-drawn traffic, motor cars, bicycles and pedestrians who wove their way through the near-chaos of the traffic with a cavalier disregard for their own – or others' – safety. The cab driver growled a curse. Annie drew a deep breath. Oddly, ever since the whirlwind set in motion by Joshua and his suggestion that she fly to join Richard and Davie, she had never really looked beyond this moment; it was almost as if she had not truly believed it to be possible that she could actually be whisked from London to Paris in less time than it would normally take her to go to an afternoon matinee at the cinema. Now, suddenly, she felt an unexpected twinge of apprehension.

They would be pleased to see her, wouldn't they?

She shook her head in nervous impatience at the thought. Of course they would. Pleased, astonished no doubt, and perhaps – who knew? – even a little proud of her daring.

The cab was crawling across a bridge now – she did not recognise which one – towards the equally crowded but much less formal Left Bank of the river. The driver grumbled picturesquely again as a plodding donkey cart obstructed him. Lights were strung out along the banks of the Seine like diamonds decking the elegant throat of a beautiful woman. The slightest of breezes lifted from the dark, moving waters. Annie had not realised just how hot it was. She glanced at the piece of paper she was carrying; Richard had given her the address of his apartment in the rue Jacob. She had taken the driver's surly grunt when she had stumblingly asked him if he knew the district as one of assent. As they swung now into the narrower streets of the Left Bank, her excitement rose.

A few minutes later the cab came to a halt. 'Here,' the driver said, 'this is the place.' His French was so heavily accented that Annie had a struggle to understand him. He pointed, unsmiling, to tall, narrow double doors that stood open onto the street. 'There.'

'Thank you.' Annie scrambled out onto the pavement, hauled her small case and the heavy coat after her, paid the man what he asked and watched the taxi for a moment as he drove away. He had said not a word to her during the entire journey, had made not the slightest effort to accommodate her obvious difficulties with the language, had neither thanked her for the money nor for the generous tip she had added; yet ridiculously, as the cab disappeared around the corner she felt, suddenly, as abandoned as a lost child. She glanced up and down the street. It was quieter here, a street of softly lighted windows and shadowed lamps. She caught her breath, startled, as a cat materialised beside her and rubbed itself against her ankles. The building the taxi driver had indicated was tall and narrow. Ornate wrought-iron balconies graced its faded but elegant façade. The hallway beyond the open doors was lit with the dim and faintly sulphurous yellow glow of an oil lamp. As she stood in the darkness she breathed in the distinctive, suddenly well-remembered scents and smells of the city: exotic, some less than savoury, heart-wrenchingly nostalgic.

As she picked up her case she glanced up at the tall building, wondering behind which lighted window her husband and son were unsuspectingly awaiting her. It had occurred to her that, despite the fact that it was late for Davie still to be up, they might well be out in the city eating. It didn't matter. She could wait for them; the surprise would be just as great, the reunion even more exciting for them all.

The concierge's shutter was propped open, inviting in the slightest breath of the suffocatingly warm air. The woman sat beyond it at an ancient desk, adding up a long column of figures in a huge, battered and dog-eared book. The light of the lamp threw grotesque shadows across her pockmarked face.

Annie cleared her throat.

Madame Colbert did not look up.

The cat, which had followed Annie into the building, jumped up onto the frame of the open shutter, balancing delicately on the narrow ledge. When the woman absently put out a dark, gnarled hand, the cat leapt lightly onto the table and arched its sinuous black back, purring. Madame Colbert, her eyes still on the column of figures, lifted it onto her lap one-handed. The cat, its almond-pupilled eyes sly on Annie, rubbed its head into its mistress's shoulder.

'Excuse me?' Annie faltered; and for an absurd, panic-stricken moment it seemed they might be the only two words of French that she would ever remember. She pulled herself together, struggled on. 'I'm looking for M'sieur Ross. M'sieur Richard Ross. Can you tell me, please, which is his apartment?'

The pen scratched. Still the woman did not look up. 'M'sieur Ross is not here,' she said at last, brusquely. She turned a page.

Annie stared at her blankly.

The cat purred like a malevolent steam engine.

'I—beg your pardon?' Annie asked.

'I said – M'sieur Ross is not here.' The concierge lifted her eyes to Annie at last. The words were slow and sarcastically emphasised.

'You mean – he's gone out to dinner?' The words were tentative.

Thin lips grew thinner. Madame Colbert sighed heavily. 'I mean,' she said with offensive patience, as if she were talking to an imbecile child, 'that M'sieur Ross is no longer here. He has left.'

Annie shook her head, spoke suddenly sharply. 'He can't have done! They aren't due to leave until next Saturday. I should know, I'm his wife.' Temper, fuelled by the stirrings of panic, was beginning to rise.

The woman shook her head dismissively, turned her eyes back to her figures. 'M'sieur Ross has no wife.'

Temper was in danger of becoming rage. Annie swallowed, controlled it. 'He didn't have,' she said, astonished at her own calmness when every nerve in her body demanded that she scream at the ghastly old witch. 'He has now. I am his wife. Davie, the little boy he has with him, is my son.'

The concierge's head came up slowly, and she studied Annie closely for a moment. A faint flicker of almost malicious interest lit the small black eyes as the woman considered this appealing piece of information.

Annie tried again. 'Have they really left?'

The woman nodded.

'Do you know where they've gone?'

The cat turned its head to eye Annie disdainfully. There was a long moment of silence while the lamplight flickered and shadows danced. The concierge, her face expressionless, gave a small, irritatingly knowing and very Gallic shrug.

'Look.' It took Annie several seconds to marshal the words she needed. She kept it simple. 'I want to know where my husband and my son are. If you know, I think you should tell me.'

The tiny twitch of the lips could just have been a smile. It was extremely unsettling. The woman turned back to her figures, pushing the cat from her lap. The animal hissed and slunk beneath the table. 'There is a house on the rue Descartes,' she said, and the pen scratched once more. 'M'sieur Ross spends a lot of time there when he is in Paris. It is possible that is where he and the boy are.'

'Rue Descartes?' Annie had never heard of it.

The woman nodded.

Once again, Annie tamped down temper. 'Would you call a cab for me, please?'

'There's no need.' The pocked face lifted again, the pen lifted, like a blackboard pointer. 'Down the street, turn left towards the river, second on the right.'

'Which house?'

The woman shrugged again. 'I have no idea.' The young Englishwoman had not asked for a telephone number. What business of hers was it to offer it?

Annie, suddenly too weary for anger, bent to lift her suitcase and hefted the heavy winter coat more securely on her arm. 'Thank you,' she said, uncharacteristically caustic, 'for your help.'

'My pleasure, Madame.' The words were unperturbed, but the eyes that followed Annie as she stepped back into the warm darkness were filled with spiteful mischief. In Madame Colbert's considered opinion, if there was trouble to be made there was never reason not to make it. She smiled as she went back to her accounting.

The air in the street was uncomfortably close; the street itself uncomfortably and suddenly intimidatingly alien. As she turned in the direction indicated by the odious concierge Annie felt sweat trickle slickly between her shoulder blades. Her mind was blank with shock. Why had Richard left the apartment? There had never been any mention of him and Davie staying anywhere else. Supposing they weren't at this house in rue Descartes? And if they were – how was she to discover which house it was?

She fought down panic. One step at a time: find the street, work out what to do from there. If worse came to worst and she couldn't find them, she had enough money to book into a hotel.

She walked on.

Whose house was this, in which Richard spent so much of his time when he was in Paris?

Two men were standing beneath a lamp, talking and smoking. They eyed her openly as she passed, their conversation falling silent. One of them made a quiet comment, the other laughed. She felt their eyes upon her back. Tensely she waited for footsteps to follow her. Nothing happened.

It was with relief that she turned left into a busier thoroughfare, with wide pavements lined with cafes. A man was playing the accordion; a small monkey dressed in white shirt, red trousers and striped neckerchief identical to his master's carried a cap from table to table. Annie hurried past. Again, curious, sometimes speculative glances followed her. She supposed that a lone woman on the streets of Paris at night could expect nothing else. She held her precarious composure, resolutely resisting panic. What had the damned woman said? Second on the right. She could see the river in the distance. She passed a right-hand turn. Was that the first? Had she missed one? She stopped, hunting for a road name, found a grimy sign: rue Flaubert. She set the case down on the pavement for a moment, hitched the coat higher on her aching arm. She was drenched in sweat; beneath her small hat her head felt damp with it, her clothes and gloves stuck uncomfortably to her skin. It took an all but superhuman effort not to burst into tired and frightened tears. Wearily she picked up the case again and walked on.

Then, there it was – rue Descartes – a narrow lane that curved away from the main thoroughfare, quiet and ill-lit. She stood uncertainly for a moment on the corner, biting her lip. Someone jostled her, and she stumbled. She spun on the man in the quick anger of fear. He held up apologetic hands. '*Pardon, Madame, pardon.*' She took a long, shaky breath, turned back to the dark lane.

At the far end of the lane a horse and cart, lamp swinging, was ambling towards her. As she watched, the light glinted upon something as it passed. She caught her breath. A car. There was a car parked in the lane; was it her imagination, or was it familiar? Was it the Wolseley? She set off, half-running.

It was indeed Richard's car, which was parked outside a wooden gate, the only break in a long, blank brick wall perhaps eight feet high. She touched the car, ran her hand along the bonnet that was warm in the night air. It was like finding an old friend in a world of strangers. She leaned against it for a moment, the pounding of her heart easing. Richard was here. And Davie. She was just a step from love, and safety. She looked around. The gate outside which the car was parked was the only obvious entrance to any of the nearby buildings. Opposite was a row of shops, closed and shuttered for the night; much further down the lane was a large church; and at the other end of the long wall was a tall apartment block. A house, the concierge had said. Not an apartment. And surely, if they had been in one of the apartments, that was where the car would have been parked?

Annie turned back to the gate. Almost light-headed with relief, she was reminded – as she had been on her wedding day – of Alice in Wonderland, and the door to the magical garden, and for a moment she found herself struggling between laughter and tears. She set her case down once again, brushed the straggle of her hair back beneath her hat, blotted the damp skin of her forehead with the back of her cotton gloves, lifted her knuckles and rapped on the wood.

Nothing happened.

She tried again, straining her ears. There was neither sound nor movement; nor was there any sign of bell or knocker or nameplate. She guessed that this must be the back entrance to the house, the front of which probably faced on to the river and the wider boulevard. Richard had obviously thought it safer to park the car in this quiet back street. She knocked once more, as loudly as she could.

Still, nothing.

Annie lifted the latch and pushed. The gate swung open, smoothly and silently. She stood uncertainly for a moment, then picked up her case and stepped through, closing it quietly behind her. 'Hello? Hello? Is anyone there?'

She was standing in an exquisite little courtyard, drowned and drenched in the perfume of its flowers. Flickering gas lamps shone on bougainvillaea, jasmine and sweet-scented lilies. A small fountain played, the clear water running from a mother-of-pearl conch shell held by a naked dryad poised upon a dolphin's back. She leaned against the closed gate for a moment, taking in her surroundings. After the emotional roller-coaster of the past few hours, the tranquillity of the place touched her like cool, soothing fingers. 'Hello?' she called again, tentatively.

The house loomed above her. Bougainvillaea scrambled up the wall and festooned a long wrought-iron balcony on the first floor. Tall slatted shutters stood open and a soft golden light fell from the window across the courtyard. She raised her voice again. 'Hello? Please – is anyone there?'

There was movement above her. A shadow fell across the balcony as a tall, wide-shouldered figure approached the balustrade and peered into the dim-lit darkness below. 'Who is it?'

'*Richard!*'

There was a moment of absolute, still silence. Then, 'Annie?' Richard's whisper was incredulous. '*Annie?* Oh, my God—!'

Annie was already hurrying across the courtyard to the door that was obviously the entrance to the house. She flung it open, found herself standing in a high-ceilinged, beautifully proportioned hallway. The panelled walls were hung with scores of paintings, soft and colourful rugs were strewn on the polished wood of the floor, a lucently gleaming silver statuette of a dancing girl with long hair streaming about her shoulders stood on a low plinth in the centre of the room, lit to an almost painful glory by the glitter of the chandelier that hung above it. Annie had eyes for none of it. A wide, sweeping staircase led to the next floor... she ran to it.

The stairs led up to a broad sweep of landing, almost a twin of the hall downstairs: paintings, statues, elegant furniture. As she reached the top of the stairs a pair of double doors opened. For a moment Richard stood, his dark figure limned in lamplight, his face in shadow. She stepped towards him, gladly. 'Richard!'

Something in his stance stopped her and she halted within arm's length of him. Her eyes were drawn over his shoulder to the room beyond. It was a very large, high-ceilinged room, furnished like the rest of the house with exquisite taste. The balcony with its open window ran along one side of it; a curtain billowed softly. The other walls were hung with pictures. As in the hall and on the landing, Annie was aware of the glint of silver, the gleam of marble. Opposite the open doors where she stood was a huge bed, draped and decked in heavy, shimmering silk. The figure propped up on silken pillows watched her, great, heavy-lidded dark eyes expressionless. Beside the bed was a huge marble fireplace within which, incredibly in the heat of the night, the embers of a fire glowed. Upon the deep mantelpiece, lit by flickering gas mantles from above, stood two large photographs in silver frames. She narrowed her eyes, disbelieving.

The silence was absolute.

Annie's suddenly numb fingers released their grip on her suitcase. It thumped to the floor, toppled over onto its side. She let her arm drop; the coat slithered after the case, the only noise in the deadly quiet.

'Annie... Annie! What in hell's name are you doing here?' Richard's voice was not much more than a harsh whisper, but its tone spoke volumes.

She ignored him; walked past him as if he were not there, into the room, to the foot of the bed.

The dark eyes beneath the great, pale, hooded lids looked into hers. 'You!' she said, her voice very quiet, and hard as stone. '*You?*' Her eyes flickered to the photographs on the mantelpiece; so familiar, so everyday. She had one of them on her own bedside table. Davie, laughing into the sun on Brighton beach; Davie, swinging on her hand, eyes bright and hair flying, in the garden at Southwold. She spun on her husband. '*Where is Davie?*'

He lifted placating hands. 'He's asleep. Upstairs. Annie—'

'Fetch him. I'm taking him home. Now!'

'Darling, he's sound asleep – you'll frighten the life out of him—'

Her head came up at that, eyes blazing. 'Don't you "darling" me, Richard Ross.' Her voice was bitterly angry. 'How dare you? How *dare* you bring my son to this house? To him?' Shaking with fury, she lifted an accusing finger and pointed at the still-silent figure in the bed.

Richard stepped towards her, put a hand on her arm. 'Annie – please – listen...'

'Don't you think I've *listened* enough?' She laid savage emphasis on the word. 'Fool – *fool!* – that I've been!' She wrenched herself free; stepped back, stood staring at him through wide, glittering eyes as her initial shock and anger ebbed and her mind began to work at least a little more logically. She saw dark colour rise in his face, and try as he might he could not sustain her gaze. He looked away. 'I think,' she said at last, 'that you owe me at least some kind of explanation. Not that it will make any difference. I see enough here' – she swept an angry hand, taking in the room, the still figure in the bed – 'to convince me that you're a liar and a cheat. And Christ alone knows what else. But why? *Why?*'

'It was my doing, Annette.' The throaty whisper came from the bed. 'I tempted him. I tempted him too far.'

Slowly she turned to look at the man, her face a mask of contempt and hatred. 'I can believe that, Lucien. Oh, yes, I can believe that.' Her voice was very low. 'You at least obviously haven't changed. You're still spawn of the devil!'

Incredibly the old man smiled a little, pale lips stretching in a gaunt face that might have been carved from ivory. 'You always were a lovely child, my dear,' he said, the whisper echoing into the darkened corners of the room, 'especially so when you were angry, as I remember. I should have known you would grow into a beautiful

282

woman.' He smiled again. 'But I must say I preferred your hair long.'

'Bastard,' she said, grimly bitter.

Richard looked at her, shocked disbelief in his eyes.

She took an almost threatening step towards the bed. 'What do you want of my son?' she asked, her voice dangerously quiet.

The old man lifted a long, thin, all but transparent hand. He was no longer smiling. 'I wanted to see the boy, Annette – is that so wrong? Surely not?'

Annie took several long, slow breaths, trying to control herself. Her hands had folded into fists. She relaxed them, caught hold of the wrought-iron rail at the foot of the bed, leaned across it to stare at the man. 'Wrong? *Wrong?*' she repeated, savagely softly. 'I would have seen him dead – stone dead! – before I let him anywhere near you. And you know it.'

'Annie!' Richard's voice was shocked.

'Shut up, Richard.' She did not even glance at him.

The great, arched lids closed for a long moment. In the silence the ashes of the fire slithered, a whisper in the quiet. The room was almost unbearably hot and stuffy; there was the smell of sickness about it. The old man opened his eyes again. 'You have a right to be angry,' he said.

'Angry? *Angry?*' Annie's laughter was so bitter that Richard physically winced. She walked round the bed, stood over the wasted body that could barely be discerned beneath the smooth silken counterpane. The lustrous, huge-lidded eyes followed her, expressionless. She bent forward, hissing into his face. 'If I had a knife, old man, I would put you out of your misery right now. I would be doing a favour to the human race.'

Again that faint stretch of a smile. 'You would be doing a favour to me.'

She straightened, mouth tight. 'Then live on. As long as possible.'

Richard was staring at her. She ignored him, turned and walked to where the photographs of her son stood upon the mantelpiece. She studied them for a moment, then turned to face Richard, the sudden pain in her face so fierce that once again he flinched from her. 'Did you have to do that?' she asked quietly. 'On top of everything else you have obviously done, did you have to do *that*?'

He said nothing. She turned back to the photographs, picked up the close-up of Davie's carefree, laughing face, looked at it for a long time. Both men watched her. She lifted her head at last, looking at Richard. 'What have you told Davie?' she asked, her voice suddenly perilously reasonable. 'Why does he think he's here?'

Something changed in Richard's face. There was a wary flicker in his eyes, a small tic in his jaw. 'I've told him the truth,' he said, his eyes holding hers. 'That I had found his grandfather for him. That the old man, not unnaturally, wanted to see him.'

Annie stared at him.

A sound like the ghost of laughter came from the bed.

'I'm sorry I didn't tell you. I'm sorry I deceived you – I knew that if I told you you'd refuse to let the boy come—'

'You were right.' Incredibly Annie was smiling, a small, tight smile with nothing in it of happiness or humour. 'But we both know that isn't the only deception you've practised on me, don't we? We both know that you've lied and you've cheated, you've put me through hell – I don't yet know how you did it, but I know as surely as I stand here that you did – and for what?' Suddenly and shockingly she had started to laugh. She choked for a moment, hand to mouth, but she could not stop the laughter.

Richard watched her in disbelief.

'You imbecile!' she said, and again her shoulders shook, again the laughter punctuated her words. 'You bloody imbecile! You thought you could get the better of *him*?' She pointed. The old man had closed his eyes again; he had begun to cough, very slightly. Still holding the photograph folded in her arms across her breast, Annie crossed the room to where Richard stood. She stopped a foot or so away from him, looking up into his face. Then she laughed again, real laughter with a cruel touch of derision in it. 'The liar, lied to,' she said. 'The deceiver deceived. Richard, I told you – Lucien is not Davie's grandfather—'

'Annie!' Richard's voice was anguished.

'—he is his father,' Annie continued inexorably. And then again, softly, into the sudden silence, 'His father,' she repeated.

The coughing had become a wet, spluttering rattle. They turned. Bright blood splattered the pale silk of the counterpane, dribbled onto the pillow.

Richard leapt to the old man's side, slipping an arm behind his shoulders, drawing him upright. 'Lucien! Lucien! Annie, there's a bell pull by the mantelpiece there – quickly!'

Annie stood stock still, watching dispassionately.

'Annie! For the love of God! He needs help.'

Again that small, mirthless smile.

'*Annie!*'

She shrugged, walked in no great haste to the fireplace and pulled at the tasselled rope.

Moments later the door opened and a plump and imperious uniformed nurse bustled in, followed by a girl in cap and apron. 'M'sieur, M'sieur, what have you been doing? Out. Out—' She spoke in rapid French, flapped her hand at Richard and Annie without looking at them. 'Marie, prop up the pillows – help M'sieur to sit up—'

Richard reached for Annie's arm; she snatched it away. 'Don't touch me.' Without so much as a look at the bloodied face of the man who lay choking in the bed, she stalked ahead of Richard through the door, past her case and coat that still lay discarded on the landing and down the elegant, sweeping staircase.

Richard passed a hand across his eyes. 'Jesus Christ,' he said faintly. 'Jesus bloody Christ!'

'Please go, M'sieur. Marie will fetch you later.'

Richard left the room, closing the doors very quietly behind him.

Chapter Eighteen

Annie sat unmoving on a small stone bench, her preoccupied eyes on the play of the fountain's water. Even under such fraught circumstances as these the musical sound of it was soothing, the sweet scent of the flowers heady. Fleetingly she remembered her thought when she had first opened the gate earlier that evening: Alice's enchanted garden. She grimaced a little. More like the Garden of Eden. Complete with serpent.

Her hat and gloves lay discarded beside her. Now she ran a hand through her sweat-damp hair. She had been sitting here alone for some minutes, and as she had turned over in her mind the events of the past weeks and months and related them to what had happened this evening, at least one small piece of the sordid puzzle had clicked into place. She remembered the words she had spoken to her mother on the beach after the incident on the *Shamrock*. '*The words that I heard in my head – so clear, so real... Something... odd—*' There was movement in the shadowed doorway. 'Is he dying?' she asked, her face and tone dispassionate. She might have been enquiring about the weather.

Richard stepped from the shadows. He was carrying a bottle and two glasses. 'Yes.'

'Now?'

He set the glasses on a small stone table, shook his head. 'Probably not. This has happened before.'

'Pity.' She turned her head to look at him. 'It would be so very fitting if I had had at least something to do with sending him to hell.'

'Annie—'

She ignored him, glanced about her. 'He's done very well for himself. As I remember, he and Philippe were comfortably off, but not this comfortably.'

'He did well out of the war, I believe.'

A faint cold smile twitched at that. 'He would.' Still her voice was calm, almost conversational. 'What did he do? Sell cardboard boots to his own side? Or supply the Germans with land mines, perhaps?' she asked pleasantly.

'I don't know.'

She watched as he poured wine, handed her a glass. She sipped it. It was good wine: clear and cold, and had about it the faint taste of gooseberries.

'Annie?'

'What?'

'How *did* you get here?'

'I flew. From Hounslow Heath. It was Joshua's idea.' The conversation was still being conducted with almost surreal normality. 'Now, tell me something. How did you persuade Charles Draper to do what he did? He didn't cure my phobia, he deliberately exacerbated it, didn't he? Didn't he?' she added again, more sharply, when he did not immediately answer.

Richard looked down into his wine glass.

'There's no need to answer. There's been something bothering me about what happened on the *Shamrock*. Something that didn't fit. I've just realised what it is: the words I heard in my head were the gypsy's words, but it wasn't his voice. That's what's been nagging at me. The words keep coming into my head; but it isn't the gypsy's voice I hear. It's Charles Draper's. He convinced me I was safe on the river, but somehow set a trigger that would terrify me when I was at sea. Isn't that it?'

He buried his face in his hands for a moment. Then, 'Yes,' he said, his voice muffled.

'You told him what the gypsy had said,' she continued inexorably, her face set in fierce concentration, 'so that he could reinforce it. But it gets worse than that, doesn't it? *You do well to fear the treacherous waters.* A fine phrase, Richard. Clever. Too clever for an itinerant fortune teller, might you think?' She watched him for a moment. 'They were your words, weren't they? You told him what to say. Didn't you? The red dress, Richard. Now that I realise what you were doing it's all so bloody simple, isn't it? The one and only time you've ever told me what to wear. The red dress. So that the gypsy would recognise me and deliver your message. Am I right?'

He neither moved nor lifted his head.

'Because I had told you that Philippe wasn't Davie's father. And you had deduced – rightly – that therefore Lucien wasn't after all his grandfather. You were unaware that Lucien, of course, already knew that.' She contemplated him for a long moment. 'So much I have worked out for myself. You might as well tell me the rest, don't you think?' The words were still oddly calm, almost detached. 'Why, Richard? Why?'

In the silence that followed, the water played musically around the feet of the nymph, gleamed and glistened on the smooth sides of the dolphin. At last Richard raised his head. His face was haggard. 'Annie, please believe me, I never – *never* – intended to hurt you. I swear it!'

The quiet sound she made was one of contempt and disbelief.

He closed his eyes for a moment, took a long, steadying breath. When he reached for his wine glass she saw that his hand was shaking. He picked it up, then quite suddenly and without drinking put it down again and stood up. 'Please. Come with me a moment.'

She shrugged, put down her own glass, rose without speaking.

He led her through the door and into the hall, crossing the polished floor beneath the magnificent chandelier to a large door opposite the staircase. He pushed it open. Annie followed him into a well-proportioned rectangular room laid out like a small gallery. There were paintings on the walls, chairs and sofas set around the room at every angle, facing the pictures. Lamps glowed softly; Richard walked around the room turning them up. 'There,' he said, pointing.

Annie walked past him to the wall he had indicated. She studied the half-dozen pictures it held, intently and for a long time. Vivid with life and colour, they dominated the room.

'Beautiful, aren't they?' Richard asked quietly from behind her.

She nodded. 'Yes. They are.'

'You've guessed who they're by?' It was barely a question.

'Toulouse-Lautrec I would think, from the style and from what you've told me.'

'Yes. Henri Toulouse-Lautrec. But not his can-can dancers, or his ugly circus girls. His first love. Horses. Racehorses. Carriage horses. Hunters, and the life that revolves around them. Aren't they the most marvellous things you've ever seen?'

She shrugged a little. There was a very long silence. At last Annie asked, very quietly, 'Tell me something. Just what do these things have to do with Davie?'

Richard took a breath. 'If I hadn't found Davie, Lucien intended to leave them to an art gallery in New York.'

'And since you have?' Her voice was now perilously soft.

'They're to go to Davie.'

'And – indirectly – to you?' The words were cold.

'No! *No!* Annie, I know you have good reason to mistrust me – but surely you don't believe that of me? That I'd somehow swindle Davie?'

She turned to look at him, coolly and steadily.

'Annie – please – I swear I wouldn't do such a thing!'

'After the things that I'm coming to realise you *have* done, you'll pardon me if I take leave to doubt that?'

He ran his hand through his thick, already untidy hair, shaking his head. 'I don't know how you can be so calm—'

She shook her head, suddenly and fiercely. 'Calm? I'm not calm. I'm very, very angry. So angry that if I let it go I'd quite probably kill you. Do you mind if we go back outside? The sight of these things nauseates me.' She stalked ahead of him out of the door and across the hall. The heavy, perfumed air enveloped her as she stepped into the courtyard. She picked up her wine, settled herself on the stone bench and sat looking up into his shadowed face. 'Tell me,' she said, her voice clipped. 'All of it.'

He reached for his cigarettes. She watched expressionless as he went through the ritual of lighting one. Even then it was a long time before he spoke. 'I've known Lucien for years,' he began finally. 'My father used to do a lot of work for him, and when Father retired I inherited him, so to speak. We had a lot in common…' He sucked his lip a moment, colouring a little at her small, derisive laugh, and turned to stare into the tumbling water. 'I always understood he had no family. I knew about Philippe being killed in the war, but he never mentioned you or Davie. He wasn't sick in those days, of course. He lived very grandly.' He glanced about him. 'Parties and dinners, soirées that were the talk of Paris. There were always people coming and going; the house was always full – artists, writers, theatre people, film-makers. Bankers. Politicians.'

'Anybody who was anybody,' she said, dry and unimpressed.

'Yes. He lived a quite frenetic social life. And he collected fine art. He commissioned me to find those pictures for him—'

'A task that you enjoyed, no doubt?' Again the cut of sarcasm.

'Yes, I did. Very much. It took me over two years. It was during that time that I began to share Lucien's passion for Lautrec—'

'Obsession, you mean,' she interjected quietly.

He stared at her. Then, abruptly, nodded. 'Yes. Obsession. I can't deny it. I have spent hours alone in that room, simply looking at them. I had come to feel' – he hesitated, glanced at her and away – 'as if in some way some small part of them was mine.'

'You were wrong,' she said flatly.

'Yes, I know. But I can't help it.'

She noted with no more comment than a raised brow the use of the present tense.

'Then Lucien had his first bout of illness. He was very sick for quite a long while, but went to Switzerland for a time and came home apparently cured. He had taken to me, we were good friends. I visited him in Switzerland, looked after his affairs here whilst he was away—'

'Especially the pictures.' She could not resist the gibe.

'When he returned, everything went back to the way it had been before – or at least so it seemed. But I've since discovered that the doctors in Switzerland had warned him that the remission was unlikely to last.' Richard dropped the spent cigarette onto the flagstones, ground it out with his heel. 'One night, sitting over brandy on the balcony up there' – he lifted his head to look at the long, wrought-iron balcony above their heads, still lit with soft lamplight from the room beyond – 'the room used to be a salon before this latest bout of illness – he told me about you and Davie. His own version, that is. He said that you and Philippe had married just before the war, that Philippe had died before his son was born. That there had been some kind of trouble between himself and you' – Annie's head came up, her eyes glittering, but she said nothing – 'and that, hating him, you had fled with your mother back to England, taking the boy with you. In the confusion of the war years he couldn't find you. After the war he was too busy, or perhaps didn't particularly care. Discovering how ill he was changed him, Annie. He truly, desperately wanted to see Davie before he died—'

'So he sent you off to look for him?'

'Yes.'

'And you found him.' Her voice was bitter. 'And me.'

'Annie – please! *Please!*' He came to her, sat beside her on the bench. She turned away from him, but he took her hand in his. 'Listen to me! I loved you the first moment I saw you. I mean it! And Davie, too. I loved you both then and I love you both now.'

'Why the deception, then? You deceived us both from the start. Why?'

'I told you – Lucien had warned me that you hated him. That you would never allow the boy to come to him. He didn't tell me the truth of that, of course. And now I can see why.'

'He was right. I would never have let Davie near him.'

'I thought – if I got to know you, I could persuade you to let him come. I didn't plan on falling in love with you.'

She turned on him. 'Love? *Love*, Richard? Are you serious? To quote the cynical Mr Forster – what *about* love? – where in hell's name is the love in any of this?' Her voice was bitter. 'Perhaps you might have showed how much you *loved* me by telling me the truth?'

He propped his elbows on his knees and again dropped his face into his hands. 'I wanted to, I swear it! I couldn't. I just couldn't. I was so very afraid of losing you; of losing both of you. And the longer I left it, the harder it became. And then, too,' his voice dropped, 'I can't deny it – there were the paintings. I couldn't bear the thought of their going to America. I had to try. I had to! They're Davie's! He should have them!'

The eyes she turned to him were flat with disbelief. 'So this has all been for Davie's good, has it?'

He was silent for a moment. 'I thought,' he said at last, 'that is, I convinced myself that it was. For his good and for Lucien's.' He lifted his head. 'I am very fond of the old man,' he added quietly.

'God preserve us all from your fondness!'

He closed his eyes and shook his head a little at the savagery of the words. 'I knew you loved me – as I loved you. I persuaded myself that if I told you while we were on honeymoon – not the entire truth, but simply that I had traced Philippe's father in Paris, that he was dying, that he wanted to see Davie – then you'd agree to let the boy come to him.'

'Then I told you that Philippe wasn't Davie's father.'

He nodded.

'And that put the cat amongst the pigeons, didn't it? You assumed that Lucien didn't know that, and that if I told him – and you guessed that I would – you'd lose your precious pictures anyway?'

'Yes.'

'And by that time you were in so deep that you couldn't bear that to happen. So you started planning to get Davie here without me.'

He rubbed at his face with his hands.

'And the only way you could do that was to exacerbate my fear of deep water whilst encouraging Davie to become virtually obsessed with the idea of driving to Paris. It's really quite clever, isn't it?' She stopped, watching him, her eyes thoughtful. 'One thing I don't understand. How did you get Charles Draper to go along with such a disgraceful scheme? Is he an art lover too?' The words were dry.

Richard shook his head. 'The Charles Draper you met wasn't the real Charles Draper. Oh, there is a Charles Draper, and he does use hypnosis in treating his patients. When I first mentioned him to you I genuinely wanted you cured, because I thought I could persuade you to come with Davie. It was, as you say, when you told me that Philippe wasn't Davie's father that I had to... change my plans. I had invited the real Charles to the wedding; I put him off—'

Annie let out a small gasp of genuine laughter as the irony of that struck her. 'And you invited Joshua instead! Now *that's* funny!'

'—and hired a stage hypnotist – the "Charles Draper" that you met – to impersonate him.'

'You set up the night at the opera, the West End consulting rooms, the bogus wife? No wonder I didn't like her.'

'Yes. He wanted to meet you first. To check if you were a suitable subject.'

'An emotional, imaginative sleepwalker. Suggestible is the word, I believe.' Her mouth twisted a little and she looked at him closer in the shadowed darkness. 'That must have cost an awful lot of money? But then – this isn't about money, is it?'

'No.'

'Nor is it about love. If you had loved me you couldn't possibly have put me through what you have. Could you?'

He could not look at her. 'I swear, Annie, I didn't realise how bad it would be for you. I would never have gone through with it if I had.'

'But you *did* go through with it. To the bitter end. Didn't you?'

'Yes.'

'You're despicable.' Her voice had dropped to a shaking whisper. All at once a fierce reaction had set in and, despite herself, tears were rising. She fought them fiercely.

'Annie—' He put a hand out to her.

She wrenched herself violently away from him, jumping to her feet. He caught her hand; furiously she struggled against him. 'Let go of me! Let *go*!' Suddenly she was crying, sobbing hopelessly and desolately. 'How *dare* you touch me! I hate you. Hate you, hate you, *hate* you!'

'Annie, don't. Please!' He stood, tried to put his arms about her.

Outraged, she stepped back and slapped his face with all her strength.

The action checked them both. Annie's sobs quietened; Richard stood quite still, his hand to his stinging cheek.

'You deserved that,' she said at last, almost defensively.

'Yes.'

'Worse,' she said. Miserable tears were sliding down her face.

'Yes. Tell me something?'

'What?'

'Could you ever forgive me?'

'No.' The answer was quick and flat.

He lifted a hand to touch her wet cheek. 'So – you really don't love me any more?'

She did not reply.

He did not press her. 'May I ask you something?'

She nodded.

'Is Lucien truly Davie's father?'

She inclined her head. 'Yes.'

'Did Philippe know?'

'No.'

'Did you love him? Philippe, I mean?'

'Yes.'

'So—' His voice was quiet and held a trace of almost helpless sadness. 'You know what it's like to deceive the one you love? Can you tell me what happened?'

She turned abruptly away and stood with her back to him, arms crossed, shoulders hunched against him. Yet when she spoke, her voice had calmed. 'Tell me something – you spoke of the high life Lucien lived in this house before he became ill. At those gatherings – those parties and soirées for the rich and the beautiful – did you ever know of drugs being used?' She glanced over her shoulder as she spoke, and caught the unguarded expression on his face. 'Ah. No need to answer.'

He stared at her. 'You... took drugs? With Lucien?'

Annie shook her head fiercely. 'No! I was tricked into taking a drug. By Lucien. From what I have read and learned since, I believe it must have been some kind of opium derivative. I was eighteen years old, a virgin, and engaged to his son.'

His eyes narrowed in shocked disbelief, 'Annie!' He stopped.

She turned to face him, lifting a hand. 'Oh, it gets worse.' She moved to the fountain, wetted her hand in it and rubbed at her face. When she started to speak, her voice was almost calm again. 'When I knew them, Lucien and Philippe lived in Billancourt, just north of here. Their house had a huge and beautiful garden that ran down to the river. There were lawns and fountains and fine statues... Lucien has always had an eye for fine things – and for pretty girls. As you obviously know, of course.' Her voice was caustic. 'The riverbank was lined with willows, and there was a small grove of trees at the back of the house which sheltered a pretty little summer house.' She turned her head to look at him. 'The summer house was almost always locked, though Philippe said that his father spent a lot of time there. Working, he said.' Her smile was mirthless. 'There was always an odd – not unpleasant – smell about that summer house. In our innocence neither of us knew, or even came near to suspecting, what it was.'

She paused for a moment, putting a finger back into the water, watching as it trickled over her skin, shining in the lamplight. 'There was a path along the riverbank. Hardly anyone used it but Philippe and me.' She half-smiled, sadly. 'We were young and silly. No one ever objected to our meeting, but sometimes we liked to pretend we were star-crossed lovers meeting secretly. There was no harm in it; it was just more... romantic, I suppose. And I often used to slip away and walk by the river, too, not telling him I was coming, just hoping to see him, to meet him "accidentally" – just for the fun of it. One summer's night' – she glanced around her – 'a night very like this one, I sneaked away, hoping he'd have the same idea and meet me in the garden. We often did that. It wasn't quite dark. There were shadows, and the water was silver—' She stopped abruptly, and closed her eyes for a moment.

'The drowned mother and child,' he said, his voice almost a whisper.

'Yes. They were caught in one of the willows. It was the most terrible thing I had ever – I have ever – seen. The child's mouth was open, the woman's arms—' She stopped, pressing a hand hard against her mouth for a moment, her eyes closed again. 'I was rooted to the spot,' she said at last. 'I couldn't look away from them. I screamed. Screamed and screamed and screamed. I heard footsteps running towards me. I thought it was Philippe. I turned and threw myself into his arms. I was utterly hysterical, but—'

'But it wasn't Philippe?'

'No. It was Lucien. He held me and comforted me. He was talking and talking, very softly, in my ear. He stroked my hair; kissed me, I think. I couldn't stop crying. I was sweating and shaking, as if I had a fever. Even with my eyes shut I could see them – see their faces and their pale, bloated flesh – the way their bodies moved in the current...' Annie drew a deep breath, shuddering. 'I still get confused when I think about what exactly happened next. I know Lucien led me away and into the garden, and that the summer house door was open. I remember that the warm glow of light coming from it was the most comforting thing I had ever seen. I don't know what gave me the idea, but I thought perhaps Philippe was in there. Perhaps Lucien said he was. I don't know. But I know that it didn't seem at all strange that he took me there. I was shaking so badly I could barely stand.'

She fell silent for a moment, remembering. 'The summer house was beautifully furnished. Even shocked as I was, I remember being vaguely surprised at that. It wasn't what I had expected. There were rugs and a big couch, with shawls and cushions. Pictures on the walls. Pictures of naked women. Very beautiful pictures, you understand. Nothing... nasty. There was a very strong, very strange scent in the air. It made my head swim. I still couldn't stop crying, still couldn't get the sight of those poor drowned creatures out of my mind. Lucien seated me on the couch and sat down beside me, holding me, stroking my hair. And still talking, whispering. I could feel his mouth against my ear... his breath. At last he got up and went to a sort of cabinet. He seemed to be there for a long time. I couldn't see what he was doing, but I heard glass chinking. Then he brought me a glass of something. I remember that it looked like Pernod and water – you know, sort of milky, I've never been able to stand the stuff since – and it smelled like it too, but... it tasted odd. He coaxed me to drink it, said it would make me feel better—'

'I don't think you need tell me any more.' Richard's voice was harsh.

'I drank it because I trusted him.' She turned to look at him levelly, her face still tear-streaked. 'Trust makes fools of us all, doesn't it, Richard?'

He did not reply.

'It was like a dream.' She turned back to the fountain, speaking softly. 'A bizarre, but at that moment not unpleasant dream. Even the pain wasn't that bad until later. He touched me, gentled me. I felt as if I were floating. The faces went away... my mind went away... everything went away. And for the moment that was all that I wanted. All that I needed. What he did to me didn't seem wrong. Nothing seemed wrong. It was like a dream,' she repeated. 'Like drifting in a dream.'

Richard waited to see if she would say more. The perfumed silence deepened. 'Did you not tell anyone?' he asked at last. 'Your mother?' He hesitated. 'Philippe?'

'No. I was quite ill for a while afterwards. Confused. People assumed that it was because of the shock of what I'd seen. Perhaps it was. Sometimes I couldn't be sure what had happened myself.' She gave the ghost of a laugh. 'Who else would believe me if I didn't entirely believe myself? It was a month or so later – when I realised that I was pregnant – that I knew I hadn't imagined it all. I was terrified. Absolutely terrified. That was when I went to see Lucien. Just the once.'

'And?'

'He suggested that it was very doubtful that anyone would believe me. He reminded me – oh, very gently of course, you know the man probably better than I do – that my illness had proved my hysteria and that he was a respected man of no small influence. He advised me to marry Philippe as quickly as possible and assured me that – since the war was obviously coming and a hasty wedding would cause little comment – he would put no obstacles in the way of my swift marriage to his son.'

'Jesus!'

'Quite.' Her voice was expressionless. 'You know the rest. Philippe was killed in the first few weeks of the war. We had only a few days together. That at least, in this miserable story of deception, is true.'

Both heard the murmur of voices above them. Both heard a door close.

'Did you ever discover who they were – the mother and child? How it had happened?'

She shook her head. 'By the time Lucien reported to the authorities the current had taken them further downstream, almost into the heart of the city. No. I never did find out who they were.' Her eyes were distant. 'I have sometimes found myself wondering if they ever truly existed, outside my nightmares.'

'M'sieur? Madame?' The little maid, Marie, had appeared at the doorway. 'M'sieur is asking for you. Madame Tilde has told him he should rest, but he will not. She asks you to come, please, but not to stay too long.'

'The longer the better,' Annie murmured beneath her breath, in English, 'as long as it hastens his passing.'

Chapter Nineteen

'So.' Lucien, propped against ivory pillows that were no paler than his skin, looked from one to the other. 'You have told each other your secrets? Go away, woman, and stop fussing.' This last, sharp-edged and dictatorial, was directed at the uniformed nurse who was plumping his pillows and smoothing the bedspread.

The woman straightened, tutting, glared at Annie and Richard. 'M'sieur must not be excited. You understand?'

Lucien's great dark eyes turned upon her. Tight-lipped, she left the room. The eyes, tranquil now, turned to Annie. 'It was clever of you to find us, my dear. I'm glad you did. I very much wanted to see you again before I died.'

'I'm sorry I can't return the compliment.' Face and voice were bleakly expressionless.

'Richard has shown you the paintings?'

'Yes.'

'What do you think of them?'

'I think it a great pity that such lovely things should be so polluted by lies and treachery.'

'And – supposing they were yours?' His voice was very soft. 'Supposing I gave them to you? What would you think of them then? What would you do with them then?'

She looked from one to the other, then spoke clearly and sombrely. 'I'd probably burn them. Just to spite the pair of you.'

'Isn't that just a little extreme?'

Annie flared. 'What do you expect? A deathbed reconciliation? I think not!' She raised an angry finger. 'Listen to me, both of you, and listen carefully. I'm taking my son and we're going home. I want neither of you near nor by him again. Or me. *Ever!*'

Richard took a step forward. 'Annie!'

'Wait.' Lucien lifted a wasted hand. His eyes were half-hidden beneath the huge, drooping lids. 'You're very self-righteous in your anger, Annette.' His voice was soft. 'Pitiless, even.'

'Why shouldn't I be?'

There was a long moment of quiet. Then, 'How clear are your memories, Annette?' the old man asked.

'Clear enough.' The words were clipped.

'And – how selective?'

'What do you mean?'

He turned his head a little, eyes now wide, to look directly and intently into her face. 'Do you, for instance, remember the splendid party at which we celebrated Philippe's nineteenth birthday? We held it in the garden at Billancourt. I recall it so very clearly. You wore a very pretty dress. White, with a wide green sash. And you had flowers in your hair. Do you remember that day?'

Annie did not for the moment answer. Richard looked at her, a faint question in his eyes. Then, 'Yes,' she said quietly. 'I remember.'

'It might surprise you to know—' Lucien broke off for a moment, fighting a coughing fit. 'It might surprise you to know that I still have the rose that you gave me that evening. It is hidden, still, in the pages of the poetry book. Do you remember that too?'

'Yes.' A very faint flush of colour had risen in Annie's cheeks.

Richard looked from one to the other, his eyes still puzzled. 'Lucien? What's this all about?'

Lucien was still looking at Annie. 'You were enchanting, Annette. Bewitching. As you were the day when we all picnicked in the Bois de Boulogne. It was spring. You wore blue that day. Do you remember? Blue always suited you well.' Voice and eyes were gently remorseless.

She stared at him stonily, and did not reply.

'Tell me – do you still have the brooch? The little bluebell brooch I gave you that day?'

'No.'

'A pity. It was a pretty thing, as I remember.'

'Lucien! Stop this.'

Pale, arched eyelids drooped again for a moment, then lifted. 'Stop what, my dear? May an old man not treasure his memories? The weekend at Honfleur, the walks on the beach – you played with the waves like a child, running barefoot on the sand. But you were not a child, Annette. Were you?'

Annie said nothing.

'The memories are strong, are they not, my dear?' He paused. 'Or have you chosen, perhaps, to forget?' he added, his voice soft.

'Lucien' – Richard broke in, his voice sharp – 'what exactly are you trying to say here?'

Annie it was who replied, bitterly, her eyes not moving from the man in the bed. 'You know exactly what he's trying to say. What he's trying to do. He's trying to say that I flirted with him, that I led him on. He's trying to imply that I was to blame for what happened.'

'And – were you?'

'No! *No!*' At last she turned away from Lucien to look at her husband. 'I was young,' she said. 'Young. Silly. Innocent. All of those things, though in my book none of them counts as a crime. And yes, I suppose my head might occasionally have been turned by his attentions, by the flattery of an older man—'

'Annette,' Lucien interrupted her. 'Listen to me. And believe me. I am not asking for forgiveness. I know that nothing – nothing! – can ever excuse what I did to you. I always was a wicked and self-centred man. But I would ask you to believe one thing. If I had not been' – he hesitated – 'indulging myself on the night when you discovered the drowned woman and child, what happened never would have occurred. Our... flirtations... would have remained as innocent and enjoyable as they always had been. As it was, I lost control of myself, took outrageous advantage of you and then abandoned you. You have every right to hate me; I'm not denying that. I'm simply asking you if, with your hand on your heart, you can swear that you did not find the small games we played as exciting as I did?'

'That doesn't excuse what you did,' she said.

'Of all the things I have done in my life, that was the one which haunted me. You at least have had Davie... he's a handsome and charming lad – and has real talent, he's a credit to you – oh, please, don't flinch from me when I mention the boy's name. I mean him no harm, Annette! On the contrary—' He stopped, his eyes flickering to the open door.

Annie heard it too. Soft, padding footsteps coming across the landing. She turned. As if conjured by the sound of his name Davie stood in the doorway, blinking and knuckling his eyes, the flushed softness of sleep on his skin and his tousled hair. 'What is it? What's happening?' His eyes moved to Annie and widened in delighted amazement. '*Mother!* How on earth did you get here? When did you come? Why didn't you wake me up?' On bare feet he flew to her. He was sleep-warm in her arms and smelled of soap. She caught him to her so hard that he squealed breathlessly, and then wriggled away. She took his hands in hers and held them tightly, looking into the bright face that was lit with delight. 'How *did* you get here? Did you manage to come by boat after all?'

She shook her head. 'I came by aeroplane.'

He stared at her, entranced. 'By *aeroplane*?' He turned excitedly to the two men. 'Richard! Grandfather! Did you hear that? By *aeroplane*! That's really *swagger*, isn't it?' And in the same excited breath, as he turned back to his mother, 'Did you know that Richard had found Grandfather for us? Wasn't it clever of him? We're having such a good time, aren't we, Grandfather? And now you're here too, Mother. Now we can stay a bit longer, can't we? You don't have to go home yet, do you?' He flashed a brilliant smile at the still figure in the bed. 'You'd like that, wouldn't you, Grandfather? I could paint some more flowers for you. And you could teach me some more French—'

'Davie...' Annie began, then stopped.

He turned the smile upon her. 'I'm getting really good. *N'est-ce pas, grandpère?*'

'*Mais oui, Bonbon.*' The old man's voice was very gentle.

Annie glanced at him. For the first time since she had seen him a faint trace of colour had risen in the waxen skin; her heart lurched suddenly at the look in the deep-sunken eyes that rested upon Davie. '*Bonbon?*' she enquired faintly.

Davie giggled. 'It's a nickname. Grandfather pretended he couldn't say "Davie".' He pronounced the word with an atrociously exaggerated French accent and laughed again. Then he pulled his hands from hers and ran to the bed. 'May I show Mother the paintings I did for you, Grandfather?'

'Of course.' The long-fingered, skeletal hand moved to rest upon a folder Annie had not noticed before, which lay upon the bedside table.

Davie dropped a quick, casually affectionate kiss on the thin cheek, and his hand lingered softly for a moment on the thick white hair. 'I can do you some more now, if Mother will stay and we don't have to go home for a week or so. I'll pick some flowers for you tomorrow, and you can choose, like you did before. Look, Mother, these are all from the courtyard – have you seen the courtyard? It's absolutely spiffing. I like this one, look, bougainvillaea, though' – he put his head on one side, frowning a little – 'I'm not sure I've got it exactly right. Perhaps I'll do another one.' He smiled at her, a smile of quite dazzling excitement and happiness. 'Oh, I'm so pleased you're here. An aeroplane! What a clever thing to think of! Wait till I tell…' Suddenly and hugely he yawned. 'Sorry.'

All at once Annie herself felt exhausted. 'Darling,' she said quietly, 'I really think you should go back to bed, don't you? We can talk in the morning.'

He pouted a little. 'O-oh – can't I just…?'

'Davie. Please. I'm pretty tired myself. We'll talk about everything tomorrow.'

He yawned again, and his eyes watered. 'Oh – all right. Will you come and tuck me in, please?'

'Of course.'

He went back to the bed, replaced the folder and gently kissed the old man. 'Good night, Grandfather. God bless.'

Lucien took the child's hand. 'Good night, *Bonbon*.'

Davie stood looking down at him in concerned affection. 'You must look after yourself, you know. You must do what the nurse says. We want you to get better.'

The man smiled faintly. 'Yes, child,' he said obediently.

Davie went to Richard, who bent to kiss him. As he did so the boy put his arms about the man's neck and stood on tiptoe to whisper something in his ear.

Richard straightened, his eyes going to Annie. When Davie tugged on his hand and whispered again, urgently, Richard nodded – a trifle reluctantly, Annie thought. Her eyes sharpened. A self-defensive worm of suspicion, swiftly awakened, curled through her mind.

'Come along, Davie.' She held out a hand.

The boy came to her. 'I'll show you where my room is.'

It was a large room at the front of the house, the shutters open to catch the breeze from the river. Davie climbed into a huge bed that dwarfed his small frame as he snuggled back tiredly beneath cool cotton sheets, reached up his arms for a cuddle. She hugged him fiercely. 'I'm ever so pleased to see you.' His voice was already on the verge of sleep. 'And I'm ever so glad that Richard found Grandfather for us. I've never had a grandfather before. He's really sw...' The rest of the word was lost in a huge yawn. But then his eyelids, which had been drooping, opened suddenly wide. His eyes were serious. 'I know he's sick,' he said, his young voice strangely reassuring, as if for a moment he were the adult and she the child. 'Richard has explained it to me. So I know that I probably won't

309

have him for very long. But Grandfather says that any time is better than no time at all. That's true, isn't it?'

'Yes,' she said, 'that's true.'

He closed his eyes, smiling.

Outside the door she leaned tiredly on the wall for a moment, her hands covering her smarting eyes.

'I've made arrangements for you to have a room of your own. I thought you'd prefer it.' Richard had come up quietly beside her.

She jumped, dropped her hand. 'Thank you,' she said stiffly.

He pointed. 'It's that one – at the end of the landing. It's quiet. You need some sleep.'

She nodded.

There was a long silence. Neither looked directly at the other.

'Annie, I'm sorry,' he said at last, very softly. 'So very sorry.'

She did look at him then, but did not speak. It was not until he turned to leave her that she said, 'Richard?'

'Yes?'

'What did Davie whisper to you? When he said good night?'

He shook his head quickly. 'Nothing important.'

'Oh?' Her voice was suddenly chill. 'Nothing important, or nothing to do with me? More secrets, Richard? Even now?'

There was undisguised pain on his face as he looked at her. 'Annie, please. Believe me. It isn't something you'd want to know about, I promise.'

She looked at him levelly. 'That's rather an odd word to use under the circumstances, don't you think? I saw the way you looked at me. It has something to do with me, doesn't it?'

He hesitated. 'Yes.'

'Then I have a right to know what it is. Especially since Davie obviously already knows. I'd really rather not have any more nasty surprises sprung on me, if you don't mind.'

His head came up sharply at that, a mix of anguish and anger in his eyes that was quickly extinguished. 'All right. I suppose I deserve that. It was only this.' He put his hand into his breast pocket. 'All that Davie said was that I'd be able to give it to you now, instead of waiting until we get home. He's been dying for you to see it. He helped design it; he was understandably excited about that. Here.' He put something small and heavy in her hand, wrapped in tissue paper. She unwrapped it, laid it carefully upon the flat palm of her hand and stared at it.

'I had it made for you. At a little shop in the Place du Tertre.' She sensed rather than saw the small, unhappy smile, the accompanying shrug. 'A belated wedding present.'

The brooch was silver, and designed in exquisitely graceful *art nouveau* style. It was a delightful study of tumbling flowers and leaves encompassing two sensuously entwined initials: 'A' and 'R'.

Annie blinked. The gleam of silver blurred in her eyes.

Richard had walked away from her. Now he turned, looked back. She did not lift her head. 'I do love you, Annie,' he said softly. 'You may find it hard to believe at this moment, but I truly do. Even I didn't realise how much.' He opened the door of the dying Lucien Sancerre's bedroom. The click of the latch as he shut it behind him was very loud in the silence.

Annie stood very still for a long time, almost absently rubbing the teardrops from the gleaming silver as they fell. They made no sound at all.

In the room behind her slept her son, having joyfully found a grandfather who, for all her fury and resentment of betrayal, Annie knew she would not be able to bring herself to tell him was not his grandfather; having excitedly collaborated with charming, deceitful, manipulative Richard, whom he adored and trusted, to create the beautiful thing she held in her hand because he knew how much she would love it. Innocence and corruption, side by side. What most would damage him? To know of it? Or not to know of it? For the briefest of moments she remembered – and forced herself to acknowledge – the undeniable and undisguised love in Lucien's gaunt face as he had looked at his son earlier. The son whom she had herself noticed with every day that passed looked so very much like the dead Philippe.

She couldn't think about it now; she couldn't. She'd think about it in the morning. Or perhaps the next day.

Salt tears ran through the wrought silver and onto the skin of her hand.

Annie went to bed; but not to sleep. Later – much later – she heard Lucien's door quietly open and close, heard soft footfalls cross the landing, hesitate for a moment outside her door before walking on. She lay for a long time after that, staring into the darkness as if staring into a pit.

–

It was a strange household for the next few days. For the first twenty-four hours Annie pleaded travel fatigue and a splitting headache – neither one of them a deception

– and stayed in bed, waited on by an anxious but still ever-ebullient Davie. Sitting on her bed he wanted to hear every single detail of the flight, several times over, and was full of praise for her ingenuity at finding them. 'Supposing you hadn't, what would you have done? Would you have gone to the police? Or would you have gone home? You'd have been ever so worried, wouldn't you? I must say, I didn't like that horrible Madame Colbert one little bit – but at least she gave you a clue, didn't she?'

Unable to stem the flow, Annie nodded.

'And now we can stay here for a while. Even that crabby old nurse told Richard that our being here was doing Grandfather loads of good. Would you like some more lemon drink? It's awfully nice, isn't it? D'you know, it's made with real lemons!'

It was on the third day that, worn out with the treadmill of her thoughts and tired of the stilted politeness and the careful avoidance of anything like real or meaningful conversation, she ventured out of doors. It was early Sunday morning. All over the city church bells rang, and people in their Sunday best hurried to their summons; scrubbed children, their boots as shiny as their scrubbed faces, being firmly marched in front of their elders. She was leaning with her elbows on the parapet of the Pont des Arts, looking out across the glittering water to the majestic magnificence of the Louvre, when the voice behind her made her start.

'Annie?'

She turned. Richard stood behind her, tall, lean, his bare head glinting like new-peeled chestnuts in the sunshine.

'I'm sorry,' he said quickly. 'I didn't mean to startle you. I hope you don't mind? I saw you leaving the house. I followed you. Annie – we need to talk. Don't we?'

She turned back to her contemplation of the river. 'Yes,' she said. 'I suppose so.'

'What are you going to do?'

'About what?' Her voice was tired.

'About Davie. And Lucien.' *About us*; he did not speak the words but they hung in the air between them.

She turned her head to look at him, her eyes narrowed against the brightness of the sun. 'I don't know.'

'Annie, I know you don't want to believe it – and I don't blame you if you don't – but Lucien really does love the boy. And Davie…' He spread his hands.

'I know. I *know*. You think I haven't seen? Haven't listened? What the hell else do you think I've been thinking about for the past three days? Whether or not to stand for Parliament?' The words were almost vicious in their despair. She pushed herself away from the wall and began to pace slowly across the bridge. Two young people rode past on bicycles; the laughing girl carried a couple of long sticks of bread under her arm.

'You surely couldn't be so cruel as to tell Davie the truth now?' His voice was intense, almost pleading. 'How would you ever explain? What would it do to Davie if you did?'

'How long can we lie?' she countered bleakly. 'Months? Years? For ever? We'll surely have to tell him sometime?' She stopped abruptly, biting her lip at the slip of her tongue.

They had both stopped walking. '"We"?' he asked quietly. 'You mean – there is a "we"?'

314

Stubbornly she turned and paced on, refusing to look at him. Refusing to answer.

He did not press the point. 'Annie,' he said after a moment, softly. 'I've talked a lot to Lucien these last few days. If it's any consolation at all, I do believe that what he said was true. What he did to you *has* haunted him in these past years. I think that was why he didn't try to find you. He genuinely thought it best for you both – you and Davie – if he stayed away from you.'

'How did he know we weren't starving in an attic?' The words were caustic.

Almost he smiled. 'He remembers Jane… very well. He knew she wouldn't allow that to happen. He knew she had the means to care for you if it had been necessary. Annie, he's dying. Can't you find some pity for him? You lost your husband – but you had your son. He lost both his sons. Why do you think he's lived the way he has? He's killed himself with his excesses—'

He stopped. Annie had turned to him; her dark eyes, huge in a pale face that had thinned in the past few days, were studying him with a sudden and disconcerting intensity.

'He spoke about the paintings yesterday…' Discomfited by her disturbing gaze he struggled on.

'No,' she said sharply, 'I don't want Davie to have the paintings.' Still her eyes did not waver. Uncomfortable warmth rose in his face. She was studying him as if she would read his mind, his soul.

'I understand that. So does Lucien. But – you do realise how valuable they are?'

'Of course I do.' Again the words were brisk and entirely dispassionate, at odds with her expression. 'Davie doesn't need that kind of money.' Her eyes were still probing his. 'Those things would bring nothing but trouble.'

His long lashes lowered, as if in defence against her fierce, intense gaze, but he did not look away. 'Lucien asked—' They were standing quite still now, eyes locked, in some strange way set entirely apart from the busy world around them. A sprucely dressed young couple in their Sunday best pushing a bouncing perambulator walked by, eyeing them curiously.

'What did Lucien ask?'

'He wants to set up a trust fund for Davie. To help with his education and with his ambition to become a botanist.'

She considered that gravely for a moment. Then shrugged and nodded. 'I can't see anything wrong with that.'

There was another long, precarious silence. Still she studied him with unsparing concentration. Suddenly Richard knew that behind those brave, steady eyes conclusions were being drawn, decisions being made: conclusions and decisions over which he could have neither influence nor control.

'He asked me,' he continued quietly, 'what I thought he should do with the paintings in the highly likely eventuality of your not wanting Davie to have them.'

'Oh? What did you say?'

'I told him to send them to America.'

Annie sucked her lip reflectively. Her gaze still had not flickered once. 'What did he think of that advice?'

Richard's expression did not change. 'He offered them to me.'

The small sound she made was almost, but not quite laughter. It held not the slightest trace of amusement. 'The only temptation the devil himself can't resist,' she said, softly, 'to tempt others, even to the last. What did you say?' She raised her eyebrows a little, questioningly.

'I refused them. Politely but firmly, I believe the phrase is.'

'Oh? I would have thought they would have looked splendid in the Hampstead house?' Her voice was suddenly and deliberately savage.

He could stand it no longer. 'Annie!' He caught her shoulders. 'Annie – don't! Please don't! And – oh, Annie, don't cry – please, don't cry?' There were hard-held tears in his own eyes now.

'I'm not crying,' she lied calmly, turning away from him to look across the water. 'I'm tired of crying.'

He came close behind her, hesitated for a moment, then put his arms tentatively and very lightly about her, barely touching her. She did not move away; even, imperceptibly, he felt she might have leaned against him a little, her head tilted to his shoulder, her hair brushing his face. She sighed wearily.

'What are we going to do?' he asked quietly. 'Will you ever forgive me?'

'I don't know,' she said. 'And I don't know. In that order.'

'We have to decide. For Davie's sake.'

She smiled the very ghost of a smile. 'For Davie's sake,' she repeated.

'And for our own.'

She closed her eyes. '"*Marriage is too absurd in any case*",' she quoted softly. '"*It begins and continues for such very slight reasons…*"'

'No.' Rough in his urgency, he turned her to face him. 'No, Annie! That isn't us.'

317

'Isn't it?' There was a moment of silence. 'Tell me something?' Annie broke it, a sudden note of true curiosity in her voice.

Richard waited.

'Was there ever a real Isobella? Or did you lie about her too?'

He flinched at that, but answered calmly. 'Yes. There was.'

'And... did you love her?'

'Yes,' he said again, with no hesitation. 'But not as I love you.'

With the tip of her finger she very precisely and delicately brushed away the tears from her cheeks. 'Really? What good luck for her.'

He shook his head despairingly. 'Annie! Listen to me! Please! I believe you love me. I know I love you. I know how badly I've treated you. I swear if you give me the chance I'll spend the rest of my life making it up to you. I don't expect you to forgive me. Not now; not soon. But one day, you'll see. Some day I'll make you understand what happened; some day you'll look at me and you'll trust me again.'

'Oh?' She had vanquished the tears; she lifted her chin. 'And just how are you planning to manage that? Do you have another tame hypnotist up your sleeve?'

He ignored the taunt. 'I'm going to start by asking you to do something for me.'

'Me? Do something for *you*?'

'Yes.' He put his hand in his pocket. 'Davie brought this to me. He found it on your dressing table. He... he thinks you don't like it.'

The silver brooch glimmered in the sunlight.

There was a long silence. Then, 'I would have loved it,' she said sombrely, and this time made no attempt to wipe away the tears.

He moved his hand a little, holding it out to her. 'Please? Wear it?'

She bent her head, looking at it. 'For Davie's sake?' she asked bleakly, at last.

'No,' he said, and there was a fierce intensity to his words. 'For ours, Annie – for yours and for mine. To let me know that at least there's some hope.' He drew a breath, plunged on. 'For if there's no hope, then there's no point in trying and I might as well give up right now. Annie – take the brooch, or tell me to leave. Now. I'll understand if you do; but I have to know.'

She made him wait for a very long time before she took the brooch from him, pensively turned it over in her fingers. When at last she lifted her head to look at him the shadows of hurt and uncertainty still had not left her eyes. 'For Davie's sake will have to do for now, I'm afraid, Richard,' she said. 'At least it's a start.' She handed the pretty thing to him. 'Will you fasten it for me, please?'

He took the brooch, pinned it carefully to her lapel; leaned tentatively to kiss her cheek.

Annie turned her head away.

Beneath them the waters of the Seine swirled about the stone stanchions of the bridge, the deceptive, bright, reflectively sunlit surface glittering and dazzling, concealing and disguising the dark chill of the swirling currents beneath.